Readers love *The Bookshop*

'I cannot recommend this book enough. I was **absolutely hooked** within the first couple of pages! I love the way the backstory is teased out little by little to give real depth and honesty to the characters. I found myself completely transported' ★★★★★

'I absolutely loved it. The characters were real from the first page and I really cared about them all. **Beautifully written** and full of family drama' ★★★★★

'A superb story with vivid descriptions of the location and the characters, who are so complex and believable. **A rollercoaster for your emotions** as you are drawn into the antics of the family and their friends. I highly recommend this book' ★★★★★

'Much more than just a summer read – it's a story which **pulls you in immediately** and keeps you hooked right to the very end, leaving you wanting to know what happens next!' ★★★★★

'Family and friendship, love and loss. It's all here in this fantastic debut novel… **A real page-turner** from start to finish' ★★★★★

Jen Mouat was born in Edinburgh and fell in love with books at an early age. She soon began to write her own stories which she kept in a suitcase under the bed. She studied Illustration and Printmaking at Duncan of Jordanstone College of Art and Design before doing a Postgrad in Education and embarking upon a successful career as a primary school teacher. Idyllic childhood summers spent on holiday in Dumfries and Galloway inspired her love of the Solway Coast, the setting for her writing. She now lives near Edinburgh with her husband and their Border Collie. This is her first novel.

The Bookshop of New Beginnings

JEN MOUAT

ONE PLACE. MANY STORIES

This novel is entirely a work of fiction. The names, characters and incidents portrayed in it are the work of the author's imagination. Any resemblance to actual persons, living or dead, events or localities is entirely coincidental.

HQ
An imprint of HarperCollins*Publishers* Ltd
1 London Bridge Street
London SE1 9GF

www.harpercollins.co.uk

HarperCollins*Publishers*
Macken House, 39/40 Mayor Street Upper,
Dublin 1, D01 C9W8, Ireland

1

First published in Great Britain by
HQ, an imprint of HarperCollins*Publishers* Ltd 2017 as *Summer at Bluebell Bank*
This edition published by HQ, an imprint of HarperCollins*Publishers* Ltd 2025

Copyright © Jen Mouat 2017

Jen Mouat asserts the moral right to be
identified as the author of this work.
A catalogue record for this book is
available from the British Library.

ISBN: 9780008737245

This book contains FSC™ certified paper and other controlled sources to ensure responsible forest management.

For more information visit: www.harpercollins.co.uk/green

Printed and bound in the UK using 100% renewable electricity at CPI Group (UK) Ltd

All rights reserved. No part of this publication may be reproduced, stored in a retrieval system, or transmitted, in any form or by any means, electronic, mechanical, photocopying, recording or otherwise, without the prior permission of the publishers.

Without limiting the author's and publisher's exclusive rights, any unauthorised use of this publication to train generative artificial intelligence (AI) technologies is expressly prohibited.
HarperCollins also exercise their rights under Article 4(3) of the Digital Single Market Directive 2019/790 and expressly reserve this publication from the text and data mining exception.

*For Chris: without you life would be just a
series of random wanderings*

and

*for Brittany, my pushy American:
you made this happen*

Chapter 1

The musty scent of old books was both damp and dry. It clogged Kate's nose and throat as soon as she stepped over the threshold, but was not entirely unpleasant. The bookshop was an old stone building set back off the main street of Wigtown, along a narrow alley dog-legging between shops; a crazy-paved path wove through an explosion of dense, free-spirited shrubbery. The shop was an unprepossessing place at first glance, viewed through a curtain of drizzle and wreathed in grey Solway mist. A peeling, hand-painted sign pointed the way to a barn filled with books, the interior almost invisible through its dirty windows. Floor-length, rickety metal shelves and overflowing tables filled up the space with no order, no arrangement, no rhyme or reason as yet; just precious words, mouldering and haphazardly stacked.

Into the midst of this muddle stepped Kate Vincent, just off a transatlantic flight. She was travel-weary, bemused, still to fathom exactly how she came to be here.

Behind the antique counter sat Emily Cotton, wearing a cable-knit fisherman sweater and a loopy scarf of pink and gold. Kate had made this for her, parcelled it up and sent it across the Atlantic – her attempt to resurrect a friendship feared long dead. She got a polite thank-you note in reply – Emily was well brought up that way – and that was their last communication. Until the email.

Emily's dark head was bent over a book, her lips moving as she read. She had an unhealthy indoor pallor and blue crescent moons of fatigue beneath grey eyes, which, when she glanced up at the sudden intrusion, seemed dull and lifeless. A weird beam of half-sun pushed through the murk and lit her face as she stared at Kate. It transformed her, burnishing her wiry curls to copper, turning her grey eyes mauve and luminous. There was a moment of confusion; then a howl of surprise and delight as she flung herself off her stool, exclaiming, 'Kate, you came!'

It was a month since the email, composed and dispatched under the influence of three-quarters of a bottle of Merlot. A summons, a plea to an old friend in time of need. Emily had begged for assistance with this hasty new enterprise of hers, this ill-conceived ploy – at least melancholy and Merlot combined to make it seem so; in brighter moments it was more like a dream. Her grand, if undefined plan, was to run a bookshop in a town already famous for them.

Emily's status as proprietor was signed and sealed, but faced with the enormity of the task ahead – and complete lack of both business experience and, she suspected, general acumen – she needed help. She also wasn't in the proper frame of mind to be taking on this venture; she had been yo-yoing between delight and despair for weeks now, procrastinating like mad. Most days Emily wandered disconsolately through the cold shop, idly shifting books from one shelf to another; or else buried herself in a novel for a few hours and avoided the hard work, the decisions.

She hadn't the heart for decisions; even the simplest of them felt beyond her. Fear and expectation of failure had diminished her, chiselled away at her resolve. Joe was in her thoughts all the time, undermining her and reminding her of her weakness.

Now – impossibly – Kate had come and Emily instinctively knew that all would be well.

'You came!' she said again, her voice fading to a whisper of incredulity, as if she doubted the evidence of her own eyes. Perhaps she had conjured this Kate-mirage out of sheer desperation. If that was the case, she really *was* in a bad way, as her family was wont to believe.

Emily threw her arms around Kate and felt the incontrovertible evidence of her friend, breathed in her perfume and shampoo – only Kate could look and smell so good after a long flight. Old envy cloaked her and hastily she pushed the feeling away; she didn't want the reminders of her worst self.

Kate closed her eyes and returned the embrace, sinking into memories: crystal clear, perfect, untainted for her by disappointment or guilt. They surged to the surface and broke through. The impulsive steamroller embrace – so typical of Emily and her affectionate family – smoothed the awkwardness of the reunion after so long apart; despite Emily's hair getting in her mouth and her clumsy tread on Kate's toes, the hug was a moment of perfection, alignment; they hadn't embraced – or even seen one another – in six years.

'Of course I came,' Kate said, when they had disentangled. She held Emily at arm's length and surveyed her. 'I was summoned.' She lifted one eyebrow and bestowed a teasing smile.

Emily was sheepish, remembering the drunken, superlative-laden email. She looked Kate up and down; Kate seemed unsuitably dressed for a rainy, Scottish summer-town, in a well-cut, navy sateen dress printed with bird motifs. Navy stockings, whisper soft, and grey suede ankle boots – now trailing mud from the path – completed the ensemble. Her hair fanned out across her shoulders like corn-silk and her smile was vibrant with vermillion gloss.

Emily smiled nervously back, her chapped lips as pale as rose petals, skin bloodless. She was utterly overwhelmed by the moment and stepped away from Kate, wrapping her arms around herself. 'Sophisti-kate,' she said wryly – an old nickname, given when Kate emerged, swan-like, from her tomboyish, ugly-duckling years, 'I didn't think you would come.' The awe in her voice revealed the magnitude of this gift of Kate's presence: a whim to buy and renovate a run-down bookshop, one drunken email, and here Kate stood. So easy. *I should have done this long ago*, Emily thought. *I should have brought Kate home.*

Kate shivered and cast another appraising look around the room, concerned mainly with the temperature, but not overlooking the dust, the cobwebby corners and the shop's general listlessness. 'Well, here I am. It's really cold in here, Em. Don't you have heating?' Emily shook her head, her face falling. Kate began to wander, already redesigning the place in her head: planning how to order and stack and present to best advantage. 'No matter,' she said briskly, and clasped her arms to her sides, suppressing a shiver.

'I can lend you a jumper,' Emily offered, glancing doubtfully at Kate's outfit, and producing from beneath the counter a hoodie that had seen a lifetime of better days. Kate made no complaint as she pulled it on over her dress, distracted by a ribbon of memory, tangled around so many others; this was Emily's hangover jumper. Adding a pair of fingerless gloves to the outfit brought further relief, and she cared not for the lack of sartorial elegance; the chill inside the barn was of old, neglected stone.

The jumper looked every bit as incongruous as Emily had feared, but Kate only tossed her head, struck a funny pose and made them both laugh. And the jumper was an invisible thread between them, bringing them snapping back together. The memories surged, unfettered, like moths shaken free from the fabric.

Laughter was the overriding memory. Laughing long and loud and often, in a succession of crumbling student flats. Wine-nights in vibrantly painted kitchens amongst the detritus of a thrown-together meal, and lazy weekend mornings watching old films on the sofa, beneath Kate's duvet because they so often couldn't afford to turn the heating on. Boys came and went and other friends hovered on the periphery. But always Emily and Kate. Together. A unit.

Since the first days at South Morningside Primary School. A playground that resonated with the cries of major victories and minor conflicts, with melodies of skipping rhymes and football feuds and the brutal games of tig – a place of conquest, chieftains and queen bees and imperative allegiances; of friendships forged that might eventually wither, and one day die.

Or else last a lifetime.

The jury was still out on whether Kate and Emily's friendship would stand the test of time – for a while both had been doubtful they'd ever see each other again – but here Kate was, which was a good start. They would need all the laughter they could muster to undertake this venture together, to repair what was broken – the barn with its rotting timbers and decaying books, and their friendship. Every word, every smile, every girlish giggle so reminiscent of old times, broke through the barricade and began the painstaking process of shoring things up.

'You could offer the customers jumpers to keep them warm,' Kate said, only half joking, plucking at the sleeve of the threadbare hoodie. 'Keep them in a basket by the door.'

Emily's tone was gloom-laden. 'That presupposes there will *be* any customers.' Kate looked stern at that and Emily quickly smoothed over her doubts with a paper-thin, unconvincing smile. 'Cup of tea?' she offered brightly.

Ah, the Emily of old, thought Kate, healing all the ills of the world with tea. And when tea failed: Merlot. 'Sure. Is there electricity?' Again, only half in jest. She was quickly realigning her ideas of this bookshop; the cheerful images that had sustained her across the ocean were fading now. This was not a bountiful business yet: nowhere near. It was not even a germ of one; it was just four walls and a roof and piles of books, and Emily so weighed down by the last few years that all the hope and verve had been squeezed out of her. Emily, who had been the schemer, the imaginative one, who had masterminded all their games and commanded Kate and the brothers to her will during Solway summers past.

Emily drew herself up with all the dignity she could manage. 'Yes. No need to look so surprised. No coffee, I'm afraid. But come and look around.' Walking Kate around the small shop, she visibly swelled with pride, a queen in her domain. For all its faults, every stone and timber of the shop was her own and she loved it. 'The electrics are actually not bad,' Emily said, leading Kate through a little door at the rear of the shop. 'The lights flicker occasionally, but . . . look, there's a kitchen here and a toilet through the back, and some outbuildings where we can keep the spare stock.'

The use of the word 'we' did not go unnoticed, but hovered in the air between them, somehow tangible and reassuring. The brightening of Emily's tone cheered Kate.

She peered through the postage-stamp window, coated with decades of dirt, and nodded, enjoying Emily's enthusiasm. Her arrival, she realised, had stoked Emily's fire, released little tendrils of optimism that flared from her like smoke – shades of the little girl with grand schemes who had learned her obstinacy at her grandmother's knee. But, at the same time, Kate could also see how fragile Emily's confidence was, how very breakable her friend had become.

They stood in the cupboard-sized kitchen, which boasted a small sink, a cracked countertop and a merrily bubbling kettle, and stared at each other, breaking into foolish, incredulous grins and feeling just as shy and unsure as that first day in the school playground, when Emily had shared her crisps for no better reason than that Kate didn't have any – and Emily had known instinctively that this wasn't an oversight but a matter of course.

Back then, Emily and the Cottons were all twelve-year-old Kate had to cling to; they had become her life raft in the maelstrom of her mother's depression and drinking. Lily Vincent had succumbed to her demons before Kate was born and even a small daughter dependent on her hadn't been enough to drag her out of the slough of despair she found herself in. Kate had learned to survive, relying on her wits and a sense that there was some other life, just waiting to be uncovered. That she had managed to do *more* than simply survive – had crafted a new life for herself and dared to dream of a future in which she could achieve something – was entirely down to the Cotton family.

Emily laid out a box of tea bags, two cracked mugs and some sour-smelling milk – they opted to drink the tea black. Wrapping their hands around the mugs, they wandered back through the shop, their thoughts unconsciously unspooling in perfect harmony. The moment had a vibration, shared thoughts humming between them. *This is awkward. This is brilliant! Why didn't we do this before?* And, *Why are we doing this now?*

They exchanged shy sidelong glances. Emily weighed her words, a furrow between her brows as she considered how to broach the question. Why *had* Kate come? She must surely have left so much behind in New York: a career, boyfriend, friends – all abandoned for a cold, damp summer in Wigtown, renovating a dilapidated bookshop with an erstwhile former friend who probably didn't deserve her sacrifice. 'I had no right to expect you would come,' Emily said finally, struggling with the enormity of her gratitude. 'Or even to ask it of you.'

Kate sipped her tea and looked at her levelly. 'You had every right to ask it, and expect it too. You're my best friend.'

'Still? After all this time?'

'Time makes no difference, Em.'

Emily's grey eyes were trembling with a mix of hope and doubt, the intensity of her gaze unnerving beneath heavy brows. 'Doesn't it?'

The look – the hope – was too much for Kate. Time was not the problem, but rather the nature of their parting; immediately after university, Emily running off with gorgeous, unreliable Joe, quite determined to make a life with him in spite of her family's objections; and Kate, tired of fighting Emily on the subject, still heart-sore over her own lost love and desperate to put as many miles between her and her mother as possible. She stuck a pin in a map and came up with New York. It seemed glossy and glamorous, ambiguous, anonymous: the ideal stage for her reinvention.

Time mattered only in as much as all the moments lost, and all the things they hadn't said.

Kate knew what she needed to say to mend the moment, what Emily needed to hear. 'Not to us.' Her words were emphatic and brooked no argument. They'd work the rest out later.

She set down her lipstick-printed mug on a nearby table and her boots rang on the flagstones as she made yet another loop of the shop.

Completing her circuit, she paused, lips compressed in contemplation as her plans began to form, spider-webbing in her mind. She had flown through the night, navigated airport queues and driven for hours in a rented car for this. She had had next to no sleep, but she barely felt tired at all now. When she turned back to Emily, her eyes were bright. 'It's going to be great,' she enthused. 'We'll start with a good clean-up. We should redesign the layout of the shop floor, get new tables, chairs, rugs. We must start thinking about our advertising strategy, our unique selling point . . .' She paused. She could already see it all – buttery light spilling from low lamps, plump cushions and overstuffed armchairs, and row upon row of books awaiting the ready smiles of the regulars and the meandering casual browsers, and, pervading it all, the smell of good coffee.

So real was the image that she could almost feel the crisp, thick covers of new books beneath her fingertips, hear the murmur of rustling pages and the hum of happy voices. Kate didn't even *like* books all that much but she was desperate to begin, to create the very best bookshop imaginable. Together.

Emily buried her head in her hands as bubbles of panic rose and burst and she began to deflate like a popped balloon. 'Please—' she began.

Kate looked confused. 'I'm sorry, should I slow down? But . . . this is why you brought me here – no?'

Emily dragged her hands from her face with a sigh. 'Yes. But it's all so fast. I need some time to get accustomed to the idea of you being here, never mind thinking about rugs and chairs and . . . and *selling points*.'

Kate gave her a cool, meditative stare, deciding that Emily's dithering ennui had best be ignored. 'Nonsense,' she said briskly. 'Find me a notebook and point me in the direction of the nearest deli. We'll make some notes over lunch.'

Equipped with legal currency and directions – it had been a long time since Kate's last visit to Wigtown and shops had come and gone in the intervening years – Kate headed for the door, only to turn back abruptly. Emily remained anxiously in the middle of the shop. 'Emily, I came all this way with no warning. I should have called . . . and I didn't even ask where I would be staying.' Suddenly it seemed impulsive and imprudent to have leapt on the plane and come on the strength of so very little.

Emily set aside the book she had picked up and pushed her hair back behind her ears. 'You'll stay with me of course.' As if it was a stupid question.

Kate spoke with exaggerated patience. 'Yes, but *where* is that exactly? Sleeping bags in one of the outbuildings?' With Emily, she wouldn't rule it out.

Emily shuddered at the prospect of the scuttling spiders. 'I live at Bluebell Bank, with Lena. You'll stay with us there.'

A thrill ran through Kate. Full circle. Back to Bluebell Bank. It was more than she could have hoped for. Missing those years with Emily had meant losing the rest of the Cottons too. Bluebell Bank was the source of the only happy, carefree memories of Kate's childhood. When she had been welcomed into the clan she had been transported from her life of poverty and loneliness and brought here to the Solway, to share the Cotton's idyllic summers with Lena, their unconventional grandmother, and all Emily's brothers.

'Will that be all right with Lena?' she asked, flinching from the prospect of coming all this distance only to be turned away, or worse, treated like an old acquaintance from an era long gone. She was *family*. She belonged. And they belonged to her.

'Yes,' Emily said stoutly, 'it'll be grand.' She was keeping something back, Kate could tell. She lingered in the doorway, watching, noting how Emily's eyes remained fixed on the floor as she reached for another book and began nervously rifling pages. A spasm of fear caught Kate in its iron grip, squeezing the breath from her lungs. For the first time since the email – the precipitous decision, the termination of her New York life and the plane ride over the ocean – she began to contemplate the dreadful possibility that the sanctuary she had returned to was not, as she had always imagined it must be, simply waiting for her, unchanged.

'Bluebell Bank,' Kate whispered, as Emily's anxious eyes rose to meet hers again. 'We were so happy there as kids, weren't we.'

Emily's smile was every bit as pale and determined as the thin beams of sun that strained through the shop windows – nearly opaque with grime. 'Yes. And we will be again.'

Chapter 2

Kate walked briskly along the street, reacquainting herself with the town: its wide cobbled roads and flowering planters pungent in the persistent rain; the county buildings at one end and the bowling green splitting the road into two forks; the arty-crafty havens all along the street; the coffee shops and newsagents.

And bookshop upon bookshop upon bookshop.

What was Emily thinking: opening a bookshop in this town?

Kate thought of the draughty old barn – rustic and romantic, Emily would say – with its mouldy books and pall of damp and cold, and lights that flickered, but only occasionally. How typical of Emily to see none of the pitfalls, but only the potential of the place shining through, like a lighthouse beacon in the fog, ready to save them all, but only if they did some serious work, fast.

Wigtown was accustomed to tourists; the book festival had gone from strength to strength since its first incarnation had drawn the town into cultural focus, and the Solway coast had long been a haven for holidaymakers, with its beaches and forests and gentle, rolling beauty. It was the beginning of June, the festival was some months away and the thick of the tourist season was not yet upon them, and today was a drab, grey Monday, so Kate found the town quiet. For a horrible moment, it seemed too small for her and she felt a wave of homesickness for her city.

And for Ben. She pictured him, luxuriating in his vast bed, giving her a lazy look from sloe-dark eyes. But, no, Ben would not be idling between his Egyptian cotton sheets waiting for her to come home and slip in beside him. He would be getting on with things, working or schmoozing clients in a bid to impress the senior partners at the firm, or having a good time in one of his favourite wine bars.

Kate bit her lip as she felt the first stab of doubt pierce her armour. She was running again, avoiding making a decision about where she and Ben were headed; as if she didn't know – had she stayed – their inevitable outcome: a glamorous wedding and another reincarnation for Kate, into beautiful, compliant wife and mother. Ben had made no secret of what he wanted – and expected – from her.

So she had come to repay a debt, yes, assuage her guilt, very possibly; but she was also, definitely, running.

*

In her rustic, romantic barn, Emily was trying to reclaim her equilibrium. Kate's arrival had unsettled her to say the least. Of course she had been in dire need of a shake-up, but she hadn't really expected this; and now she was worried Kate would be disappointed – in her and in the shop. Dan had been nagging her for weeks to write a proper business plan, get things moving; she had been dodging phone calls from her uber-organised mother who would just love to get her hands on Emily's project. Ally had been sending polite, cheerful email enquiries, fishing for information and evidence that Emily was on the mend, recovering from the divorce everyone seemed to think she should have put behind her by now. Even Noah had had something to say on the matters of Joe and the bookshop, but Emily wasn't about to take advice from her youngest brother on any subject, especially given the mess *he'd* made of things lately. Fergus was keeping out of it, but probably only because he was on the other side of the world and contact with him was sporadic. Her family's sympathy had run out fast.

Emily sat on the stool behind the counter and took a few calming breaths. Kate felt like a stranger, but achingly familiar at the same time. Emily both wanted her here and feared her presence too. There were things to put right and Emily wasn't sure she felt equal to doing so; she was still raw and bruised from the divorce, and the inglorious premature end to her teaching career, no matter what they said about it being time to move on.

Kate might expect them all to be the same, Bluebell Bank to be the haven it had always been. What would she make of the changes? Of Lena?

She heard Kate's tread on the path outside and quickly found a smile. Kate shouldered the door to the shop and burst in. 'We need to get a shop bell, a cheerful impressive one,' she said. 'Say, Em, what was the big idea, opening *another* bookshop in this town?'

'You noticed?' Emily bit her lip. Trust Kate to jump straight into the practicalities of the thing.

'The *hundred* other bookshops in this town? Yeah, Em, I noticed.'

'Only a dozen or so. Not a hundred. It's a *book town*. That's what it's all about. Don't you remember? Here, I found a notepad for all your ideas, so hit me.' Fanning the pages invitingly, pale blue lines whispering past Kate's eyes like a flip book animation, Emily slipped behind the counter and took her seat expectantly on the stool.

Kate looked at the virgin paper awaiting her inspiration, and at Emily's trusting face.

Placing her coffee on the counter, she unpacked slices of oozing cake. 'I forgot,' she grumbled. 'Never paid much attention to the bookshops. You were the one always with your nose in a book, remember? Dessert first, I think. Then lunch, then planning. That's the best way round to do things.' Hoisting herself onto the desk, she crossed her legs. 'This is not a bad counter, you know. We should keep it.'

They were rendered speechless for several minutes, savouring and salivating. Licking the last of the frosting off her fingers, Kate glanced down at the notepad. On the top line, Emily had written: *Keep the counter*. She supposed it was a start.

After they'd eaten they traded ideas, words pouring onto the page in Emily's loopy cursive. The list was extensive – and probably expensive, but Emily didn't want to think about that. Not yet, not when this dream she'd spun was still so fragile and imperative. The bookshop. She and Kate working side by side.

Kate scanned the list and tapped the page with a manicured fingernail. 'That,' she said with satisfaction, 'is how we make this place work.'

'All of it?' It was exhausting merely to contemplate. Emily chewed the end of her pencil.

Kate reached across and took it. 'Eventually. We'll start small. One step at a time. A good clean-up is our first priority, and building better shelving.' She annotated the list with criss-cross stars to show the order of importance, and handed it back. 'So, are you quite sure you don't like my bookstore-boudoir idea? We could be draped over chaise longues in our lingerie, reading Jane Austen aloud and wearing sexy reading glasses? It would certainly make us stand out in this town full of bookshops.' She grinned.

Emily thought of her grey brassieres and garish pants with cartoon characters and cheeky appliquéd messages. 'I don't do draped,' she said firmly. 'Or lingerie. And you don't do Jane Austen.'

Kate sighed theatrically. 'No, that's perfectly true. But chaise longues are not a bad idea frankly. Along with the big, comfy armchairs around a wood-burning stove. We could pick them up cheaply and do the reupholstering ourselves. Write that down, Em,' she ordered.

Kate leapt off the desk to pace. She picked up a book at random and fanned the pages, making a face at the dust clouds blooming from the spine. Picking up book after book, she created unsteady, leaning towers. 'Some of this furniture is good,' she said, when she had revealed the wood beneath. Funny, Emily thought, *she* saw the jewels in the piles of words and stories whereas Kate saw the books as decoration, focusing on the structures and substance beneath.

Kate turned and leaned against the rickety table she had cleared. The book towers wobbled. 'This probably isn't the time to mention it, but I'll need to take a look at the business plan . . . see the financials, that sort of thing. It would help to know what kind of budget we're working with.'

Emily paled visibly. 'Business plan?'

'Yes. You do have one, right?'

'Not exactly.' She dragged out the words reluctantly; she had hoped this moment would not come so soon.

She hadn't been thinking business plans when she was halfway through the bottle of wine, typing her plea to Kate to come and rescue her. She hadn't been thinking of anything except how, once upon a time, Kate had made everything better.

'How did you convince the bank to lend you money without a business plan?' Kate tamped down a swarm of panic, frowning at her friend. This *was* Emily; she hadn't had any grand expectations of fully formed plans, but still . . . 'I was expecting it to be rough around the edges, in need of some tweaking, but . . .'

Emily folded her arms on the counter and regarded Kate calmly. 'It needs a lot of tweaking. As in, there isn't one. I didn't borrow money from the bank.'

Kate raised one eyebrow. 'O-*kay*.' Her doubtful expression asked more questions of Emily.

There was a long, uncomfortable pause. 'The money came from Joe,' Emily said, taken by surprise when her voice became a ragged gasp – just the mention of his name could still undo her.

Kate glanced at the glaringly empty space on Emily's finger, devoid of engagement and wedding rings. Emily rubbed the spot unconsciously as if the absence caused her a physical ache. Even after so short a marriage there was a faint white mark where they had been.

'I see.' Kate was gentle now. 'The divorce settlement? The sale of the house?'

'Sort of.' Emily shifted position and didn't meet Kate's eye. She didn't want to be pitied, and yet she knew she had become pitiable: a shade of her former self. Never more so than when thinking or speaking of him. 'He . . . he came into some money just after we broke up. He made me a one-off payment; it was enough to buy this place. I moved in with Lena. She . . . It was a mutually beneficial arrangement.'

Kate pressed her lips together; she had never liked Joe. 'Yes, I've heard him on the radio, quite the star now. So, tell me there's enough cash left over to make this a viable business.'

'I guess.'

Kate was wide-eyed. 'You *guess*? Emily, don't you know how much money there is left in the bank?'

Emily shrugged defensively. 'All that stuff makes me anxious. I don't care about money like you do.' The words came out before she could stop them, tumbling off her tongue in an avalanche to swamp them.

'Right,' Kate muttered. 'Thanks.'

'I didn't mean . . .' Emily raised a hand, gestured wearily at Kate's expensive cut and colour, the vintage dress more costly surely than the entirety of Emily's wardrobe, the bracelet she suspected contained real diamonds glittering on one slim, tan wrist. 'You know . . .'

'Sure you meant it, but it's OK. You're wrong, though, Emily. I *don't* care about money the way you think I do. I have enough. I don't have to struggle and I'm not going to pretend I do. God knows I did enough struggling to last a lifetime. You remember when getting new clothes for me meant wearing your old cast-offs, don't you? Taking charity from your parents like a beggar. Scraping together coppers I found down the back of the sofa to buy food?' Kate's voice rose and she clenched her hands, already regretting the brief outburst, the loss of cool.

Emily nodded, remorsefully. 'I know. I'm sorry. Oh shit, what was that – two hours? You haven't even been here a whole day and I've managed to put my foot in it. I'm not good company at the moment. The others will tell you. They think I'm losing it, since . . . you know.'

'Joe,' Kate said sighing softly. 'It's fine. We don't have to talk about all that now. And we don't have to talk about the financial stuff either. Like you said, I only just got here.'

Emily nodded. 'I know it might not look much, Kate, but this place is a dream come true.'

Kate held Emily by the shoulders. 'It doesn't look like it *yet*,' she said. 'But it will.'

Emily smiled weakly. 'OK. Why don't we call it a day and go home?'

Chapter 3

Kate picked up the notebook: their recipe for success. She felt better with a plan; she needn't worry about anything beyond the last bullet point on the final page, and that was comforting. Emily grabbed a bin liner from the kitchen and chucked the detritus of their lunch inside.

'I have a hire car outside,' Kate said, slipping the notebook into her bag. 'I have to return it in three days. The nearest branch is just outside Glasgow.'

Emily called over her shoulder as she carried the rubbish into the kitchen. 'That's fine, I can follow you up in the Land Rover. We can make a day of it, scout around auctions or something.'

Suddenly it seemed too final. As if returning the car meant she was committed for the summer. Kate quickly pushed her uncertainty to one side and focused again on their plans for the shop, and sorting out Emily, who was clearly in just as much need of repair. 'Not the same Land Rover, surely?' She remembered a green, lumbering brute of a vehicle, mud spattered and temperamental; Lena ferrying them all down from Edinburgh in it all those times Kate gatecrashed the Cottons's holidays, escaping the loneliness of the tenement. Every Easter and summer they would all pile in and chunter along the scenic route through Moffat and Dumfries, past the swooping valley of the Devil's Beef Tub.

Emily returned from the kitchen, ducking beneath the strap of an old suede shoulder bag, her jacket over one arm. 'Jasper? Yep, he still runs like a dream.'

Kate snorted. 'He never did before.'

'Don't be mean about poor Jasper. Do you remember when Lena told us she'd named him after one of her old boyfriends? She said they were each as ornery as the other.' She grinned at this memory; Lena was a woman who spoke openly of errant past lovers to her grandchildren, who smoked fulsomely and cursed and was generally considered (by Emily's mother) to be *a bad example*. When in fact she was the best example of all; an example of how to be oneself in a world where all too often one was expected to twist and contort and conform to fit in.

Kate remembered being fourteen, squashed in the back of Jasper with Emily, Fergus and Ally; she and Em reading *Just Seventeen* and giggling over the problem pages, fascinated by sex. Dan and Fergus had come to blows over the front seat and were nursing their wounds and lingering tempers. Kate was eyeing Dan surreptitiously when she didn't think anyone was watching, a strange, new fluttering of longing in her belly that summer – for what she didn't know. Willing him to notice her *that* way. Lena was singing badly to The Kinks and the dog was stinking out the car with his breath.

That was the summer Kate met Luke Ross and everything changed.

'Come on, let's go home to Lena,' Emily said, cutting through Kate's reverie. Kate flushed with the heat of her remembered crush on Dan – fading in the face of her greater obsession with Luke. It had been one of the best times of her life and they had repeated it year on year, those hot, languid summers on the Solway becoming synonymous with love, and Luke.

Bluebell Bank had never grown old or lost its appeal. They

kept coming back long after most kids gave up on family holidays, especially with a curmudgeonly old grandmother. Lena understood young folk, never patronised them or interfered, and they loved her for it.

Every year they'd gathered, right up until Emily went off with Joe and Kate left for New York. They'd convened at Bluebell Bank, place of peace and beauty, and relive those blissful younger days.

She was nervous and excited now in equal measure. Bluebell Bank conjured up nostalgic images of corniced rooms and patterned carpets, of salads on hot summer days and net curtains blowing into the garden on the breeze; of paddling pools and rope swings and gnarled apple trees and children's shrieks carried on warm currents of air; a place where time slowed and stopped and real world problems could not touch her. Bluebell Bank was a parallel universe; it had always seemed impossible to her that the same old life was continuing unabated while she was there; far easier to believe she had slipped through a crack in time, into a new world altogether. A world where she didn't have to worry about her mother, or where the next meal was coming from.

Kate pictured the indomitable Lena, with her penchant for wearing men's work trousers and battered sandals on her leathery feet, overseeing the Cotton family chaos, her wild, white hair sticking up around her face and shrewd blue eyes seeing to the heart of them all. She was always ready to listen to childish woes and her puckish sense of adventure kept the children coming back for more. Kate could not wait to be reunited with the Cotton matriarch, a woman who had been more of a mother to her than anyone. Emily's mother, Melanie, was always supremely kind, but she was so polished and perfect that Kate had never quite got over her awe of her.

They locked up the shop, inserting a heavy, rusted key into a door warped by damp. The small yard and corkscrew path were overrun with lush, rain-drenched foliage. A wet, summery smell wrapped itself around them as they squeezed between the dripping bushes, heading up the lane towards the high street.

'Tomorrow the hard work starts,' Kate said, shooting a warning look at Emily. She didn't want Emily to lose sight of the road ahead, the hurdles they must vanquish along the way.

They drove in convoy out of town, past the Bladnoch Inn and distillery and along narrow, tree-lined roads. Bluebell Bank was a mile from town, sitting atop a small rise with its gardens spilling down towards the river. A twisting drive led through a thicket of steadfast old trees.

Turning off the road, negotiating the bumps and turns of the track in her too-pristine car, Kate had a sudden vision of these woods filled with children. She could see herself and Emily darting through the long grass, barefoot, hair flying, grabbing the old gnarled trunks to peer out and glimpse their pursuers. She could hear their gasping laughter, feel the twigs and rough grass catch at her feet; Fergus, cursing as he stumbled gracelessly through the woods in pursuit, while Dan laughed complacently, calling out that he was wasting his time, they'd be better off lying in wait for the girls to risk a final flight towards the house – Lena's protection being the only safety net in this ferocious game of chase and catch. Kate had *wanted* Dan to catch her; she had longed to feel the crush of his arms as if in embrace, to be swung off her feet. Dan had seemed so tall and handsome and brave, everything her girlish soul could desire.

The garden opened up before Kate as she took the final bend and pulled the hire car to a stop on the square of gravel out front. The house, backlit by late afternoon sunshine, radiated all the warmth and happiness of those perfect childish interludes.

She felt a fresh flood of nerves as she stepped out of the car. There were birds singing in the trees and the air smelled of summer: honeysuckle and manure-fields and rain-soaked vegetation. *Here I am*, she thought. *I am here.* They were two distinct sentiments, representing both what she had come to offer and the absolution she hoped to receive.

The front door opened and a figure hovered on the bowed step. Long white hair formed a cotton-wool halo around her head and her expression was curious, eyes squinting in the afternoon sun. Her sinewy frame was familiar, clad in an over-large blue shirt with the sleeves rolled up over gnarled forearms.

'Lena,' Kate cried joyously, and hastened across the drive as a russet brown dog squeezed around Lena and limped down the steps, wagging a feathery tail: an old man now, with greying muzzle and stiff legs.

Emily called Kate's name softly: a warning. That, and some other instinct, made Kate stop short before she reached the steps. Lena stared at her, unsmiling. 'Who is it?' she asked querulously, looking past Kate to her granddaughter. Kate turned to glance at Emily, who was still dragging her suitcase out of the boot of the rental car, then bent and wound her fingers in the dog's fur for comfort.

'Lena,' Emily said softly. 'This is Kate. She's my friend. She's come to stay for a while.'

Kate stared at Emily. Why on earth would she introduce her as a stranger? She turned to Lena, who was searching her face, a veneer of polite friendliness replacing her former suspicion. That scared Kate more than anything – Lena was rarely polite. Gruff, unrelentingly honest, fiercely loving, but not polite. 'Come in,' Lena said. 'Would you like some tea?'

Emily pushed gently past Kate, who was frozen on the drive, and set her suitcase on the step. She stretched and kissed Lena's weathered cheek. 'I didn't know Kate was coming until the last minute,' she said.

'I should have called,' Kate began, baffled, floundering. 'I wanted to surprise Em . . .'

'There's plenty of room,' Lena said laconically. She took a step back and her tone turned petulant. 'Where's my hat?' She shuffled off down the hall muttering, the dog at her heels.

Emily met Kate's questioning gaze fiercely; the answers she

sought would have to wait. 'I'll find it for you,' she called out, hurrying after Lena, bumping the suitcase behind her. Perplexed, Kate followed.

The downstairs hallway had not changed in all the years Kate had been away. The walls were apple green and covered with framed pictures of Cottons through the ages: Emily and the brothers, their parents, Jonathon and Melanie, photos of Jonathon and his sister Val as children, a sepia snap of Lena's brother Austin in military uniform, a smiling couple on their wedding day some eighty years ago, Lena's own wedding to James, now twenty years dead. Kate traced the dusty generations along the wall with a wistful fingertip.

Then she spotted a photograph of herself. She and Emily were squeezed onto a rock with Rigg Bay resplendent behind them, squinting and staring at the camera and dangling their dirty bare feet. Their arms were wrapped around each other, heads pressed close – Kate's honey-blonde plaits and Emily's wiry curls intermingling. Emily was grinning into the lens; Kate looked unrelentingly serious. She stopped short and stared at the picture and suddenly Emily was beside her, unhooking it from the wall, carrying it into the kitchen. Kate stepped over her abandoned suitcase and followed.

Lena stood at the counter heaping tea bags into a pot, her immediate need of her hat forgotten. 'Look, Lena.' Emily tapped her on the shoulder, pushed the picture in front of her and gestured from the photograph Kate to the real-life version lurking anxiously in the doorway. The dog wagged and weaved between them, tongue lolling.

Lena looked from Kate to the picture version, recognition dawning like an opening bud at first sun. 'It's you,' she said, wonderingly. Something changed in her face and she was the Lena Kate remembered. 'The bangle girl.' The realisation brightened her immeasurably, but there was strain there still, a moment of uncertainty, a veneer of lingering pretence.

For a second, Kate was baffled, then Lena pointed to the picture and held it out to Kate with a grunt. When she looked more closely, Kate noticed them: numerous plastic bands in fluorescent pink, yellow, green, looped around her wrist. Emily gave them to her for her twelfth birthday and she refused to take them off, even when she slept. They were just pocket money toys from the paper shop in Wigtown, but they were as precious to Kate as diamonds. The first piece of jewellery anyone ever bought for her. 'Oh yes,' she cried. 'I'd forgotten those. I still have them somewhere.'

'Sit down. Sit down.' Lena flapped a big, bony hand, directing them both to the scrubbed refectory table in the midst of the untidy kitchen. She sounded more resolutely herself.

Kate sat. Emily took the chair opposite her and set the photograph between them. 'Thanks.' She accepted a cup from Lena and sloshed in some milk, took a sip, winced as it burned her tongue. 'Kate's come to help me set up the bookshop.'

Lena banged a tin of biscuits down on the table and gave a grunt which might have been encouragement. Emily continued, describing their plans. She was eager, a child spinning dreams, and Kate felt the weight of her impending success or failure resting squarely on her own shoulders. Several minutes into the conversation, Lena's eyes clouded over and her face changed, adopting a baffled smile, nodding politely. At the next mention of the shop, Lena said, 'A bookshop? How lovely.' As if it was the first she'd heard of it. Kate's anxiety ratcheted up another notch.

They finished their tea and custard creams, then Emily pushed back her chair. She plucked Lena's ancient hat from the dresser where it rested on a hook meant for cups and handed it to her. 'Why don't you go and potter in the garden with Bracken? I'll show Kate to her room and then make dinner.'

Lena put on the hat, the wide brim of it almost concealing her face entirely. She stood up obediently, whistled to the dog who was curled up under the table waiting hopefully for crumbs, and they both departed through the back door. Kate could hear her voice as she proceeded down the path, a gruff, comforting hum, and through the open door she could see the dog wagging his tail in response as he trotted faithfully at her side. Emily got up and started to clear the tea things. 'I guess you remember Bracken, he was probably just a pup last time you saw him.' Her tone was guarded, overshadowed by words she didn't say.

Without warning Kate found herself overwhelmed by exhaustion, the flight catching up with her at once; she was in no mood for Emily's prevarication. 'What's going on, Em?'

Emily dumped the cups into the sink with a jarring clatter of china. 'All right. Not here. Let's go upstairs.' Between them they lugged Kate's suitcase up the creaking stairs and sat side by side on Emily's bed in a room almost entirely overlooked by time. Emily had yet to make the mark of her adult self on a room that still anchored her securely to her childhood.

'So?' Kate prompted, kicking off her boots and drawing her legs up beneath her, feeling the jet lag tug at her like the pull of a strong current as soon as the softness of the bed embraced her.

Emily stroked the seams of her patchwork quilt and took a deep breath, looking as if she was about to make a dire confession. She fixed Kate with a solemn, grey-eyed gaze. 'Lena has Alzheimer's,' she said.

The thought of Lena being sick was a blow to Kate, and she reeled from the impact. Lena was one of the formative pillars of her childhood, the foundation upon which she had crafted herself. Six lost years . . . so much of Lena gone, and continuing to be lost – moment by moment, slipping away.

'Mostly, she's frightened about forgetting,' Emily said softly. 'It's little things: beginning a sentence and forgetting the end, losing words for ordinary things, forgetting the names of people she knows, or recent conversations. Older stuff she's better with. It was easier to introduce you as if she'd never met you because she'd be upset if she thought she should know you and didn't. Sometimes photographs help her to make the connections. And sometimes you just have to accept that she doesn't remember, and ride out the episode until she comes back. She always comes back.' Emily met Kate's eyes with a fierce flare of defiance, then dropped her gaze to her hands, knotting them into fists. 'So far she has, anyway. Suddenly, there she is . . . and then gone again.' Emily's voice was careful and controlled now, but Kate could hear the pain flexing beneath the surface.

Kate was silent for a long time, thoughts and questions spinning too fast; everything she knew about the condition – admittedly, not much – was depressing and inevitable. A slow, indecorous decline: was that to be Lena's future? 'When did you find out?' she asked, when she couldn't think of anything more helpful to say.

Emily picked at her bitten, unloved fingernails and heaved a sigh. 'She was diagnosed about a year ago. She was living alone and my parents were worried it might not be safe in the long term. There were other options, such as selling the house and taking her to live with them in Edinburgh, or . . . a home. But . . .'

Kate raised an eyebrow. 'I can't imagine Lena being very happy with either of those options.'

Emily shook her head. 'We didn't even suggest them to her. I had just quit teaching – I was terrible at it! – and had no idea what I was going to do and I needed a place to stay. It was convenient for me too – I wasn't being entirely altruistic. It puts Mum and Dad's minds at rest having me here keeping an eye on her. And we rub along together all right. We play Scrabble and do crosswords and keep her garden going and sell her vegetables at the market. Just trying to keep everything normal for as long as possible. We're lucky, at the moment she's mostly still Lena. Sometimes it feels like there are bits of her missing, but mostly she's the same. And she's physically very well. We have to accept that will change in the future, though. She will get worse, and when she loses her sense of self entirely . . . I guess it's something we have to be ready for.'

Kate frowned; Emily might have resigned herself to Lena's illness, but this was all new to Kate and it eroded some of the joy of reunion. 'How do you prepare for something like that?'

Emily's mouth wobbled in a pale smile. 'I don't know. I'll tell you when I have it figured out.'

Kate studied her closely. 'Do you think it will confuse Lena more having me here? I wouldn't want that.'

'Sometimes it confuses her having *me* here. She forgets I live with her. Forgets she has children, or grandchildren. I don't think having you around will make things worse. It's more company for her and talking to people is good. Plus, *I* need you here.'

Kate pictured again the Lena of her childhood, tough, rough around the edges, desperately caring in her own unorthodox way, and was haunted by regret. The sense of loss was too big, too impossible to wrap her mind around. How she wished she hadn't lost those years. 'It was very good of you to do this,' she said. 'Really, Em. Lena's lucky to have you.'

They had *all* been lucky to have had Lena.

Emily stopped pacing and pulled the cuffs of her jumper down over her hands to hide her ruined nails. She nodded. 'I needed somewhere safe to go. After—'

'Joe.' His name, once again, shaped the very air, changing its texture and altering Emily, making her shrink. She turned to her dresser and began rearranging items in the film of dust that covered its surface.

She shook her head quickly. 'Look, I don't want to talk about him. Not yet.' She sounded brittle, as if she might snap at any moment, fracturing along old fault lines like an ancient piece of china. 'Why don't you tell me about Ben, and your life in New York? It all looks so wonderful.'

Emily thought about the pictures she'd ogled on Kate's Instagram: the fantasy perfection of Ben, with his designer suits, model-esque physique and artfully scruffy hair. How could a relationship with such a man be anything less than perfect? She'd studied every photo Kate posted online in minute detail, when that were all she had left of Kate: the skiing holidays and nightclub posing; the fancy restaurants and gallery openings; the whole rich, luxuriant life Kate had immersed herself in, slipping into a new persona like a new skin. Emily was just one of hundreds of thumbnail friends to grace her page – a fragment of memory clinging steadfast as a barnacle to a rock. Ignored, just another insignificant face. Until now.

Kate must have reasons for coming beyond old loyalty and the desire to rekindle their friendship. She couldn't have been altogether happy with her life if it was so easy to shed that glossy new skin and leave it all behind.

Kate played with a strand of hair. 'I will tell you,' she said, 'but not now. I don't really want to talk about Ben yet either. It's complicated. He's there . . . and I'm here.'

'At least you didn't marry him.' Emily's habit of saying the first thing that popped into her head without a thought was in some respects an admirable trait, but it didn't always win her friends.

Kate was used to it. 'No, not yet.' She gave a shaky laugh. 'So, the subject of men is off the table for us both.'

Emily gave her a rueful smile. 'I suppose so. What do you mean *not yet*?'

Kate gave a languid wave, deftly dismissive. 'A question for another time. When I don't feel like I'm drowning with tiredness.'

Emily nodded. 'Of course, sorry. Actually now would be a good opportunity for you to have a rest while I make dinner. I was thinking after we eat we might take a walk over to the farm and visit Dan.'

Kate was half consumed by a jaw-cracking yawn. She felt a shiver of trepidation and pleasure at the prospect of seeing Dan again. 'Fine. Not the resting part. I think maybe a shower instead. If I fell asleep now I'd be out for hours.'

'OK. You know where the bathroom is. And your room – it's the same one you always had. Do you need me to show you?'

Kate shook her head and got up from the bed, the soft quilt and pillow doing their utmost to drag her back.

*

As Emily clattered down the stairs, Kate tugged the suitcase across the hall and stepped into the bedroom that had always been hers – stepping back in time. Nothing had changed: not the blue forget-me-knots on the bedspread or the candlewick blanket; not the walls painted the colour of cornflowers or the tarnished silver mirror hanging a little askew above a rickety chest of drawers; not the little, wooden bed beneath the window or the smell of fabric softener and dust, or the windows that could do with a clean, but still revealed the most beautiful, picture-perfect view in the world. However far she travelled, Kate did not think it was possible to top the view from her Bluebell Bank bedroom.

A hard lump of emotion invaded her chest, pushing into her throat and threatening to undo her. A heavy cloak of nostalgia settled around her, shimmering all shades of happy and sad, and every hue between. Knowing better than to let jet lag and wistfulness hook her, Kate made herself busy. She unzipped her case and dug around for her toilet bag, which she carried down the hall as she went to take a shower.

The bathroom had got an overhaul since her last visit, thank goodness: new shower, fresh paint, pristine white porcelain. The shower itself used to be a trickle of lukewarm water from the rubber tube that attached to the taps, in an ancient, freezing stone bath so scratched and stained it was impossible to tell what colour it really was. Not that Kate had cared back then. She would have made do with a daily dip in the river if Lena hadn't forced her to bathe occasionally. Now she lined up an array of expensive products and stepped into the steamy cubicle with a luxuriant sigh.

As she soaped and shampooed, she felt the last vestiges of

tension from that final fight with Ben ebb away. His incredulity had rung in her ears all the way across the Atlantic ('You're going to quit your job to go and run some mouldy old bookshop! Why? You don't even read books. And who *is* this girl you never talk about whom you claim is your best friend all of a sudden?')

Fair points, both. Kate couldn't adequately explain the inexorable pull across the ocean. The Cottons. Bluebell Bank. Emily.

She had known she would come the instant she opened the email, sitting in the middle of Ben's big bed wearing silk sleep shorts and an Edinburgh university T-shirt as she waited for him to return, framed by the New York night sky through the picture window: velvet and purple and polluted with the glow of a million firefly lights.

The email was so perfectly Emily that she could hear Em's voice in every typed word, could hear the Merlot talking, and she wanted to laugh and cry at the same time.

For six years, Emily had been no more than a fragment of memory; a stab of guilt that pierced in the depths of a sleepless night; the unbidden thought that came to mind when least expected – hurrying through Time Square late for work, or boarding the subway and catching sight of a countenance or gesture that tipped her headlong into reminiscence.

No messages, not a single word, save the depressingly formal thank-you note. Until that email.

Quitting her job, telling Ben, purchasing the ticket, saying goodbye to her friends – all of those things were items to tick off her list, and she did them all with a brisk, unemotional vigour. It was accomplished quickly, simply. Before she knew what was happening she had a suitcase by the door of Ben's apartment, a one-way ticket tucked between the pages of her passport and a lot of confused people clamouring for a better explanation.

Kate did not fully understand her choice either, but she knew enough: this was redemption, for both of them; the joy of rediscovering a simpler time, retracing their steps. Emily had been the key to Kate's salvation, enveloping her in her big, loving family when all she knew was neglect and cold and that sinking feeling accompanying the clink of wine bottles.

Now it was Kate's turn to do the saving.

Kate hadn't packed the right clothes, didn't *own* the right clothes: she was now a city girl through and through. But now that she was here that didn't seem to matter. Nothing mattered: not the differences between her and Emily, the way they'd let circumstances come between them or the divergence of their paths; not the doubts and uncertainties Ben had exploited to try to convince her to stay.

Stepping from the shower, Kate still felt bone-achingly tired – neither the tight confines of her airplane seat nor the snoring of her supersized seatmate had been remotely conducive to sleep as they hummed over the vast grey of the ocean – but she was able to push the tiredness aside for a little longer. She rummaged through her suitcase again, seeing the lovely dresses and designer labels with a critical eye. Nothing suitable for Bluebell Bank. In the end she pulled on a pair of jeans and Emily's hoodie, avoided the bed after one long, yearning glance then set off downstairs in search of Emily.

Chapter 4

With ghosts popping up at every turn, Kate descended the stairs, feeling like an imposter. For the first time the unwelcome thought rose to torment her: what if the email had been a drunken whim and Emily neither expected nor truly *wanted* her to come? Then she recalled how Emily had flung her arms around her in the bookshop and was somewhat reassured.

Kate was unused to doubting herself these days – such prevarication was relegated to a time long gone – and the sense of uncertainty unsettled her.

Life with Lily in the dismal tenement flat in Edinburgh had been terribly grim, a battle for survival sometimes. It was thanks to the Cottons that she had prevailed, made a success of herself; thanks to one night in fact, when she had been driven to seek their help. The nights were always the worst; it was then that her mother's demeanour was at its most precarious. It wasn't so bad when Lily went out – the parties back at the tenement were far more frightening. Kate would lie rigid and sleepless beneath her thin sheet, listening to raucous voices in the sitting room. A man had invaded her bedroom once, lurched towards her bed slurring sibilantly, shushing her, grinning drunkenly. Kate had lain frozen, heart thundering and body useless, until Lily had come in and laughingly dragged him out by the shirt. After that Kate always made sure the chair was firmly beneath the door handle.

The nights when Lily went off who-knew-where with people she called friends were usually something of a relief. But not this particular night. After years of trying to keep the stark truth of her mother's drinking locked tightly within, Kate was forced to throw herself upon the Cottons's mercy. She hadn't been able to sleep. She had been up for hours waiting for Lily to come home, tormented by some ambiguous terror. They'd had a fight earlier – a raging argument about Lily spending all her money on booze, too little left over to feed them – and Kate was nursing lingering resentment and the dull thud of pain from a developing bruise where Lily had swiped at her on the way past.

Lily didn't come. The electricity was off again and there was no money to feed the meter. Kate was cold, wrapped in a blanket, watching raindrops slide down the dark, curtain-less windows and street lights bleed in the wet that patterned the glass. Waiting, waiting, for her mum to come home and be safe. She had her shoebox on her knee – the contents might have seemed like junk to anyone else but to Kate they were treasures and she had them still, carrying them through adulthood with her, carefully preserved: shells from Rigg Bay, the plastic bangles from Emily, a birthday card Dan had given her scribbled in his messy boyish handwriting, a piece of turquoise sea glass and other such oddments.

Kate listened to the sounds of car tyres sluicing through puddles until there were fewer and fewer of them and the street below was almost deserted. When she checked the clock by her mother's bed it was 4 a.m. She did the only thing she could think of.

She hadn't any money for the bus, but anyway, she felt safer walking than she would on the night bus with the drunks and weirdos. When she arrived on the Cottons's peaceful, sleeping, suburban street only a mile from her own dark, uncared-for tenement, she was a mess: hair in rattails, stark white face, eyes like holes burned in cloth. No wonder Dan had looked so shocked when he opened the door, his father appearing behind him, rumpled and helpless, with glasses askew. Kate remembered, despite the overriding cold and fear and loneliness of that night, the warmth of Dan's hand as he pulled her inside, as he put his arm so gently around her and guided her into the kitchen; the concern and anger on his face as he sat across the table from her listening to her story, while Ally made lumpy hot chocolate and Fergus buttered toast, and Emily sat as close to Kate as it was possible to be. Later, Jonathon had driven her to the tenement to check on her mother – passed out and snoring on the sofa – and collect her things. She had stayed with the Cottons for a week, begged them not to call social services upon her return; she didn't want to be taken away from Emily and the brothers. From then on, she spent most of her time at the Cottons's house anyway, and it was worth putting up with the occasional night with her mother to preserve her sanctum.

It was the first time Kate had asked for anything. She had shown the Cottons the worst of herself and they hadn't shunned her. Kate – hitherto so closed and wary, so protectively curled around the shame of her home life – had opened up like an unfolding flower.

It was the first the Cotton siblings had glimpsed the reality of Kate's life; the first they knew of any lives lived like hers: without refrigerators filled with an endless availability of food, or nagging parents complaining about picking up laundry, but always remembering to pack lunches or sign forms for school trips; homes like Kate's that were not warm and safe, where adult responsibilities and fear came much too soon. This enlightenment was sobering and all four Cottons became fiercely protective from there on in.

Kate hadn't been afraid after that because she had never again felt alone; their acceptance sparked new confidence in her, and helped to determine a different course. Afterwards, she joked that the brothers were as much hers as Emily's, to which Emily was wont to reply that she was welcome to them. At thirteen, Emily was at the age to despise her family: Dan was supercilious by dint of being eldest; Fergus was a pain in the neck, always playing practical jokes and taking the piss; Ally trailed after Kate and Emily like a lost puppy most of the time; and Noah was too young to be of any use.

Kate wouldn't have traded them for anything.

Now, she hovered in the hall, memories of that miserable night, and others, too close for comfort. This was the home of her heart, these were the Cottons; and she couldn't remember their beneficence without feeling fragments of that old pain.

It was frightening, this change, turning her back on everything she had cultivated and embarking on a path so uncertain, but it was also exhilarating, necessary. Kate squared her shoulders as she descended the last two steps. She had been the chameleon all her life, forced to adapt, to make her own way. She'd managed to secure a place at university to study art, bolstering her mediocre grades with a heap of hard work and a little help from Emily; left Lily and the tenement and all they represented behind to forge a new life in America – playing the part of someone confident and carefree from the outset and being surprised when everyone seemed taken in by this new incarnation.

Emily was in the kitchen, making noisy dinner preparations. Kate stood in the doorway for a moment and observed the scene of domestic . . . well, *bliss* wasn't precisely the right word . . . with a smile. 'Need a hand?' She wasn't sure what Emily was making, but it seemed to involve using most of the utensils and pans in the kitchen.

'Oh, hi. No, I'm good thanks. Sit and talk to me by all means. Do you still like Bolognese?'

'Yes.' Kate studied the unique array of ingredients on the bench. 'But are you quite certain that's what you're making?'

'Well, a version of it. I just chuck everything in.'

'So I see.' Kate slid into a seat at the table and looked around the room. Besides the unfolding dinner carnage, the room was clean, but cluttered; she hadn't taken the time to look around properly earlier, too preoccupied. She studied a pinboard neatly arranged with little slips of paper, thick black pen in Emily's hand marking out instructions and appointments: a manual for getting through the day. Alongside that was another board of photographs, each carefully labelled. Kate rose and went to study the board. If not for those labels it might have been any ordinary display of family pictures, in an ordinary kitchen, rather than a glaring reminder of Lena's illness.

These photographs were recent and she eyed them with interest, updating her mental picture of them all. 'Tell me about the boys,' she said, tapping a photo showing all five Cotton siblings – at an airport by the looks of things, if backdrop and baggage were anything to go by. Fergus was in the middle, his red hair vibrant and a grin on his face, his arms spread wide to pull all his siblings into the frame of the picture.

'The boys? There's not much to tell really. They're the same.'

Kate laughed. 'They can't be; it's been six years.' The boys in the picture were men now, every one; only Noah, the youngest, still clung to the vestiges of boyhood.

Emily dumped a can of tomatoes into the strange concoction in a pan on the Aga. She gave it a cursory stir and turned to look at Kate, frowning as she tried to summarise six years in a single sentence apiece. The first came as a blow to Kate, though she hadn't any right to care. 'Well, Dan got married a couple of years ago. He and Abby run the farm together and Abby's pregnant with their first child. Noah lives with them just now; he's working on the farm this summer – he was having a hard time at home. He got expelled from school. I can't *believe* he's seventeen, can you?'

Kate thought of the boy she had known, a gentle, shy eleven-year old. 'No. Wait . . . *expelled*?'

Emily nodded. 'It's a long story and one you should hear from him. He'll probably tell you, he always liked you more than the rest of us. He won't talk about it,' she added with a scowl that suggested it was an ongoing battle.

Kate put this knowledge aside to be considered later. 'What about Fergus?'

'Went to Australia eight months ago. He's having a ball. He and Dan had a falling-out over the running of the business. It was always Dan's farm – Lena gave it to *him* to run when her last tenants pulled out – and Fergus's interference didn't go down too well. Ferg's happier setting out on his own anyway. Alistair's fine. He's in London. He got his law degree and now he's working towards making partner in his firm. We barely see him.' She smiled ruefully. 'You know what it's like, everyone's busy.' Her tone was brisk as she turned her back and stirred the saucepan's contents again.

'You're scattered, aren't you? I suppose it was stupid to think you'd all still be here.' In contradiction to her words, Kate felt discomfited. 'I suppose people move on,' she said vaguely.

'Yeah, like to *New York*.' Emily couldn't help herself.

Kate conceded the point. 'Fair enough. It'll be great to see Dan and Noah again. I'm glad they're here. I missed your brothers almost as much as I missed you.'

Emily turned to look at her. 'I was right here,' she said. An awkward silence fell. She had no right to mind, really; Kate might bear the brunt of the blame for being the one to flee the country, but strictly speaking Emily left first; though there wasn't anything to be gained by that kind of petty point scoring.

Emily did what she did best and changed the subject swiftly. 'You know when we were kids I always wanted you to marry one of my brothers?'

Kate accepted the conversational olive branch. 'So you told me. Frequently.'

She didn't want to talk about her feelings for Dan, or their inevitable conclusion. Exactly how much Emily knew, Kate wasn't sure; it was one of the few secrets she had kept, but she couldn't be sure Dan had been as circumspect. She kept her tone light-hearted as she continued. 'Ally was like a brother to me, Fergus was just too busy being a grumpy teenager to notice me like that. Noah's a *wee* bit young, and Dan . . .' Here, she trailed off. There was nothing to say about Dan now, or rather there was, but it was all too late. Married! A baby!

She couldn't help but voice the thought. 'It's so strange to think of him being *married*.' It seemed such a grown-up thing to do – never mind that he was almost thirty and had been running his own business for the past ten years. But, also, hadn't she always hung on to the vague, selfish idea that he was *hers*? Though *she* had let him go.

Emily gave her a wry smile. 'My money would have been on Dan, if you were going to hook up with any of them, but I suppose that ship has sailed now. You know, I'm sure he had a crush on you. I just wanted you to be part of the family, but of course you already are.'

Kate's heart raced as she tried to fathom if Emily knew more than she was letting on about her and Dan. Perhaps it was one of the many things they must lay bare, to clear the air between them. But not yet.

Emily's use of present tense felt good, reminding Kate that she had earned her place on the wall of family photographs, that her bedroom was waiting for her as if she had only stepped out momentarily. She watched as Emily picked up the framed picture again of the two of them on the beach at Rigg Bay, rummaged in a drawer for a slip of paper and a felt tip, wrote a label and added Kate to Lena's memory board with a flourish.

She turned to look at Kate, her expression innocently content, as if in that moment all her cares had melted. She smiled. 'Wait here a moment. I've something for you. Oh, and open a bottle of wine. In the cupboard, there.' She directed Kate towards the larder and then whisked out of the room in a whirl of knotty curls; she had shed the fisherman's jumper in favour of more seasonal attire and her red T-shirt was vibrant against the dark of her hair.

Kate wandered past the Aga, sniffing cautiously at the contents of the pan, which smelled surprisingly good – better than the sum of the ingredients haphazardly thrown in – and opened the larder door. She selected a bottle at random from the wine rack – Merlot, of course, but taking her back all the same to those student days sharing a bottle or three with Em, when the wine was rank and cost a few quid from the local newsagent.

The cupboards in the Bluebell Bank kitchen were well ordered, despite the clutter covering the surfaces: the folded newspapers open at the crossword page, old yellowed recipes, receipts and lists and piles of glossy junk mail. The place had always had an air of lived-in untidiness, which had contrasted with the sharp cleanliness of Emily's parents' home and the fetid mess of Kate's. It was comfortable and familiar to sink into a chair here, to look around at the lingering debris of Cotton family life and revel in the unchangeable-ness of this house.

Kate had just twisted the cap off the bottle when Emily returned, bouncing into the kitchen with a heavy book in her hand. 'Glasses are in there,' she said. 'Lena doesn't like wine. She prefers a whisky, but it's strictly rationed – medication, you know.' Emily swept aside a sheaf of papers and sat down at the table. She accepted her glass of wine from Kate and, hesitating for just a moment, pushed the book across the table towards her. 'Here. I made this for you. In case I ever saw you again. I was feeling sentimental one night.'

Kate set down her own glass, and opened the leather cover. It looked like an old hardback book, but inside the pages were crisp and new: a photograph album disguised as an antiquarian book. 'Is "sentimental" a euphemism for "drunk"?'

Emily shrugged, with the beginnings of a grin. 'Maybe.'

Kate turned the pages slowly. Emily had documented their

life together, gifted the book to her to smooth the turbulence of her return: there were school portraits in rumpled sweatshirts; summers at Bluebell Bank and hot days on the beach – in garish Bermuda shorts and Mickey Mouse sunglasses – and playing in the old orange dinghy with Ally and Fergus; then as young teenagers, posing provocatively, wearing the wrong shades of lipstick and heavy eye make-up. A bonfire party, their first purloined cigarettes held proudly between dark-painted fingernails.

Next came the university days: nights out in cheap student bars around the city; sunbathing in Princes Street Gardens with various hangers-on they had once called friends; a weekend clubbing in London; a week in a backpacker's in Rome.

It was all there, every important moment in the timeline of their friendship and, because of the significance of that friendship, their lives: so entwined and tangled you could barely see the join. Where Emily ended and Kate began.

And then, it all came to an abrupt end, like a sentence without a full stop. Kate turned the page after the final photograph – a day trip in someone's car to the sands of St Andrews – and was met with nothing but blank paper. All those empty pages were a glaring reminder of the sudden fracture.

There was something missing too. Some*one*. Luke.

Made more conspicuous by his absence, Luke's name hovered on her lips as Kate flipped back to the place where he should have appeared – it couldn't have been more obvious if Emily had left an empty space for him. Kate looked up, noted how Emily's eyes slid away from hers as she realised her mistake. Perhaps she was only trying to protect Kate, shield her from the remembered pain of losing him, but erasing him wasn't the answer; as if Kate could possibly forget.

'Thanks,' Kate said softly, pushing the book aside. 'This is great.'

Emily feigned interest in her ragged fingernails, hands curled around the stem of her wine glass. She took a gulp, realising too late that the gesture of the album had served as a nod to darker times just as surely as rekindling the gentle, happy reminiscences. No Luke, no Joe; but they were there all the same. 'No problem. I had boxes of pictures lying about and I thought they should be in an album. All the photographs were taken on my camera. I didn't think you would have any.'

Boxes of pictures? So where was Luke? 'I don't. Thank you,' Kate repeated. She lifted her glass to her lips and slowly took a sip.

Emily stood up, almost knocking over her glass in her haste. 'Better check on dinner,' she said. 'It's probably ready. Oh, I gave Dan a call. He's expecting us later. I didn't tell him about you. I wanted it to be a surprise. He won't be able to believe his eyes.'

Kate, lost in thoughts stirred up by the album like a gust of autumn leaves, only murmured in assent. She was realising that two worlds could not collide and be expected to mesh. She could not be the New York Kate here at Bluebell Bank, with these people and these memories.

And in New York she had eschewed the memories of this place, this version of herself, in order to be a completely new person: a better one, or so she had thought.

But such a split couldn't continue; she was either *new* Kate, aloof and unattached and capable, or *old* Kate, immersed in this world and these people. One must prevail.

She would have to *choose*.

Losing the new self she had crafted so carefully seemed like too great a loss, a betrayal, but she wanted to be the girl with the bangles again, the Kate who hoarded simple treasures and clung to the Cottons. Alarmingly, she didn't feel like Ben's Kate any more – not here, awash with the memories of love and loss, of Luke and Dan; and not when the person Ben had fallen in love with was a phoney. The Kate the Cottons remembered was the real one.

*

Emily watched Kate leaf through the photograph album and knew her mistake; she had omitted Luke from the annals, which was stupid – also difficult because he was in nearly every bloody photograph! She had been trying to save Kate the pain of seeing him, and also – if she was honest – to save herself too. Luke Ross was dangerous territory; they definitely didn't need to venture there tonight.

Kate's expression was soft as she studied the images of her teenaged self, Emily and the brothers never far from her side. The album had achieved the desired effect of reminding her that once they had been her world.

And they could be again. She and Kate could start fresh, put past differences behind them. They would make the bookshop work together. And maybe *everything* else would be easier with Kate here: bearing Lena's illness; bridging the ever-widening gulf between Noah and Dan – permanently at each other's throat; forgetting Joe. For the first time since she had fled home to Bluebell Bank, Emily felt wildly optimistic.

Chapter 5

They ate in the dining room – not quite one of the epic dinners of family lore; not enough people seated around the table for that – but comfortingly evocative all the same. The walls were cherry red, the bay windows shrouded in net curtains that danced in the breeze, and the paisley-patterned carpet was wearing thin in places. They ate Emily's unconventional Bolognese, though for authenticity's sake they should have been eating salad and cold cuts; with cherry tomatoes and avocado, little octagons of cucumber, folds of pink meat and shiny, quartered hard-boiled eggs. If they ever ate anything else those summer days at Bluebell Bank, Kate didn't remember it.

Kate reached for her wine glass, watching Emily and Lena laugh over recounting one of Fergus's famous temper tantrums. 'Red hair,' Lena said sagely. 'I should know, I was a redhead myself. I once threw James's plate of dinner at the wall when I was in a temper over something or other.'

'You didn't?' Emily's eyes widened. 'That should go in the memory book.' She sprang up from the table and went over to an ancient sideboard. A moment later, she returned with a pad of Post-it notes and a pen. She hastily scribbled. 'I don't want to forget,' she explained, glancing up from her writing to see Kate watching her curiously.

'Memory book?' Kate enquired.

Emily nodded. 'The story of Lena's life. I'm preserving it all for her.' *And for all of us.* The matter-of-fact way she said this, and the unspoken addendum, laid Lena's illness before them.

Kate looked at Lena, but she was unconcerned. Lena caught the look and grinned irreverently. 'Like downloading me onto one of those memory stick thingies. On a computer. She's making a backup.'

Kate wasn't sure how to deal with this candour. She hid her face in her wine glass to avoid having to reply. Emily and her grandmother had always been close and, watching them now, Kate felt the depths of their bond still. Emily seemed unfazed by the indisputable evidence of Lena's illness; she faced the moments when Lena's lucidity slipped with unfailing calm and gentleness, barely a crack in her composure. This was a good sign, for Emily had always been highly strung.

After dinner, carrying the glasses to the kitchen to be washed, Kate overheard Lena in the kitchen saying petulantly, 'But who is she? Has she come to clean? I told you I don't need a cleaner.'

'No, she's not the cleaner. She's an old friend of mine, Lena. She's Kate.'

'Kate? Don't be silly. Kate's just a child.'

Kate had to return the glasses to the dining room to catch her breath, feeling dizzy and thrown off orbit. How on earth did Emily cope?

By the time they set out to Dan's farm, Lena was back to herself again. It was a perfectly lazy summer evening, the air sweet and heavy. A last slice of sunlight spilled over the rain-damp fields, the long grass was bowed with the weight of water and soft mud sucked at Kate's borrowed wellingtons as they walked beneath the cool shade of the trees. The woods were alive: chirruping, rustling, crunching, squelching.

'We walk this way most evenings after dinner,' Emily said. 'Even if we don't go to the farm to see Dan and Abby. It's a good walk for Bracken and Lena knows it like the back of her hand. She's been doing it for seventy years so I don't worry about her losing her way.'

True, but Lena had also been handling cutlery for more than seventy years, yet earlier when she tried to set the table Kate had seen her freeze, bewildered, staring from the silverware in her hand to the empty space on the table, as if she had been asked to complete a puzzle, the key to which hovered beyond her ken, before finally dumping the whole pile in the middle in frustration. Everyone had extricated their own and it didn't matter. Except, of course, that it did.

The path from Bluebell Bank to the farm – shaped mostly by generations of Cottons – led down through the woods at the bottom of the garden, crossed stream and stile and skirted the fields, leading eventually down the slope of the lower pasture to the farmhouse nestled in the valley in the lea of two rolling hills.

A lifetime of tramping the fields and hills of Galloway had made Lena thin and rangy and fit. She looked so strong striding out ahead of them in her manly boots, her wide-brimmed hat squashed on top of her wild, white hair, that Kate could imagine for a few moments that she was completely well. This physical wellness seemed unfair in the face of the insidious disease creeping at the corners of her mind, erasing parts of her. Kate wondered if Emily would have traded the mental disease for a physical, debilitating one, if it meant keeping Lena sharp and clever and *herself*? Would Lena? If she got to choose. She tried not to think about it as they walked. Lena led the way: hawk-eyed and stealthy as ever, naming the birds she spotted in the forest with mechanical ease; a woman who didn't always remember what a fork was for could point out crossbills, goldcrests and great spotted woodpeckers without having to think about it.

Now, trailing Lena and Bracken through the cool, dappled shade of the trees, Emily walked close enough to Kate to link arms affectionately. 'So, tell me all about your job,' she said.

Kate pushed back her sleeves. The evening air had a strange, early summer feel to it: both warm and cool. She grinned. 'There isn't much to tell. I quit. I felt the commute from Wigtown would just be too much.'

Emily rewarded her attempt at humour with a smile. 'I hardly know what you did. Advertising or something, wasn't it?'

'Advertising, yes. It was a good company, some big campaigns. I was a junior assistant, but I was working my way up. I was working on a campaign for a big lingerie brand before I left.'

'You were selling knickers?' Emily sounded gleeful.

Kate gave her a look. 'Not knickers. *Lingerie.*'

'Knickers are knickers,' Emily said sagely. 'However you dress them up.'

Kate punched her arm lightly. 'Perhaps that should have been my slogan. *Knickers are knickers.*' She sighed. She had certainly felt like that sometimes, when she emerged from hours of interminable meetings, wilted and disillusioned: what was it all about? Haggling over wording to make even more millions for a company that paid pennies to the workers who actually *made* the underwear – the last word in delicate decadence: all manner of froth and lace and ribbons and carefully constructed artifice and the illusion of beauty – sex in a designer bag. And now, *here*, describing it to Emily, it all seemed utterly pointless.

'Should I be feeling guilty?' Emily asked. 'I mean, have you given up a potentially lucrative career as a high-powered advertising executive for me and my bookshop?'

Kate shuddered. 'Yes, probably. But thank God for that. Oh, I don't mean the feeling guilty part, it was entirely my decision to come. But honestly, Em, the job was so freaking boring, so futile. I'd spend my days in meetings wrangling over stuff that seemed so important at the time, surrounded by people who all acted like the world would stop turning if we didn't get it just so . . . then I'd come home and wonder what it had all been about. There was no drawing involved, very little creativity. Hand it to corporate types to kill creativity stone dead. But . . . no, I had to leave anyway. You just gave me the impetus.'

'Well, *lingerie's* loss is my gain,' Emily said. 'If you start getting withdrawal, there's a stall at the market sells knickers, I'm sure we could get you a job hawking granny pants.'

They both laughed. 'Gee, thanks, Em, it's good to know you're in my corner.'

Emily smiled. 'You know,' she said, treading carefully now, 'I can't imagine you doing a job that doesn't involve art. You were so sure, when we graduated, that you wanted to be a designer. And your stuff was *good*, Kate. Really good. Remember the degree show?'

Kate nodded, her smile vanishing. The degree show was the pinnacle: everything to show for all the years of hard work, the socialising sacrificed, the long days and longer nights devoted to the studio. Three years of textile design and Kate had been *immersed*, and nothing else had mattered. 'It's . . . hard,' she said vaguely.

'I'm sure.' Emily knew about that. She'd done a job she hated – though what had possessed her to take up teacher training remained a mystery to everyone – and she knew that real passion for one's work was hard to come by. 'What are your plans? For after the bookshop.' Her tone betrayed her anxiety that Kate might drift away once more.

'I have no plans. After the end of the summer, after the bookshop . . . well, we'll see.' Kate tried to keep her tone light, as if her whole future didn't hinge on that very conundrum. The truth was she hadn't a clue.

They emerged from the shade of the forest and crossed the stile over a crumbling dry stone dyke, paused to look down on the farmhouse at the bottom of the slope. This field was empty, the cows having been transferred to one of the upper pastures. Emily glanced at Kate in her clumsy, borrowed boots and suddenly took off at a gleeful sprint, running with childlike enthusiasm and complete lack of grace. 'Race you to the house,' she yelled over her shoulder.

Kate frowned in surprise. Emily running? Challenging her. She took off in pursuit. As they tore down the hill, gathering speed, she reflected that she hadn't run like this in years. The running machine at the gym really didn't compare to this feeling of the breeze in her hair, earthy farm smells in her nose and her quarry firmly in her sights. Kate had once prided herself on her athletic ability – which could not exactly be said of Emily – but this wasn't about skill, it was just running. Kate accelerated, eyes fixed on the bright red of Emily's T-shirt, a laugh bubbling and escaping from her, stealing precious breath. She was running faster than she had in years and it felt amazing. It felt like childhood: running for running's sake, for pure joy. She eased past Emily and slowed at the last minute for the gate, collapsing against it, breathing in strangled gasps.

Emily reached her, bent double over the gate. 'Ow-ow-ow,' she complained. 'That . . . really . . . hurt. Can't breathe.' She flipped the hair out of her sweaty face and grinned at Kate. 'I let you win for old times' sake, but actually I'm pretty athletic these days.'

'Sure you are.' Recovering first, Kate stood up. She felt the flush of heat on her face and knew she must look a mess, but she really didn't care.

Emily retied her ponytail and grabbed Kate's arm. 'I can't wait to see my brother's face when he sees you.'

They hung on the open gate recovering their breath and waiting for Lena, gazing towards Dan and Abby's farmhouse, which was surrounded by a scattering of low outbuildings and a tall, silver silo. Two young dogs rushed up the track to meet Lena. They were calmed by a gruff word and the briefest touch of her hand. They whined at Kate when they reached her. Dan's dogs and Bracken sniffed their greetings to one another.

'Daft kids,' Lena said with a swift shake of her head when she reached them. Emily and Kate exchanged smiles.

Abby, heavily pregnant, opened the door. 'Hi Lena, Em,' she said, balancing the weight of her stomach with care, caressing her bump. She looked curiously at Kate. 'Hello there.'

'Abby, this is my friend, Kate,' Emily said. She found her eyes drawn downwards as always, to the immense bulge of baby, and took a quick, shallow breath; it was almost impossible to look at Abby without a sharp stab of longing.

They kicked off their wellingtons on the mat and were ushered into the big kitchen, which was the focal point of the house. Lena dropped into a favoured tweed armchair immediately, propping her socked feet on a stool. Emily smiled affectionately; this used to be Lena's farmhouse, hers and James's. Before they built Bluebell Bank, before James died and Lena leased it out to a series of unsatisfactory tenants; before she gifted it to Dan when he was twenty-one and directionless, resisting university and all of his mother's attempts to corral him into academia. Lena could see the way the wind was blowing even then, could see that Dan needed something to get his teeth into, and he wasn't going to find his future in a library. Emily and Ally, perhaps. But not Dan, not Ferg either.

'Welcome, Kate. Can I get everyone some tea or something?' Abby seemed open and friendly, her soft, fair hair curling around her chin. Her skin was pale gold, dusted with freckles.

'Brandy,' Lena declared. Bracken was at her side, his big russet head resting on her knee, gazing up at her adoringly.

Abby smiled indulgently. 'Sure. Kate?'

Before Kate could reply, a voice boomed out behind them. 'Kate Vincent? Is that really you?'

Kate spun round to find Dan framed in the doorway; a bigger, broader Dan than she recalled, with muscles and limbs honed from hard labour, and wrinkles creasing the wind-burned skin at the corners of his eyes, and a scruff of beard across his chin. Warm, brown eyes bored into her and for a split second, time stood still.

'It's me.' Kate was quite breathless with joy and nerves, and Dan crossed the room in three giant strides to scoop her into a hug that lifted her off her feet.

'Well, thank God for that; it's about time.' Dan put her down and stared. 'Jesus, Kate, it's good to see you.' His smile was as infectious as ever: a flash of white amongst the dark, untidy beard.

Kate was embarrassed by the effusive welcome, discomfited by her reaction to him. With his pregnant wife looking on, here she was remembering things she had no right to. 'It's good to see you too.' She tucked her hair behind her ears and glanced from Dan to the flagstone floor and back again, sneaking looks at him and searching his eyes for signs of intimacy, for recognition of the hurt she had wrought. It was there in spades. She looked quickly away again.

'Kate's come to help with the bookshop,' Emily said, oblivious, and they all sat around the big table, except for Lena who had taken root in her armchair and was quite content, Bracken already snoozing at her side.

'Good,' Abby said. 'You certainly need a hand with it.' She smiled at Emily and reached to pat the head of the nearest sheepdog. Kate couldn't keep from staring at Abby, marvelling at the changes these past six years had wrought. Dan's wife. Dan's *child*. And the look in Dan's eyes saying he felt the bonds of connection still.

But Dan was no longer a boy. The creases around his eyes implied a life of laughter and smiles; he was happy and Kate was glad – of course she was. Except for the flicker of envy, the memory of his throaty laugh, so intimate, once hers alone.

Dan was staring; Kate had forgotten how forceful his gaze could be. 'About bloody time,' he said wonderingly. Abby laughed and chided him gently about minding his language in front of the bump – how could she not feel the tension and wonder?

Because Abby was secure, certain – in Dan, and herself.

'I know,' Kate said calmly, directing her reply at Abby. 'My visit is certainly overdue.'

Dan rubbed his hands together, stood up. 'Let's open a bottle of something to celebrate. Jeez, Kate, I still can't believe it. So, where did you spring from?'

'New York.'

'I want to know what the hell you were doing there and what brought you back, but hold that thought. I'm going to open a bottle of wine. Red?'

'Sure.' She nodded. Usually she didn't drink mid-week – she was strict with herself about that – but here she felt as if all her rules had been suspended along with reality.

'She's my knight in shining armour, come to save my sanity and my business,' Emily called, getting up from her seat and brushing Kate's shoulder. 'I'll give you a hand, Dan.'

When Dan and Emily were on the other side of the vast kitchen getting wine, bickering amiably, Abby leaned forward and touched Kate lightly on the arm. She lowered her voice. 'I'm glad you've come. Emily needs help with this venture. Things haven't been easy for her, I suppose you know that.'

'I'm here to help,' Kate said, a little uneasy; she didn't want to discuss Emily's divorce behind her back. 'I can't wait for us to get started,' she added.

Abby nodded. 'Emily's not the most practical person, you know. Dan's worried she hasn't really thought this through. It was all so sudden.'

Kate smiled. 'I lived with her at university. I know everything there is to know about her. And she'll be fine. She just needs help to get out the starting blocks, that's all.'

Abby's eyes held curiosity, but that was all. Obviously Kate had been seldom discussed.

Dan brought their wine and a cup of peppermint tea for Abby, who screwed up her face. 'I am so sick of this stuff,' she grumbled.

Dan sat beside Abby and rested a hand on the back of her neck, a casually affectionate gesture, but also a significant one. He took a gulp of wine. 'We should have a family dinner,' he said. 'Give Ally a call and see if he can make it up, eh, Lena?'

'At Bluebell Bank,' Lena said, nodding vigorously and looking up at him. 'A proper family dinner, with everyone; Austin will be home.' Her eyes were clouded with the ghosts of her past, until the realisation of her mistake swept them away.

'We can have it here,' Dan said, his eyes locking onto his sister's, holding her gaze for a moment. 'You can all come here and then you wouldn't have to worry about cooking, Lena.'

Lena shook her head. 'It should be at Bluebell Bank. Silly me, of course: not Austin at all. *Jonathon*, and Alistair, and . . . what *is* her name?'

Dan frowned and Kate remembered his stubbornness, his need for control in every situation. He was fighting Lena's disease instead of rolling with its punches. 'Dan.' Em reproved him in a gentle voice. Dan's frown deepened.

Kate intervened. 'Actually, it really *should* be Bluebell Bank. It just wouldn't be the same for me if not. I can help Lena with the meal and that way Abby doesn't have to worry about cooking.' She glanced at Lena. 'Melanie,' she supplied quietly, the name of Lena's daughter-in-law hovering so elusively on the tip of Lena's tongue.

Lena nodded, satisfied. 'That's the one.'

Abby smiled and rapped Dan smartly on the arm. 'That would be brilliant, Kate. The more pregnant I get the more Dan seems inclined to invite people for impromptu parties.'

Dan was repentant as he leaned down to kiss her forehead, brushing a strand of hair out of her eyes; Kate had to look away from the intimacy of their joined gaze. 'I guess I keep forgetting,' Dan said.

'Lucky you,' Abby replied, rubbing the bump. They all laughed.

'Where is Noah? I was looking forward to seeing him.' Kate remembered a skinny little boy, a little isolated from the rest of his family by the age gap. Of all of them, he would have changed the most.

'Out with his mates,' Dan said scowling darkly. 'If he comes home drunk again I swear I'll kill him this time.'

Abby laughed, but it sounded a little forced, like this was a common thread of dissent. 'If he does and he has any sense, he'll sleep in the barn sooner than face you again.'

'Hmm,' Kate interjected with a knowing smile. 'Underage drinking, how *awful*. You *never* did that of course.'

Dan softened. 'All right, I know I'm an old hypocrite. I was hardly perfect. Nor were any of us. But it's different when you're responsible for them.'

'Better get used to it,' said Emily.

'We're having a girl and she won't be allowed to leave the house until her twenty-first birthday. I'm planning to be a very old-fashioned father.'

'Poor kid,' Emily teased. She drank the last of her wine. 'You want some help bringing the cows down for milking?'

'That would be great. Thanks.'

As Dan and Emily steered the cows down from the pasture to the milking sheds, Kate followed at a safe distance, keeping out of the way of the great, inquisitive beasts who gazed at her as they sauntered past, flicking their tails against their haunches and swaying from side to side. She was watching Dan from a distance and marvelling again at how strange it was to be here. The cows would not be hurried, but took their time, no matter how much Dan and Em shouted and ran at them as they meandered this way and that.

Kate lingered by the gate for a few moments of peace, trying to put together all the various pieces of Bluebell Bank and its inhabitants to form a new image, trying to process the inevitable changes. The image jarred with memory. Much as she liked Abby – and she did – it was difficult to fit her into the picture.

*

Before it grew dark, they walked home with Lena across the fields, both giddy from the wine.

Home.

It actually *felt* like home, as Kate was afforded her first glimpse of the slate rooftops of Bluebell Bank through the canopy of trees. She had never felt this way about any other place. And no one but the Cottons had come so close to being family.

Chapter 6

Kate washed her face in the bathroom sink. Blinking, she blotted her face on a towel and peered at her reflection in the mirror. Her eyes were more green than blue in the half-light, her hair was scraped back from her face and her skin, washed clean of make-up, made her seem younger, despite the blurring of fatigue. She swayed as she gripped the edge of the porcelain sink and stared, seeing herself as a child again, when coming here had felt like stepping into a fairy-tale world.

She wondered what Ben was doing. Would she be replaced? They had parted on awkward, ambiguous terms, neither making any promises, despite the recent introduction to his parents and his casual mentions of marriage – too offhand to ever be considered a real proposal.

Kate wasn't under any illusions about Ben. It had begun as physical desire, nothing more; then had morphed into something neither of them felt able to define. Lately it had felt like they were travelling down well-worn patterns, transforming the relationship into something serious by dint of time served and convenience. Kate was attractive, successful – both decorative and engaging on his arm at parties: the perfect wife for a city boy with old money and its accompanying reputation to uphold. And Ben was gorgeous, solicitous, good company. And rich.

But it probably wasn't love, and Kate didn't feel certain that Ben would wait six days for her, let alone six weeks, or six months, or however long she stayed away.

Ben had been unattainable when Kate snagged him; there was a certain thrill in the hunt and acquisition of such a man. And he lingered in her thoughts now, his slow, sexy smile reaching out to taunt and tease across oceans. She definitely still wanted him.

Her fingers itched to reach for her phone and check her email. *If he has sent me a message it means he loves me, he is waiting for me. I will go home immediately*, she decided.

But she was home already, so how could she?

Kate grimaced at herself in the mirror. Being here had reminded her of a more primal, urgent sort of love. With Dan she had felt the throes of schoolgirl infatuation; with Luke Ross she had fallen fast and hard.

She didn't feel comfortable with the possibility that she was succumbing to the allure of marriage for money, for practicality – not wanting to struggle as she had all through her childhood. But did she really love Ben? She wasn't sure.

Financial security and the promise of a certain kind of life were not good enough reasons.

Kate threw a robe over her vest and shorts and padded barefoot across the quiet hall to her bedroom. After closing the door softly behind her, she sat on the bed, curled her legs beneath her and reached for her iPhone, cursing her eagerness and the anticipatory flutter in her belly.

A message from Ben. Her fingers trembled and tripped over themselves, fumbling as the message was revealed. *Kate, baby, I fucking miss you. B.*

That was all. Kate hated pet names, especially *baby,* as well Ben knew. And was that really *all* he had to say to her? The man who had lavished her with champagne and diamonds and made her feel safe.

The message was inadequate and infuriating.

Ben's world would continue without Kate in it: working hard and playing hard. He loved to bitch about how stressful his job was, but he wasn't happy without the pressure. He needed to feel important; if there had been a major fault line running through their relationship, it was that Kate wasn't needy enough for Ben's liking. Too independent for his taste. He'd asked her not to leave, but now what had seemed like an entreaty felt more like a threat.

For the last year, being Ben's girlfriend had consumed her. All of her friends had been under Ben's spell, encouraging the match, and there had been no one – no *Emily* – to point out the hard truths: that Ben was arrogant, emotionally illiterate, egotistical. Of course he was hot, he could make her feel like the only person in his universe with just a glance. But he could charm anyone thus; he wouldn't be pining for her, or drowning his sorrows alone. Ben would be indulging in a little gentle flirtation along with his martinis, despite his reluctant concession to long-distance love.

'I won't have much time to talk to you,' he had warned.

Kate, her ire up, had answered smartly, 'No change there, then.' Their parting had not been the gushing, embracing, kissing airport spectacle she had envisaged. Ben had had an important meeting to go to and said a hasty goodbye in the cab and she had wandered disconsolately into the terminal alone.

Kate leaned over and set the phone on the bedside table. She welcomed the return of her natural cynicism; *yes, he misses me in his bed, keeping his sheets warm.*

Not a good enough reason either – sex. She slid deeper beneath the covers and faced the fact that their relationship had probably been doomed the moment she set foot on that plane. She turned on her side and closed her eyes, seeking oblivion, but she sensed that sleep, jet lag or no, was going to be a long time coming.

In the darkness the face she saw was not Ben's, but an amalgam of two, long relegated to the very depths of her mind: Luke who had stolen her heart and broken it; and Dan, whose heart *she* had broken in turn.

*

The next morning, Kate stood before the contents of her suitcase, dressed in her underwear, and sighed. She had a suitcase full of beautiful clothes but none of them were right for Bluebell Bank. Designer labels, expensive fabrics – they were fine for New York, but here they seemed like artifice, reminding her of just how comprehensive a metamorphosis she had managed.

Standing clothes-less, homeless and directionless in front of her shell case – spilling its sophisticated contents onto the bed – Kate was caught between two homes, two identities.

She dug around in her case for the plainest thing she could find – a long white vest top – and tugged it over her head. She picked up last night's jeans and discarded them. Outside, the sky was blue, with the promise of summer warmth. Kate opened the bedroom door and yelled for Em.

Emily emerged from her room down the hallway, clutching a bath towel to her chest. Wet corkscrew curls spiralled on her shoulders. She looked startled. 'What's wrong?'

'Nothing. I was just wondering if you have a pair of shorts I could borrow?'

Emily's eyebrows shot upwards. 'Me?'

'Yes, it looks like it might be hot today and I didn't bring any.'

Emily screwed up her face in doubt. 'I guess.' She whisked back into the bedroom and reappeared a few moments later with a pair of navy cargo shorts which she tossed to Kate. 'They're kind of plain but the only other kind I have are towelling ones and they only look right on the beach.'

Kate caught the shorts in one hand. She didn't look at them. 'They're great.'

'Right.' Emily looked and sounded unconvinced, but her eyes sparked with inspiration as she leaned past Kate to peep into the bedroom, where Kate's suitcase sat on the bed: a treasure chest spilling out riches. 'I don't suppose I could borrow something of yours, could I?'

Kate opened her mouth and swallowed her words just in time. She didn't want to offend Emily, but ever since they had reached puberty they had been blessed with quite different body shapes. Emily seemed to wake one morning with ready-made curves, much to her dismay, and she was always a dress size – or two, depending on the strictness of the latest dieting regime – larger than Kate. But, as Kate was struggling to find a way to point this out, she looked at her friend anew and stifled her surprise. Noticed that Emily, clad only in her towel, had knobs of bone in place of rounded flesh. Her ribs popped out like bicycle spokes and her legs were too thin. Kate raised her eyes to Em's face and saw for the first time the hollowness of her cheeks, the way the bones jutted and protruded around her eyes. Sadness and turmoil had stripped her of flesh, a diet not to be recommended and, honestly, it didn't quite suit Emily. Kate thought she better suited her softness and curves. 'Of course,' she said. 'Take whatever you want.' She measured the new, slender Emily with a dressmaker's eye. 'Actually, I have a maxi-dress that would look great with your hair.' She rummaged in her suitcase and produced the sundress, patterned teal and bronze in a bold flower print. She found a pair of sandals and handed these over too. 'Put them on,' she instructed. 'Let me see you.'

Emily departed, smiling, with her loot. Kate stepped into the shorts and zipped them. They sat loose on her hips. She was vain enough to be glad that her last spray tan was holding, her long legs were still golden and smooth. She shoved her feet into a pair of red thongs – *flip-flops,* she reminded herself and the name sounded childlike and cheerful, evocative of half-baked summers, buckets and spades and cheap, plastic crab lines from the pocket money section of the newsagent.

She smiled to herself, loving the onomatopoeia of the word as she flipped and flopped around the room, brushing her hair and putting on the white-gold bangle Ben gave her one birthday.

Emily looked good in the dress; she knew it and couldn't help smiling. For once she carried herself with confidence, a self-assured tilt to her chin. She twirled, enjoying the diaphanous swirl of her skirt around her calves. The dress was soft and floaty, tight over the bust and flaring from the waist. Gold sandals peeped out from under the hem. 'You look amazing,' she said, only a little disgruntled that Kate had made an ugly pair of shorts look so good.

They linked arms and walked down the stairs together, following the clink of crockery that signalled a presence in the kitchen. Emily paused by the mirror in the hall to examine her reflection again, fiddling with her hair, and Kate proceeded into the kitchen alone.

She was tentative as she entered the room, not wanting to startle Lena, a little afraid that Lena might have forgotten her again. But it was not Lena she found in the kitchen, clattering crockery and making a messy breakfast, scraping a chair across the flagstones and banging down a bowl of cereal in a puddle of spilled milk. It was a young man – a boy, Kate realised, paying him closer inspection: a boy with the Cotton features and the eyes of a child she used to know, tucking into a breakfast of builder's tea and Cheerios.

'Noah!' she exclaimed, genuinely shocked. Here was the physical evidence of her six-year absence. There was not such a huge difference in Emily between the ages of twenty-one and twenty-seven, and physically Dan had changed little; but between eleven and seventeen, one changed beyond recognition; as indeed Noah had – from boy to nearly man. He still had the lanky frame of a teenager, skinny in places, burgeoning with muscle in others. He wore the uniform of his generation: jeans riding low, T-shirt from Abercrombie & Fitch. He had the bed-head look of someone who didn't really care about his appearance. His eyes were clear and bright, and his skin scrubbed and clean, with only a few pimples, a faint shadow where he had begun to shave, a crescent of fatigue smudged beneath each eye as if he hadn't slept much; but he possessed the resilience of youth, and on him the look was endearing and boyish.

He looked up from his cereal. 'Kate,' he said with excited inflection. 'Dan said you were here. I came over to see for myself.' He glanced down at his bowl and gestured with his spoon. 'And because I needed breakfast.'

'Dan doesn't feed you?' Kate asked, pulling out a seat and sliding into it. She wanted to hug Noah, but she felt too awkward; for him it had been a long time. What memory did Noah have of her after all this time? Eleven was formative, hovering on the brink of teenagedom, with childhood memories lingering long.

'It wasn't the lack of breakfast,' Noah explained, digging his spoon into the soggy mess of cereal. 'It was the fact that Dan seemed to feel the best accompaniment to it was a morning lecture.'

Kate smiled. 'Was it deserved, this lecture?'

Noah considered. He chewed and shrugged with easy grace. 'Maybe. But that doesn't mean I had to sit and listen to it.'

Kate filed away his response to think about later. There was something lost and fragile about Noah; she thought back to what Emily had told her about his expulsion, and Dan's acerbic comments about him getting drunk with his mates. 'Did you have a good time last night? You were out with friends, right?'

'Yeah.'

'So, did you have a good time?'

He shrugged again. 'Yeah. You know. It's really good to see you. We're all glad you came.'

'Oh?' Kate was a little taken aback.

Noah nodded. 'You're here and everything is going to be different for Em.'

The kitchen door swung open and Emily entered. 'Hey, Noah,' she said, ruffling her brother's hair as she walked past. Noah recoiled, scowling, as if this were a common annoyance. 'What you up to?' Her tone held a sing-song cadence that seemed to irk her brother.

'What does it look like? Eating breakfast, talking to Kate.'

Emily gave him a measured look. 'I mean, what are you doing *here*? Aren't you supposed to be working? Dan's your boss, you know.'

'Like I could ever forget.' Noah pushed his cereal bowl to one side and stood. He went over to the kettle, filled it and put it on to boil again. 'Tea?' he offered, glancing over his shoulder. 'I made Lena one. She's already out in the garden with Bracken.'

'Is she all right?' Emily's voice grew sharp.

'Of course. Why wouldn't she be? Tea?' He turned away from his sister and aimed the question at Kate.

'Sure. Thanks.' Kate knew there was no point asking for coffee; this was Bluebell Bank, where no one could go longer than an hour without another cup of tea, and coffee was considered the devil's own drink.

'So,' Emily persisted, again with the bright, enquiring lilt that seemed to so irritate her little brother. 'Tell me why you're not at work.'

'Because if I had to spend another hour in Dan's company we would have hurt each other. Abby doesn't need the stress of that in her condition.'

Emily made an impatient, teacherish noise. 'You really should make more effort with him. Like I said, he's your boss. He pays your wages.'

'That doesn't give him the right to tell me what to do with my life.'

She frowned. 'Actually it does. You do live under his roof and you're only seventeen.'

Noah filled the mugs with boiling water. He crossed to the fridge and took out the milk carton. There was something deliberate about his movements. Kate watched them both, dismayed at the skin of tension that flexed and rippled between them. She cast around for something to say to ease the atmosphere.

'If you're not working today,' she said, with sudden inspiration, 'what *are* you doing?'

'Getting over his hangover, probably,' Emily said in a derisive tone.

Noah sighed and slammed Kate's mug down on the table, tea slopping over the rim. He threw himself into his seat and resumed his breakfast. 'I don't have a hangover,' he said, tight-lipped and sulky.

'Don't talk with your mouth full,' Emily scolded, swatting him, smiling as if she really had no idea how annoying she was being.

Noah met Kate's gaze with a resigned expression and something flared between them: an immediate kinship. Kate could sense his relief at having her here – someone to talk to who wasn't a Cotton

'Why do you ask?' Noah addressed himself to Kate, ignoring Emily completely. 'Did you have something in mind?'

'Yes.' Kate glanced briefly at Emily. 'We could really use some help.'

'We can manage,' Emily said.

'Emily, we can *use his help*.' Kate looked reproachfully at Emily, her tone steely. 'We're going shopping,' she told Noah. 'We need to go and pick up wood for some shelves for the bookshop.'

Noah nodded. 'I can help with that. And I can build shelves.'

'So can we,' Emily said tersely.

Kate looked at her. 'Really? *Can* we?'

'Well, we can figure it out,' Emily qualified. 'You can learn anything from the internet.'

'Sure,' Kate agreed. 'But are we really going to turn down the help?'

'I suppose it would keep him out of trouble,' Emily mused.

Kate bridled at her admonishing tone, but Noah only rolled his eyes.

'You know, if you're buying wood you're going to need better transport than Jasper. I've got a mate in the town owes me a favour. I can get us a van if you want.'

'That sounds great. Can you drive it too?'

'I've got my licence. I learned to drive on the farm. Of course, Dan never lends me his truck and since Emily appeared on the scene Jasper is always spoken for. But I'm a good driver.'

'That's a matter of opinion,' put in Emily. She may have been trying for humour, but her sarcasm fell woefully short of the mark. Kate sighed as Noah set his jaw.

'*You* don't have to come,' he said to Emily in a tight voice. 'If you have other plans, Kate and I can manage.'

Emily frowned; she knew she had gone too far, but was loath to apologise. 'Of *course* I don't have other plans. I guess it would be good to have the use of a van, and if you want to come along that would be helpful.' She was less than magnanimous.

'We could use the muscle,' Kate said, to make up for Emily's waspishness, and Noah flushed with pleasure.

'I'll give my mate a call and I'll meet you guys back here with the van in a while. Okay?'

'That sounds perfect. Doesn't it, Emily?'

Emily gave a non-committal grunt. 'You need to check with Dan, make sure it's all right. You can't just leave him in the lurch. He'll sack you.'

'Like that would be a hardship,' Noah said, and he disappeared out of the room before Emily could retort.

When Noah exited the kitchen, he left behind a tense silence. Emily wore a buttoned-up look that did little to encourage Kate in overtures of conversation; she sipped her mug of tea, picked up a newspaper – which, Kate noticed, was several days old – and began to read with great deliberation. She might have preferred a novel but, none being to hand, a newspaper would suffice; to Emily, reading *anything* was always preferable to not reading at all. Kate felt awkward, having observed the perplexing exchanges and felt the earth shift beneath her feet again – her Emily of old was warm, funny, loquacious: sometimes impulsive, often abrupt, but never unkind.

She watched Emily until she could bear the silence no longer and had to speak. They had been reunited not twenty-four hours – yesterday everything had seemed so exciting and strange, every moment budding with possibility. Now it was different, strained.

'So,' Kate said cautiously. 'I think it will be good to have Noah's help. And, of course, it will be nice for me to get to know him properly.'

Emily barely looked up from the pages of her newspaper. 'Mmm.'

'I thought you were a little hard on him before, to be honest.'

Emily's head snapped up and she set aside the newspaper. 'You don't know,' she said, not harshly, but it still stung. 'I mean, he was exp*elled* from school, Kate. And everything . . . everything's just been such a mess.' She ran a hand through her hair, working at its knots and tangles.

Kate knew Emily was not only talking about her brother. She nodded slowly. 'OK,' she said. 'I suppose it must be tough for you all, Noah's expulsion, and Lena . . . but everyone seems to be on Noah's case. That's just my opinion. As an outsider, observing.' She held up her hands and surrendered with a small smile. She wasn't here to upset the apple cart, unless it needed upsetting – perhaps that was her purpose after all.

Emily sighed with a long-suffering air. 'You're not an outsider,' she said. She didn't argue with the rest of Kate's assessment 'The thing is . . .' She paused. 'Look, it's not my place to tell you about Noah. I hope he'll tell you himself. Mum and Dad sent him to Dan to get him away from all the unpleasantness, but he won't talk to any of us. He needs to talk to somebody, but it obviously isn't going to be Dan or me. I think maybe it could be you.'

'I hardly know him,' Kate objected. 'I haven't seen him since he was a kid.'

'Yes, but you and he had a bond.' Emily looked bleak. 'You know, sometimes I think you were a better sister to him than I was.'

Kate shook her head, exasperated. 'No,' she said. '*You're* his sister. You just need to let up on him a bit.'

Emily didn't say anything for a while. When she did, her voice was small. 'Well, I was still hoping that you could speak to him.'

'I will, if you think it will help. But only if Noah wants to talk to me.'

'If you hear the full story, perhaps you'll understand why Dan and I are so anxious about him.' She stood quickly. 'I'm going to see Lena,' she said. 'To check on her before we leave.'

Kate was left alone in the kitchen with a mug of cooling tea she didn't want, a pile of unwashed dishes surrounding her and the creeping knowledge that when she had clicked that link on the airline website to book her ticket, she really hadn't had the first idea what she was getting herself into.

*

Half an hour later, Noah reappeared in a beat-up van. Kate was enjoying the pale gold of the morning sunshine and a moment of solitude, as she allowed the world to settle down a bit after her hasty hurtle across the Atlantic and the revelations of disquiet at Bluebell Bank; sitting on a bench outside Bluebell Bank in front of the gravel drive where Jasper was parked alongside her shiny rental car. The gravel gave way to grass – much too unruly to be called a lawn – which thickened and straggled as it merged into the edge of the wood, which in turn grew more dense as it sloped downwards towards the stream. To the other side lay the hill which, carpeted blue in spring, gave the house its name.

Noah lurched up the drive and crunched to a halt in front of her. He leaned out the open window, amid a blast of loud music, looking ridiculously pleased with himself. 'Kate, are you ready? C'mon, let's go. Where's Em?'

Kate stood up with a languid stretch and a yawn. 'She's still in the garden with Lena. Shall I go and get her?'

'No need.' Noah pressed his foot down and the engine revved throatily beneath the bonnet. 'C'mon,' he urged again, eager to begin what was something of an adventure to him.

Kate, not entirely devoid of adventuresome spirit this morning either, was looking forward to the trip too. She left her bench and went to open the passenger door, spotting Emily coming round the side of the house, latching the gate behind her. She scrunched across the gravel and got in the van without a word. Noah backed out of the drive and executed a rough turn with a spray of gravel.

Kate sat in the middle. On one side of her was Noah, eyes fixed on the road, on the other Emily stared out the window, her body angled away and a discouraging expression on her face. They drove for several minutes before anyone spoke, the thrumming bass of the music vibrating through Kate's bones and the jerky lurching of the van's suspension shoogling her.

Noah turned to Kate and yelled over the music, 'So, where are we headed first?'

Kate glanced at Emily; this was *her* enterprise. When Emily didn't reply, Kate leaned across to turn the music down. 'I thought the nearest hardware store, wherever that is.'

'I know a place. It's not far. Do you think we could stop in town for a coffee before we get on the road?' He slowed hopefully as they approached the turning for Wigtown.

Without turning her head, Emily said, 'We don't have time for that.'

Kate leaned forward, trying to catch Emily's eye, but Emily wouldn't look at her. 'I guess we have time,' she said mildly. 'We're not in a hurry, are we? I could definitely use a coffee. I'm sure you'd *love* one, Em.' Teasing, trying to mollify her.

Kate could only see a sliver of Emily's face but she glimpsed the glimmer of a grin. Emily turned. 'Tea,' she said with exaggerated patience. 'I'd like tea. Obviously.'

'Tea it is then. So we'll stop?'

'Actually.' Emily's sudden change in demeanour was like the sun emerging from behind a cloud: welcome but bewildering. Kate felt she could barely keep up with this new mercurial Emily. 'Actually, we have to stop by the shop. I forgot to measure up for shelves yesterday.'

Noah leaned forward to eye his sister askance as he slowed at a junction. 'Seriously? You were going to buy wood for shelves with no idea how much you need?'

'Yesterday was kind of an eventful day,' Emily said. There was sarcasm, but no malice now. 'You know: long-lost best friend turns up out of the blue and announces she's here for the summer and you forget to measure the shelves. A common error, I'm sure.'

Kate laughed aloud and the tension lifted. Emily's words lingered. *Here for the summer*: a delightfully vague description of her future. The thought made her lurch between contentment and fear once more.

Noah continued teasing Emily, as delighted in her change of humour as Kate, as he made the turn and accelerated again. 'Have you found this wonderful YouTube tutorial that's going to teach you how to build these shelves with no measurements?'

'We're not completely inept,' Emily answered, with a mock-severe glare. 'We're both highly skilled individuals.'

Noah smiled and slanted a look at her. 'No,' he agreed, 'not *completely* inept.'

Kate leaned back in her seat and let the words flow around her – the teasing camaraderie felt good, much better than Emily's snappishness. She closed her eyes, let the sound of their voices entwine with the music, the throb of the engine and thrum of tarmac meld into a melee that dulled her thoughts.

All these little faults, rips in the fabric of the place, doubts. And still, the overwhelming certainty that this was where she was supposed to be.

Chapter 7

Emily stayed in the bookshop to make measurements while Kate and Noah went to collect refreshments. She busied herself quickly, feeling ashamed for this morning's altercation with Noah. Not that it was a rare occurrence, but she hadn't meant to let the mask slip in front of Kate so soon, and Kate had obviously been perturbed.

The sun was streaming through the shop and it looked fresher and brighter than it had twenty-four hours previously. Emily had to admit that if not for Kate there was no way she'd have mustered the energy to set about building shelves and buying paint today. Nor would she have accepted, or even considered asking for, Noah's help.

She wondered when things had become so strained between her and Noah. It wasn't just her annoyance at him for what had happened at school. She used to be his advocate whenever Dan and their parents were on his back about what he was going to do with his life, but now she was as bad as the rest of them. It would do them good to work together today.

She watched Kate and Noah set off up the street together, laughing easily. He had been morose and spiky since his ignominious exile here, but now he seemed more like his old self.

Kate had achieved that in just a few hours. Emily was so very glad that Kate was here.

Noah must be scared, she thought: of what he'd done and the uncertainty of his future. They weren't so different, really. If only she had been more sympathetic. But Emily had become used to silence, to staying locked inside her head and her books, and she hardly remembered how to open up to people; only with Lena could she relax, because Lena didn't look at her with constant pity and concern – probably because Lena didn't remember what had happened to Emily most of the time.

Emily had been sitting in a dank, empty bookshop for weeks, wondering when she would find the courage to start living again. With Kate's arrival came the return of some spark.

But still the fear was there, lying in wait. She felt the shadow of it looming over her, even now, in the brilliant sunshine of a day carefully planned out ahead of her – the sickening waves of anxiety that claimed her for no reason, with no warning. She didn't want Kate to know just how bad it was, to see how badly damaged she was. She'd been keeping them hidden for months – her panic attacks. It was why she felt so dissociated from them all, constantly having to keep her terror secret.

It was so stupid, when there was nothing to fear. No reason to feel like this. Emily berated herself once more for being so weak, so unable to get over him. She'd had no one to confide in since Kate. Was it too much to expect that Kate could fix everything?

*

In the café, once the waitress had fulfilled their order, Kate tried to get Noah talking. 'Tell me how you are,' she said, fixing him with a hard stare that left him in no doubt what she was talking about.

Noah gave her a guarded look as they stepped out into the street amongst a riot of flowers spilling from hanging baskets and window boxes. 'Emily already told you, I guess.'

'No. She hinted. I mean, yes, she told me about you getting . . .' She paused, the word 'expelled' was weighty and unwieldy.

Noah drew his lower lip between his teeth and sucked in a breath. 'Yeah.' He turned away from her and stared ahead, but she caught a glimpse of his frustration hidden behind the mask of teenage malaise and carelessness. He was the youngest of the Cottons, with all the weight of his parents and siblings on him; all that optimism and expectation. As an only child, and a lover of all things Cotton, Kate couldn't really relate to his predicament – there was a time she wanted nothing more than to be part of this family; you had to take the rough with the smooth, that was what family was about. But she could sympathise and understand that the pressure of living up to what other people expected of you might get tiresome at times.

'If you want to talk about it . . .' she offered clumsily, handling things with less aplomb than she had envisaged – had she fancied that Noah would jump eagerly at the chance of a willing confidante? No, she was doing this for Emily. And, she supposed, for Noah, who needed to talk it out even if he didn't realise it himself yet.

They threaded their way slowly back up the street towards the shop. 'Look,' Kate said, 'I'm not going to force the issue—' Noah smiled ironically '—obviously I'm here to help Em but I'm here if *you* want to talk too. I think you and Emily need—'

'Our heads banging together?' Noah's laugh held a hint of self-deprecation. 'I got that impression at breakfast.'

'Well, the three of us are going to be spending time together while I'm here. It could be really good fun, but not if you and Emily are at each other's throat.'

'Tell that to her.' There was an unmistakeable whine in Noah's voice: like a child who didn't want to take his share of the blame; but he smiled ruefully enough when Kate fixed him with a stern look. 'I know,' he conceded. 'It's both of us. It's just . . . I want my sister back. Not the schoolteacher – not that she was ever particularly good at *that*.'

'There you go again,' Kate said. 'Undermining her. Dan does it too. No one seems to have much faith in her. So, teaching didn't work out, but don't you think she can make this bookshop work?'

Noah stopped in the middle of the street and stared at her, his frown deepening at the reproach. 'The evidence would suggest not. She's sat in that shop doing nothing for months now.'

'Maybe she *couldn't* do anything. Maybe she wasn't ready. Maybe she needed help.' Kate rose immediately to the defence of her friend, although she too had been wondering about Emily's lengthy procrastination.

'We would have helped,' Noah said, wounded.

'Would you? You and Dan are busy with the farm, Abby's about to have a baby and Lena—' she stopped. It wasn't fair to use Lena's illness against him. 'I'm not saying it's your fault, Noah. I'm just saying that Emily needs help to get out of this slump . . . and that's where I come in. But it would help if the rest of you could be a bit kinder—'

'Kinder?' Noah was incredulous. 'Have you *heard* the way she speaks to us lately? She nags at me all the time. If you can get her to stop doing that then I'll be more supportive.'

Kate sighed. 'How very adolescent of you,' she said, remembering too late that that was exactly what he was. She was berating him simply for acting his age, when, in fact, hadn't he had to grow up rather fast lately? She paused, about to turn down the vennel towards the shop.

Noah stopped her with a hand on her arm. He shook his head. 'OK, ugh, I get your point, I'll try.'

'I'm just saying you're not a child any more.' But this too felt like an attack, a reminder of what he had lost. She seemed to be saying everything wrong. 'I'm sorry. Look, let's just try and enjoy today.'

The bookshop, devoid of its stock save a single pile of books on the counter, was a blank canvas, and Kate felt the spark of inspiration strike her anew as she and Noah stepped inside. Noah, too, seemed intrigued by this measure of progress. He looked around eagerly, seeing its potential for the first time.

Emily, sweat-damp curls sticking to her forehead, glanced up from where she was tugging the rickety old metal shelving away from one wall. She studied her hands, thick with dust, then looked mournfully down at her dress. 'This outfit was made for wandering around glamorous shops and having lunch in a lovely wine bar, not messing about with shelves.' Her tragic expression made Kate laugh; Emily had never been one to worry about clothes.

'How about a compromise? If we find a pub with a decent beer garden, I'll treat you both to lunch after we've picked up the wood?'

Emily nodded happily and came across to take her tea from Noah. She gave him a small, uncertain smile, but her tone was resolute. 'Right, shall we get to work then? I was thinking shelves round all three of the walls. Floor to ceiling. Of course I'd really love one of those ladders on runners that slides along . . .'

'You've wandered into a Jane Austen novel again,' Noah said, waving a hand in front of her face. 'Earth to Emily.'

Emily smiled at him and batted at his arm. 'Aww, you know who Jane Austen is! And there I was thinking my family never listened to me.'

'Like I could be related to you and *not* know who Jane Austen is.'

Emily reached for the pile of books she'd set aside on the counter and unearthed a volume, grinning. 'Say the word and you can borrow.'

'When hell freezes over. I'd sooner read *Twilight*.'

Emily bared her teeth and hissed. 'Blasphemy,' she cried. 'Get out.'

Kate, laughing as she watched this exchange, said, 'I know in your world preferring *Twilight* to Austen is a crime punishable by immediate banishment from all bookshops for ever, but I don't think we can afford to lose his muscle.'

Noah preened. 'Yeah, my *muscle*.' He struck a pose.

Emily rolled her eyes. 'Don't encourage him,' she said. 'He already thinks he's God's gift to women since he got a girlfriend.'

'How do you know about that?' Noah demanded, flushing pink.

'This is all very interesting,' Kate intervened. 'And truly, I intend to quiz you mercilessly about your love life later, Noah, but perhaps we should get to work.' She picked up the tape measure from the counter and tossed it to Emily, who fumbled the catch and spilled her tea.

As Emily and Noah got to work measuring up the shop, Kate had the more enviable job of sitting on the counter sipping her extra-strong coffee and jotting down the figures they called out to her. She flipped idly through the books on the countertop while she waited, picking up a photo book about Galloway and leafing through the colour plate images.

'There are so many things I want to do while I'm here,' she mused. The book painted the Solway Coast in so many shades of beauty: soft sunsets, and storm-tossed seas beneath transient, rolling cloud; the sparkling firth scattered with diamonds. It was the picture-perfect Solway of her best memories. 'I want to go to Kirroughtree and drive the Raiders' Road, visit St Ninian's Cave and the Dark Sky Observatory, walk through the Galloway Forest, go to Rigg Bay and walk the clifftop to Cruggleton. I want to see the shops in Kirkcudbright and Gatehouse – all the places we went as kids.'

Emily glanced up from a crouch on the dusty floor, letting the tape measure snap back. Noah yelped as it caught his fingers. 'We can do all those things,' she said, sounding surprised, as if she had never thought of doing any of them, despite living here with such treasures right on her doorstep. Kate had three thousand miles and six years of separation as her excuse for not revisiting all the special places of their childhood; Emily had nothing. 'It'll be like old times.'

But they both knew that it wouldn't; nothing was ever quite

like old times, no matter how much one tried to recreate them. But they would create new times, make new memories. 'What else?' Kate said, closing the book with a snap and stretching her arms above her head impatiently. 'What else did we used to do? I'm sure I've forgotten things.'

Emily laughed. '*I* seem to remember spending most of my time either sequestered in a bookshop, or reading some place or other, so what you and the brothers got up to I can't exactly recall. I was there in body most of the time, but my mind was elsewhere, at Green Gables or Pemberley or Hogwarts. There was a lot of cricket, and a lot of very long walks. I remember those particularly because Lena would never let me read as we walked in case I tripped over my feet.'

'I loved to walk. I used to wish we could walk and walk and never stop.' Kate slipped into the feeling she had once had that if she walked far enough and deep enough into the Galloway countryside she would finally leave all her problems behind. All those school holidays, little escapes from reality, slipping into the storybook world of Bluebell Bank. Just her, Emily and the brothers, with Em's parents making fleeting cameos, popping down from Edinburgh at weekends when work allowed. Trusting their offspring to Lena's loving, no-nonsense guardianship.

'Do you remember the otter pool?' Emily asked. 'That was fun.'

Noah sat back on his heels and listened, getting a glimpse of the world of Bluebell Bank he had missed. The childhood shared by Kate and Emily, Dan, Ally and Fergus was a mystery to him. In that sense, Noah was almost an only child; the gap was so great that his childhood had been largely solitary, the last of his siblings departing the family home by the time he was eight. 'I want to come with,' Noah said. 'All those places sound kind of cool. I've mostly ignored the fact that I'm here at all, but I really should see something of the place.'

Kate gave him a sympathetic smile; he was so young, so vulnerable, pretending the whole mess with school had never happened and punishing the Solway and his siblings because he didn't want to be here. He was looking hopefully at Kate and his sister now: the little kid hanging on their coat-tails again, wanting to be included in their excursions.

'Of course you can come,' Kate said. 'It'll be fun, showing you *our* Solway, won't it, Em?'

'Yes,' Emily said, sounding surprised. 'I dare say it will.'

Kate slid off the counter. 'Are we done here?' She was anxious to be off now, to distract herself from thoughts of Luke. Inevitably, thinking of all those places, her escapades with Emily and the brothers, led her back to him.

'Um, I think so.' Emily frowned as she studied the scrawl of figures and brushed down her dress. Kate went on ahead of them while they faffed about putting away tape measure and notebook, chucking out empty cups and locking the door. She pushed impatiently through the branches that caught at her hair.

Luke. She had been days from her fifteenth birthday when she met him, and he was only a few months older.

Dan had just turned seventeen and was badgering Lena to let him learn to drive in Jasper, and Kate's infatuation with him had become almost painful. Until she met Luke, she had been wondering how she was going to survive a summer of being so close to Dan, without the relief of being able to talk through the crazy feelings with Emily – it seemed important to Kate to keep her desire for Dan secret; she sensed it might somehow spoil everything otherwise. Emily was beginning to grow prickly about such things, occasional burst of possessiveness over Kate alienating her from her brothers; jealousy beginning to colour their relationship and a general dissatisfaction with her new adolescence emerging. While Kate found it easy to make friends and was popular at school, Emily was spiky, always a bit different.

Kate had met Luke in the town square as she was returning from a mad dash to the public toilet. Lena had driven up to

Edinburgh to pick them all up for the summer, but they hadn't quite made it to Bluebell Bank, stopping en route to pop into the Co-op for whatever food fads they currently couldn't live without – Lena had no compunctions about feeding them junk. Emily, of course, had taken advantage of the opportunity to dive into her favourite bookshop, but Kate had been concerned only with her bladder. She was too embarrassed to admit in front of the boys that she needed to go, but Lena looked at her askance as she jumped down from the car. 'What's wrong with you? Dancing about like a scalded cat.'

'Bathroom,' Kate muttered.

Lena grinned and pointed her in the right direction,

Coming back across the road at a more leisurely pace, she got her first glimpse of the boy with the skateboard. He had long, tanned limbs and baggy board shorts. His gaze was almost fierce, eyes icy blue beneath hunched, dark brows. She shoved her hands in the pockets of her jean shorts, her tummy wriggling with butterflies. She took a step backwards, feeling awkward, turned and started to walk quickly in the opposite direction.

Her crush on Dan aside, Kate had little experience of boys. Dan was her friend, first and foremost, despite the fact he sometimes rendered her speechless – like that morning when she bumped into him coming out of the bathroom wearing just a towel and she had been overwhelmed by the desire to touch his bare, damp skin. She felt the same way now, looking at the skater boy, a heady and confusing concoction of fear, anticipation and pleasure.

Kate quickened her step away from him, feeling shy and out of her depth. 'Hey,' the boy shouted. He scooted round in front of her on his board so that she had no choice but to stop. He grinned, stepped off the board and flipped it. 'Do I know you? Do you live here?'

Kate shook her head, tongue-tied. She stared at him; with his close-cropped black hair and brilliant blue eyes he was gorgeous.

Emily would disagree with Kate's assessment, being obsessed by an older, Darcy-esque, romantic-hero type Kate wasn't sure existed in the real world. 'I come here most summers.'

He had a dimple at one corner of his mouth when he smiled. 'Oh, a tourist.'

'Not exactly. I'm visiting. Family.'

The boy's eyes travelled over her. She could feel his gaze burning hot on her skin. It blazed through her self-consciousness and she didn't feel exposed or vulnerable, but warm and brave and whole, basking in his attention.

'I'm Luke, I live here and it's pretty boring to be honest. Are you here with your folks then?'

Discussing her own familial situation was never going to be a good opening gambit so she was deliberately vague. 'My best friend and her brothers. Do you live here in town?' It felt as if her tongue no longer fitted her mouth; her words were clumsy and imprecise, but the boy seemed not to notice. He continued to stare at her, fascinated.

'Down that way.' He pointed vaguely behind him. 'Then I suppose we'll see each other around.'

She tugged on her ponytail. 'I suppose. It's a small place.'

'There's a bunch of us hanging out tonight if you fancy coming, instead of just leaving it to chance.' Luke's tone was casual, but as he stared at her from beneath his long dark lashes, his eyes flared with intense blue fire, and Kate felt the dizzying sensation of everything – the whole summer, perhaps her whole life – hanging in the balance as he waited for her answer.

She wanted to agree immediately, but she wasn't sure what Lena would think. And it wasn't just the logistics of it – groups of teenagers meant drinking and Kate didn't do alcohol.

Before she could reply, a sound startled her: her name bellowed out as Dan jogged across the road towards her. She struggled to drag her eyes from Luke's.

'There you are,' Dan said and looked the boy up and down

warily, bristling a little in the way that teenage boys did. Luke returned his gaze steadily.

'I was just . . . Is everyone finished in the shops so soon?'

'Em needs to be prised out of whichever bookshop she's hidden herself in, but the rest of us are ready to go. Lena was worried you might have got lost on the way back from the toilet.' Kate stared at the ground, embarrassed. 'Let's go.' Dan was tugging at her arm, a touch that any other time would have sent her into paroxysms of joy.

'See you around,' she told Luke.

He nodded, tapped his skateboard against the kerb. 'What about tonight?'

Beside her, Dan's head snapped up. Kate ignored him. 'Maybe,' she said. 'When, where?'

Luke pointed at the fountain behind them. 'Seven?'

She nodded. Luke's eyes drew hers and held them unnervingly. Her stomach twisted. She wondered what it would be like to kiss him; she had never kissed a boy. Coming to her senses, staring at his mouth – his full bottom lip and straight white teeth – she quickly averted her gaze, surrendered to the pressure on her elbow and turned to walk away, unable to keep from glancing back over her shoulder.

Dan teased her mercilessly as soon as they were out of Luke's earshot. 'So, what *about* tonight, Kate?'

Kate said nothing. She wanted to be alone to relive those precious moments with Luke, or in the sanctuary of her bedroom at Bluebell Bank with Emily, regaling her with the tale and working out what to do. Emily might have preferred her men old-fashioned and fictional, but if there was one thing her romantic soul would understand it was love at first sight. Which was what this undoubtedly was.

In the car, she cradled the encounter with Luke close. She recalled everything she could – the shape of his lips, the intense blue of his eyes, the long, lean form, the way his body swivelled sinuously as he weaved the skateboard side to side. Em dug her in the ribs with a sharp poke, shattering her love-struck daydreams. Dan was twisting round and grinning at her from the front seat. She looked daggers at Dan, but he grinned back, unabashed.

'Kate has a date. Some skater kid was chatting her up in the square. He asked her out.' There was something else in his tone besides glee at the opportunity to tease: was it possible that Dan was jealous?

Kate felt the weight of their scrutiny. She was disappointed that Dan would choose to torment her so. She caught Lena's cool gaze in the rear-view mirror. 'Enough, Daniel,' Lena said, stamping her foot on the brake as the turning for Bluebell Bank loomed and she swung a sharp left. 'If you keep that behaviour up, I might just change my mind about letting you drive my precious Jasper.'

Dan looked at her in disbelief. 'I was only messing about,' he said. Lena so rarely admonished him, and certainly not over sibling banter. He looked at Kate and a hint of remorse crept into his expression.

Dan slammed his door and headed for the house without stopping to help unpack. Kate looked around, lingering to enjoy the first moments of Bluebell Bank magic; the air was so sweet and clear and distinctive here. Emily grabbed her arm and hustled her towards the house. 'I need to know *everything*,' she declared.

Dan was waiting for her at the door, frowning at his feet. 'Sorry,' he muttered; sometimes he forgot that Kate was not Emily, that she took his teasing more to heart. She pardoned him with a nod, but Emily shoulder-barged him out the way as they passed by. 'You're going to regret that,' Dan warned with a laugh. Kate scooted out of the way as Dan chased Emily back down the drive, past Lena who muttered about *teenagers* under her breath, as they narrowly avoided bowling her over.

Now Kate stood in the shade of the alley, staring across the street at the very place where they had all met that night: she and Emily, Luke and his friends. Lena had consented to drive them and they had made her drop them off up the road so they could sneak into the toilet and put on their make-up. There had been beer – a six-pack under Luke's arm – and the sounds of youth ringing clear in the summer-sweet evening air.

It had seemed so easy. Luke had an arm around Kate's shoulders in an easy, proprietorial fashion before she knew it, introducing her to everyone like they were old friends, leading her down the road towards the Martyr's Stake. She couldn't have cared less who the others were, or where they were going, or even that there was beer (she didn't drink any and neither did Luke, but Emily got spectacularly intoxicated for the first time); she was love-drunk, infatuated, weak with desire, and when Luke kissed her it felt both incredible and unsettling. It was a small moment of epic proportion; big enough to consume the universe with the scale of her feeling – fleeting sensation that lasted long, forever cemented in memory.

Noah shattered Kate's reverie as he and Emily clattered up the path behind her. 'Come on.' Kate was staring at the fountain, her fingers brushing her lips which still tingled at the memory of that first clumsy, incredible kiss.

'I'm coming.'

If Kate had been an ordinary girl, with an ordinary childhood, she and Luke might not have fallen quite so hard. As it was he was infatuated, drawn in by the web of mystery that clung to her. She was ripe, ready for him, driven by her desire for acceptance and love. Luke's own home life was far from ideal; in him she found acceptance, understanding and affection that transcended even the Cottons's concern.

The conditions were perfectly apposite, the timing exactly right. And Kate and Luke were perfectly doomed.

Chapter 8

In the van, Emily was silent while Noah and Kate argued about the music. Eventually, Noah gave in and let Kate plug her iPhone into the speakers. Emily leaned her head against the window and felt the vibrations of the road run through her, the glass cool against her forehead. Sunshine filtered through the canopy of leaves overhead.

The panic, which had been kept at bay all morning by ensuring she stayed busy and distracted, reared its head again. Joe rushed into her mind. She tried to banish him from a day that was so full of promise, but she felt defenceless against the pull of the tide. Her heart sank; she was so tired of feeling this way.

Her phone was a grenade waiting to explode in her hand; she should have wiped his number and changed hers. She should have stopped herself tracking him on social media and reading about him online, but she was weak. It wasn't so easy to expunge an ex who had actually managed to achieve fame just as they'd split up. His band, after years of diligence and dull gigs, had finally made it and the music world was going crazy for him; it made him hard to ignore.

Noah drove into the parking lot outside the DIY store. His and Kate's conversation seemed muffled and removed from her.

Emily felt too hot, trapped inside the van. She pushed at the door, feeling a spurt of panic: the hot ache against her eyeballs, the all-too-familiar compulsion, her breath quick in her chest. *Not again. Not now.*

The panic pushed up into her head; her vision blurred and her blood roared. She had to escape, seek the only comfort she could, even though she knew it was wrong.

She got the door open and stumbled out, lurching away from them. She wasn't sure if she said anything. She *thought* she told them she'd be back in a minute, but from the matching looks of concern on Noah's and Kate's faces, she wasn't sure the words made it out coherently before she took off across the car park.

She ran frantically up the steps at the other side, sandals slapping the pavement, and dodged the people meandering along the street. She took herself to the riverbank, to a secluded spot beneath a yew tree where she watched the soothing gush of the rain-heavy river. She looked down at the phone clutched in her hand and wanted to hurl it into the river. She didn't.

Already sighing with relief, she dialled the familiar number. Anticipation as the staccato tone sounded in her ear, then his voice: deep, resonant, resigned.

'Joe?' she whispered.

*

From the beginning Kate had not liked Joe. She didn't trust his sides: his soulful looks and philosophising one minute, the dirty jokes and laddish laughter the next, how he was always the centre of attention. Ignoring Emily, and then monopolising her, lavishing her with his attention and tempting her away from her friends as the fancy took him.

He dangled Emily like a puppet and Emily, for her part, was all too happy to dance. Kate had tried to tell her this more than once, but to no avail; Emily was unwavering in her conviction

– she had never had a boyfriend before. Emily and Joe had met in a bar a couple of weeks after matriculation, and flirted over a pint of lager and a game of pool. Emily had been taught to hustle by Dan; Joe had been impressed and swaggered over to challenge her. University suited Emily; she found like-minded people, didn't feel like such a freak for her literary obsessions and strong opinions. She had perfected the art of flirtation; she wore tight T-shirts and lots of eyeliner.

'I just don't think he wants you for your intellectual capacity,' Kate grumbled to Emily as they were sitting on the steps by the front door of the Art College, wearing bobble hats and scarves and nursing steaming polystyrene cups of hot chocolate.

It was a few weeks before Christmas break and Emily had been dating Joe for almost two months. Not that it could be called dating, really; there was no formal acknowledgement of each other as boyfriend or girlfriend, but they did seem to hook up at every party, drawn like moths to a flame, and they kissed in dark corners of the student union bar. They had spent an amorous weekend holed up in Joe's messy, fetid bedroom. But, boyfriend? No. For some time Emily was scared to label him.

'I don't think I care to be honest,' Emily said lightly. She put her head on one side and looked at Kate wonderingly. 'Can't you be happy for me?'

Kate set her cup down on the step and squeezed Emily's knee. 'Of course,' she said. 'If you're happy, I'm happy.' But this was not true and they both knew it. Emily resented this; for some reason she could not quite fathom, her relationship with Joe did not carry the same weight as Kate's with Luke. Although Kate was resolutely single by then and would not allow anyone to even *try* to measure up to Luke.

Emily knew she was insecure and that this made Kate doubt the validity of her feelings; she didn't trust her to know her own mind. 'You don't have to go for the first guy who pays you any attention,' Kate said. 'You're gorgeous, Em, but looks are surface and if that's all someone loves about you, well, the love isn't authentic.'

Easy for Kate to say. She had become effortlessly beautiful as soon as she shed the grime of the tenement and shook off her tomboyish ways.

Emily spoke quietly, but there was an emphatic undertone to her words that made Kate pay attention. 'You don't have the first idea how it feels to have him adore me. It's *amazing*. I feel . . . I don't really know what love is *supposed* to feel like, but this is the closest I've ever been to knowing. And you don't know him like I do. He's wonderful – funny, sweet, passionate. Sometimes I feel sick just waiting for him to arrive at the door, or wondering if I'll see him when I step into the pub. I never knew love made you feel this way – half nauseous, half delirious, half anxious, all at the same time.'

She was lit up, glowing, believing what she said with every fibre of her being. She had languished in Kate's shadow for too many years, been the plain one, ignored. Joe was hers and it was her time to shine.

'That's too many halves,' Kate pointed out.

Emily laughed. 'So it is.' She paused. 'I meant nauseous and anxious in a *good* way, you know?'

Kate's smile was strained. 'Yeah,' she said. 'Of course.'

Joe was Emily's fate and there was not a damn thing either one of them could do about it.

A lot had happened since then. She'd run off with him, married him, followed him around the country supporting his dream. She'd let him cheat on her and demean her, she'd lost her job and her self-respect. Now Emily didn't know how else to quell the panic except by hearing his voice.

The problem was that no one had known Joe the way she had. She hadn't bothered integrating him into her family; her friends hadn't liked him and she hadn't tried to make them. Instead, she'd let the bonds of friendship and family loosen, drifted away from them all until she had nothing and no one but Joe.

He wasn't all bad. He was insecure too. Driven by the desire to make music, to be someone. It was intense between them but it felt so right. So real. She'd stand in damp basement bars, vibrating with the bass of the music, Joe's voice soaring above the dingy surroundings, raising the roof of the mediocre little bar, lifting his listeners up and taking them one by one to some higher, far-flung place.

With every beat and strum and note, he captivated. Emily would be swallowed up by the dark, drawn in by his song. She would feel his words in her *soul*. A combined sense of calm and euphoria washing over her, raising the hairs on the back of her neck, tingling down the length of her spine. Joe, singing the words like every syllable defined him, clasping the microphone, sweat gleaming on his face, his eyes never leaving hers, singing songs he wrote for her alone.

'I'm not always good at saying how I feel,' Joe would say. 'Especially in front of other folk.' Then he'd pick up his guitar in the dark of his bedroom and pour his heart out.

Kate saw a lazy, arrogant boy with greasy hair and stubble; Emily saw the man he would become. Or might have become, but didn't.

She had loved him. She hadn't wanted to give up on him, but in the end she'd had no choice.

*

'Well,' Kate remarked, watching Emily fly across the parking lot. 'What do you suppose that was all about?'

Noah slammed the driver's door and came round the side of the van. 'Panic attack,' he said laconically.

Kate stared at him. '*What*?'

'She's been having them for a while. She thinks we don't know. She always takes off when it happens. She's sad, depressed or whatever. That's why everyone is so happy that you've come.'

'I can't work miracles.' Kate was starting to feel like everyone's fairy godmother.

I chose this, she reminded herself; but she hadn't truly known what she was getting into or how deeply and quickly invested in the Cottons she would become.

Noah's eyes were trusting. 'But it's been awful, and now it's better.'

Kate sighed. 'I can see that,' she said softly. 'But Emily doesn't want to talk about what happened with Joe.'

Noah nodded. 'She turned up on the doorstep out of the blue one day looking like she hadn't slept or eaten in weeks. She wouldn't go back for her stuff, even when Dan offered to go with her. She wouldn't say a word and no one dared mention Joe's name. She just lay in bed. It was only the fact that Lena needed her that brought her round. Next thing anybody knew she had bought the bookshop. She goes there every day, but she does bugger all. Just sits and reads. She's bought her own personal library, not a business.'

'Well, that's certainly going to change. I might not be able to fix Emily, but I can certainly sort out her business.'

Noah gave her a beseeching look. 'I hope you can fix her too.'

'I'll do what I can, but you need to understand, Noah, that Emily and I haven't spoken in six years. Things happened.'

Noah folded his arms across his chest. 'But you can sort it out, right? You wouldn't be here otherwise.'

'I'm going to try.'

His shrug was philosophical. 'That's good enough.' He slouched against the side of the van, scraping the toe of his sneakers in the gravel. He sighed expectantly, an opening.

Kate cast an appraising glance at him, inspected the van for grubbiness, then decided she didn't care and leaned beside him. 'What's up?'

'Nothing . . . just being seventeen, everything sucks, you know?'

'Being seventeen is the greatest. You just won't realise that until it's too late.' She snapped her fingers. 'Gone. The best times. Just like that.' Though she had meant to sound matter of fact and wise, she was aware of a wistful undertone that belied her intention.

Noah glanced at her with narrow-eyed suspicion. 'Are you about to tell me I should live in the present and hug trees and stuff? I'm really not into that shit.'

Kate wrinkled her nose and laughed. 'How can you live anywhere else *but* the present? I always wonder that. But, appreciating what you have, I guess that's important. The tree hugging is entirely optional.' She gave him a confidential smile, dug him lightly in the ribs. He was fascinated by his trainers for a moment and she knew he was thinking about what had happened. Her steady silence worked its magic.

Noah glanced up and began to speak. 'No one trusts me any more,' he said. 'Which is fair, considering I got expelled from school a month before my exams. Emily, she's the worst. She and Dan are always on my back about something. They're all at it. Except for Ferg and that's only because he's on the other side of the world.'

'I guess they feel justified. You know they're just worried, right? Maybe you have to weather it for a bit, let them all have their say. They'll blow themselves out like any storm.' Kate could imagine the combined force of the Cottons in all their righteous dismay, desperate to help Noah find a way forward and only succeeding in alienating him in the process. Talking, remonstrating, inveigling themselves into the nitty-gritty of each other's lives: she had once loved that about them, but she supposed it might also be overwhelming.

He echoed her unspoken sentiment. 'You know us Cottons; everyone's business is everyone's business.'

'Time to fess up, Noah, what *did* you do? Seeing how everyone's business is everyone's business and I'm *practically* a Cotton. Plus, I'd rather hear it from you. We were friends once.' A sort-of friendship between a gawky kid and his almost-sister. In the kitchen this morning Kate had recognised a connection of kindred souls. Even in the jolly maelstrom of brisk Cotton life, she could see that Noah was every bit as lonely as she had once been.

'You *are* a Cotton,' Noah said and kicked at a loose stone. He turned and repositioned his shoulder against the van, wedging his hands beneath his armpits. He was so sweet, so vulnerable, but Kate could see in his eyes that he was fed up of being so, of being the child. When he spoke his voice was flat and emotionless. 'I went to school one day with a knife,' he said.

'A *knife*?' Kate couldn't help it.

He looked at her. 'Yes.' Again the curious monotone, unsuitable.

'Keep talking, Noah,' Kate said softly, trying to quash the urge to shake him and demand to know what he had been thinking. 'Because that sentence is *not* finished.'

'I didn't do anything with it. Just had it in my bag.'

'Why?'

There was another lengthy pause. 'I was sick of the hassle I was getting from this bunch of guys. They wouldn't leave me alone. Everywhere I turned, there they were, making comments, shoving me about, trying to piss me off. It had been going on for months – I was going out with one of their ex-girlfriends – and I lost it, grabbed the knife one morning and shoved it in my bag. I don't know what I was thinking. But I was too much of a pussy even to take it out—'

'Good!' Kate exclaimed, but he only raised his eyebrows wryly.

'Things kicked off again and I punched one of the guys in the face in the lunch room and we got into it, a couple of teachers split us up and hauled me off to the office. They searched my bag. Found the knife. Called the police, called my parents. Expelled me. That's it.'

Kate could see through the transparent layers of carelessness to the vibrations of that day still rocking him, fissures spreading and cracking, until the gap between the Noah he had been before he put that knife in his bag and the Noah he was afterwards, was a chasm. 'I'm sorry,' she said, laying a hand on his arm, feeling his tremor. 'That must have been horrible.' Noah pressed his lips together, his composure harder to maintain in the face of her kindness. He had anticipated condemnation; her sternness would have been easier to deal with, and more what he was used to. 'They were bullying you for a long time?' she probed.

His brow furrowed. She could see the word jarred him. Bullying was for other people, for victims. Not for him. His shoulders hunched. 'They hated me after I started going out with Charley. I didn't know she dumped him for me, I swear. And then I got picked for the rugby team and . . . they just started this campaign. Got everyone against me without anyone even realising they were doing it.' He shrugged. 'It was smart. Horrible.'

'So you bottled it all up and eventually exploded. Hardly surprising. What *is* surprising is that they expelled you. I mean, if there was clear provocation and it was a first offence—'

He looked at her bleakly. 'I had a *knife*, Kate. There's no going back after that. If it had just been the fight I would have got off with a suspension, but . . .' He shook his head. 'Stupid, stupid, stupid.' With each epithet he slammed his fist against the door, then took a couple of steps away from her, turned – eyes hard, shoulders hunched. 'They all treat me like I'm broken now, watch me constantly, scared I'm going to snap.' A bitter laugh. 'The thing is, it wasn't even a very good punch. I guess I'm not the punching kind. It looks easy on TV, but . . . have you ever tried to punch anyone?' Kate shook her head. Noah smiled weakly. 'I got expelled for the world's worst punch. And a moment of complete madness.' He looked down at her, serious now. 'I *wasn't* going to do anything with that knife. They all think I was, maybe just for a second. Premeditation, the police called it. Said if I'd used it I'd have been looking at attempted murder . . . They made me see a counsellor . . . Mum thought I was going mad or something. *But I wasn't going to use it. Never.*'

'I believe you,' Kate said softly, and hugged him.

'No one else does.' He was rigid in her arms. 'It was a mistake. A stupid mistake. They couldn't see it.'

'Trust can be earned back, Noah. Not easily, but it can. You have to be patient. And calm – no more moments of madness. No knives, no punches – however lousy.'

Finally, he relaxed enough to hug her back.

Noah's confession had drained the energy from them both. They leaned against the van waiting for Emily. 'Any theories about where your sister went?' Kate asked.

Noah shrugged. 'I have a theory. But you're not going to like it.'

'Go on.'

'I think she's calling Joe.'

'Joe? Why would you think that? It's over. It *is* over, isn't it?'

Noah nodded. 'I checked her phone,' he admitted. 'She was acting really weird, jumping like she'd seen a ghost every time her phone rang.' He shrugged. 'And I was pissed at her. So I grabbed her phone when she was in the shower. Her call log is full of him. Outgoing calls only. Not long, sometimes just a few seconds.'

'He never calls her back?'

Noah shook his head. 'Should we be worried?'

'I don't know. Maybe. You know checking her phone is a crappy thing to do, right?'

'She hacked my email,' Noah offered as explanation.

Kate gave him her most dubious stare. '*Emily*, who can barely use a word processor, hacked your email?'

A small concessionary smile. 'Well, maybe not *hacked*. I might have left my email open on my laptop. But she definitely read it. Private stuff, you know? That's out of order. I was messaging someone and she teased me about it. She needn't have been so high and mighty when she was running off to make nuisance calls to her ex. I'm surprised he hasn't changed his number by now.'

'Noah,' she said with gentle reproach in her voice. 'Have a heart. She's hurting.'

'Yeah, and don't we know it.'

After a while of waiting beneath the warm sun, sticky backs pressed against hot metal, Noah and Kate gave up waiting and wandered into the air-conditioned cool of the hardware store. The mood of confession might have deserted Noah, but Kate wasn't quite finished with him yet and pursued him round the aisles. 'So,' she said, keeping pace with his loping glide with the trolley, catching at his elbow to force him to stop. 'What now? You said Dan and Emily were driving you mad. I guess your parents aren't breezy about the whole thing either . . .'

Noah stopped and looked at her, face rippling in an anxious frown. 'They're not the only ones,' he mumbled. 'And now *you* want to know my future as well? Like I have to map out the next twenty years and I have to do it right now or I'm a total screw-up.' His voice rose and she could feel the sharp edge of anger beneath the surface of his fragile calm. He was sick of being defined by that moment.

'Easy, Noah,' she murmured. 'That's not it at all. I'm talking about mending your relationships with your family, and the next couple of weeks, not twenty years. I want to help ease your way with them. I can do that. I have Emily's ear . . . and Dan's.'

She must have frowned then, or got the faraway look of old secrets in her eyes, because Noah, with unexpected perspicacity, said, 'Did you and Dan have some kind of thing going on?'

'What? No!' Kate shook her head swiftly for emphasis, an overdone denial. 'Why do you ask?'

'No reason. Just a look he gets whenever your name is mentioned.'

Whenever her name was mentioned?

Kate shuddered; she had not been entirely omitted from collective memory after all. 'We were friends,' she said swiftly. She changed the subject. 'So *you* have a new girlfriend?' She needed to steer them away from her relationship with Dan: a series of non-events; all those mismatched moments, turning points, their terrible timing, and her worry about what coming back might mean.

Noah hid a shy grin. 'Ye-ah, maybe.'

Kate saw him through teenage girl eyes: floppy hair, deep blue eyes, soft heart. 'Tell me more.'

'It's complicated.'

'Why? She's not pregnant, is she?'

'No! It's nothing like that.' Noah was shocked that she'd asked, then managed a half-embarrassed leer. 'We so don't need to have *that* conversation. It's just . . . I'm not certain she even likes me.' He was the picture of awkwardness, shifting from one foot to the other, staring at the ground and looking so incredibly young.

She and Luke had been in love at Noah's age, younger even.

She reached to ruffle his hair. 'What's not to like,' she said, which earned another shy smile. 'Seriously, Noah, you're a catch. Tell me about her.'

'OK, but *don't* tell Emily. She'll only give me a hard time again. Her name's Becca. She's smart. Like, scary smart.' He hesitated. 'She doesn't know about . . . about what happened. I'm kind of scared she won't want anything to do with me when she finds out. Charley couldn't dump me fast enough. The whole girls liking bad boys thing is a myth, you know.'

'Girls only like the *idea* of a bad boy. Which you aren't. The thing is, honesty is really important in relationships. It would be better just to tell her.'

Noah nodded. 'I know. I will. So, are we finished with the counselling now?' He gave her a cheeky grin, certain of his forgiveness.

She laughed. 'Yes, my work with you is done. For now.'

Noah nudged her gently with his elbow and said, half embarrassed, 'Missed you, Kate.'

'Missed you too.' She gave him another quick hug. It felt natural; he was still the little boy she'd read bedtime stories to and plastered grazed knees.

But he wasn't; he was hovering on the edge of adulthood with so much to figure out about himself.

'Mum and Dad want me to keep going to counselling,' he

said, slumping over the trolley. 'I don't need some doctor telling me what's going on in my head.' When Kate didn't respond, he added, 'Seriously, I'm not violent or anything.' But she knew that he was questioning it, scared of his own self. He looked away, eyes darkening again. 'It all got messed up so quickly,' he said. 'And I don't know how it happened. One minute, life was just normal, and then—'

'Things will be normal again,' Kate soothed. 'And you don't have to know what you want to do with the rest of your life. I don't know that either. I don't know past the end of the summer.' It sounded scary when she put it like that. 'Just the next few weeks. Emily and I could sure do with your help but your work on the farm has to come first . . .'

'No. I'm close to outstaying my welcome with him. Dan and I will end up hating each other if we go on like this much longer. And the baby is coming soon.'

'Yes, but Dan will need you more than ever then.'

'I s'pose.'

'Do you have money?' Kate asked.

'I save some of what Dan pays me.'

'So see out the summer, maybe Christmas even. Then you could travel if you wanted. A couple of years down the line all this will be a distant memory of a stupid thing you did once. And there'll be plenty more of them, believe me.'

'I wish you could convince the rest of my family.'

Kate laughed. 'You're a Cotton, you're everyone's property, you should know that by now. Come on, let's get this wood sorted out before Em comes back. I really want to make a start on the shop this afternoon.'

The clock was ticking on the bookshop now, and on her summer: this brief interlude to recapture, to remould, to decide . . . Kate was in a hurry, except she didn't really know what she was rushing towards.

She looked around, hoping to catch sight of Emily tripping

along in her borrowed dress and sandals, sparkling from the ill-gotten pleasure of the phone call. 'Perhaps I should go look for her,' she muttered.

Noah steered the cart up against a display and left it there, turning into an aisle where floor-to-ceiling shelves displayed stacks of fragrant wood. He glanced back at her as he paused to examine the merchandise. 'She'll be back when she's ready. How about you, Kate? How come you decided to leave everything behind for the summer? Don't you have a boyfriend back home?'

The scent of sawn wood was thick and heady, pine and resin mingling with the tang of outdoors. Kate took a deep breath and closed her eyes. She didn't like the reversal of roles. Noah ran his thumb along the edge of a board and looked up at her, curious. 'It's complicated,' Kate said, echoing his words, her tone discouraging him from probing.

Noah didn't heed the warning. 'You moved out there on your own. That must have been cool. Brave. I'd love to travel. What made you pick New York?'

It hadn't been about being brave, or striking out on her own, or any overwhelming desire to live in New York; it had been nothing more than distancing herself from her mother for good, putting space between them. Becoming someone new – and here she was discovering that she couldn't, not really.

'It was just something I did.' Her tone was clipped. She stared him down until he quailed, confused.

'I'll go talk to this guy about the best sort of wood.' He pointed to where a middle-aged man in a crumpled apron was checking off stock on a clipboard. 'Em needs to hurry up, we can't choose without her,' he added.

'I doubt she'll know one sheet of wood from another, or care. But we do need her credit card.' Kate felt like crossing her fingers, wondering if Emily had enough money left to make this project viable. 'Right. You check out things here, I'm going to make a start looking at paint, OK?'

When Noah nodded, Kate headed to the paint aisle. Closing her eyes, she projected the image of the finished bookshop in her mind's eye, then she began to mark colours on the chart: duck egg blue, sage green, claret red, cream. Paint was her domain: all those rich, precise colours combining and contrasting to tell a story. The bookshop was going to be beautiful when it was finished and it would be just what everyone needed.

Chapter 9

Joe was busy, distracted and didn't say much. Of course, once she hung up, Emily was furious with herself. She should still be furious with *him*; she should never want to speak to him again; she was pathetic. Shame helped her to get herself together.

What possessed him to go on answering her calls? She kept waiting for him to change his number, half hoping for a bland, electronic voice telling her the number had not been recognised. A signal that he was letting her go, jettisoning her because she hadn't the strength or dignity to do it herself.

Soon, she was rushing impatiently along the street towards the store.

She had Kate and Noah and the bookshop to think about today. Things were happening. She had purpose, a plan; a van waiting to be filled with stuff and an empty shop like a blank canvas poised to be transformed with life and colour and energy. The bookshop Emily had dreamed of was becoming a reality. When she had first signed the missives, still trembling with excitement at her own audacity, she had felt hope flutter in her belly: a second chance. But it wasn't so easy. She just sat in the shop, dithering, the task insurmountable.

Her mother called it depression. As if labelling made it better somehow; that was the trouble with having a doctor for a mother, never mind *both* parents. She knew Dan and Abby talked about her behind her back as well, about how brittle she had become. Lena was steadfast; even in entirely her right mind, Lena had been inclined to let people manage themselves, minded her own business. But Emily couldn't help but think that the Lena of old would have given her a damn good talking-to, and perhaps she needed it.

Emily tried to do it herself, hearing Lena's voice in her head, but she was so tired – some days it was hard to drag herself out of bed. Hard to watch Dan and Abby so in love, building their family, hard to face her parents who were so disappointed – *in* her or *for* her, it didn't much matter. Hard to hear of Ally's success. Only looking after Lena gave her any purpose and she threw herself into the task.

Her parents were trusting the Lena-wisdom, the magic of Bluebell Bank and the healing Solway air to cure Emily.

Joe's voice jarred her today. Usually there was the illicit thrill of wrongdoing, then a rush of guilty pleasure flooding her veins. Today, she just felt ashamed and his voice had done nothing but increase the jangling of her nerves, the ache of dissatisfaction.

Not wanting to waste any more time, Emily rushed through the automatic doors. She caught a glimpse of herself in the reflection before they parted and split her in two: her dress was a bright splash of confidence and she looked taller, sleeker and more assured, with her sunglasses perched on top of her dark curls and her feet dainty in the gold sandals: not at all like someone just emerging from her latest panic attack, someone who couldn't get through the day without hearing the disembodied voice on the end of the phone of an ex-lover who had nothing left for her but pity.

Strange, Emily thought, turning from her reflection, that the outside and inside selves could be so mismatched.

She was running through hasty apologies in her mind as she

dashed through the turnstile. She took a deep breath and went up and down the aisles looking for them. She should be more grateful, she thought. *Show* Kate her gratitude. She resolved to text Ally later and start organising that family dinner in Kate's honour, show her how welcome she was, that her place in the family was never usurped; there was a Kate-shaped hole in their lives all those years, an empty chair at their table.

She turned a corner, raised her eyes to scan the shelves, took in the soothing stripes of so many colours and textures of wood. Noah was talking to a man with an apron and a name badge. They appeared deep in conversation, discussing the merits of different slabs of wood. Of Kate there was no sign. Emily let her fingers trail across the shelves, and put her nose to the wood.

She had just about reached Noah when someone called her name, in the wondering manner of a long-lost acquaintance. 'Emily *Cotton*?'

She turned and almost tripped on the spinning hem of her dress. All the breath left her body and her limbs turned weak and rubbery: standing in front of her was Luke Ross.

Of all things, Emily had feared this most – her, Luke and Kate in the same space once more.

Luke Ross had the power to derail everything.

*

Kate was lingering in the paint aisle. With an artist's eye she scanned the shelves, drinking in the hues and shades and crazy colour names: not quite as good as the rows of glossy oil tubes in her favourite art store in Manhattan, but almost.

That was her first New York–related thought all day, and it wasn't about Ben, or missing her job, at all, but about paint. The Ben conundrum already felt less pressing.

Kate selected a few more colours she liked and folded the paint chart to a page to show Emily, then went in search of Noah.

When she turned the corner into the wide timber aisle – tinny music drowned out by the droning of a buzz saw – she could see Noah and Emily leaning over a trolley heaped high with wood. There was someone else with them, a man with his back to her. At first, Kate took him to be another assistant, helping. Until she got closer and, even from the back, he began to sharpen into familiarity.

Emily stared past him and her eyes widened, mouth dropping into a gape as she met Kate's eyes. 'Kate,' she called, far too loud and cheerful, waving down the empty aisle. 'Look who it is!'

Kate knew exactly who it was. After ten years she still knew the shape of his shoulders, every line of his features even before he turned. She knew the long, tanned legs beneath the khaki work shorts, the black hair and thick, straight brows, and those piercing blue eyes: the perfect melding of his Celtic and Italian genes.

Luke.

His shorts were smeared with plaster and he wore a black T-shirt and a pair of battered hiking boots. As he turned, his eyes locked on hers, burning and fierce and as blue as the Solway Firth on a sparkling hot day. Kate's legs trembled, all the air shuddered out of her lungs, and she couldn't breathe. Her heart slammed against her ribs. Every nerve ending, every inch of skin he'd ever touched or kissed or coveted shivered in response to him. His eyes swept her up and down and settled on her face again, that burning blue gaze much too intense.

'Kate.' His voice banished any last lingering trace of doubt; any hint of the boy was gone now. In every muscle and line of his body, in voice and the set of his jaw, he was a man – with the shadow of stubble and the faint tracings of lines around his eyes. Her heart jolted.

'Ugh,' she croaked – all she could manage.

'It's Luke,' trilled Emily, her eyes wide with shock. They hadn't yet prepared for this.

Kate, still incapable of speech, nodded. She wished to be

whisked away from this moment, to a time when she was not expected to stand in front of Luke – the grown-up, even lovelier version of the beautiful boy who won her fifteen-year-old, fledgling heart so completely – and make inconsequential conversation.

Luke's smile faltered, the amusement faded from his eyes and he seemed a little unsure of himself. Kate remembered how fierceness and vulnerability vied within him, and the cloak of confidence and humour he wore to shield himself from the hurt of his father's disregard.

She stared at his face, following the line of his jaw and cheekbones with her eyes, remembering the way the planes of him felt beneath her fingertips as they lay in the long beach grass together beneath the stars, lost in velvety darkness and each other. 'Hi,' Kate managed, long past the moment she ought to have replied.

'Luke is renovating his father's old place.' Emily had taken on the over-bright tone of a tour-group leader, and she seemed less than delighted at the fact. Noah was confused, glancing between each of them and trying to figure out the dynamics.

'Oh?'

Luke didn't take his eyes off Kate. 'He died six months back. Cancer. It took me a while to work out what to do, but I decided to come back. I just finished my degree in architecture, so it seemed like a good opportunity to put theory into practice. I like doing some of the work myself; it's fun. And cathartic, you know?'

Was he nervous too? He was talking fast. Perhaps he was as apprehensive as her. 'I'm sorry about your father,' Kate said, wondering if she peeled back the layers would she find his grief, raw and exposed.

And would she find a part of Luke that loved her still?

'How about you?' His voice was soft, his eyes searching hers as if he was trying to find her core. She remembered that about him too: how his gaze would make her feel exposed, interesting. As if he had seen right into her soul found all the truths that lingered there, and liked them. Sometimes she'd thought he could read her mind. Could he do that? Could he find her secrets – that she never got over losing him, never felt that way about anyone since; never loved so deeply, so innocently, so completely and had begun to think she never would?

'It's a long story,' Kate said, wanting to take him through every moment between then and now: no simple summary could suffice. 'But the short version is that I've come to help Emily set up a bookshop in town.'

'We're putting up shelves,' said Emily, hovering awkwardly. 'This is my brother, Noah. He's helping us out.'

Noah and Luke shook hands. 'I'm the hired help,' Noah said. 'Just drive the van and do the heavy lifting. They promised me lunch though.' It helped that Noah hadn't a clue what was going on; his easy innocence was a balm to the loaded moment, history shimmering and shuddering between them.

'I don't want to keep you from your lunch, or your shelves,' Luke said, looking at Kate again. 'You'll be here for a while?' She nodded. 'Then I suppose we'll see each other around.'

Kate bit her lip, feeling fifteen again. Who knew seeing Luke would be like this – like the tattered pieces of her heart were shredded anew? Now she remembered one major reason New York had seemed like such a great place to be: it was several thousand miles from a chance encounter with Luke Ross. Never mind escaping from her mother, she'd been running away from this too.

See each other around. Those same words he'd said to her in the street in Wigtown all those years ago, doing tricks with his skateboard and staring at Kate like she was the most interesting thing to happen to his town.

'I should go,' Luke said.

Was she imagining the regret in his voice? She couldn't trust her judgement where he was concerned; her thoughts were hummingbirds, flitting around her brain, melodic and out of control.

Luke seemed to take a long time to walk away from her, turning to look back twice before he turned the corner.

Kate's feet were cemented to the floor. She wanted to run after him and make him stop, erase all the hurt they had caused each other, but she couldn't move.

'Who was that guy?' Noah was shifting the weight of the wood to balance the trolley better, pushing against it with all his strength to get it moving. Emily joined in and together they slithered the load around the corner towards the tills.

'Just someone we used to know when we were kids,' Emily said. The worst understatement Kate had ever heard.

Kate followed slowly. *A complication*: that's what Luke Ross was. And from the way Emily kept shooting those not-so-surreptitious glances at her as they queued and paid and loaded up, she knew it too.

'Sorry,' Emily said, when they were back in the cab of the van and trundling along. 'For running off like that. I just needed a minute, you know?' She hadn't managed the rehearsed apology earlier, too busy being surprised and horrified by Luke, trilling and twittering like an idiot to ease their passage through the moment. Emily could not shake her unease at seeing Luke and Kate together again.

'It's fine.' Kate dismissed Emily's moment of madness with a deft flick of her hand. Of course it wasn't fine; there would be a reckoning later. Explanations were owed.

Fighting her conscience and the sudden need for disclosure, Emily bit her lip. 'It's just—'

Kate leaned towards her, gave her a little poke with her elbow, a confidential smile that said it all: *I know. I don't like it, but I know.* They would weather this together. 'Later, Em,' she whispered. She turned her head and stared out the window with a dreamy smile on her face.

That was not good, Emily thought, not good at all.

Chapter 10

The days lapsed into a comforting rhythm with the three of them working companionably side by side in the bookshop. The first afternoon, Noah announced his intention of helping to see the renovations through. 'I won't get in the way of your painting,' he said. 'I'll work out the back in one of the outbuildings. I'll just get the wood cut to size and treated.' They had all changed into old clothes and were back in the shop, which was now draped in dust sheets.

'What about your job?' Kate said, seeing that Emily, prising open the first tin of sage paint, wanted to ask. Noah's help would be invaluable, but not worth causing a rift over. 'Shouldn't you check with Dan?'

'Fine.' Noah took out his phone and tapped it twice, sighing. Emily looked up from the paint in alarm.

'I'm not coming,' Noah said calmly, no doubt in response to an irate *where are you/when are you coming home* rant. A lengthy pause for some contribution from the other end and Kate found herself holding her breath. 'I don't mean just today,' Noah said, his tone hard. 'I mean ever. I don't want to work for you any more. I'm going to work here, at the shop with Kate and Emily.'

'What?' Emily spun around and tried to wrestle the phone from her brother, but he was a head taller and held it aloft. 'What are you doing? I can't *pay* you. This isn't a job.'

'What are *you* doing, Emily? Get off.'

Dan's furious voice could be heard clearly down the phone now, although Kate couldn't discern his words. Emily pulled at Noah's arm, trying to snatch the phone from his hand, unable to reach as he twisted away from her with a grin.

'Tough,' Noah was saying into the phone, shrugging out of Emily's hold. 'I quit,' he yelled. 'I told you. Yeah, well, maybe you should work on being a better boss.' He ended the call and shoved the phone back in his jeans pocket. 'I'm all yours.' He held out his arms with a happy grin, like a puppy expecting praise for peeing on the carpet.

Emily exploded. 'Bloody hell, Noah, what are you thinking? What will you do for money?'

The smile slipped, his jaw set stubbornly. 'I'll think of something. No worries.'

'*Yes* worries. Jeez, you're an idiot. You need to grow up.'

'You sound just like Dan,' Noah said curtly, a dangerous note in his voice. 'Piss off, Em, I've got work to do for *your* shop.' He hefted a plank of wood and headed for the outbuildings, whistling carelessly.

'Leave him,' Kate advised, seeing how Emily itched to continue the argument. 'He'll come to his senses and I guess Dan'll take him back. Look, you make a start with the painting. I'm going to nip out for bottled water. The stuff in the tap tastes like crap.' She wanted to get out of the shop for a bit and let everyone cool off.

It certainly wasn't going to be boring, being here.

Kate took a slow stroll round across the town square. She was idly gazing in a shop window when she was very nearly knocked off her feet by Dan, who had screeched to a halt by the kerb in his old truck. 'Woah,' Kate said, taking a step back as he slammed the door and barrelled into her.

Dan blushed. 'Sorry, Kate. I didn't see you there.'

'Too busy thinking of all the ways to murder your little brother and get away with it?'

'Something like that. You heard?'

'Yes. So you hotfooted it over here to give him a piece of your mind?'

Dan was defensive. 'Yes.'

Kate sighed and took his arm, steering him in the opposite direction to the bookshop. 'Don't you think perhaps that should wait until later, when everyone has simmered down?' Dan had always had a hint of temper, had liked to debate and argue with his siblings, but this was different. This was Dan being forced into a fatherly role he wasn't yet ready for.

He deflated a little. 'That's what Abs said.'

'Perhaps you should heed her advice.' Kate smiled up at him. He was still flushed and she suddenly felt uneasy about holding onto his arm; she didn't want there to be any misgivings between her and Dan. She had felt it the other night at the farm – shared history and things that might have been. 'Look, why don't we go and grab a coffee? Then, if you still feel the need, you can go to the shop and talk to Noah. At least you'll have calmed down a bit.'

To her surprise, Dan's cheeks flooded with yet more colour, as if she'd suggested making out with him in the back of his truck. 'I . . . um . . .' he stuttered. It was not like him to be short of words.

'It's just coffee,' Kate said, deciding to be brazen. 'Not like I'm going to seduce you amongst the old worthies and the cream cakes.'

Her brash attempt at humour didn't work; this time her own face blazed to match Dan's. She hastily dropped his arm.

'So, coffee, sure.' He put his hands in his pockets, took them out again, shuffled his feet and studied his boots. 'Nowhere fancy, look at the state of me.'

'You look like a farmer,' Kate said. 'Come on. We'll go to the Reading Lasses.' It was always busy in there: easy to make it innocent and incongruous, just two old friends having coffee.

Except, it *was* innocent, so why did she feel the need to create an impression of it being so? 'I don't think they'll turn up their noses at your attire. You might want to wipe your boots though.'

They crossed the road, Dan waving at the folk they passed on the way. Somehow, he managed to look guilty, like they were doing something wrong, which irked Kate. He opened the door for her and she ducked under his arm. He smelled loamy: of animals and maleness and work sweat. They squeezed through the narrow front room, along a corridor and into the café proper. The walls were covered with bookshelves. Kate found them a sofa and perched on one end. Dan sat at the other, hands resting on his knees, ill at ease. Kate looked at the dirt ingrained in the whorls of his fingers. 'Bathroom's there, if you want to wash up,' she said.

'Oh, yeah.' Dan got up. Kate perused the menu. She had wanted to grab these few minutes alone with Dan, not just to keep him from killing Noah, but to prove to herself that there was nothing weird going on between them. That her crush had been just that, and that he hadn't really been hurt by her carelessness all those years ago.

Now she was starting to think this wasn't her brightest idea. There *was* still something there, something undeniable; a quiver of longing, recognition and the sense of *what if*.

She remonstrated with herself as she waited for his return. He was a married man now with a baby on the way. It didn't matter what they had once felt; it didn't matter how nostalgically she viewed it, through the rosy veil of the past.

She ordered herself a strong cup of coffee and a tea for Dan. When he returned, marginally cleaner, she was sitting up straight, as breezy and casual as she could manage. *Just old friends having coffee together.*

'So,' she said with a smile. 'Calmed down a bit?'

'I guess.' Dan looked abashed. 'You must think I'm an arse, driving down here just to have a go at him. But you don't know how it's been . . .'

'So everyone keeps telling me,' Kate said. 'I took the liberty and ordered for us both. Tea's OK, I hope.'

Dan nodded. 'This is weird,' he said, gesturing between them. 'You and me. Here.'

Kate shook her head. 'No,' she said. 'It's not. It's totally normal. Two old friends catching up.'

Dan was startled by her vehemence. 'I just meant it's been a long time . . .'

'Yes. A *very* long time. Look at you, all married and expecting a baby. That must be very exciting.'

'Ye-es,' said Dan.

Kate grimaced. Was that doubt in his voice? *Don't sound doubtful. Sound sure of yourself and unrelentingly happy.* 'Abby seems lovely,' she pressed.

'Abs is amazing.' Dan frowned. 'Let's talk about Noah and what the hell I'm going to do about him.'

The waitress brought their drinks and there was the usual hiatus of *thank yous* and adding sugar, stirring and sipping. 'Why does everyone seem to think I should know what to do about Noah? Why doesn't anybody just ask *him*?'

'Because he's seventeen and not thinking straight.'

'I seem to remember you being fairly headstrong at seventeen. Didn't you refuse all your parents' attempts to get you to go to university?'

'Well, yeah. But Noah's clever.'

'As are you. That's hardly the point.'

Dan looked up. 'Then what is?'

'Everyone telling him what he should think and feel and do. Just give him some space. He's had a terrible thing happen to him—'

'Which was his own doing.'

Kate carried on as if he hadn't spoken. 'It's bound to take some time to get over. You want my advice? Go home, don't even let him know you came to talk to him today. Leave him until he's ready to talk to you, keep the job open for him.'

Dan gaped at her. 'And what am I supposed to do in the meantime? Abby can't exactly help out on the farm at the moment.'

'You can't hire a temporary worker? Come on. Noah will realise he needs that job with you, or else he'll find something else. Something that's his. But it's better if he comes back to you of his own accord.'

Dan was silent for a moment, considering. Kate sipped her coffee, dark and bitter, and closed her eyes with pleasure.

'You're pretty smart, you know,' Dan said, and her eyes flew open. He was studying her, a softening expression that alarmed her. 'You were always smart when it came to people, Kate. I'll do that. I'll go home and leave it to him to come and talk to me when he's ready. How's that?'

Kate nodded, uncomfortable with his admiration. 'Good.'

'I hope Emily's got in touch with Ally. We need to arrange that family dinner for you. It'll be good to be all together.'

*

When Kate had waved Dan off, she strolled back to the shop.

Emily had painted all the way along one wall. She had a scarf round her hair and a smudge of paint on her cheek. From the back came sharp sounds of industry. 'Where did you get to?'

'Just a walk,' Kate said breezily, reaching for a roller. *And a little Cotton diplomacy.* As she started to paint she thought of how it might appear, she and Dan and their clandestine visit, and wondered if she should tell Emily, make it all above board, but Emily was painting and reminiscing about the time Fergus had got himself tangled in a barbed wire fence on a walk along the Carrick shore, so she didn't bother.

The moment didn't seem right later either, or the next day, or the one after that. Kate decided just to let it go.

Chapter 11

It was evening – Emily's favourite time of day in the shop. The radio was playing, Noah had gone out to meet a friend and it was just her and Kate putting the finishing touches to the paintwork. One stone wall was left exposed, the other three alternated cream and sage green. The shop looked and smelled fresh, clean.

'So,' Emily said, the moment the door had closed behind her brother, 'you talked to Noah yet?'

'Yes.' Kate was cautious.

'Well?' Emily had been itching to ask, but Noah was always there and by the time they returned to Bluebell Bank at night they were exhausted; she had made time for Lena's nightly Scrabble matches, but she had been so tired Lena had beaten her easily.

She was a little nervous to ask about Noah in case it inspired the conversation about where Emily had run off to and what she had been doing. She would tell Kate about the panic attacks, about Joe, but she was happy to postpone her confession for a while longer.

'Emily, you can't ask me to wheedle my way into Noah's confidences then expect me to betray them.'

'He's a kid,' Emily said. 'I'm his sister. I need to know if he's OK.'

'He deserves some privacy. He *needs* it.' Kate looked uncomfortable. 'But, yes, I think he's OK.'

Emily pushed her hair off her face with the heel of her hand and dropped her paintbrush into the tray. Kate was lying on her belly painting skirting boards painstakingly. 'Good, because, honestly, we were all pretty worried there for a while. He told you what he did, right?' Kate nodded. 'Well? What do you think?'

'I think he must have been feeling pretty desperate. And I'm sure a day doesn't go past when he doesn't regret it.'

Emily threw herself down on the floor beside Kate and watched her careful progress along the wall.

Kate looked up. 'I don't want to tittle-tattle about him, Em. You wanted me to be a willing ear for Noah and I am, but I won't gossip about him.'

'Of course not,' Emily grumbled, disgruntled. 'I'm his sister, Kate, not some stranger. I just meant . . . well, you know, getting expelled is pretty major, and what he did is kind of scary, don't you think? Mum and Dad don't know what to do with him.' She sat back and looped her arms around her legs.

Kate reached the end of the skirting, set her brush aside and came over to join her, throwing herself on the ground with a sigh, stretching her back. 'He isn't going to do anything stupid, if that's what you're worried about,' she said. 'I think he just wants to be left alone for a bit.'

Emily glanced around the walls. 'That is an amazing colour, like a herb garden, or the sea in stormy light. You were totally right about it. And you're probably right about Noah too, don't listen to me, I'm just grumpy because he'd rather talk to you than his own sister.'

'You asked me to—'

Emily waved a paint-spattered hand. 'I know. I know. I didn't say it necessarily made sense, it's just how I feel.'

'Talking of things that don't make sense,' Kate said. Emily's heart sank. 'Want to tell me what you were doing when you ran off the other day?'

Emily became very intent in scraping the paint that had dried around her nails.

'You sound as if you have some idea what you *think* I was doing.' If they were going to make this work, they had to be honest with one another.

'Phoning Joe?'

Emily looked at her. 'Bloody Noah,' she said, getting up and wiping her hands on her jeans. 'Cup of tea?'

'No,' Kate said sternly. 'Sit down, Em. No running off to make tea as an avoidance tactic. And it was just a theory of his, but I guess it was true, huh?' Emily gave a non-committal grunt which was all the confirmation Kate needed. 'Seems like a strange thing to do is all.'

'It's just a thing I do, it calms me down.' Emily felt her hands shake and leapt up again. 'I'm not avoiding anything, but I will talk better with a paintbrush in my hands. I'm going to start the second coat of the cream.'

She reached for a roller. She dipped and swiped, taking pleasure in the lush sweep of paint.

'It's not my place to judge,' Kate said. She got a brush too and did the fiddly bits along her neat gloss work so that Emily didn't make a mess. 'Just sounds like an odd way to get over him. You get to worry about Noah, and we both get to worry about you.'

Emily paused and glanced at her. 'I know,' she said. 'On all counts, I know. But, I saw your face today in the store when we met Luke. You can't tell me you don't recognise the pull of first love, or that you don't understand how downright impossible it can be to truly get over someone who once mattered so much. It's just . . . hard, you know.'

What was she doing? She hadn't meant to bring up Luke and she'd been delighted when Kate hadn't either. She had been quite happy to pretend he didn't exist at all, or at least that he wasn't here, his very proximity threatening this tentative thing she and

Kate were building. Emily jabbed her roller savagely into the paint and sprayed an arc of paint onto the wall.

Kate opened her mouth to deny, perhaps to opine that being vaguely overwhelmed by a chance sighting of her childhood sweetheart was very different indeed from clinging to the threads of a worn-out marriage long after they ought to have been let go.

Kate had been trying to put Luke out of her mind, but it wasn't easy to banish him from her thoughts – not now that they had stood face to face in the same spot, covering the gaps in their histories with those inadequate, enticing synopses of the lost years; and yes, she wanted to know more. But Luke hadn't just broken her heart, he'd crushed it; turned her into the ice queen she'd become all through university, when she let no one get close.

It had been love at first glance, from that very first kiss in the woods at the Martyr's Stake to Kate's birthday dinner, when Luke first ran the gauntlet of Lena and the brothers; and all the rest of that long, heavenly hot summer, and beyond.

Falling in love and feeling that nothing else mattered, that time was elongated; some moments lasting a lifetime, while hours passed in a heartbeat. And every kiss, every touch, every hungry, lingering glance seemed so significant, so memorable. Which made it all the more impossible to accept when it ended.

Lena had been tight-lipped that night when she picked them up in town, Emily slumping in the back seat: an inebriated Pre-Raphaelite heroine with hair spilling over her face, barely able to control her drunken glee. Kate had been worried Lena would hold Emily's drunkenness against Luke, but she had liked Luke when she met him – when she realised he hadn't been the one to ply her granddaughter with drink. Lena was a good judge of character and her approval mattered to Kate more than anyone's.

On Kate's fifteenth birthday, after a family dinner at which Luke was guest of honour and Kate could barely eat for awe of him, they had all piled into the woods to light a campfire. Dan remonstrated with Fergus for purloining a bottle of cider from

Lena's cellar with which to toast the special occasion since he, more than the others, was perceptive enough to make the link between the liquor Fergus was trying to press upon them and the mess of Kate's childhood.

Dan's sensitivity might have touched Kate, had not she been so wrapped up in Luke, sitting by the fire with the heat licking their faces and the smoky, orange light of the flames in their eyes. That Dan was jealous did not occur to her until much later, when it was too late; she was already completely embroiled. At the end of the summer Dan started seeing some girl from school anyway.

When Luke rode away on his bicycle that night, lights blinking through the blackness between the trees, Kate had returned to the house to find Dan on the doorstep waiting. 'Be careful,' he warned; but she only smiled beatifically and hugged him with none of the coyness she would have previously felt, and then dashed up the stairs to regale Emily with a starry-eyed account of Luke's kisses.

Kate realised she had lapsed into daydream, her brush frozen midway between tray and wall. Emily was looking at her as if she had just proved her point for her. 'It's different,' Kate said reprovingly, leaning over to replenish the paint. 'You don't want to talk about him yet, that's fine, but trust me, it's different. And what you're doing is not cool, Em.'

Emily wore the mulish expression she always did when she felt she was being told off. 'You don't—'

'I don't understand,' Kate groaned. 'I'm sick of you telling me I don't understand because I wasn't here. Look, Emily, I plan to help you. With all of it. The shop, Lena, Joe . . . I know we've got a lot to talk about, but I just think it's important to be straight with each other. You've never told me what happened between you—'

The shop door swung open and Noah breezed in, putting an end to the conversation: a welcome interruption for Emily, but not so for Kate. She hadn't liked Joe in the beginning and she didn't like him now that he was a phantom hovering around and getting in the way. She didn't like what he'd done to Emily, turning her into this shadow of herself. She intended to get to the bottom of it and help Emily exorcise Joe for good.

*

The following days passed in a blur of laughter, reminiscences and hard work. In the evenings, Kate immersed herself in fabric samples and design ideas on Pinterest, while Emily entertained Lena by recounting their progress; it wasn't always clear if Lena was taking any of this in, but Emily never gave up telling.

Lena spent her days in the garden amongst her rows of lettuce, kale and cabbage, her raised flower beds and blue tepees of climbing plants. Perhaps the ingrained knowledge of how to turn the soil and commune with her plants would be one of the last things to go, and here Lena felt anchored and solid in her shifting world.

One evening Lena, with her straw hat pulled down over her eyes and wisps of wild, white hair sticking out, noticed Kate meandering among the fruit trees and stopped what she was doing. She tugged off her gardening gloves and threw them to one side.

She reached out to take the proffered mug from Kate. 'Thank you,' she said, and Kate looked at her warily, searching for presence, for a trace of the strong woman she had known.

Lena might easily have forgotten her again, think she was the cleaner they had had for a while – a disaster, according to Emily; Lena kept shouting at her and making her cry. Today, in this precious moment, Lena was lucid; she seemed to know Kate, and herself. She sipped her tea with relish and looked around the garden. 'What do you think?'

'It's wonderful, Lena. You've got a proper business going on here.'

Lena smiled wryly. 'I always loved gardening. You know where you are with plants.'

People had sometimes confused Lena, with their obfuscations and petty insecurities. She had taught the girls that it didn't matter what anyone thought of them, only what they thought of themselves. She had taught them to be straightforward. *Always be able to meet your own eyes in the mirror.*

When Emily got drunk that first night at the Martyr's Stake, it was not the drinking itself that irritated Lena. 'So long as you did it because you wanted to, and not to impress anybody,' she said severely. 'And so long as you don't tell your mother this happened on my watch.'

Fergus had been furious at her lenience, claiming it would have been an entirely different story if it was him, or one of the other boys, and perhaps it would.

Emily, who wasn't precisely sure of her motivations – other than the enticement of Luke's cute friend named Cam – only that she never meant to let a drop of alcohol pass her lips again, had certainly no intention of telling her mother.

Lena didn't disapprove of romance of course, only the dissipation of self that sometimes accompanies love. She liked Luke, Kate suspected, mainly because he adored Kate exactly as she was, required no contortions of her personality to suit him. Too often, Kate had learned – post-Luke – that this wasn't the case with relationships. Lena would have been horrified, had she known, by the girls' – well, *Emily's* – doubtful dithering and nervous vigils by the phone during their university days.

Questioning herself over a man would have been anathema to Lena. Or maybe not, Kate thought, maybe it hadn't always been that way. Perhaps Lena had once been a love-struck young girl too, desperate to impress.

What Lena might have thought of Joe was a source of wild curiosity to Kate – perhaps eloping was the far easier option when the alternative was having to face Lena's shrewd stare and explain herself; explain Joe – dissolute, self-indulgent and irresponsible; explain a tumultuous present and an uncertain future. *But he has cheekbones to die for, Granny! And when he sings I want to jump his bones right there on the stage.*

Somehow, Kate fancied Lena would have forgiven Emily for sleeping with Joe, but not for caring about him, and not for valuing his opinion of her or making herself miserable in marriage.

Sitting in the garden, Kate leaned her head against Lena's shoulder, just as she would have done as a girl. Automatically, responding to muscle memory and some deep-rooted instinct, Lena put an arm around her and rested one calloused palm against the soft silk of Kate's hair. There was a hole in Kate's heart, the size and shape of Lena's illness. She hated the wavering uncertainty she felt every time she looked at Lena; the capricious whimsy of an illness which seemed simply to please itself. Day to day; moment to moment: unpredictable, cruel in its voracious appetite for memories and personality.

Kate didn't know the right thing to say. Would Lena be offended if she mentioned her Alzheimer's? Or more offended if she didn't. It was difficult to know what was right. Lena would laugh at herself if she could, would find the humour and face the disease with stoic disdain, but she couldn't because the disease was attacking the very parts of her that made her Lena.

Lena looked down at her, eyes piercing and clear, at the very same moment Kate glanced up. Kate took a breath and sat up straight. 'What does it feel like?' she asked.

Lena stretched her booted feet in front of her. 'That's not something people ask,' she said. 'They're all too afraid of offending me. You've gone all direct and American on us, haven't you?'

Kate blushed. 'Sorry,' she said. 'You don't have to answer that.'

'It's . . .' Lena paused and looked down the garden, as if seeing through the layers of history she had created; life and love in this house, the rabble of children, grandchildren and dogs she'd raised.

Kate thought she had gone, lost the sense of the moment and the question. Lena looked back at her with eyebrows raised. 'If people talk about it at all it's to give me the benefit of their well-meant advice. Treatments, old wives' tales.' She smiled grimly. 'No one ever asks how it feels. And mostly they talk over my head as if I am . . . dissipating, like smoke.' She waved a hand, took a breath and let it out slowly. Lena was never one to talk about feelings, but now Kate could see a chink in her armour, a glimpse of the loneliness and fear beneath. 'I am always waiting to be asked a question to which I will not know the answer,' Lena said. She drained her cup. 'It makes you stupid, this infernal disease.' Her frustration was ripe, sharp on her tongue. She made an impatient, guttural sound then lapsed into silence.

For a while they just sat, letting Lena's words settle like sediment. Then Lena said, so quietly Kate had to strain to hear, 'I wonder if you've made things right with that mother of yours yet?'

Kate stilled and said nothing; the question sounded rhetorical but it had hit the mark. She sat for a long moment, contemplating her answer.

She sensed the moment's passing, between one heartbeat and the next; Lena's attention wavering and the conversation sinking into the soup of lost things. Lena began to fidget beside her.

She changed the subject quickly. 'Emily phoned Ally earlier. He's coming at the weekend. And Jonathon.'

Lena nodded vaguely, a flower nodding in the breeze, but Kate could detect the frantic searching: who were these people? Her kin? Impossible.

'Thanks, Lena.' Kate uncurled her legs and stood, her heart breaking a little. She collected Lena's mug and headed up the path. When she glanced back, Lena had taken up her hoe again and was lost in her work.

Kate was restless as she wound her way up the garden path towards the house. The sun was low, a soft, pale gold light infusing the air and painting the shadows purple. There was still a warmth to it. Kate wanted to find Emily, to ask her to do something: take a walk, have a glass of wine, talk.

Wine was probably a bad idea; she felt heady enough as it was.

Perhaps a walk, she thought, but not to the farm, she didn't want to see Dan again, not until she had squared away her troublesome feelings.

One of their meandering talks, then, about nothing much, dissolving into laughter, finding everything funny; Emily, acerbic and sharp of wit, not ceasing until Kate was doubled over, holding her ribs and begging her to stop.

But talking no longer seemed as loose and easy as it once had; not when there were so many topics being skirted, half discussed. She was aware of how deftly Emily had dodged the Joe conversation the other day, hiding her obfuscation by launching Luke into the exchange to distract her.

She desperately wanted to spill her heart to Emily about Luke, as she used to; to tell her how she hadn't been able to put him out of her mind, how the old heartbreak felt fresh, as raw as if it had happened yesterday. And Ben – she needed Emily's advice about him. Something was holding her back.

Her mobile buzzed in her pocket and Kate pulled it out. Of course, just what she needed right now – a message from her mother.

Kate scrolled through their recent text conversation – misleading to call it that since it was almost entirely one-sided, with only occasional, curt replies from Kate. Lily never stopped trying. She had joined a church, she was busy with a fundraiser, she had a new job as a florist; all breezy, little clean-living proclamations punctuated with smiley faces and exclamation points. The latest read: *Just wanted to let you know that I've been promoted to manager!!! A real step up. Very exciting!! Hope you are well, how is the Big Apple?*

Her mother had begun straightening herself out when Kate went off to uni, completed the turnaround with Kate out of the country. Now she hovered on the fringes, poised like a butterfly, waiting for Kate to notice her new wings. It wasn't that Kate hadn't noticed. She just hadn't a clue how to go about repairing things, or even if she wanted to. She was so afraid of being hurt, and still so angry.

As she set the message aside for later – a time that never seemed to come – Kate realised she hadn't even told her mother she was in Scotland.

Chapter 12

The first fortnight at Bluebell Bank passed in a blink and Kate could scarcely have said where the time had gone, but she had to admit to herself that it had all been quite wonderful. Like slipping on a comfortable old jumper, she had settled back into the gentle rhythms of Bluebell Bank life. There were a few bumps along the way: Noah's continued refusal to return to the farm or countenance any discussion with his brother; her bewildering turmoil about Ben and Luke and Dan – which she hadn't found herself able to tell Emily – how could she when she didn't understand it herself? Lena frightened everyone half to death by wandering off one afternoon while they were all at the bookshop. She was escorted home in a police car after being found walking about Garlieston – a local resident recognised her from her Saturday morning market stall and called the police as soon as she realised how disoriented and upset Lena was.

There had been no word from Ben since that one desultory email her first night. There had been no word *for* Ben either. No reassurances; no reason to hope. Kate knew her silence was a reply of sorts; an answer of omission. As was his. They were damned by unsaid things, by their charade of a relationship.

The spectre of him hovered at the back of her mind. She knew she ought to free him, free them both, but rather selfishly she didn't feel like burning her bridges, still clinging to the notion that she would have a life to return to back in New York should she so choose.

*

Emily and Noah had established an unspoken truce; they didn't mention Noah's future, his job at the farm, or the fact that he had moved uninvited into one of the spare rooms at Bluebell Bank and had no apparent plans to leave. But Emily felt happier: she had Kate by her side, their friendship painstakingly piecing back together; Noah was occupied and behaving himself, no longer moping around picking fights or looking as if such a great weight rested on his shoulders; and her shop was being transformed, though not yet finished. The shelves were taking shape, stretching floor to ceiling along one wall. Noah, with a pencil wedged jauntily behind his ear, was looking very pleased with himself today, whistling as he checked the shelves with his spirit level. The work had been good for him, giving him purpose and a chance to explore his talents, and his presence around the shop was cheerful. 'Jeez,' she muttered as she walked past him, tugging at his waistband where it sat low on his hips revealing several inches of plaid boxers. He grinned, flipped her the finger. Emily responded in kind. There was no malice in the exchange.

'Let's take a break,' Kate said, pulling out a camping chair. She was leafing through the pages of her new favourite book – the one full of colour plates of the glorious Solway – and sat with her feet propped on a paint tin. Emily took the other chair, placing her laptop on her knees – she was starting to get the hang of the spreadsheets and costings – while Noah sprawled out on the floor.

Kate was smiling as she studied the now familiar images. They had been busy in the shop and there hadn't been much time for exploring, so she was still hankering to revisit some of those precious places of her youth. Noah sat up and leaned over her shoulder to look at the book. 'We still haven't done most of those things on your list,' he said. 'I guess it'll have to wait now until the shop is sorted.' He seemed restless, Emily thought at times, as if being trapped within any four walls didn't suit him. Kate had been like that as a teenager too – outgrowing her spaces and confines, while Emily had preferred to hide in corners.

Emily glanced up from her laptop, frowning over a spreadsheet. 'We shouldn't wait till then,' she said, closing the lid of the computer. 'We should do it. Otherwise we'll go crazy cooped up in here. We've barely taken a break except to eat and sleep. How about we start tonight? We could drive to Rigg Bay. Lena can come too. A game of cricket on the beach for old times' sake?'

Kate was nodding and Noah looked eager, but before either could reply, the door opened. 'We're closed,' Emily yelled, without looking round.

'I'm not a customer. I came to say hello, and to offer my carpentry skills.'

There he was: Luke Ross.

Standing in the doorway in a bright yellow T-shirt, his dark hair damp from a recent shower. The book tumbled off Kate's lap and she and Luke bent simultaneously to retrieve it, freezing for an instant with their heads close, faces nearly touching, Luke's eyes burning blue fire into hers. Luke straightened, looked around the shop.

Emily couldn't move. 'Looks like you don't need me after all,' Luke said softly. 'Nice job on the shelves,' he added to Noah.

'Thanks,' Noah said, puffing his chest out a little. 'They're coming along. It was kind of tough, you know? Since the floors aren't even.'

'Yeah, I had that same problem at my dad's place.'

'Hold on a minute,' Emily said, breaking out of her trance. 'Before you get *all-boys-together* about this, Kate and I helped with the shelves too.'

Luke's smile was infectious, even as he pressed his lips together to suppress it. Was he laughing at her? Emily narrowed her eyes.

Kate hid a smirk behind her hand; when Emily used her school-ma'am voice it didn't do to laugh at her, but it was hard not to. 'Are shelves the extent of your DIY skills?' Luke asked, looking only at Kate. 'I could use a hand with some plasterboarding. I just stripped out the bathroom in my dad's house.' His voice, slightly teasing, was deep, melodious, and Kate fought the urge to close her eyes and be transported back. It was a goosebump voice, warm and rounded, with just enough Scottish rasp in it, vying with the barest lilt of his mother's heritage.

'I never tried,' she said. 'But I'm a dab hand with grouting tiles. Had to learn to do stuff like that.'

Luke's expression grew sombre, though Kate hadn't been looking for sympathy. 'How is your mother?' he asked, the question not exactly intimate, but a reminder all the same of how well he had once known her. He was gazing intently, too close for the comfort of casual acquaintance. Kate was aware that Emily and Noah were both staring.

'Good,' she said lightly, which was strictly speaking true. 'It sounds like you've got your hands full with all the cottage renovations without offering your services to us too?' Kate felt flustered, not something she was accustomed to. She scooped her hair into a rough ponytail. All the subtleties of Luke's voice and face and body were slipping through the cracks in her composure, reminding her so acutely of the boy she had loved and lost. His seeking her out was unnerving, but she found she liked it.

Luke shrugged self-deprecatingly and tried another excuse. 'Well, it seemed like the thing to do – to help support the new local business.'

Emily set her laptop aside and stood up. 'You could do that by coming in and buying lots of books once we're open,' she said sourly.

He ignored her tone. 'I don't get much time to read, what with work and the cottage.'

'Would you like a coffee?' Kate interrupted. It seemed essential that Luke not leave yet; she wanted more of him: his smile, his voice, the steady interest in his cobalt eyes. She felt so warm, wanted again. 'I was just going to make a pot.'

'Sure. Thanks.'

He followed her into the kitchen, little realising how small and intimate the space was. Kate could barely turn round without brushing his arm, feeling him bearing down on her and blocking the doorway. He tensed, tried to back away and bumped his head on the low door lintel. 'Ow.'

Kate laughed. She settled back against the counter and crossed her arms, wished she was wearing something more glamorous than paint-covered flannel shorts and a vest that showed too much of her. Slowly, her rhythms were returning to normal – if it could ever be considered normal to be conversing casually with Luke Ross in a half-renovated bookshop in a forgotten corner of the Solway Coast.

How the hell had all this happened? The email, the plane ticket, Emily, Bluebell Bank, the bookshop: hurtling her towards *this* moment with a disconcerting inevitability. Towards Luke.

She made a cafetière, poured out cups and handed one to Luke. She wanted to preserve this moment alone with him in the tiny kitchen, enjoying his closeness, his smell of mint and pine, the mellow outdoorsiness. He didn't seem in a hurry to leave either.

'You know I didn't just come in to offer to help with the shelves, right?' Luke said softly, setting his cup down. 'Or for the coffee.'

Kate's face was hot. 'No?' A smile tugged at her lips. 'So you really do want my help with the plasterboarding then?'

'I was curious,' Luke said, voice softening further, dipping below the level which Emily and Noah might overhear, slipping into a more intimate timbre. 'Seeing you the other day made me curious.'

'Me too. It's been a long time.' The ending of their relationship was so brutal and abrupt that Kate had never sought him out. It was rare, in this day and age, to really lose touch with anyone. You had to really *want* to lose touch and Kate had.

So hurt was she that for a time the mere thought of Luke was agony. Never mind seeing him. Worse still would have been hearing of his happiness with someone else. She sneaked a look at his left hand. No ring, but of course that didn't mean anything. Dan being married was bad; Luke would be unbearable. She felt wary of him, even as her younger self turned somersaults with excitement.

'So,' Luke went on, rushing to get the words out. 'Now we're both here, I think we owe it to ourselves to have a drink together.'

'We do.' A decade and she had managed to completely, deliberately expunge Luke Ross from her life, and thoughts. Now everything was rushing back: love and loss and all those giddy moments in between.

He nodded, grinned with a trace of his old, boyish confidence. He tried to make his tone light and inconsequential when he spoke. He failed. His words were heavy with significance, laced with the nuance of old feelings. 'It's odd how things work, isn't it? We've both been away from the Solway for so long, and we return within a couple of months of each other. We walk into the same store on the same day. You're here. I'm here.' He shrugged then, catching her alarm. 'Just a drink, Kate, and a chance to catch up.'

Such an overused euphemism, Kate thought, and for what, exactly? The inevitable ping-pong of news, filling each other in on the minutiae of lives missed over the past decade. Tit for tat. Competing and one-upmanship. Kate didn't think it would be like that with Luke. With him, she felt she could take up exactly where they left off – except where they left off was her heartbroken and alone; Luke distant and cold.

Ben! A warning voice was screaming in her mind. She ignored it. 'Yes,' she said. 'I think I would like that.'

Luke was relieved. He picked up his cup with a grin. 'Great. When?'

'This weekend is out. Big family thing at Bluebell Bank. How about Tuesday?'

'Works for me. I'll pick you up at seven?'

Kate nodded. She picked up her own coffee and another for Noah – Emily wouldn't thank her for the stuff of course.

Back in the main shop with Noah and Emily they talked civilly about the shop and house renovations and Luke's job – he was employed by a firm of architects in Edinburgh, but was taking a sabbatical to finish his father's house, doing the plans for another renovation in Newton Stewart to make enough money to finish his own project.

When he'd finished his coffee, Kate walked him to the door. He gave her an awkward wave and a crooked smile, before heading down the alley to the main street. Kate sighed and leaned against the door frame.

The attraction, after all this time, was in Luke's humility; he had so few expectations of others, and was always ready to give of himself. She had loved his open-hearted interest in people, his instant warmth. She remembered how he would talk to strangers wherever they went – anyone, any age. She would lose him in the market, find him chatting to some guy doing a tourist survey, or a well-heeled elderly lady down from Glasgow for the day, or the ageing hippy who wanted to extol the virtues of fruit beer. Kate had had a teenager's impatience for adult chit-chat, and was interested only in Luke, but Luke always had time for others.

She turned to Emily and Noah, bracing herself for the onslaught of teasing.

'So?' Emily said pointedly.

Kate feigned interest in the Solway photographs again. 'So . . . nothing.'

'Are you going out with him?' Emily put her hands on her hips.

'As friends. To have a drink and a catch-up.'

'Oh,' Emily said. '*To catch up*. You like him all over again, don't you?'

Kate pushed her hair out of her face, losing patience. 'Emily,' she snapped, 'I'm not sure I ever stopped.'

It felt like such a relief to admit it, the mark of Ben fading almost instantly from her heart.

Emily's lips formed a perfect *o* of surprise; she hadn't expected the blunt force honesty. Noah looked up with interest. 'What about your boyfriend?' Emily said; her voice was trembling, though Kate couldn't figure why it should matter so much to her. 'What about Ben?'

Kate wanted get out of the shop, to process her thoughts. She beat a hasty retreat towards the door. 'I'll catch you guys back at Bluebell Bank. I'll walk home; the fresh air will do me good.'

'Don't forget Rigg Bay tonight,' Emily called after her, as if Kate was planning to do a complete runner.

And maybe she was right to be worried. Kate couldn't honestly say the thought hadn't entered her head a few times since she'd arrived: wondering what the hell she was doing here, and at the same time falling for the place all over again, feeling the invisible cords of the Solway coil around her, holding her in place.

*

Emily watched her go, her happiness deflating. What right had Luke Ross to come and stir things up again? She found herself angry at the world for the unfortunate convergence of events that had brought him here.

She should tell Kate the truth; she *must* tell her, before it was too late.

She tried not to panic at the sight of Kate's retreating form. Kate wasn't going to run again. Kate had fled the farthest – hopping a flight to New York when it was easier to go, to start over – but they were both pretty good at running away when things got tough. Emily knew she had plenty to answer for: the casual, selfish ease with which she had turned her back. She had chosen a giddy love affair over a lifetime of friendship and now she had a chance to put that right.

Friendship was love of a different sort: the type you built over decades of little moments, the kind that was stronger than family. The kind that *became* family.

How could she have given up on that? She couldn't fathom it now but at the time Joe had filled her senses and her mind until she couldn't see anything but him.

'Emily!' Noah was saying impatiently; he'd been trying to attract her attention for a while but had been ignored. She turned swiftly. 'Gonna to give me a hand to get these shelves in place or what?' He shook his head at her distraction and flashed her an indulgent smile – they really were getting on so much better now, working together, cementing the relationship they ought to have had if Emily hadn't been so preoccupied over Joe.

*

Later, Emily lay in bed with the pleasant feeling of fresh-air tiredness washing over her, the catharsis of confession leaving her languid and relaxed.

It had been a perfect summer evening at the beach: warmth still lingering in the air from the former heat of the day and the unchanging landscape of rocks and tree-sculpted shore soothing her with soft sands, the laughing whispers of the sea and a lazy, lilac sky dotted with fluff-ball clouds.

Kate's arrival had sparked a Solway heatwave like those of their childhood. The girls had strolled along the beach, arm in arm, talking, laughing and re-strengthening the bond between them. Noah hurled sticks into the sea for the dog and Bracken, despite his age, plunged valiantly after them. Lena stood in silent contemplation, her head tipped to the last vestiges of the sun.

They bowled a ball or two in the magical light of gloaming – cricket was the game of Lena's childhood and therefore the

Cottons's too. Kate had lost none of her natural athleticism despite having not wielded a bat in a decade, while Emily managed to be every bit as clumsy and ungainly as she had, squealing and diving out of the way when Lena bowled a wicked curve ball her way. Noah was a rugby player, but had the boy-grace that made transitioning from one sport to another a matter of ease. Bracken barked with puppyish excitement and danced around them in the sand. For an hour or so nothing mattered, nothing could trouble them.

As they played, Emily could hear their voices echoing back at her through the years: Lena saying with dismay, 'What grandchild of mine can't bowl a decent ball'; competitive Fergus screaming at Ally to run faster; her own careless laughter at her ineptitude as she retreated behind the pages of a Judy Blume book; Dan laughing as he tried to bowl Kate out, rarely succeeding.

While Noah and Lena walked one way, along the wooded path towards Garlieston, Kate and Emily hiked across the rocks towards the Cruggleton cliffs. Here Emily finally opened up about her divorce.

'I suppose you want to know what happened?' she said, offhand.

There was no doubt she meant Joe. 'If you want to tell me,' Kate said, smiling at her Emily-ness.

They picked their way over seaweed and rock; Emily's face was bleak and still. 'I suppose I should start with the last time I saw you, in that bar in Morningside.'

'We were just about to sign the lease on that flat.'

University over, Kate had a bar job and was sending out her work to every design company and fashion house she could find while Emily was about to embark on her first year of teaching. 'I was a little crazy. Joe's band had had their first small taste of success and I was scared about what it meant for me, for us. I was terrified about starting teaching.'

'You left me with an unsigned lease and a half-drunk bottle of wine, and you never came back,' Kate remarked, without rancour.

Emily nodded. 'I shouldn't have done that. I don't know how to explain it. You know how things were between us . . .'

'Intense.'

She nodded. 'He asked me to go with him. To get married. I felt that I was nothing without Joe . . .'

'That's not true.' Kate couldn't keep the anger at bay now. 'You couldn't see your worth, Em.'

'I know. I let *him* define my worth.' The bleakness of tone told of six years of introspection and analysis, winding up at this truth Kate had always known – from a very young age Emily had judged herself by the perceptions of others, despite Lena's best teachings.

'But, marriage, Emily? Wanting to feel better is a stupid reason to marry.'

'I know, but I thought if I refused he would go off on tour and—'

'Find someone else,' Kate finished.

'Yes. I thought if I broke up with him I would never find anyone again. I'd be alone for ever.'

'You thought that at twenty-one with everything ahead of you? You don't believe that still, do you?'

'I left him, didn't I?' Defensive now. Kate raised her eyebrows. 'OK. A bit. I still think it a bit. I'm still on my own, aren't I? You don't understand, it's always come easy to you. Men are attracted to you, but you don't care. You act indifferent and it only makes them more keen. It's not like that for me.'

'Confidence is a state of mind, Em. Besides, I resent that; it doesn't seem that way to me. There hasn't been anyone but Ben in a long time. I can count on the fingers of one hand how many guys I dated at uni and none of them ever lived up to Luke . . .' Her voice trailed off into the gentle sounds of evening: the shush of the waves at their backs.

'I'm sorry. I know. I was always envious of you which didn't help matters.'

Kate's tone softened. 'What happened after you and Joe left?'

Emily's smile was bitter. 'It wasn't very glamorous; we moved in with Joe's cousin in East Kilbride. The flat was a bit of a dive but we didn't care, we were too wrapped up in each other. We got married at a registry office. It felt so romantic and irresponsible and I was happy, I really was.'

'What about family? Why didn't you want any of us there to see you get married?'

'None of you approved and I couldn't bear to have anything spoil . . .' She paused and frowned, weighing her words – how much should she reveal?

There were parts of the truth that hurt even to think about, parts she had pushed down. Feeling like a terrible person every time she saw Abby and another spear of resentment pierced deep.

'I thought you all were wrong and I was right. The family was appalled, of course, when they found out what I'd done. Dan was furious. He ranted, told me how selfish I was – how upset Mum and Dad were.' She shrugged. 'By then it was too late. I hardly cared. Ally was the only one I really saw for a long time. He wasn't mad at me and it felt like he understood better how I felt, perhaps because he's my twin.'

'Were you ever happy?'

'I was. Joe was focused on the band, but for a while everything was good. I joined them on their tour – just small venues and little festivals, nothing major, but with an album coming out it felt like they were on their way. Oh . . . there were cracks appearing – artistic differences, Joe said. Secretly I think it was just that Joe wanted complete control and the others didn't like that. The album bombed, their performances started to suffer. Then the label dropped them. Joe was devastated, went on a month-long binge drowning his sorrows. I didn't have a clue how to comfort him. His dream was crumbling around him. We ended up back with the cousin for a time. He got over the initial disappointment and cleaned himself up, resolved to go on. But he and the rest of the band were arguing. They attempted to keep working together, to get on with the next album, a better one, but by the following Christmas it had got too much and the band split.

'We moved back to Edinburgh, but I was still mostly estranged from the family – my choice, I couldn't bear them to be smug.'

'They wouldn't have—'

'It was just how I felt. We went on that way for a couple of years. I drifted in and out of various jobs, then I decided enough was enough. We needed stability. I started teaching, but I hated it. High schools are full of teenagers, you know.'

Kate laughed. 'You didn't get an inkling about that on your course?'

'Things went from bad to worse with Joe. Some days he barely spoke to me. He was inconsiderate, playing his music or staying out all night. No concern for me whatsoever. Of course, he was cheating. Lots. Then, suddenly, he had a new band. They got signed and things started to improve.

'Then . . . then he met Bronwyn.'

'Bronwyn?' Kate was quiet; this was the crux of the matter right here. She could see it in Emily's eyes, hear the tremor in her voice.

'She was just a girl. Actually, no, she wasn't. It was much worse than that. She was also the reason I had to quit teaching.'

Kate said nothing so Emily would keep talking, in that curiously flat tone – all the horror and self-loathing from that time hidden beneath the surface. 'Bronwyn was one of my students. She was seventeen. She was a fan of the band and when she found out I was Joe's wife, she was so excited; she thought it was really cool. I had no idea how deep her feelings for him went; or that he'd be stupid enough to . . .' A lungful of air, preparing to go on. 'I introduced them after a gig. I didn't know Bronwyn was going to be there; I didn't know she'd started following me, found me on social media. I didn't have a clue about any of it and Joe's fame was so new. He hooked up with her, Kate – actually started *sleeping* with her! She began trashing me online. I had to leave work. I'd put a child in danger—'

'Joe's fault, not yours,' Kate said quickly, terrible anger settling deep in her belly. She'd been *right* to hate him.

'I know, but I had to leave all the same. I couldn't stay. The kids were laughing behind my back, the other teachers talking about me. And Joe and Bronwyn got serious. It wasn't just sex, he really fell for her.'

'He had no business, what was he – twenty-five?'

'Yeah. It was wrong, but you know Joe; he does what he wants and gets away with it with a smile. She was of age, thankfully, but still . . . it was the end of everything.'

'You left him immediately? Good for you.'

'No-o . . . I wish. I left *teaching* immediately, but I believed Joe when he said it was over. I stayed for another six months while they carried on behind my back, having a good laugh at me no doubt.'

'Oh Emily.'

Emily held up a hand. 'No sympathy, Kate, not yet. I need to finish telling this and I won't be able to if you're kind. Go back to stern and *what were you thinking?*'

'What were you thinking?' Kate echoed, but her voice was warm and kind.

'I still thought we were . . . fated, I suppose, is the only way to explain it. That I just had to put up with anything because he was my destiny.'

Kate smiled. 'Star-crossed lovers? Emily, you really do read far too many books.'

'Technically, that's a play, not a book. I know it sounds ridiculous, but I felt stuck.'

'I wish you had called me. I could have helped.'

'I couldn't call you. I couldn't call anyone. I couldn't admit that it had all been a mistake, such a waste. Plus, you were living an amazing life in America.'

'None of us wanted you to get hurt.'

Unwillingly – 'I know.'

'So what changed?'

Emily blew out a breath. 'It was Christmas. I was so homesick, but I didn't feel like I *could* go home. Joe wouldn't really be welcome at my parents' house and I didn't want to go alone. I didn't want them to see me unhappy. I was exhausted – I'd got a job in a library, which should have been great, but I was always tired. Joe was out rehearsing with the band all the time. Even at Christmas I hardly saw him and I was so lonely; all I could think of was the fun I was missing at home. You remember – Dad stuffing the turkey in the kitchen, drinking port and singing along to a Christmas compilation; Mum stringing up hundreds of Christmas cards; Lena watching the carols from King's College on the telly; the trying to bribe me to do their wrapping. I was lonely for them.'

'You spent Christmas Day on your own?' Kate was horrified. She remembered cold, long-ago Christmases when the festivities going on around her served only to emphasise what was missing; but these were distant memories, hazy, overwritten with happier ones she had shared with the Cottons.

'I tried to make a Christmas meal for us but I burned the lot and I was sure he was texting *her* during the day. Later, the guys came over and they just wanted to sit around and drink beer and smoke weed and I couldn't bear it, so I took a taxi to Mum and Dad's. I didn't care what they thought any more; I just wanted to be home. When I arrived, I burst into tears and threw myself at Lena. It just exploded out of me and wouldn't be kept in – how unhappy I was, Joe and Bronwyn, teaching, the flat; how I just wanted to go home.'

'Emily,' Kate said, finally breaching the gulf between them with a sympathetic hand.

Em grimaced. 'I know. Pathetic, isn't it?'

'No. I just wish I had been there.'

'It was my own fault you weren't. I pushed you away.'

'So that was it? You didn't go back?'

'Nope, at first it was such a relief to be free. I started divorce proceedings straight away. Ironically, that year proved to be a turning point for the band. The media circus around them was crazy. They were everywhere. Every time I picked up a magazine or turned on the radio, there he was. I was pleased for him, I honestly was. But I was also relieved to be out of it.'

Kate slipped her hand into Emily's and they teetered over rocks, supporting one another. Dusk was falling, soft and velvety. Emily's confession had fashioned the closeness of old. 'I suppose we'd best get back. Emily, you are done with him, aren't you?'

Emily looked up with worried eyes. 'Honestly, Kate, I have no idea.'

'Well, at least you didn't have kids,' Kate said. 'Divorce is one thing, but kids would be worse. He'd always be in your life then. At least you can erase him for good, never have to see him again.'

*

Later, yawning in her bed from the fresh air and exercise, Kate gazed out of the open curtains at the clear, star-scattered sky – the arrangement of pinpricks so haphazard and yet so perfectly placed – and engaged in guilty daydreams of Luke. Luke the boy. Luke the man. In part she understood the obsessive nature of Emily's love for Joe – she had fallen hard for Luke; but he had been kind, had treated her well.

Until he dumped her without ceremony or explanation.

Her feelings for him had been kept locked away for so long she had almost managed to deny them. Now they demanded to be considered, like sifting through her treasure trove of mementoes and wondering afresh at things forgotten.

Remembering the bubble-like perfection of those holidays,

Kate would always wonder what might have been, what she had done wrong.

The boy she had loved was gone and in his place was a man: a man who could be anywhere in the world at that moment in time but wasn't. He was here.

A man with a career and old lovers – possibly present lovers; a man with a dead father and memories and pain of his own; a man she did not know.

But she could not deny her excitement at the sight of him, the pleasure of these thoughts of him as she lay alone in her childhood bed. No longer did it seem unlikely, impossible even, that Luke and she should both end up back here. Rather, it felt precisely perfect.

Chapter 13

The family dinner promised to be a lavish affair and Kate was on tenterhooks awaiting it. She and Emily made careful preparations under Lena's watchful eye. Melanie couldn't get the weekend off work, but Jonathon was coming and Ally had booked a flight for Friday evening, as soon as he got out of court. Jonathon was going to pick his son up at the airport and bring him to Bluebell Bank; it would be Ally and Jonathon's first trip down to the Solway in many months.

'No one talks about Ally much,' Kate said, as she and Emily were making up the guest beds with Lena's lavender-scented sheets.

Emily shrugged. 'He's just Ally. You know. He always keeps himself to himself. Gets on with stuff. He's fine.'

'Yes, but . . .' Kate wasn't satisfied. Ally and Emily were twins, Emily should show a little more interest in his life. Alistair had always been the quiet brother, on the periphery of everything, never fully part of their escapades. Dan and Fergus were so boisterous, the best of friends despite their frequent, vicious disputes. And Emily had had Kate, had no need of her twin's company.

'Look, I guess we've all been preoccupied with our own shit. It's possible he's got some crazy exciting life down in London, but I think he just works mostly. You know how driven he is.'

'Well, I guess I'll see him for myself tomorrow.'

Fergus would be missing from the reunion, but she and Emily had Skyped him more than once since her arrival and she was satisfied that he was much the same – a little more tanned, a little more laid-back and with a strange Aussie twang to his accent, but essentially Ferg.

Lena marvelled at the miracles of modern science that allowed her to sit in her easy chair at Bluebell Bank with Em's laptop on her knees and see her grandson half a world away. But the next time they Skyped she didn't know to whom she was talking, and it unsettled her for hours.

On Friday evening, Kate laid the table with the good lace cloth and Lena's best pottery goblets, and the old wedding china carefully preserved for sixty years. She folded napkins, tied them with ribbon, set out the decanters and the place mats with prints of Solway seascapes, and flicked a napkin at the dust gathering on the mantelpiece. 'You're going to a lot of trouble,' Emily observed, watching her.

'So would Lena, if she could.' If Lena could hold in her head for longer than a few minutes what was happening, who was coming and what it was all in aid of. Kate knew Emily was concerned the party would be too much for Lena.

Jonathon duly picked up Ally at Glasgow airport and they arrived at Bluebell Bank just before ten, finding the occupants gathered expectantly in the sitting room. Lena nursed a whisky as she looked out on the last of the sun sinking behind the black outlines of the trees, low slanting beams all shades of gold, burnished orange flames licking at the horizon. Emily was curled up in the rocking chair, frowning in concentration over lists on her laptop, and Kate had fabric samples laid out on the floor amongst the pages of her open sketchbook. Occasionally she thrust some idea for consideration under Emily's nose, but mostly they worked in silence, each engrossed in their own part of the planning.

Lena opened the door to Jonathon and Ally and returned to the living room with them, wiping her face with a piece of folded kitchen towel. It was the first time Kate had ever seen her crying and it brought a lump to her throat. They had all been so worried she wouldn't know them, that the reunion would be upsetting, underwhelming. Emily had prepared everyone for the worst.

For days Emily had been talking to Lena about them, taking down pictures from the wall and weaving Ally and her father into their dinner conversations. This strategy had worked, and Kate was glad; Jonathon hadn't managed to come down to visit his mother for a while and it would have been a shock to find her much deteriorated.

If Kate thought the greatest transformation to take place in the Cottons was in Noah, she was proved wrong when she saw Ally. He was every inch the successful city lawyer now: pinstriped suit, polished shoes, blond hair styled in a cut that probably cost more than Kate's own. He broke into a familiar grin and swept her into a warm hug. 'Hello, stranger,' he said, and their meeting was as smooth as if they had seen each other yesterday. Ally was easy company, secure in himself. Kate basked in the pleasure of seeing him again. 'When Emily emailed to say you were back, I was so glad. What do you make of this bookshop idea of hers?'

Kate glanced at Emily, smiling confidently. 'It's going to be brilliant,' she said. 'I guess the next time you come up will be for our grand opening. If you can make it. It'll be the start of August we think.'

'And are you going to stay?'

Kate hesitated. 'For the opening, of course. I don't know what will happen after that.'

Lena brought out the whisky bottle and four glasses and poured them each a measure, and Jonathon had them raise their glasses in a toast. 'To family,' he said and they echoed his words as they drank, their tumblers clinking together companionably and

Bracken wagging his tail from his basket by the hearth. Kate and Emily wrinkled their noses at the whisky, grinning at each other over their glasses, like kids stealing furtive sips of the grown-ups' booze – except, Kate had never really done that; she had been eighteen before she was persuaded to have a drink and she had never been comfortable with the booze culture that dominated university life, too well versed in the darker side of drinking and all it could destroy.

'How are you, Kate? And how is your mum?' Jonathon asked, taking off his glasses and wiping them on his shirt, getting comfortable on the settee nursing his drink. There were a few more lines around his eyes and his hair was now completely grey, but he wore the same slightly rumpled, surprised look that was so familiar to Kate. The closest thing to a father figure she had known – Lily had remained steadfast in her refusal to grant Kate the details of her own father – a gentle, calm presence in all their lives, so unlike his livewire wife.

'Good, thanks,' Kate replied politely, discouraging him as surely as she did everyone else from probing further. Of all topics, her mother was off limits. There had been another cheerful text update yesterday – Lily never seemed put out that Kate didn't reply; maybe just biding her time, confident that Kate would concede eventually. Kate wasn't so sure she would. She was scared of letting her mother back into her life; scared of opening the floodgates. If she began to talk to Lily, she wasn't sure she'd be able to stop, or where she'd draw the line. The anger was long suppressed, but it was there.

Kate was so afraid of opening herself up, of being let down again.

She *couldn't* be let down again.

To take the sting from her taciturn reply, Kate launched into a more thorough depiction of New York, describing her job, her apartment, her friends, skating over the surface of her life, barely mentioning Ben.

'I'll make us something to eat,' Lena said suddenly, getting up. 'You must all be hungry.'

'Don't bother for me, Mum,' Jonathon said.

'Rubbish. It's no bother. Won't be long.'

Jonathon watched her go with a frown, then turned to his daughter. 'How is she?' he asked in a low voice.

'We don't talk about her behind her back, she's not a child or an invalid,' Emily said firmly. 'But she's fine, Dad. It's still early days. Sometimes you wouldn't really notice any difference. She struggles with people's names, doesn't recognise folk from time to time. She makes endless lists in case she forgets and I write everything down for her too.'

Lena's list-making comprised scraps of paper, receipts, the back of old envelopes, none of it seeming particularly organised. The kitchen was strewn with notes and labels, all Blu-tacked on cupboard doors and pinned to the cork board. Jonathon and Ally had yet to see the evidence of how differently life at Bluebell Bank was forced to unfold these days. Emily understood Lena's mind better than anyone.

Jonathon nodded slowly and Kate wondered how he felt about handing over his mother's care to his daughter. Lena and Emily needed each other, both requiring something only the other could provide. 'And Noah. How is he?'

Emily glanced to Kate for help. Noah had absented himself when he realised his father's arrival was imminent, despite Emily's entreaties to him to stay. 'He's doing fine, Mr Cotton. He's been helping us out at the shop,' Kate said.

Jonathon smiled. 'I think we're long past such formalities, Kate. Jonathon, please. So, I guess I can thank you for looking after two of my children.'

'*D-ad*,' Emily complained, rolling her eyes like Noah. 'I'm a grown woman, and so is Noah – grown, I mean, not a woman obviously.'

'Grown or not, your mother and I are still allowed to worry about you all. In fact, it's non-negotiable.'

Emily was silent, considering the disproportionate amount of worry she had caused her parents: running off to get married, disappearing almost entirely for all those years, landing on their doorstep broken, now mired in a depression that wouldn't lift. 'I hope Noah re-evaluates things while he is here, and takes some responsibility for himself,' Jonathon continued. 'He isn't a child any longer.'

'Do me a favour, Dad, don't lecture him when you see him tomorrow.' It was strange to be defending him, but Emily felt suddenly protective of her brother, coming round to Kate's notion that Noah just needed to be left alone to heal.

Jonathon made an impatient sound and sighed. 'Credit me with a little tact and diplomacy, Emily,' he said in a pontificating tone that riled Emily – lecturing was much more her mother's style. 'Noah is my seventeen-year-old son and I reserve the right to enquire about his plans.'

'Well, *I'm* only home for a flying visit,' Ally cut in, before a father–daughter argument had time to break out. 'And we haven't seen Kate here in . . . what is it, six years? So *I* reserve the right to tell you all to shut up if you start getting all serious and argumentative. This is a family dinner, the first for a long time, so play nicely please.'

They were laughing when Lena came back into the living room carrying her sewing box and a pair of slacks that she had been meaning to sew the button on for several weeks. No one mentioned that food hadn't materialised, but Kate could see the concern in Jonathon's eyes.

Emily sat in the rocking chair with her legs curled beneath her, letting their conversation flow over her, basking in the comforting hum of their words. There was a warmth at her core that was nothing to do with the whisky. For the first time in so long she was relaxed, content, free of the iron grip of fear and despair, released from the shackles of her panic attacks.

The darkness was receding now, and only as it diminished was she aware of the true horror of it.

She had felt deep gloom before – the summer when Kate first met Luke and Emily hadn't wanted to be jealous of Luke's place in Kate's affections, but was all the same.

Emily's teenage years had been dotted with despair.

It had felt like she was losing Kate. Kate's Technicolor happiness seemed only to magnify Emily's dissatisfaction. She wasn't comfortable in her skin, wasn't adept at making casual conversation or meeting new people. The initial flirtation with Cam had petered out, nothing of substance beyond that first sloppy, drunken kiss.

While Emily had to content herself with simply reading about romance that summer, Kate was living it. Kate's feelings for Luke emulated the sort of heady, consuming affairs Emily had only encountered in novels, far exceeding the ordinary, teenage liaisons they read about in *Just Seventeen*. Listening to Kate, Luke might have been any one of the romantic heroes of Emily's books.

The awareness of her jealousy did not make it any easier to deal with. It was repugnant and she disliked herself for it. Cam had been far from Emily's dream – frankly, he bored her – but when things fizzled out between them, Emily still wondered what was wrong with *her* that she couldn't keep his interest.

It was an alarming new development that summer: the tendency to turn on herself, one she'd never completely lost. It was the first time she remembered looking in the mirror and despising what she saw. She resented her burgeoning womanhood and felt constantly out of sorts. Kate, by contrast, seemed to glow: growing golden, ethereal and oh-so desirable.

Over the course of that summer Emily had grown more and more remote, locking herself away in a fictional world, putting up a barrier of words between herself and real life. This had the inevitable outcome of pushing Kate and Luke even closer together and isolating Emily further. It had other consequences too, ones she didn't like to think about, but which she might have to face now that Luke was back on the scene. His appearance in the bookshop had unsettled her.

Emily met Kate's eyes across the room. She raised her whisky glass in a silent toast, with a ghost of a smile. *We're all right*, the smile said. *We're getting somewhere.*

And they were. Apart from the nagging worry about Luke, Emily hadn't felt real panic since the episode in the car park. She hadn't called Joe either, which was something of an achievement. She was, she decided, doing all right.

Chapter 14

Kate cradled her wine goblet and looked at the noisy gathering of Cottons clustered around the dining table, feeling a web of warmth and comfort enclose her. *This is what I came here for.* This was family and all she had missed. These people were not her blood, but she felt as if they were.

Late evening sunbeams danced across the table, gilding their faces, burnishing the coppery highlights in Abby's hair, lighting up Lena's smile, setting fire to the ruby contents of the wine bottle and streaking its reflections on the wall. The meal was finished and still they lingered, taking every last gasp of succour from the table and company.

Lena was at the head of the table, currently slapping her palms on the cloth and throwing back her scarecrow head, roaring with unrestrained laughter; Jonathon had made her laugh talking over old times and they all joined her.

Lena had saved her best for when it mattered. If this was all there was, if tonight was the last dinner that Lena was truly *here*, it would be worth it, Kate thought. She felt tipsy and nostalgic, expansive with her affection, trying not to watch Dan out of the corner of her eye.

Emily, too, seated at Lena's right, studied her family – Dan and

Ally throwing easy jokes around, happily drunk and brotherly; Lena, holding court; Abby, glowing and massive; her father getting along with everyone, even with Noah; and Kate – just her being here was enough.

There was a time when her grandmother had been the only person who came close to understanding Emily, but now she was forging stronger bonds with the rest of them. She felt a surge of affection for Lena, the familiar urge to write some more in her memoir. It was a stubborn itch, the desire to write and preserve the past. It was a torment, how time ticked away, grains of sand slipping beneath her feet. Her time with Lena was precious, Emily knew. Riches beyond anything one could put a price to.

She reached for her wine goblet, caught Kate's eye and grinned. Not tonight. Tonight was no time for fretting or regretting the past. Tonight was a time to relax, wrap herself in the peace and love of her family and have fun, and banish all other thoughts for later.

Dan, with his penchant for making bad jokes and laughing uproariously at himself when he was drunk, was verbose tonight and the more red wine he and Ally put away, the louder, more voluble and glib they became. Abby patted Dan's knee indulgently as she watched him mess around with his brother. Dan missed Fergus and it was nice for him to have this bond with Ally.

Kate couldn't help but notice how their camaraderie excluded Noah, who sat beside her silently for the most part, glancing at his father and siblings from time to time. When the plates were picked clean and the decanters almost empty, Abby and Lena went into the kitchen to make a pot of tea. Ally picked up the last decanter, hovering it over Kate's glass questioningly. When she shook her head, he moved on to Emily, sharing the dregs between them. 'So, Kate, Em says you sell knickers for a living, is that so?' He and Dan sniggered like schoolboys and Kate rolled her eyes.

'I prefer the term lingerie,' Kate said indignantly. 'And it's pretty classy stuff, a top designer, but yes, I guess you could say that at the moment I sell underwear for a living.'

'I thought you studied textile design,' Ally persisted.

'Yes.' Kate sighed; she knew where this was heading.

'So, how did you end up—?'

'It's hard work breaking into fashion,' she said defensively. 'I got into advertising almost by accident and I like it, really I do.' She shrugged. 'But, you're right, it's not exactly utilising my creativity. Maybe I'm ready for a change.'

'Hence the *bookshop*?' Dan sounded doubtful.

Kate laughed. 'I plan to make some very nice cushion covers for the bookshop and advertise the place to within an inch of its life,' she said with dignity. 'Who knows, I might set up my own business at some point in the future. I do still want to design. I'm tired of selling other people's knickers.' It got a laugh, but sparked something less jovial in Kate: decisions, again. They couldn't be put off for good. Anxiety ticked in her brain: for if not now, when?

Jonathon leaned forward, serious behind his thick specs. 'It's like Emily,' he said, loosened by a glass or three of wine. 'She was always such a good writer. I expected her to write her own books, instead of teaching about other people's.'

Emily had the grace to smile, with a hint of self-deprecation. 'Teaching was a momentary aberration. I don't know what made me think *I* could have the patience for dealing with recalcitrant teenagers who aren't remotely interested in literature all day long.' This made them all laugh, but she caught Kate's eye – the only one who knew the whole story.

'And now you're going to *sell* other people's books,' Ally pointed out. 'You think one day we might see an original Emily Cotton on the shelves?'

Emily merely shrugged.

'Are you writing?' Kate asked. Emily hadn't mentioned doing any writing since she'd been here, but she'd dabbled as a child.

Emily shrugged again, thinking of the memory book, bursting with Lena's words. 'A little. Sometimes. Right now the shop is my focus.' She spoke a hint of defiance, as if daring anyone to contradict her. No one did. 'Actually,' she said. 'I have an idea for the name. The Book Nook. What do you think?'

A murmur of assent ran round the table, everyone agreeing that this was just the thing. Of course, lubricated by Merlot, they weren't the most sober of judges.

Dan drained the last of his wine. 'Is anyone up for a pint after dinner? Noah can be designated driver.' He reached across to slap Noah on the back and his brother jerked away from his touch. They had yet to resolve the difference of opinion over Noah's employment and Emily guessed the source of Noah's discomfort over dinner was the fear that Dan would tell his father before he got the chance to confess it himself.

'Sure,' Emily said. 'That sounds good. It's been ages since I went out – even if it is just the local pub. I'm sure Kate is used to far more glamorous night life.'

'Perhaps. But as I didn't come here for the night life, it's fine. I think the pub sounds like a great idea. You sure you don't mind driving, Noah?'

Noah nodded. 'It's fine. I've got to get up early so I can't drink. We've work to do at the shop.' He was taking his new – unpaid – job seriously. This was the moment Jonathon might have asked why on earth his son was involved in the shop instead of being gainfully employed milking Dan's cows, and if it hadn't been for the wine perhaps he would have. But Jonathon was feeling gently mellow and missed the opportunity.

However, he was not so mellow that the mention of underage drinking went uncommented upon. He cleared his throat. 'Ahem, I think you'll find not drinking has absolutely nothing to do with how early you have to get up and everything to do with the fact that you are *seventeen*.' He looked at Dan. 'Daniel, I hope you haven't been letting him drink?'

'It has nothing to do with whether I let him or not,' Dan retorted, leaning back in his chair. Noah gave his brother a glare and they eyeballed each other in silence for a few moments.

Kate was about to weigh in on Noah's behalf, thinking she might be his only defence, but Emily beat her to it. 'Lighten up, both of you.' She put a hand on Noah's arm. 'He's seventeen, not seven, the odd pint or two isn't going to hurt him.'

Noah looked at her in surprise, but before anyone could say anything further on the matter, Lena and Abby returned with the tea.

*

Kate shuffled along the bench to make room for Dan as he returned from the bar with two pints. It was just the two of them in the lounge. The party had fragmented; Noah had found some mates in the bar, Ally had nipped outside for a fag and Emily was hustling some unsuspecting guy on the pool table. The growing audience looked increasingly impressed as she sank ball after ball – therein lay the proof of Emily's misspent youth; she sucked at sports, but her knack for pool had made her a legend in the student union bar.

Dan knocked his leg against the table as he sat down, spilling a pool of beer that soaked through the cardboard mat. 'Sorry.' He slurped the foam from his pint, slid Kate's across the table to her, and wiped his lips. He was drunk, but not totally pissed: just the thickening of his vowels, clumsy fingers, slightly glazed eyes. But there was a nervous intensity about him too that made Kate uncomfortable, made this moment seem too significant.

'Thanks. *She's* having a good time,' Kate said, pointing to the pool table. Emily rocketed the black ball into the pocket and slapped high-fives around the table, with a Cheshire-cat grin and sparkling eyes. The door opened and Ally strode in; he had rolled up his shirtsleeves and shed his suit jacket, but he still looked dressed for London.

Dan followed her gaze. 'Ally doesn't make it home often

enough. He's good for Emily. You are too,' he added. 'That's why it's so good that you're home.'

Kate smiled. 'It's a long time since I considered Bluebell Bank to be my home. I didn't realise how much I missed it until I came back. It's nice to be made so welcome.'

'Were things so bad in New York?'

Kate shook her head. 'No-o,' she said, trying to find the words to explain. 'They weren't *bad* at all. Just very different.'

'So you just packed up and left just because Emily asked you to? I don't get it.'

They were jammed onto the end of a bench. The pub was loud, heaving with humanity and the thrum of drink-loosened laughter, and he had to lean close to be heard. The press of his leg against hers, their arms brushing, his breath on her neck. Kate shifted and tried to make space, but there was none to be had. It was Saturday and the joint was jumping – for Wigtown.

This was one of those heady, imperative moments, when everything seemed right and proper and vital, and the future seemed to hinge on every word; Dan filled her senses and everything about him was so familiar she was fifteen again, in the grip of her first crush, and this boy was her whole world – awareness of him had plagued her every waking moment. Before Luke, Dan had been the first big love of her life. And he hadn't even known it.

And then, later. Seventeen years old and stupid; she thought she was over the infatuation until that night. Scarcely did she allow herself to think of it, but here, with Dan clouding her vision, her thoughts, it was hard not to.

They had been in the empty Cotton house by candlelight, April storms raging outside and the fire stoked; opening a bottle of Jonathon's best Pinot Noir set aside for a rainy day or a special occasion – it was both.

She was freshly heartbroken, searching for something. Dan had been waiting for her for too long. The sofa was cushioned with blankets and at first they sat demurely side by side, still believing in the pretence, then slowly unbending with the wine.

Kate had just returned from her Easter holiday visiting a friend in Oxford and the rest of the Cottons were at Bluebell Bank.

The darkness, the meandering conversation; the encroaching, entwining limbs and words, bodies and lips. The whole evening building to the crescendo of their first kiss. And beyond, into the unknown. Into a forever land from which they could not turn back.

She remembered the heat of Dan's skin on hers, how her name gasped from his lips made her quiver, the weight and press of him, the sofa cushions thrown on the floor as they shed their clothes and inhibitions and good sense. Sex with Dan had been illicit, thrilling, breathtaking. It had also been her first. She and Luke had been waiting – for what she could no longer recall.

Kate, still reeling from Luke's dismissal, had felt the wrongness of it immediately – it had already been too late for her and Dan – but by then Dan fancied himself in love with her.

She pushed him away – too hurt and confused to know what she was doing – and it was soon afterwards that Dan took himself off to the Solway to take on the farm with Fergus. Then Kate was off to university. They tried to forget and continue on in a platonic way – not that they saw each other much after that, just the occasional uni holiday, when they couldn't help repeating the pattern, drawn inexorably back by the lure of attraction and sex. It was never the same, it was never easy to ignore what they had done and they had never managed to be entirely platonic.

It was difficult to ignore what it had meant to him. Even now.

It had meant something to Kate too; she just hadn't been in a position to make something of it, too lovelorn over Luke. She looked up at Dan and he was staring back at her intently, the frowning, stubborn earnestness she still found so attractive. Her stomach churned and her head spun, even though she was nowhere near as well lubricated as he was. 'I owed her,' she told him – she owed them all. 'It seemed like a chance to repay the debt.'

'It's a pretty extreme way. What did you do, kill her cat?' Kate didn't laugh. 'You couldn't send a card, or a bouquet of flowers?'

'It's the kind of debt you need to pay in person,' Kate replied. 'Long overdue. Also, Emily hates cats, as well you know.'

'You sound serious.' Dan's easy grin faded.

'I am.'

She saved me. You all did. You showed me a different path.

She shivered. It always scared her to think of those turning points, each lucky escape. The small moments when fate had intervened and took her in another direction altogether. She didn't like to think about what she might have become without the solidity of the Cottons behind her, without their care.

Dan seemed uncomfortable with the weight of Kate's words. 'I know Em's not perfect either, so I'm sure you're even,' he said. He was missing the point, she thought. He was so close: a lazy smile, dark eyes she could lose herself in, broad shoulders and strong arms that had once wrapped around her in friendship, protection and, finally, passion.

This was dangerous.

'I'm really glad everything worked out for you,' Kate said, reminding them both that he was not hers, *could not be hers*. She put a hand on his arm, which was a mistake. She felt him flinch at her touch, and drew in a deep breath. She snatched her hand away. 'I hoped you were happy.'

Dan raised an eyebrow, gave her his boyish grin. 'So you finally got over your crush on me?'

Kate blushed. 'I don't know what you mean.'

'Yeah. Right.' His voice was soft and intimate. Now his hand found hers and neither pulled away. 'What do you mean, you *hoped I was happy*?'

Kate was confused by things she had no business feeling. 'I

hoped you were happy. In that I hoped you weren't *un*happy. I hoped you had a nice life. I'm glad to find you do.'

For her, *happy* meant not *un*happy. It was clear, black and white. No grey. Just depths of despair or delirium. Not so for Dan, for him there were all shades between and this was a great big grey area, blurred beyond reason.

'What about those moments when you are neither happy nor unhappy. Just nothing. Do you think that everything in my life is perfect, Kate? You can't put people into boxes like that. You can't assume you know how it is for someone. I mean you can't live their *life* for them, every day, see them in those transparent moments when you can see right through . . . or when everything is turned to shit.' He paused to draw breath. 'No one knows that they're doing the right thing day in, day out, not for sure.' There was a seam of truth in his words, depths of doubt and reality that troubled them both. '*It's not a fucking fairy tale, Kate.*'

She flinched at his words, his slow-burning anger. He was still holding her hand under the table. She was quiet, letting it sink in slowly, and swirl, unwelcome, stirring up unwanted thoughts of her own, of what might have been. 'But, you love the farm, don't you?' She felt desperate; needed to keep him in his box for the world to make sense. For this moment to be safe.

'Sure. I love farming: it's in my blood. My grandfather was a dairy man, he farmed there before me and *his* grandfather before him. But that doesn't make it easy, doesn't mean I don't question it sometimes, or wonder . . .' He paused. The conversation was too much for Kate; it was swirling with undercurrents and old attractions and suddenly this wasn't about farming, it wasn't about happy or not happy, it was about *what if . . . What if we'd got our acts together, and said the words that needed saying? What if I hadn't pushed you away?*

They were right on the edge of something now, of saying things that would forever then be *said*; things they might regret in the cold light of tomorrow, and the day after. Things that would change them intrinsically, turn them into different people, and affect everyone around them.

They weren't callous or careless with people's emotions; they weren't so irresponsible, not now there were others to consider, people who would be irreparably damaged if they selfishly dived into this moment; for a split second Kate wanted to be selfish, to let her heart rule . . .

'Abby . . .' Kate began and stopped, leaving another sentence hanging. They toed the edge of the precipice, not daring to look down.

Her name changed everything.

'I love Abby,' Dan growled, dropping her hand. 'But there's always uncertainty when it comes to other people, right? I mean, you can't predict how they might feel in five years' time, or how *you* might feel.'

He was staring at his hands, twisting a beer mat, already full of shame for the almost-thing he had almost done. 'You . . .' he said, and stopped.

Kate was reeling. She needed Dan to stay what he had become: a past attraction, a married man, a father-to-be content with his life; a girlhood crush to take out and admire sometimes. Not a complex man with complex feelings.

She took a shallow breath, wedged her hands beneath her thighs. This was the conversation she had imagined when she was twelve years old, before she realised the nature of her admiration of Dan, when he was still oblivious. If only he'd stayed that way.

It was the conversation he had tried to have when she was seventeen and lying in his arms, when she was too confused by Luke's defection to heed his words or care.

She looked into his eyes and her heart soared and for a second she allowed herself to wonder. Memories of him that were far too intimate surged unfettered to the surface of her mind. His skin, his sighs, his fervour.

What if . . .

Dan sighed and broke eye contact, rubbing his hands over his face; he had managed to create new space on the bench because suddenly they weren't touching any more. 'Look, whatever it sounds like I'm saying, I'm not really saying it, OK? I've had a bit much to drink and . . . I just, well, you can't help but wonder sometimes, if things were different. You broke my fucking heart, you know that?' Kate swallowed and dropped her gaze. She breathed deeply. His voice was low. 'There were so many times I thought we were on the verge of something. Our timing was never quite right, was it?'

She raised an eyebrow and risked a glance. 'It's *lousy* now.'

'Yeah.' They laughed, shattered the tension.

It would be so easy, Kate thought, to take advantage of their history and the weight of all those almost-moments. To turn upon this instant and change the course of their worlds for ever.

But their timing *was* lousy. Their time had been and gone. She was not that woman, someone who could take something so precious without a second thought, bring Abby's world crashing down for the sake of a selfish second. She would hate herself. Dan would hate her too. Plus, she had things to do here, and so did he.

Kate drained her beer, stood up. 'Sometimes,' she said, 'you just have to let it go, accept you won't ever know what might have been. I'm going to see Ally for a bit. Why don't you go and rescue that poor guy from your sister before she demoralises him any more? At least get her drunk enough she can't shoot so well.' It took great effort to drag herself away from the bench, from him. She felt his eyes on her as she went.

Ally was leaning against the bar watching Emily shoot pool when Kate grabbed his arm and hustled him outside. 'Need a cigarette,' she demanded, making impatient gestures with her fingers.

Bemused, he took out his packet, slid a cigarette free and offered it to her. 'You don't smoke.'

'I do sometimes. Very rarely. When I'm drunk and upset.'

'Bad girl.' Ally touched his lighter to the tip, watched the tobacco curl and burn, glowing orange as she sucked. A thin stream of smoke meandered into the evening sky. 'What are you upset about?'

'Nothing.'

'Right.' Ally grinned. 'You know what, Kate Vincent, I never did understand you. I was crazy about you, but I didn't understand you.'

'Crazy about me. Yes. And so delightfully platonic.' Kate nudged at him. 'You're an angel, Alistair Cotton. I'm so bloody glad you're normal. Everyone else around here is fucked up, but you're just you. Totally cool and sorted, all great career, smart suit. Suave and sophisticated and uncomplicatedly happy.' She glared at him, daring him to defy her.

'Are you a wee bit pissed, do you think?'

'I'm a big bit pissed,' Kate declared.

'So, what's with the Ally fan club stuff? Not that I'm complaining. No one minds a bit of hero worship, but . . .'

'Just . . .' She shrugged like a kid, sulky and woeful. 'I came back needing you all to be the same. Constant, you know. And everything's messed up.' She shook her head. 'Doesn't matter.' She didn't want to get into the Dan thing with Ally and if they talked about Lena, she was pretty sure she would cry. 'Let's talk about you and how sorted and happy you are. I bet you've got a great boyfriend too.' A look that could only be described as fear passed over Ally's face and he glanced reflexively over his shoulder.

'Ssh. Keep your voice down. I don't want Dan or Noah to hear you.'

Kate's voice crescendoed. 'What? Don't mess with me, Ally, I'm not in the mood.'

Ally closed his eyes. 'I'm not messing. I . . . I never quite got round to telling them I'm gay.'

Kate threw up her hands, cigarette and all. 'Fucksake, Ally.'

He took a draw on his cigarette, blew the smoke away from her. 'I know. I know.'

'It was ten years ago that you told *me*. Why the hell not?'

'Just not the right time.'

'In ten years?'

'Kate, would you please keep your voice down? You're yelling like a fishwife.'

She gave him a shove, laughed. 'Don't call me a fishwife.' She lowered her voice. 'Seriously, Al? You really haven't told them? Don't you think they've maybe guessed?'

'No.' He studied the ground, scraped the pavement with his highly polished shoe. 'I invent very believable imaginary girlfriends.'

Kate flattened the cigarette butt beneath her foot. 'Wow. Well, thanks a bunch. You've blown my big theory about you being the only one with his shit together. The Cottons are all officially nuts.'

'Yeah. We are. But you love us anyway.' He tried to coax a smile. 'Seriously, though, you won't tell them, will you? I *will* do it, just . . . in my own time.'

Kate bit her lip. 'The thing is, Emily already knows. I accidentally outed you on a trip to Rome when we had some stupid argument. I'm so sorry, I totally didn't mean it.'

He groaned. 'When?'

She pursed her lips. 'Six years ago. Not long before she went off with Joe. She hasn't said anything?'

'No! Oh, jeez, she must feel horrible. Like I don't trust her. She must've been waiting all this time for me to tell her myself.'

'Yes, you are officially a shitty brother. Now just bloody talk to her, Ally.' She took his arm again and began to tow him back towards the pub.

*

They'd gone to Rome at the end of their final year, just before Emily commenced her probation year and Kate set about getting a job. They'd already agreed to stay in Edinburgh and flat-share for another year. A week of blissful sunshine beneath a cobalt Roman sky, lounging in the Villa Borghese side amongst the trees and the greenery, was just what they needed; they toured all the important places Emily's guidebook recommended: the Coliseum, the Roman Forum, the Vatican, and the fountains and piazzas, gardens and palaces. The hostel was cheap – you got what you paid for – and they ate inexpensively each night in street-side trattorias serving sharp, tangy wine in rustic earthenware jugs.

Kate had hoped to tempt Emily away from Joe, mellow her out with Merlot and make her face facts: she didn't have to pursue a career she disliked just to prove a point, and she could do better than Joe; she was allowed to admit defeat, they'd all support her a hundred per cent.

But it hadn't gone to plan. Emily had kept wittering on about missing Joe, begun to talk about their future together, how Joe had hinted at marriage. Finally, one evening, washing down pasta with a jug of wine, Kate had lost patience. 'For God's sake, Em, it's only a few months since you were heartbroken about Anya and here you are mooning about marriage—'

'Don't mention her,' Emily said sharply. 'I don't even want to hear her name. That was all a big mistake. Joe got scared and she was there, seducing him, getting him all confused and distracted. He realised that it's me he wants and he came back.'

'Good for him.'

Emily's eyes pleaded with her. 'Let's not argue about this again,' she said. 'Not here.'

Kate felt a surge of frustration and couldn't let it go. 'If not here, when? You're making a mistake, Emily.'

'It was a blip, all couples have them.'

Kate knew she was being cruel, but perhaps that was what Emily needed. No more appeasement. 'Not in the form of sexy, Swedish beauties they don't. Anya was a sign of things to come.'

'Perhaps you're jealous,' Emily had interrupted in a brittle voice. 'You lost Luke and—'

'Luke is off limits,' Kate said sternly.

Emily scoffed. 'Even my brothers seem half daft for you. When are you going to face the fact that Luke isn't coming back for you and move on. I'm sure Ally would jump at the chance.'

That Emily could have overlooked the still simmering sexual tension between Kate and Dan and supposed instead that there was something between her and *Ally* was just ludicrous; but Emily had always nursed a secret fear that her brothers liked Kate more than her and she wasn't thinking straight.

Kate's temper got the better of her. 'Emily, your twin brother is *gay*, or are you too self-absorbed to have figured that out yet?'

There was silence. Kate's barb had found its mark; she had wounded Emily. Emily had drained the rest of her wine and stormed off into the Italian night, punishing Kate by staying out late, alone.

The next day Emily pretended nothing had happened. 'I'm sorry,' Kate said, over a breakfast of pastries and coffee. 'What are you going to do about Ally?'

'Nothing. I'd rather wait for him to tell me himself. When he's ready.'

And that was that.

A few months later, Emily and Joe were gone and Kate had been left haunted by her prophetic talk of marriage beneath the stars. It seemed Ally had never been ready.

Chapter 15

Luke's home life, Kate had discovered, was bleak and loveless since his mother decided that life as the wife of a small-town Scottish fisherman was not as romantic as she had hoped, absented herself from the family and returned to her homeland. She left ten-year-old Luke and his brother, Nick, with their father, a dyed-in-the-wool Galloway trawlerman, who quickly became stone-hearted and curmudgeonly at the loss of his vibrant bride. He spent a lot of time on the boat, leaving Luke to the none-too-tender care of his brother. Luke didn't mind that very much; he had the freedom to come and go as he pleased which was an advantage. But he missed his mother; she had been generous with love and smiles. And he missed conversation – the Ross house became a solitary, silent place even with three people living in it; hence his eagerness to make new acquaintances wherever he went, talking to anyone and everyone. His father drank to drown his sorrows – when he was home from the boat which wasn't often. Not seriously, like Kate's mother, but enough that Luke understood.

It was easy for him to love Kate and become another stray at Bluebell Bank, almost as beloved by Lena and the brothers as Kate was. Even Dan warmed to him eventually, though he never completely lost his protectiveness; Kate knew that if Luke hurt her, he'd happily have punched him in the face.

Of course, Luke did hurt her; but by then Dan's ardour had transformed into something else and he took Kate to bed as revenge instead. Tried to possess her more thoroughly, to make her his love; but Kate wasn't his for the taking. She wasn't ever fully anybody's after Luke.

Holidays became a blur of sunshine and picnics and piling into Jasper with all manner of beach paraphernalia; long walks to St Ninian's Cave and Cruggleton Castle, and she and Luke sneaking off to snatch a moment or two alone and steal kisses. Fooling no one. Lena turned a blind eye; leading Kate to surmise that she too had known the all-consuming passions of youth.

When the summer came to a close, as all summers did in the end, Kate and Luke parted in a flurry of tortuous goodbyes and fervent promises. Kate cried most of the way back to Edinburgh, clutching the slip of paper upon which Luke had written his phone number so tightly in her hand that the digits began to smudge from the sweat of her palm.

Every holiday for the next two years followed the same pattern: October, Easter, summer; the interminable times between them were grey, empty periods of waiting. Lessons and exams; losing herself in art while her mother slept off her latest binge; weekends and evenings in between hanging out with Emily and the Cottons. Phone calls with Luke from the pay phone down the street when she saved up enough money, or from the Cottons's house when she grew desperate. Kate didn't own a mobile until she was old enough to earn money to buy one herself.

The memories of those in-between times were hazy now, as if Kate only truly came alive during her Solway holidays.

*

When Kate woke on Sunday the wave of a hangover crashed over her. Confused dreams about Dan and Luke haunted her half-awake thoughts. She lay tossing and turning for several minutes, until she realised sleep was an impossibility. She sat up, swung her legs out of bed and reached for the glass of water on her bedside table; she had drunk a lot more than she intended last night, more than she usually allowed. She went downstairs, made a cup of coffee and took it into the garden where she sat on the bench beneath the rowan tree. Early morning sunbeams slanted through the trees, birdsong stirred the air and drops of dew gleamed on the grass, delineating each blade. The bench bore a silver plaque dedicated to James, the grandfather who had died before Emily's birth. Kate sat, toes curled in the damp grass and sipped her coffee.

How close she had come to making an egregious mistake – it was a misstep well avoided. The forks in the road were like that: subtle, not always clearly signposted. Just quiet little moments, one's whole life hovering on a sudden change in conversation, a look, a touch, a memory: that special sense of something shared.

She thought about Dan and Abby's baby and wondered, would things have been different, what might she have been willing to do?

The morning was hers alone. She drew in her sketchbook and thought instead of her non-date with Luke on Tuesday. Emily seemed weird around Luke, or even when his name was mentioned. Was it simply her disillusionment with love? Or was she afraid for Kate's heart?

Should *she* be afraid? Should she demand answers before she let herself go any deeper? That might kill any hope of rekindling romance stone-dead. Not, of course, that she had any such hope . . .

Emily interrupted her thoughts, wandering down the garden with a mug of tea. She was barefoot, wearing a pair of rolled-up jeans too big for her. Her hair hung in loose braids. 'Hey,' she said, throwing herself down on the bench beside Kate with a pained sigh. She stretched out her legs and wiggled her toes. 'Last night was fun, wasn't it? You hungover?'

'A bit. You?'

'Tired, but I couldn't sleep. Let's head over to the Book Nook early, shall we?'

'We've a lot to do today. Especially if your father and Alistair are going to come and check it out before they head back. Have we got Noah's help for much longer do you think?'

'As long as he continues punishing Dan, I guess, until he comes to his senses.' Emily blew on her tea and took a sip. 'Was it weird?' she asked. 'Seeing him again?' For a dreadful moment Kate thought she meant Dan and felt her cheeks flame. Emily leaned back against the bench, gazing up at the canopy of sun-glazed leaves, stretching and languishing and sipping tea. 'Luke,' she said thoughtfully. 'Who would have guessed he'd be back in town.'

'Mmm.'

'So, what was it like, seeing him?' Emily pressed. She turned to look at her, grey eyes serious, searching. Kate was silent for so long that Emily grew impatient. 'You aren't going to answer the question?'

Kate smiled. 'Not if I can help it, no. It was a long time ago, Emily.'

'Yes.' Emily was relieved. 'It was, wasn't it? We were just kids. But that's still not an answer. I mean, you and he were crazy about each other.' Emily wasn't sure what she was doing, picking at this particular scab. She just wanted to know how real Kate's feelings were, she supposed. Whether Luke Ross really was a credible threat.

Kate shrugged. 'I guess it was pretty weird,' she admitted.

'See, that wasn't so hard was it?'

'We haven't talked about it, have we?' Emily cradled her mug and drew her legs beneath her, avoiding looking directly at Kate. 'How devastated you were.' She traced the grain of the wooden bench beneath her leg with her fingertip. Slow, rhythmic, compulsive. Time stuttered, holding its breath.

Kate held her breath too. It had been the absolute worst of times; the loss of Luke had outweighed all the misery of the tenement and her mother's inability to love her; the loss of him had left scars that would never leave her.

Emily was waiting. She had put Kate back together again after Luke dumped her so unexpectedly.

Kate had chosen to go to Oxford to spend Easter with another school friend instead of going to Bluebell Bank. She had begun branching out in her social circle, something that discomfited Emily who didn't feel like she fitted. Emily had been upset and moping that holiday and so had Luke.

Calls between Kate and Luke had been strained and silent, which was unusual. And then, after two weeks of silence, Luke had called and told Kate it wasn't working out. Emily remembered how Kate's world had tipped and plummeted, how it had seemed like the end of everything.

'I . . . I still don't get it. I still want to know what I did.'

'Perhaps it's best not to know. Some things are best left in the past.' Emily tried to sound comforting, but didn't quite manage it; Kate gave her a strange look.

'I thought it was just that I didn't come that holiday, maybe he was jealous I had other friends, or thought I was interested in someone else. I wondered if it was because I was going off to uni when he had decided to ditch it and work on his father's boat – a stupid thing to do when he always hated fishing. I'm glad he saw sense and went to study architecture, aren't you?'

'Um, yeah, sure.' Emily cleared her throat. She knew it was down to her that Kate had managed to sort herself out in time to start her course. She had consoled and maligned by turns, pieced Kate back together.

Kate had got over it, after a fashion, only now Emily knew she hadn't, not really.

Kate shrugged and squinted at Emily, backlit by morning sun. 'We were young. It was aeons ago.'

'Are you sure?'

'Yes.' Kate didn't sound sure. 'I'm going to see him on Tuesday, but I don't have any expectations.'

She had thought she'd buried those feelings, left them here on the Solway, but it turned out they had lingered here, waiting for her all this time.

Emily remained unconvinced. 'So if he asked you out now, you'd say no?'

'He's probably married with four children.' But they'd both seen the way he looked at her, the memories and regret showing in his eyes.

'No ring. I looked.'

Kate dimpled. 'Yeah, me too, but that doesn't mean he's single.'

'Hypothetically speaking, if he was single and he asked you out, would you say no?' Emily had to know.

'Hypothetically it doesn't matter. *I'm* not single. We're catching up, it's not a date or anything.'

'Right. Of course. Ben.'

'Yes, Ben.' She'd choose Luke over Ben in a heartbeat, but it wasn't even an option. She shouldn't even be thinking it.

Emily pursed her lips and tossed one of her braids over her shoulder, catching it and examining the end. 'I think you'd say yes,' she said. 'I think this *is* a date, or you *hope* it is. I think you still have feelings for him and you should stop lying to yourself.'

'Do you really?' Kate enquired, dangerously polite.

'Yes, I do. You said yourself you never stopped liking him.'

She had; she regretted the burst of confidence. 'OK.'

'OK?'

'Yes, OK. Think what you like, it doesn't matter. I'm not here for a relationship. I'm here to focus on helping you set up your business. I won't be staying, so I certainly can't get attached. We've got more important things to focus on now.'

Kate had hit just the right chord to distract Emily from her pursuit of truth: the bookshop and its potential success. 'Emily Cotton, businesswoman. It doesn't feel real.' Emily grinned. 'I'm so excited now. Before, it was terrifying.'

Kate stood and stretched, her sketchbook falling to the ground. 'Let's stop sitting around philosophising and get on with it. I was doing some thinking last night and I think the only way the Book Nook is going to stand out in this town is if it is unique. You're not going after a particular book market, so it's all about the image. We have to make it a beautiful, sumptuous place where people come to relax with a book. It has to be all about the experience as well as the books. Tomorrow we'll trawl second-hand shops and antique dealers and see if we can pick up some bargains. I'm going to draw up a list of places. What do you think about selling some art too? Postcard prints and greetings cards. Maybe a few gifts too? Did you price wood burners the other night?'

The questions were quick-fire and demanding, designed to distract. Emily, somewhat overwhelmed, picked the last one to answer. She had, at Kate's insistence, conducted a thorough inventory of her finances and now knew exactly how much there was left to spend – not as much as Kate would like, but more than she had feared. 'Yes, they're not cheap but I think the budget can stretch. You think it's necessary?'

'Definitely,' Kate said. 'In winter, the place will be freezing and a wood burner, a comfy chair and a decent cup of coffee will definitely pull in the customers.'

'And tea.'

'Pardon?'

'Tea. Lots of people don't drink coffee, you know.'

Kate rolled her eyes, grabbed Emily's hand and pulled her to her feet. 'You and your tea. Yes, if you like. Now, I saw you and Ally deep in conversation at the bar last night. Everything all right?'

Emily gave her a look. 'Like you don't know.'

Kate shrugged. 'I didn't do anything, only gave him a helping hand. You have to help him tell the others, Em. He can't honestly believe they'll have a problem with him being gay?'

'He just doesn't think it's the right time, with Lena . . .'

Kate snorted. 'I think we've established that, where Ally is concerned, it's *never* going to be the right time. I'm just glad he told you, Em. It wasn't right that he hadn't talked to you about it. I mean, it's who he *is*. The thing is, he only told me because I was in the right place at the right time.'

'Yeah, I know. It's OK. I'm not offended that he confided in you. I've been . . . preoccupied, I s'pose. For a long time. I should have spoken to him years ago. We're too good at not talking about stuff in this family.'

They left a note in the kitchen for the others, who were still sleeping off a heavy night – Emily always left notes for Lena anyway in case she forgot where they were. She always put her mobile number on the bottom and sometimes Lena called, petulant and confused.

They climbed into Jasper. The day still held the special quietude of early morning: fresh and clean. There was barely a car on the road between Bluebell Bank and Wigtown. In the car, Kate turned up the heater to clear the screen and cast Emily a sly look. 'So,' she said, 'want to spill the beans about that guy you were flirting *mercilessly* with in the pub last night?'

Emily looked shocked. 'Mike? He's just the local vet. Only just moved here. He's too old for me. I so *wasn't* flirting.'

'Oh please. Emily, you seem to forget I know your seduction technique and it nearly always involves pool. Besides, he isn't too old at all. He's what – thirty-three, tops?'

'Thereabouts,' Emily said. 'I don't know, that was the first time we talked.' Emily concentrated on watching the road, but Kate could see the flicker of a smile.

At the shop they concentrated on clearing up the painting detritus and making the place ready for visitors – namely Ally and Jonathon. Then they set about sanding down some of the old pieces of furniture and giving them a new lease of life with paint and varnish. Kate was immersed in her task when the new shop bell chimed. 'About time, Noah,' she chided, not bothering to look up.

'Sorry to disappoint.'

Kate spun round. It was Dan, looking sheepish, his hands in his pockets. He was hangover pale, but fresh from a shower by the looks of it. 'Can we talk?'

Kate glanced wildly around for Emily, who had slipped out the back to bring in a rocking chair they had found in one of the outbuildings and were considering renovating. 'Dan . . .'

'Please, Kate.'

'I . . . oh, all right.'

Emily came in lugging the chair. 'What do you think? Worth saving? Oh, hey, Dan, what do you think of the place?'

Dan glanced around. 'Yeah, it looks great, Em.' His tone was flat and Kate could have hit him; what was he doing, showing up here all morose and miserable, wearing his guilt like a badge, as if they'd done something wrong last night. Something worse.

'Dan and I are just going to . . .' Kate grabbed her sweatshirt and tried to think.

'Get a bacon roll,' Dan said. 'My hangover is killing.'

'You're such an old man,' Emily teased. Curiously, she watched Kate bundle her brother out of the shop.

They walked down the street towards the churchyard. 'What are you doing here?' Kate demanded, all too aware that it was a tiny town and too many eyes were upon them.

'I don't know,' Dan admitted. He opened the gate and let them in to the cemetery. 'I wanted to say sorry, about last night.'

'Nothing happened last night.'

Dan gave her a penetrating look. 'I know.'

'So . . .'

'I'm scared. Kate. I didn't want to feel like this.' Dan ran his hands over his face and the scruff of his beard, dragging at his pallid skin.

'Like what?'

'I don't know. Like I'm twenty-one again.' He took a small, barely perceptible step towards her and Kate retreated.

'You're not.'

'I know.' He frowned and balled his fists, backed up a few steps.

'You're just nervous about the baby . . . You have to think about Abby and the baby. Whatever you think this is, it isn't. It never was.'

Dan gave her a hard stare. 'It was once.'

Oh God, it would be so easy, Kate thought; to close the gap between them, to grab his T-shirt and pull him against her, to feel his hands tangle in her hair. But she wasn't standing in front of the teenage boy she'd had a crush on. This was the cold light of day and it was all shades of wrong.

'Go home, Dan,' she said sternly. 'Don't talk about this, or even think it, ever again.'

Dan nodded miserably. He knew it. Kate left him leaning against a gravestone and strode out of the cemetery and up the street, her heart pounding. She felt compelled to stop for bacon rolls for her and Emily to give credence to the lie.

Emily looked up from her phone when Kate came in. 'That was quick,' she said. 'What's Dan like, eh? Can't handle his drink these days.'

'Yeah,' Kate mumbled. She set her roll down on the table, feeling a wave of confusion wash over her. She had to sort herself out, figure out what she was doing – Ben, Luke, now Dan! This was madness, and it wasn't her.

'Kate,' Emily said, waving her mobile. For a moment she was gripped by the fear that Emily had been conversing with Joe again, but Emily couldn't wipe the grin from her face as she said, 'Mike has a couple of old armchairs in his garage, from his gran's house clearance. Thought we might want to take a look at them for the shop.'

Chapter 16

Luke lifted his beer bottle to his lips and drank slowly. Kate leaned her chin on her hand and watched him, distracted by the beads of moisture forming on his lips, the trace of stubble he had missed while shaving; the stark, navy outline of his brilliantly blue eyes as he stared back at her. 'So,' he said, clearing his throat, setting the bottle down on the picnic table. They were sitting out the front of the Bladnoch Inn in the cooling evening, with occasional cars driving past and the river burbling gently beneath the bridge. 'You and Emily went to university together like you planned.' He was trying to get a feel for all those lost years.

Kate traced a drop of condensation. The sky had the clean, bright hue of lilac that preceded twilight and, despite the butterfly nerves zinging in her belly, she felt relaxed and comfortable in Luke's company. 'Yes,' she said. 'We lived in the same hall of residence. We were firm friends right through to graduation.'

If Kate had believed her friendship with Emily was solid when they were children, it had been unbreakable during those university years, cemented by history and heartbreak. Until Joe.

'But you lost touch? How on earth did that happen?'

'I moved to the States after I graduated, after Emily . . .' She hesitated. The marriage wasn't exactly a secret, but it still felt wrong to talk about it. 'Well, Emily was all set to start teaching. She'd had this mad idea to switch courses in third year and begin teacher training, which no one really understood. But there was a guy . . . Joe. No one really approved of him. She ran off and married him. That was the last anyone heard of her for a while.'

'Wow,' Luke said. 'I never heard of anyone actually doing that. Eloping.'

'She was obsessed with him. It was a kind of madness.'

'I assume it didn't work out.'

'They're divorced.' She decided not to mention Joe's full name, or the band; Emily was managing to keep that to herself round here.

When Luke had arrived to collect her from Bluebell Bank in his truck for the date that wasn't a date, Kate had been peering out the net curtains in the dining room – no matter that it was just friends, no matter that she had spent two hours yesterday messaging back and forth with him, and the rest of the night worrying about Ben. She wondered if Emily's reticence about the whole thing was down to her not wanting Kate to be hurt again, or disapproval over Ben.

Kate disapproved of herself. This felt like a date. All the hallmarks were there: the anticipatory butterflies; the indecision over what to wear.

Kate felt light as air as she tripped across the drive – she'd eventually settled on jeans, a yellow vest top and her hair in its trademark ponytail – and climbed into the passenger seat beside him, inhaling the clean, mint scent of him, meeting his nervous smile with one of her own.

Now, Luke clasped his hands on the scarred wood of the picnic table and looked at her – the butterflies went crazy. 'It's sad you guys lost contact at all; you were always thick as thieves when we were kids.'

Kate nodded. 'I hadn't heard a thing from her until a few

weeks ago. Emily sent me a message, asking for my help with the shop. I came.'

'I'm really glad you did.' He reached across the gulf of the table and touched her hand, tracing his fingers over her knuckles. Kate raised her eyes to his, hesitated a beat, a breath, unfurled her fingers and wound them around his.

'I guess I wasn't entirely settled in New York,' she said, admitting it for the first time. 'I was ready for change and maybe the timing of it was right.' She paused and shrugged, felt the goosebumps stir on her bare shoulders.

Luke met her eyes. 'Maybe it was,' he agreed softly, tightening his grip.

'But tell me about you. I want to hear everything.' Kate leaned forward.

He shook his head. 'There isn't much to tell.'

'Everyone says that, but it's never true. I don't only want to hear the big stuff. Just the everyday. I'm curious. I haven't seen you since we were eighteen and you're telling me *nothing* noteworthy has happened to you in all that time?'

Luke's eyes crinkled when he smiled. Kate studied the slope of his dark lashes, how they bled into the creases at the corners. His brows were black and straight, hair so black as to appear blue in some lights. She wanted to reach out and trace the plane of his nose as it flared and narrowed, press her finger against the cleft of his full top lip, feel the hard, square edge of his jaw and dip into the dimple to the left of his mouth, slide her lips just under his ear, tracing the blood vessels and feeling the pummelling of blood beneath his skin, against her lips. She wanted to press and coorie and nuzzle and feel his arms tighten round her.

Kate blushed and took a gulp of beer to quell her longing.

Was he reserved because he didn't want to confess to some all-consuming love affair? Had she read his signals all wrong? Perhaps this really was nothing more to him than old friends *catching up*.

Luke exhaled. 'All right. I'll give you the summary. Um, so I went to university in Dundee, studied architecture. Got a job up near Perth my last year, then after I graduated I went travelling for a bit – had to get it out my system before I signed up for a lifetime of work, you know? I've worked part-time in construction since I was eighteen; my uncle Davy was in the building trade, so it made sense to combine my skills. I can design and build houses. Cut out the middleman.'

'That's impressive.' Their hands were still clasped, but loosely now and he was absently tracing the shape of her fingernails.

Luke's face softened into a guilty smile. 'I exaggerate a bit. I can't *actually* build an entire house from scratch. But I am doing most of the renovation on my father's cottage. I did the plans myself. I'm adding an extra bedroom and an en suite, trying to make it blend a bit better with the landscape. I'm really doing as much of the work myself as I can to save money.'

Kate nodded; it used to be skateboarding, now his passion was for buildings. 'Like *Grand Designs*,' she said brightly. Emily had been making her watch late-night episodes of her favourite programmes since Kate returned.

He laughed. 'Similar. But way, way less expensive.'

'So the life as a fisherman wasn't for you then?'

Luke shook his head. 'Definitely not. I was mad to think it. I s'pose I was just trying to find some common ground with my old man, trying to make him respect me.' He shrugged. 'Considering I spent the whole of our first trip leaning off the back of the boat hurling into the waves, that didn't work so well. I didn't last long. Then I applied for uni, started working with Uncle Davy to raise the funds and went to college part-time to get my maths grade up.'

'And where did you go travelling?'

'Southeast Asia, New Zealand, Australia, America. That was fun. I spent a few months in Italy with my mother. When I came back to Scotland, Dad was sick. Lung cancer.' He let go of her hands, picked at the label on his bottle with a thumbnail, loosening a corner of the condensation-damp paper. His brow creased. 'I hadn't seen him in a long time. I came home, but by then he was already in the hospice. The cancer spread fast and he died earlier this year. I inherited the cottage so I decided to set about renovating the place. It needed a lot of work; Dad had never really done anything to it. I basically ripped everything out and started again.'

'Where do you live now if the house isn't habitable?'

Luke grinned. 'A caravan in the garden. It's not so bad. I work pretty hard though. This is my first night off in a long while.'

'I'm honoured.' She smiled. 'I'm really sorry about your dad.'

'It's fine. I'm doing OK.'

Kate realised then that in all his narrative he hadn't mentioned anyone significant. He had painted a picture of a solitary existence, but that couldn't be the case, not for all these years. 'You went travelling alone?' she asked, probing discreetly.

Luke's eyebrows arched, then compressed firmly in an anxious furrow: he had an honest, expressive face. He knew what she was asking and it was the same thing he wanted to ask of her. 'I did,' he said. 'But I was with someone before I went – a girl I met my third year of uni. We had a flat together. It was kind of serious for a while, but when we split up, I decided it was as good a time as any to travel while I still could.' He fixed her with a profound look. 'I'm single now,' he said, as if these words needed to be laid on the table between them like a hand of cards. He looked up at her, expectant.

Kate cringed. '*I'm* not . . . exactly.' She wanted to tell him that she could be, he had only to say the word, but then the old hurt reared up and she remembered the pain of his desertion, after all their plans and promises, how she'd analysed every inch of herself to find what was wrong, how Luke had never explained . . . 'It's not serious,' she couldn't help saying, dismissing Ben so easily.

With Ben, she could easily cut herself out of all of those prospective images – the fancy restaurant proposal, the champagne celebrations, the engagement party in his parents' country club, the socialite wedding pictures – and paste anyone else in her place. Any old face, so long as it was pretty.

His parents wouldn't be exactly disappointed either, Kate thought. They had been polite enough, but Kate knew she fell below the mark of their expectations. Next time he'd find someone with money and family: equal footing. She had never told Ben about Lily – certainly hadn't mentioned her to his parents. Instead, she had invented a fantasy family – not too well heeled but not too poor either – and killed them off in a tragic accident when she was nineteen. She had posed as an orphan, which was how she considered herself sometimes. This was not, Kate knew, the best basis for a lasting relationship, but, in her defence, she had never presumed the affair with Ben would be anything more than a passing fancy.

Kate took a sip of her beer and wondered if she had been too presumptuous. *It's not serious.* Dismissing her boyfriend, practically offering herself to Luke on a plate; she was certain she couldn't handle his rejection again. She felt herself flush.

'Your dad,' she said. 'Did you get on better terms with him before he died?'

Luke lowered his eyes. 'Not particularly. He was stuck in a time and a way of life that made no sense to me. I guess my mother leaving changed him, took all the pleasure out of him. He became a grumpy old man when he was still young. He and I never found much in common. I think I reminded him of her.' His eyes flicked upwards, full of barely concealed pain.

Kate wanted him in her arms, wanted to press her face against his skin and breathe him in. Her heart thrummed with desire; she felt the blood race to her cheeks and lips again – she must be scarlet by now. She pressed on, distracting herself from the pull of him. 'And your mum? You said you lived in Italy with her for a time?'

'Yeah, I lived with her for a bit after I was done with travelling. We get on well.' He shrugged. 'I mean, she has a whole new family, a completely different life from the one she lived with my dad. I have lots of little half-brothers and sisters running around the place now. Her new husband is great – laid-back, jovial – very different from Dad, but I suppose that was the point. They have a great life. They're not rich but they live well, they have lots of friends and extended family popping round, they practically *live* outdoors, the kids playing and all that sky and sunshine . . . It's great, but it's not for me. Not full time. I don't really belong there.' A sense of isolation swirled around Luke, settling on his shoulders; as if he didn't really belong anywhere, hadn't discovered his place yet.

Home, Kate was beginning to think, was defined not by the place, but by the people you chose to be with.

'So are you going to live in your dad's cottage, once it's renovated, or will you sell it?'

'I haven't got that far yet, I don't know.'

'And your brother?'

'Dad left Nick the fishing business and me the house. He knew we would each do something with our respective inheritances. Nick has some idea to sell the business as a going concern and move out to Italy to work there. I think mainly he dreams of an Italian girl making him pasta, and lots of olive-skinned children running around.'

Kate smiled and propped her chin on one hand. 'There are worse dreams to have.'

'True. So how about you, did you not reconcile with your mother?'

How much he knew, how disconcerting that no one in her new life ever got so deep since, so perfectly maintained was her shield. Old hurts were buried and the angry, neglected little girl from the tenement was long gone. But not really.

'Yes and no,' she said. 'We're civil. Pleasant even sometimes. She's sober and healthy and I'm glad. But we don't catch a movie together or meet for coffee and we never will.' She thought of her dutiful replies to her mother; everything so unemotional and matter of fact.

'Never is a long time,' Luke said quietly, peeling at his label again, no doubt thinking of his dad and the things he hadn't had time to say.

Kate looked down at her splayed fingers; her nails were neat aqua-coloured ovals without a chip or blemish. She balled her fists and dug the nails into palms, gouged deep. Luke noticed, reached out across the table and unfurled her hands. They uncurled for him, like fronds opening to the sun. His fingers on her skin, her knuckles, the pads of her thumbs. He didn't let go this time. 'You're glad you came back?' He traced the crescent scars across her palms as they disappeared.

'I always used to dream of one more Solway summer.'

'And here you are, the fairy godmother of bookshops. Will you disappear in a puff of smoke once your work is done?' The question was weighty, the answer of great import, shaping everything: the coming minutes and hours, the next sentence or three, and the night to come – the next one and the one after that, next week, and maybe even Kate's future.

Tonight was magical and full of possibilities. It didn't matter why he left her, only that he was here now.

She borrowed his words. 'I don't know, I haven't got that far yet.'

'Do you remember the sunsets out by St Ninian's Cave?' Luke asked.

She nodded. They went there many times with Lena, Emily and the brothers. Kate and Luke would sit and watch the sunset from a vantage point on a rock by the dark mouth of the cave: the cold nip of evening, the warmth of his breath and his arms, the hushed whispers and happy silence; and her back pressed into his chest as his body curled over hers. The sun sinking, liquid and luminous, the cliff face towering at their backs, the whispering, lapping waves. 'So do you want to take a drive there?'

The movie reel of moments continued to play through Kate's mind, sharp and clear: the dank coolness of Physgill Glen, the stones shifting and clattering beneath her feet, the thick smell of the sea.

She nodded again. 'Yes,' she said, because taking a drive with Luke to revisit one of the most romantic spots she had ever known seemed like an excellent idea, and the only thing to do.

It would mean something. It would take them way beyond the realm of old friends, take them someplace else entirely.

*

The path from the car park to the beach took longer than Kate remembered, weaving in a shady meander through the leafy glades of the glen. They raced the sun to get there before the last embers died. The sky was alive, a-flicker and a-glow, burnishing and enveloping the clouds in fire.

In fact, they had plenty of time, a good hour of daylight left. They would have to make the walk back in full darkness, but Luke had a flashlight and a blanket. Kate was grateful for the flashlight, but the blanket – with its promise of intimacy – made her stomach curl and curdle with delightful anticipation.

Luke's two border collies, Morse and Caber, released from captivity in the truck, ran ahead of them through the wood with a sweeping, lupine trot, happy tails and lolling tongues. 'If I'd known we were going to do this, I'd have brought a flask of coffee,' Luke said, smiling at her in the greenish semi-dark beneath the overhanging trees.

'For a pair of coffee junkies, to be caffeine-less is practically a crime.' Kate skirted the boggiest parts of the track, hardly caring about the fate of her pink ballet flats. She could hear Emily's mocking: *ballet flats, in deepest, darkest Galloway.* But, in her defence, she had thought they were only nipping to the Bladnoch for a beer.

When at last they stepped out onto the beach the majesty of it stole Kate's breath. Memory had not done this place justice.

It was a stony beach, the pebbles slithering and scattering beneath their feet. Through the soles of her shoes Kate could feel the bite of every stone. She was not the sort of girl to own hiking boots, but she could have borrowed a pair from Emily if she'd known. But it was the fact that they did *not* know that made this moment special. The romance was in the spontaneity of it – no clumsy attempt to recreate something, just two people in the right place and the right time. Finally.

Ben. His name was a drum-throb in her head, following the beat of her heart.

She didn't want Ben. Imagine him here, a fish out of water, an alien in a strange, unknown land, turning up his nose at everything that made Kate feel so alive. She would laugh at his ineptitude and arrogance, she would wonder why didn't he just piss off back to his big city.

She belonged *here*. And that was why she could not be with Ben.

Luke's arm bumped hers as they trammelled along the stony beach, sky and sea opening up before them. Her heart was full and her blood was vital and singing in her veins and everything was just as it should be.

St Ninian, to whom the cave was attributed, was a vague figure about whom history knew surprisingly little. He was the holy man credited with bringing Christianity to Scotland, according to writings dating back to the eighth century. Kate remembered Lena teaching her that on her first visit.

The Catholic Diocese of Galloway held an annual pilgrimage to this spot. What Kate and Luke were doing now seemed as significant as any religious pilgrimage could. His hand touched hers and there was the barest brush of fingers. Smiles exchanged: secretive, intimate, guilty. *Is this OK? Yes, definitely.*

When they reached the cave, Kate went inside to read the writings on the walls: pleas and prayers stuffed into cracks and crevices and crude crosses carved in the rock or made from sticks and driftwood and placed around as offerings. Luke remained outside. When she emerged into the evening sun, he was sitting on a rock, leaning on his arms, smiling, gazing skyward. Morse lay at his feet while Caber raced off into the waves with a high-pitched yip. 'What's wrong?' Kate said. 'You don't like the cave?'

'I don't like *any* small spaces. Nick persuaded me to go potholing in Italy and I haven't been the same since.'

Laughing, Kate climbed up on the rock beside him. The very same rock they had sat on as teenagers, young lovers. 'This is lovely,' she said, sweeping her gaze around the bay, resplendent before them, orchestrated with them in mind.

'Yeah,' Luke said. Without realising it, they had entwined their fingers again; their hands remembering and searching out their rightful partners. 'Is this weird?' he asked, quiet suddenly in the face of nature's glory. Pink sky, blue and lilac clouds, light like liquid gold.

She glanced at him. 'Maybe a bit. But let's just enjoy it, shall we? We'll worry about the weirdness later.'

There was a seam of light beneath the clouds, as the sun made its final descent towards the sea, the surface of the water rippling and writhing, golden and glorious. He took her at her word and fell silent and they appreciated the moment: the sunset, the blanket wrapped around them, their closeness.

Chapter 17

Emily, sitting in her shop, was distracted, unable to concentrate on work. Kate was out with Luke. On their non-date. It shouldn't bother her, but it did.

It had been a tough day. Lena was fretful. Noah was sulking. Abby had come by earlier looking for a sympathetic ear, regaling her with pregnancy woes until Emily wanted to put her hands over her ears. Eventually, she'd confessed the real reason for her visit – she was worried about Dan. He'd been weird lately, too quiet, not himself. Emily didn't know what to tell her; it was anyone's guess what was going on with Dan. It troubled her a little; Dan was the easy-going one, the Cotton sibling with his life on track. He was usually pretty uncomplicated.

Exhausted, feeling fretful herself, Emily drove home. At Bluebell Bank she curled in an armchair in the living room. Strangely she felt more alone than ever. Her brothers were concerned with their own things; Kate's presence only magnified her absence now; Lena was upstairs and so remote, so removed.

She let the room darken round her, gave up trying to read and let herself think about Luke, remembering a moment she so heartily wished she could erase.

A moment that could have cost her Kate's friendship, and still might.

Kate and Luke were together right now, reminiscing, talking over old times, and it felt so precarious – an inevitable slide towards the confession that would implicate Emily. *She* ought to be the one to tell Kate, but how could she, when everything that had come after, her silence for all those years, would seem so deliberate? Traitorous and catastrophic.

She hadn't meant it to happen. She told herself that over and over, as though it made it better somehow: her lack of intent, no malice aforethought. Luke was gone so swiftly from Kate's life, a clean slicing break for him. But not for Kate, and Emily held the key to the knowledge Kate still sought.

Emily set her book aside, the spine splayed on the carpet. She had never revealed the truth. As the years passed, and put time between her and that night, between Kate and Luke, she lost the sharp edge of panic that had been her companion – fear that Kate would discover the truth and Emily would lose her.

Kate got over Luke, or it had seemed she had. Emily reassured herself so, though there hadn't really been anyone of any significance for Kate all through university; a few flings and liaisons that fizzled quickly, but nothing that mattered. That was partly why Emily had been so relieved by the Facebook photos of Ben; they looked so happy and in love with their idyllic holidays and glamorous lifestyle. Surely, she had thought, it was safe now to bring Kate home, when Luke was but a distant memory.

But, no. Apparently not. Emily only had to glimpse the starry look in Kate's eyes, the softening of her features when his name was mentioned to know that Luke still mattered: a lot.

And so, therefore, did Emily's shame. Was she betraying Kate still, with every word she *didn't* say?

She and Luke hadn't spoken until the other day in the hardware store – when she had wished him a million miles away; not here, standing before Kate in all his glory. Yes, it was dangerous indeed; past mistakes had the power to destroy everything. Even the beauty of her new shop, and the frissons she felt when an innocuous little text message arrived from Mike, couldn't comfort her.

When Kate returned, she found Emily sitting in the darkened living room ruminating, her book abandoned on the floor. Lena was long abed; she had been so lost to Emily this evening, no attempts to coax her into lucidity with the help of the memory book had been fruitful. Which was a shame, because Emily could have done with the distraction.

Kate set her bag on the floor and went around switching on the lamps as she regaled Emily with the details. 'He took you to St Ninian's Cave to watch the sunset?' Emily hardly sounded surprised.

Kate flopped in a chair. 'Yes.'

'But he didn't kiss you?'

'No, but I didn't *want* him to kiss me. It would have ruined it. He knew that.'

'You didn't *want* him to kiss you?'

'Now you're just repeating things, Emily.' Kate was weary and ready to be alone with her thoughts. 'No, I didn't want him to kiss me. It would have been all wrong, as if he only took me there because he wanted to kiss me, or to get me into bed.'

Emily turned to Kate, wide-eyed. 'You want to go to bed with him?'

'I didn't *say* that.'

'You're the one that mentioned Luke and bed in the same sentence. I'm just pointing that out.'

Kate managed a smile. 'How old are we? Don't you think we're past all this over-analysing every second of a date?'

'Hah, so it *was* a date, I knew it.' Emily sat up.

Kate sighed and conceded. 'OK, maybe. He's coming to the shop tomorrow to help us out and have a scout around for any other structural stuff needs doing. And he's going to take me sailing soon.' Emily was silent, musing. Kate needed her approval. 'I know it's strange, but be happy for me. Please.'

'I . . . I don't think it's such a good idea, Kate. I don't want you to be hurt again. And what about Ben?'

Kate nodded. 'I'll call him tomorrow. This has dragged on long enough. We both know it's over. It won't break his heart or anything, our relationship wasn't like that. You mustn't worry about me, Em. I won't be hurt. I'm not even sure this is a thing between Luke and me, but, if it is, we're adults now, it's different. Now, I'm tired. Time for bed.'

*

Emily looked up at the square of navy through the skylight window in the bathroom, water cascading over her body. Soothing. She stuck her head under the stream and cupped her hands, throwing handfuls of water over her face, gasping as she came up for air.

The stars were visible, pinpricks of silver in the velvet black. She finished showering and stepped out of the bath, wrapping a towel around herself, trying to shake her cloak of melancholy. This time of night was hers and hers alone: just the ritual creaking of the old house and the pattering of Bracken's claws on the kitchen floor as he settled to sleep.

As she showered she was thinking about the Book Nook and how far they had come, pushing the less comfortable thoughts of Kate and Luke aside. The barn looked great, and Emily felt equal now to the task of running this business.

She had no cravings for the smooth gravel of Joe's voice in her ear, but her healing still felt fragile – she couldn't afford to lose Kate again now.

Emily was nervous, feeling everything moving beyond her control.

She put on pyjama bottoms and a grey T-shirt, towelled her

hair and brushed it, letting it fall in damp ringlets down her back. Then she left the bathroom and decided to go downstairs for a last cup of tea before bed.

Lena was standing in the hall, startling Emily in the dark. A thin, knobbly, white-haired ghost looming at her from the shadows. Wearing an old shirt of her late husband's, her bare, skinny legs all bone and flabby muscle beneath.

'What are you doing?' Emily asked, sharper than she had intended. There was a bowl of dog biscuits in Lena's hand.

Lena looked up, with bristling impatience. 'I'm feeding the dog, what does it look like?'

Emily debated whether to let it go. A second dinner in the middle of the night this once wouldn't hurt Bracken much, but it felt like the start of something, a slope gathering momentum: slide and slither and slip and before she knew it she'd be hiding medication and sharp objects, bathing her grandmother and feeding her like a baby. A wave of depression washed over Emily. She thought of the endless lists, the name-tag photo-montage, the childlike petulance when Lena didn't get her own way, how she had to hide cigarettes from her because Lena – who had given up smoking years ago – would never remember she'd lit one, leave them burning ominously in any room of the house.

A swirl of panic began at her core: it would be incontinence and insults, irrational behaviour and forgetting the very basics of how to live: Lena's ignominious future.

Was there any less dignified an end for someone of such . . . *stature*, such vitality?

A lump rose in her throat. 'Lena,' she said softly, reaching for the bowl. 'You already fed him.'

Lena's face creased with confusion. 'No, I didn't. I'm quite sure I . . .'

'You did. I saw you. After dinner.'

Lena's face collapsed in dismay. 'Oh. Yes.'

She didn't remember. 'It's OK,' Emily said. 'It's not a big deal.

We'll put up a schedule in the kitchen, on the pinboard. A space for each day and we can just tick it whenever we feed him, to stop us getting mixed up.'

Lena nodded, but she was uncomforted by the pretence. She looked at the bowl Emily had taken from her. 'Yes,' she said in a hollow-sounding voice. 'Good idea.' She glanced down at her strange attire, with cheerful bluster to match Emily's. 'Is it bedtime? Yes? Right, I'll be off. Sleep tight, don't let the bed bugs bite.'

''Night,' Emily murmured, watching her go. At her feet Bracken whined disconsolately, not understanding. Emily scratched his matted ears. 'I'm sorry, boy,' she whispered, and bent down to hide her tears in the dog's fur. It was a thousand little deaths, this illness: a long, protracted grief.

She went to her bedroom and sat in the darkness, took out her mobile and weighed it in her hand. She wouldn't call him. She didn't *think* she would call him – she didn't *want* to call him.

A text message. Mike:

1984 or Brave New World?

He had been doing this for days – texting her book titles and making her choose. 'For my files,' he'd joked. 'You can tell a lot about a person from their book preferences.'

Emily texted back:

1984 is better, Brave New World is scarier

Cop out, Mike replied. *Choose.*

I'll have to think about it and let you know.

Can I come by the shop tomorrow after work and get your answer over a pint?

Emily considered for only a second, made herself wait another minute, then responded.

Yes.

Chapter 18

In the morning Emily was up with the dawn, listening to the birds through the open back door as she breakfasted. She hadn't slept well – her dreams a viscous soup of Lena's loss and Kate's outrage, flashes of Mike shining through the fog of dread. She yawned and leaned her head on her hand. If Kate found out . . .

Find out she must, but when, how? Emily must grasp the nettle and do it. Soon . . . Today?

Lena came into the kitchen in a voluminous, threadbare grey dressing gown. She paused by Emily and surveyed her. 'Good morning, girl. What's up with you?'

Emily glanced up and found Lena's sharp gaze steady. She smiled. 'Nothing, Lena. Just tired.'

Lena dropped into a seat. 'He isn't worth it, you know. That husband of yours, the musician fellow.'

The air sharpened and hummed; Emily wanted to hold on to this moment and never let go. 'I know,' she said. 'I know that now.'

'So why so blue?'

It felt alien to confide, but Emily couldn't resist. This was the woman to whom she had brought all her adolescent woes, to be considered, dismissed with ease, vanquished in flames of righteous anger on Em's behalf. She missed that woman. *God*, how she missed her!

'I've done something,' Emily said. 'It was a long time ago, but it still might matter . . . The guilt is driving me mad, and I guess I'm scared of it being told.'

'I did something once,' Lena said quietly. 'Never told anyone, only James.'

Emily felt the mood of confession overtake Lena. She wanted to reach for a pen, but this didn't feel like a usual memory-book tale; this was two women talking, baring souls. She folded her arms on the table and leaned in.

'I had a sister.'

'Wait, what? I thought there was only you and Austin?'

Lena said severely, 'Don't go interrupting and asking your infernal questions, girl,' so Emily shut up.

'Her name was Annabelle.' The name was precious, sweet as honey tumbling from Lena's tongue.

As she spoke, it was like a film playing out on the screen of her mind; she was transported, no longer here in the kitchen with Emily, but in a house far away in time, living through every second of tragedy again. 'She was seven years younger than me and she adored me, wanted to do everything I did. I had little patience for her trailing after me. I wanted to be out in the fields and woods playing with James and the other boys.' Emily already knew much about Lena's early life – the man who would become her husband had once been her childhood playmate.

'I was always telling her to go away,' Lena said, her voice fading to a low thrum which resonated through Emily and filled the room. 'I just meant to go back to the house, to play with her dolls, to leave me and James to our own devices. She wanted to be like her big sister. I told her she was too small to be any fun. She couldn't do the things we did.'

There was a pause, which Emily knew better than to interrupt.

'One day she must have followed us deep into the woods, hid

from us so we wouldn't catch her and send her home. She must have stayed very quiet and watched us play. We were climbing our favourite tree – daring each other to further heights and feats of bravery. I liked to prove that I was every bit as brave as James; he knew it, but he'd tease me and call me a girl to make me mad.'

Another pause. 'We'd tired of climbing and were heading through the woods towards the river when we heard the scream. We raced back to our tree and there was Annabelle – on the ground, like a pale, broken doll. She'd tried to climb, to be like her sister.

'We had the good sense not to move her – it was obvious her back was broken – and James ran for help while I stayed with Annabelle. She was unconscious then and I thought she was dead. I sat by her in the grass and leaves and promised that if she would only live I'd never send her home again. I suppose I was in shock myself for I was numb when the men came running through the woods. I couldn't move even after they got her on a board and began to carry her home. James stayed with me; I remember he was crying and it seemed odd to me – I'd never seen James cry. Eventually, he persuaded me to get up and he walked me home. We could hear my mother's screams when we reached my house.'

This time the silence stretched so long Emily couldn't help prompting. 'Did she . . .?'

'She lived. She never walked again. She couldn't run after me, or climb trees. I got my wish.' The bleakness in Lena's voice made tears sting Emily's eyes but she wouldn't let them fall in front of Lena. 'My mother never fully forgave me, I think. I never forgave myself.'

'But—'

'No, girl. I know. It wasn't my fault, but also, it was. Six months after her accident, Annabelle caught scarlet fever; she was very ill and then she died.' The word had weight and shape and texture. This time the pause felt right, reverent.

'I learned from Annabelle to always listen to people's desires.

Not to dismiss them as stupid, or childish, or pretend they don't matter because you think you know best. I could have let her play, shown her our woods, taught her to climb safely like James taught me. Maybe then she wouldn't have hidden from me, wouldn't have followed me a step too far. I never told a soul this story and there is no one left alive who remembers my sister.' She looked at Emily, her expression heavy, old, significant. 'I chose to erase her, but now I don't want to.'

Emily was glad she knew it, even though she felt the sting of Lena's grief and knew she'd carry a trace of Lena's burden of guilt now. Every snippet and revelation of the girl her grandmother had been was precious and helped her to understand the woman she had become – the granny who had never stopped them doing what they wanted, but had been there every step of the way to make sure they were safe; and who had taught them to believe in all possibility.

A girl who didn't fit – in a different time, when not fitting was harder: a girl who played with boys and came home covered in mud. A young woman with fierce independence and a determination not to conform. The boy who'd loved her as a child and become her husband, but only after she spread her wings, went off adventuring while he patiently waited for her to come back to him. The little country church where they'd married was the same one in which they'd whispered and passed notes in as children.

The Lena Emily was discovering through the memory book was a changeling to her mother's eyes, source of so much bemused pride to her father – a girl who liked to dismantle engines to see how they worked, who argued and battled and fought to carve her own way in the world. A free bird.

When the mood deserted Lena so too did her awareness of the present. The interlude was over much too soon and Emily felt the ache of its passing, but also the import of the story, her time with Lena and the message Lena was once again trying to convey: life was too short to waste on guilt, or on trying to be someone else.

Emily understood. It was time to be true, time for her authentic self to shine through.

It was as well Emily had Mike and her work at the Book Nook to distract her over the coming days, since Lena retreated into an impenetrable fog and Luke kept showing up at the shop. It was innocent enough, just hanging out, helping where he could, but any fool could see the romance blossoming between him and Kate, a constant reminder to Emily of her resolve to reveal all in the wake of the Annabelle story. She still hadn't managed to have the conversation.

*

By Friday Kate was starting to worry that Luke was neglecting the work on his father's cottage, but she didn't want to mention it because she was already growing far too attached to his presence. They hadn't spoken about what, if anything, was happening between them, but she had told him, awkwardly, when she ended things with Ben and Luke had seemed quietly pleased.

'I'm not the person you think I am,' she had told Ben. 'And I don't think that's fair to either of us.'

Ben had been silent for so long, Kate had wondered if they'd lost the connection. 'So you're not coming back?'

It had been Kate's turn to be stuck for words. 'I have no idea,' she'd said, and the madness of it hit her. It was more than Luke; it was Emily and the Cottons, and maybe it was her mother too.

Kate could feel herself getting closer and closer to tapping a reply, telling Lily she was in Scotland, making that first terrifying overture, and getting further and further from New York.

'There's someone else,' Ben said, matter of fact.

'Yes.' Kate felt a tug of guilt. 'There is.'

'No,' Ben said. 'I mean me. There's someone else. Since we're being honest and all. It was fun while it lasted, Kate. Good luck to you.'

'You too.' Kate felt curiously like they were ending a business meeting. 'Take care, Ben.'

Kate returned from a chocolate run late on Friday afternoon to find Emily with a book spread out on her lap; it was a weighty tome, spotted with age. 'It's a tea anthology,' she said, flipping it to show Kate as she squeezed past. They were taking a break from reupholstering the armchairs from Mike's grandmother's house clearance, armed with a stapler and lengths of uncooperative tweed – Emily was taking an unsanctioned break while Kate had nipped out for the victuals.

'A *what* now?'

'I'm thinking of doing tea tastings.'

'Is that a thing?'

'Yeah, it's like wine tastings only—'

'A lot less fun,' Noah interrupted, with a huff as he hefted and manhandled another piece of wood. He and Luke were sweatily sawing and hammering, building a new bookshelf from reclaimed timber Luke had sourced for them. Luke laughed and straightened up.

'Coffee time?' he said. 'Did you get chocolate, Kate?'

Emily yawned and perked up as Kate proffered chocolate from the depths of her pockets. 'Put the kettle on, will you, Luke? Mine's a—'

Luke nodded. 'Tea. Strong enough to stand a spoon in, dash of milk, no sugar. Yep, I got the memo.'

Kate went to help him, touching his arm, his back, just for the sake of it; to feel the flex of muscle, the sweat where his T-shirt adhered to his shoulder blades. He had arrived as usual with his bag of tools, ready to help. 'Are you sure you can spare the time?' she had asked anxiously, as she did every day.

'It gets lonely working out on the house by myself,' Luke had said. 'This will be fun.'

And it had been fun, the four of them working in surprisingly easy harmony. Upholstering chairs, however, was proving to be a lot harder than it looked and Kate was quite content to extend her break for a bit. They sat on the floor and surveyed their handiwork; the shop was bright and clean, a seamless blend of rustic and modern. The tables and counters had been sanded and smoothed and painted, the shelves gleamed, the wood syrupy and sleek, awaiting precious books.

'You've all done a great job,' Luke said, stretching out his legs as he propped his back against the wall. 'And the place is in good shape. No damp or anything.' He and Kate had been trying not to stare too obviously at one another, but their eyes kept drifting, connecting, remembering: the beach, the cave, the hand-holding, the slip and shush of the waves in the gathering dark.

'So, d'you fancy getting something to eat after this?' Luke asked. He opened the invitation gallantly to the others, but it was obviously meant for her.

Emily shook her head. 'Nah. Can't. Lena isn't expecting me to be out for dinner.'

This wasn't strictly true – Lena wouldn't notice and Emily had put leftovers in the fridge as usual – but Emily had been a third wheel often enough. She was unwilling to confess that Mike might pop round as he had done on two previous occasions – once to take her out for a pint and once to bring pizza. She wasn't sure why she was keeping him secret.

'Noah?'

Noah was flushed, his eyes fixed on the picture window where a figure could be seen coming down the path.

Emily had her back to the window and couldn't see what was obvious to Kate; Noah was transfixed by the sight of a girl weaving her way along the path towards the shop. She pushed the door open and stepped inside. She was very pretty, with a shy smile, caramel skin and huge, brown eyes. Her dark hair was tied back in a swishy ponytail.

'Hello, Noah,' she murmured, half hiding beneath the sweep of her fringe. 'I hope you don't mind me gatecrashing like this. You told me about working in your sister's new shop and I thought...' She gave a shrug and wrapped her arms about herself.

Noah couldn't hide his grin. 'It's fine,' he said. 'Brilliant. Everyone, this is Becca.'

The girl looked nervous. She was tiny beside Noah, with skinny bird's legs tucked into Ugg boots. She bit her lip, flicked her fringe out of her eyes and shook hands with everyone.

Kate and Emily shared a smirk. Noah was so sweet and attentive, glancing at Becca so proudly, that it was difficult to muster the required teasing.

'It's lovely to meet you, Emily,' said Becca. 'I love what you've done with the place. It's beautiful.'

'Thanks.' Emily was surprised. This girl was different from the last one Noah had brought home; Charley was an unprepossessing creature, hard-eyed and insolent. She had been mixed up in all that business at school.

'It must be daunting,' Becca continued. 'Starting up a bookshop *here*. Personally, I think you can never have too many bookshops.'

Emily raised an eyebrow. 'I couldn't agree more,' she said, looking approvingly at her brother.

'Sorry if this is a bit cheeky, but I was wondering if you're going to be hiring soon?' Becca's smile was embarrassed.

'I hadn't thought about it yet, but I suppose I might be.'

'Great. I'd love if you could keep me in mind. I could give you a CV. I want to start saving money for university and I'd rather work in a bookshop than anywhere else.'

'Sure, drop in a CV and I'll let you know.'

Becca smiled again and Emily could see why Noah was mesmerised by her – with her dimples and dewy skin, dark eyes sparkling like a scatter of stars. Becca darted another coy look at Noah. 'So, Noah, I wanted to ask you over to dinner tonight. Mum said it was OK.'

Noah gaped. 'At your house? With your parents?'

Becca nodded. 'If you like.'

'Sure.' Noah couldn't agree fast enough. Kate didn't think he had anything to worry about – it was patently clear that Becca was smitten. She and Luke watched their first sparks of young love, remembering how it felt.

Noah's attempted nonchalance was funny. 'Do you need me in the shop much longer?'

Emily dismissed him. 'Go on. Have fun.'

Noah did not need to be told twice. He took Becca's hand and led her to the door. A moment later, the two of them could be seen framed in foliage on the path, laughing.

'Well,' Emily said. 'What do you make of that?'

'It's great. Becca seems lovely and Noah needs something good to happen.'

'She is . . . surprising. I think I like her,' Emily said.

'It's hard to believe we were ever that young,' Luke said, giving Kate a sidelong look.

She smiled at him. 'Shall we go and get something to eat, then? Emily, are you sure you won't come?'

Emily shook her head. She was looking forward to some alone time in the shop. She was feeling so much more positive about it lately and it would be a pleasure just to wander around and contemplate, and dare to dream about what her little bookshop might become. She might even start setting out books on the shelves – and there was always the possibility of Mike . . .

'Where shall we go?' Kate considered the eateries Wigtown had to offer.

Luke shoved his hands in his pockets, looking like his teenage self again; all he needed was his skateboard and she'd trip off to the Martyr's Stake to make out amongst the nettles. 'I was thinking maybe I would cook for you?'

'In your caravan?'

'Yeah. It's got a decent kitchen.'

Kate blushed, thinking of the close confines of the caravan and being alone with him in a small, intimate space. He held out a hand to her and she took it, shivering where their skin touched.

Kate glanced over her shoulder as they left. 'Later, Emily.'

Emily stayed at the shop to continue working on the armchairs, playing her music loud. It wasn't like she had anything better to do with her Friday night, with Noah out with Becca and Kate having dinner at Luke's. She was content enough as she cut and folded and stapled lengths of material – so long as she didn't give too much thought to Kate being with Luke, the conversations they might be having. She'd been waiting for her moment all day, but it hadn't arrived.

Just after nine, there was a tap on the door. Hoping for it, she leapt up, smoothed her hair and all but ran to unlock the door. There was Mike, holding a bottle of whisky and a pizza box. 'Hungry?' he asked with a grin.

They'd been texting back and forth and he'd dropped by the shop the other day after Kate and Noah had left; they'd shared a pizza and a dram, but nothing had happened yet – nothing decisive. Perhaps Mike could tell that Emily needed time to get used to the idea of a new relationship; the thought of even kissing him still terrified her, but she had to admit she was rapidly coming round to the idea.

'You're a bad influence,' Emily said, finding napkins and digging into the pizza. 'I can't keep eating junk like this.'

Mike smiled. 'Well, you'll have to agree to come out for a meal with me, or let me cook.'

'You'll have to ask me. You cook?'

'No, I'm a terrible cook, but it's the thought that counts.'

Emily was still laughing when her phone rang. When she finally unearthed it from beneath a length of tweed, the caller had rung off. She checked her log: Lena. She quickly called back.

'It's Bracken,' Lena said, without preamble. 'Something's happened to him.'

'What?'

'Come home,' Lena said, and hung up.

Emily sighed. She grabbed her bag, offering a hasty explanation to Mike, left her tools where they were and locked up the shop. She didn't think there was really much wrong with the dog, but once Lena got into a flap, she quickly descended into confused panic. She would have to go home and try to sort things out. She watched Mike walk back down the street towards his flat above the vet's, suppressing a sigh of disappointment. Tonight had been shaping up nicely. 'Call me,' he'd said, touching her arm as he'd left. 'If there really is something wrong with your dog.'

'I'm sure he'll be fine.'

'Call me anyway,' Mike said. 'So we can arrange for me to cook you a truly terrible meal.'

Emily found Lena in the kitchen, standing over Bracken's basket with her hands on her hips. The dog looked up with pathetic eyes, dropped his muzzle onto his paws and sighed expansively.

'He looks normal to me,' Emily said. 'How about a cup of tea?'

'No. He's off his food. He didn't want his dinner last night or his breakfast this morning. And when I tried to coax him outside, he wouldn't get out of his basket. He's been like this all day.'

'You never said.' Emily sneaked a glance towards the pinboard where Bracken's new feeding schedule was displayed; both last night and this morning were ticked. 'I'm sure it's nothing serious,' she said, and tried to calculate Bracken's age in her head; at least eleven, she thought – not young. She knelt by the basket and stroked the silky head. Bracken looked up at her with puppy eyes.

'Perhaps we should take him to the vet,' Lena said.

'It's late.' A glance at the kitchen clock revealed that it was a little after 9 p.m. Of course Mike wouldn't mind being disturbed . . .

'We mustn't wait.' Lena was anxious and mutinous, wringing her hands.

Emily sighed, sat back on her heels. 'OK.'

'I don't remember the vet's name. I have a card somewhere.' Lena opened the drawer beneath the kitchen table and stuff tumbled out as she began to rummage: receipts and postcards and rubber bands, notebooks, playing cards, stained recipes, loose change, batteries.

'It's fine,' Em said. 'I know the vet's number.' She pulled up Mike's number on her phone. 'Mike McKendrick is his name.'

'No,' Lena says. 'It definitely wasn't McKendrick. I'd remember.'

That was debatable, Emily thought uncharitably. 'When was the last time you had Bracken at the vet?'

'I think about five years ago.'

'What about check-ups, flea treatments, worming, booster injections?'

Lena harrumphed. 'Bracken has the constitution of an ox, never had to bother with vets much.' Just like Lena's attitude towards doctors.

'Well, I think it's safe to say that there have been some changes at the vet practice in five years, so don't worry about *who* the vet is. Mike is very nice.'

Lena muttered about not understanding why things had to change. 'Henderson,' she said. 'I think his name is Henderson. Old Jim Henderson. Or *Herriot*.'

'No. That's *All Creatures Great and Small*, Lena. It's a television programme.'

'Don't be ridiculous,' Lena snapped. She crouched by Bracken's head and stroked his sides, trying to coax him to eat a few biscuits from the palm of her hand.

'It's Emily,' Emily said.

'Hello again, so either the dog is really not well or you're pretty desperate for my cooking.'

'That's right.' Emily carried the phone outside where Lena couldn't hear her. 'The dog part. I think perhaps I'd best do the cooking.' She explained about Lena's condition. 'You see, she can't wait. Now she's got in her head that we need a vet now, there's no arguing with her. She'll just get agitated. So I was wondering if you could see him. The dog is very important to her.'

'Of course,' Mike said. 'It's no problem. Bring him straight down to the surgery and I'll meet you there.'

Emily sighed with relief. 'That's perfect, thank you.'

She returned to the kitchen. Lena was sitting on the floor by Bracken's bed, her expression deep and faraway. Emily hardly liked to disturb her manner of reflection, almost prayer.

'It's fine,' she said softly. 'If we take him to the surgery, the vet will meet us there. Now, what about something to eat; did you have dinner? I called, remember, because I was staying late at the shop.' She crossed the room to the fridge and opened it, found the Tupperware of leftovers was still where she'd left it. She pulled it out. 'I told you there was dinner in the fridge for you.'

'Not hungry.'

'You have to eat something. You have to look after yourself.'

'Why should I when you're doing such a great job of it for me,' Lena snapped. 'Always the infernal nagging: can't you just leave me alone? I'm not a child.' She stamped out of the room.

Emily sliced bread and made herself a sandwich. She hadn't managed more than a few bites of pizza. She found Lena in the sitting room, wearing her dressing gown. 'Lena, it's time to go.'

Lena frowned. 'Where are we going?'

'The vet, with Bracken.'

Panic flared. 'Is he sick?'

'What? He . . . um, no. It's nothing to worry about. Just a routine check. Must've forgotten to write it on the calendar. So, do you want to go and get dressed?'

'I don't think so, dear. I don't feel like going out. You go ahead.'

Emily suppressed a sigh and sucked her teeth. 'Right.'

With Lena refusing to move, and Kate and Noah both out, it fell to Emily to manoeuvre the malcontent dog into the car alone.

Emily drove carefully into the village, feeling the first tinges of anxiety as she pulled into town. She parked as near to the vet practice as she could. Still, when she tried to persuade Bracken to jump out of the back, he looked at her despondently and pressed himself deeper into his folds of his blanket. She closed the door and went inside. 'Hello?' Emily called.

The place was eerily silent, save for the banging of a door somewhere and Mike's voice calling, 'Back here. Just a minute.'

Emily hovered around the door to the reception, glancing down the unlit corridor from whence the voice came. The door at the end of the corridor opened and Mike came out, drying his hands on a towel. 'Hi,' he said.

'Emily Cotton,' she said with a grin. 'I called about my dog.'

He grinned back. 'The hustler.'

'Sorry about bailing, and to have dragged you back to work at this hour.'

'No worries. I'm used to it. Sleep and eat with one ear open, waiting for a call to go and stick my hand up a cow's bottom or something equally lovely. Besides, at least this way I still get to see you.'

In the close quarters, she could smell his soapy, herby scent. She blushed.

'I buy my vegetables from Lena at the farmers' market on a Saturday. She often has a lovely looking Irish setter with her – is he the patient?'

'Yes.' Emily gestured over her shoulder. 'He's in the car. I can't lift him I'm afraid. I'm also ashamed to tell you that he hasn't been to the vet in five years.'

'Don't worry. I'll come and give you a hand, shall I?'

'Thank you.' Emily put her bag on a plastic chair in the waiting room and led the way.

Mike stroked the dog, had a cursory look at his eyes, mouth and paws, felt along his ribcage and abdomen. 'What's the problem?'

'Maybe nothing. Lena is convinced he's off his food, but she may be overreacting. Her illness impairs her judgement at times and can make her irrational. But I guess Bracken won't get up to go outside, which *is* unusual.'

Mike's smile was gentle. 'Nothing irrational about being concerned for her dog. Most people are attached to their animals. I know I am. Let's get him inside and take a better look.'

When Bracken was stretched out on the examination room in Mike's consulting room, his paws drooping over the edge of the metal table, Emily's anxiety ratcheted up a notch: if something happened to Bracken, how would Lena cope?

She chewed her nails while Mike worked. He was thorough. 'This might take some time,' he warned. 'There are no obvious signs so I'd like to run some tests. Why don't I give you a ring once I know more?'

'OK.' Emily was reluctant to leave. 'Um, I hate to sound callous, but any idea of the cost?'

'I won't do anything expensive yet, this is just a preliminary check so I'll ring and discuss options with you later.'

'Options?' Visions of protracted goodbyes and vicious needles swam in her mind. Emily felt her eyes sting.

'Payment options, I mean, treatments,' Mike said quickly. 'It's not time to panic yet.'

'But he's old, isn't he?'

'He's not a young pup, but he could have a few years left.'

*

Emily wandered disconsolately down the street. Everywhere was closed and she wondered what to do. She could go home and wait for Mike to call, but that would mean dealing with Lena, which in her current frame of mind she didn't relish.

She decided the best thing would be to go back to the Book Nook and wait there.

She loved to walk down the little lane leading from the high street to her shop, to duck beneath the leafy arch and see the shop appear magically before her, nestling amongst the trees and hawthorns. The wooden sign was still blank, sanded clean and awaiting their attention – Kate was designing the logo and lettering for her.

Emily let herself into the shop; it felt reassuring to step inside in the solitude, breathe in the scent of paint and varnish and new wood – mixed with pizza now – and enjoy soaking up the atmosphere of the shop. Her place. She set her bag on the counter and imagined that in the months and years to come it would become such a familiar ritual; drop her bag, switch on the kettle, lights, computer.

She checked her phone – she didn't want to miss Mike's call.

She nearly dropped it when she saw the display: the text message, the name she had fantasised about seeing . . .

Joe.

She opened it, fingers shaking, her breath shuddering uneasily in and out.

We could meet, just name a time and place. I miss you. I'm ready to talk about the future, Em.

Emily set the phone on the counter. Waves of nausea rolled through her. He was still hers if she wanted him; he wanted her, she knew it. Finally, he was willing to talk – but was *she*?

After all these months of wanting, when the only thing she longed for was contact, hope, a second chance – or was it third, fourth, or fifth chance by now? Such a tempestuous match, when was she going to get the message that it just wasn't right? The divorce ought to have done it, but hadn't. And now, Joe was offering her another go-round, and Emily was finally moving on.

She wanted to talk to Kate, but Kate was with Luke. She longed for Lena, but Lena wasn't an option any more. There was no one else she could imagine discussing him with.

The divorce was finalised, signed and sealed and uncontested; it was too late. She had made the right decision leaving him when she did, she knew it, but she had been so miserable since, so dreary and wretched without him. All these months, nothing made sense.

Emily paced the shop. *What am I thinking? It's crazy even to consider it.*

She wasn't considering it, surely. They didn't work. They had established that. But the pull of him, the yearning, the undeniable pleasure of knowing he wanted her again . . .

Emily sat at her laptop, her thoughts in turmoil, anchoring herself at the desk, *her* place. The screen saver was a photograph of a pile of her favourite childhood books.

This was what mattered: the Book Nook.

It was all hers, her future, and it had nothing at all to do with Joe. Well, apart from the money, but she had always been able to put that deftly out of her mind. She looked around with pride at the green walls, smooth and lush against the pale wood of the shelves; at the flagstones, clean and draped with new rugs; at the dark wood beams over her head.

Every brushstroke and nail reminded her how far from Joe she had come.

Was she willing to take a step backwards – into Joe's arms and into a past in which she was so unhappy with herself?

On the questions swirled. Mike came into her mind, his honest face and gorgeous eyes. Mike would be uncomplicated and loving, she knew it.

As a distraction, she got back to work, taking out her frustrations on the armchair. An hour in, her mobile rang and her heart skipped again.

Not Joe.

Mike.

Her heart accelerated. She was happy just to hear his voice. 'Can you come over?' he said.

'I'm on my way.' Emily quickly locked the shop. She ran all the way to the clinic, her plimsolls slapping on the pavement, ponytail bouncing. It was dark out now and Wigtown was quiet but for the murmuring buzz of the pub.

'Is it bad news?' Emily gasped, bursting into Mike's consulting room.

'Not exactly,' Mike said, looking up from his computer screen. 'It is treatable, so don't panic. Take a seat.'

Emily shook her head and went to the table where Bracken lay, asleep or sedated. She ran a hand over his shaggy head, wishing he would open his eyes and give her his usual dopey look. 'Tell me.'

They stood with table and dog between them. 'Does Bracken ever get human food, leftovers or cooking scraps?'

'No. Lena has always been adamant about that . . .' Emily hesitated. 'But she has Alzheimer's. I can't tell what she'll do any more. She doesn't remember feeding him sometimes.'

'I'm thinking specifically about onion poisoning. The signs suggest it at the moment although there are still some tests to run. Onions are toxic to dogs even in small quantities, but it's rarely fatal. Chocolate on the other hand *is* fatal, so I've given him an emetic to make him sick, just to be on the safe side.'

'But you *can* treat him?'

'I'd like to keep him here for a few days just to be sure.'

'OK.' Emily rubbed her forehead. 'I don't know how to stop Lena from feeding him scraps.' Suddenly she was exhausted, overwhelmed with the responsibility for looking after her grandmother and Bracken, and the feeling that everything was only going to get worse. Tears gathered in her eyes.

Mike washed his hands carefully at the sink, looking at Emily over his shoulder. 'My granny had Alzheimer's . . .' he began. He didn't finish the sentence. No happy ending there – there never was.

'It's bad enough that she's losing her memories, I don't want her to lose her dignity as well.' Emily didn't know where the words were coming from. She felt the pressure building behind her eyes and clenched her teeth. Before she knew it, she was crying, silent, soft tears slipping down her cheeks. Mike came around the table and pulled her gently into his arms. It wasn't quite the romantic embrace she had been imagining, but still.

He reached behind him for a tissue.

'I'm sorry about your granny.' Em pressed the tissue to the rim of each eye, stemming the flow.

'I'm sorry about yours too. At least Bracken's going to be there to look after her a while longer.' Mike smiled and stepped back.

Emily gave the dog a last pat. 'Thanks for your help. And for this.' She balled the tissue. 'I didn't mean to . . .'

He smiled. 'It's no problem, Emily.'

She turned towards the door, then paused and turned back. He was watching her, smiling. She met his eyes and felt human again, capable of love. She felt light and playful, able to converse normally with a man, able to want him and not be bound by her attachment to Joe. She walked back across the consulting room and into Mike's arms. Before she had time to question it, she was kissing him.

She was more than the pieces Joe left behind, scattered shrapnel from the explosion of their war-torn love; she was whole.

They broke away from each other with goofy grins. Emily realised she was still crying, and was mortified. Mike wiped her tears. 'It's been a tough day,' he said. 'You should go home and let me look after Bracken. I am going to hold you to that offer of dinner really soon, though. You can even use my kitchen – it's pristine, never been used except to make toast and beans.'

Emily smiled, scrubbed away the last of her tears and left.

Chapter 19

Kate woke slowly to silence, the mustiness of Bluebell Bank mingled with honeysuckle sweetness drifting through the open window, and the resounding realisation that Ben was a feature of her past and Luke might just be her future.

Dinner had been good; Luke was a decent cook – what he lacked in culinary expertise he made up for in enthusiasm, a certain hearty appeal and an excellent bottle of Pinot Noir.

He gave a quick tour of the project, shrouded in scaffolding, then settled her in a deckchair in the garden with a large glass of wine. They ate outside – steaks in pepper sauce with lumpy mash and garden peas he proudly claimed were home-grown. Morse, the oldest of the dogs, was content to lie sedately at Luke's feet, while Caber, who hadn't quite outgrown puppyhood, ran around the garden barking at sticks.

The conversation moved up a gear, getting close to the important stuff. Luke told her about Louisa, the girlfriend he broke up with before going travelling. Kate told him about Ben. 'It was over the second I made the decision to come here,' she said, not wanting him to think the break-up was necessarily to do with him, or that it wasn't.

Luke just smiled, drank his wine and stroked the furry pile of dog at his feet.

Later, they walked down to the Martyr's Stake, skirting the spot where they had first kissed. Holding hands, saying nothing. Back at the caravan, they finished the wine, sitting in the deckchairs surrounded by long grass and weeds – which Luke optimistically called his wild flower meadow – and talked about the futures they imagined, in that awkward way of new love, where one tried so hard neither to include, nor exclude, but left a space like a promise in the projected future: a checking of ideals and values, without assuming too much. Luke could see the future only in so far as it concerned the renovation of his father's house and Kate the opening of the bookshop; beyond that was a question mark.

They did not kiss, save a clumsy brush of lips when they parted. Luke, not quite sure whether to aim for lips or cheek, managed to land somewhere in between. In the brief moment when he was close – the brush of his stubble and soft warmth of his lips – all those feelings long dormant surged to the surface.

It would have been too easy to slip her arms around his neck, to turn the kiss into something. Not yet; she wasn't entirely sure why she was holding back now. She was still fired with the need to know what had scared him away all those years ago; she wasn't sure she could move past that moment without an explanation.

Today, Luke was taking her sailing.

Lena was in the garden, her old straw hat bobbing between the leaves of giant rhubarb, visible from the hall window as Kate descended the stairs.

Emily was having tea in the kitchen with Abby. Kate could hear them. Abby was telling Emily that Dan wasn't himself – he was snappy with her, she was worried he'd lost interest, what with the pregnancy. 'The baby wasn't exactly planned,' Abby was saying. 'But we were over the moon when we found out . . .'

Emily was trying to reassure her. Kate imagined Dan was in for a tough conversation with his sister if she caught up with him anytime soon. She shuddered at her part in things and wished she could take it back, whatever she had done to Dan.

Wanting to hide, Kate decided against coffee; she could pick one up in town.

Had she given him hope? She thought she'd been clear. She thought Dan was too, beyond the paranoia of a hangover and the vestiges of feelings resurrected from too long ago. She thought Dan loved Abby, understood that he had made a choice. They both had. But perhaps it wasn't so simple. How could she put things right?

She walked quickly into town, nursing her vague guilt.

She hadn't had time to tell Emily about dinner with Luke, or to talk over her confused feelings; Emily had been heading for bed when Kate returned last night and there was a faint air of panic about Bracken permeating the place.

'I'm sure he's all right,' Kate had said as they conversed briefly in the hall on the way to their respective bedrooms.

'Yeah, it's not too serious. Mike says we can go and visit him today.'

'*Mike*?' Kate said.

'The vet.'

'You're on first name terms with the vet?'

'I've met him a couple of times. He's the guy I was playing pool with that night . . .'

'This conversation isn't over,' Kate said firmly, with a smile, as Emily whisked into her bedroom and bade her a hasty goodnight.

Tomorrow, Kate thought, she'd pick up a nice bottle of red and she and Emily would put the world to rights. They'd talk about Mike and Luke. She was so happy that Emily had something new to focus on, someone who wasn't Joe.

*

Luke's brother owned a Wayfarer sailing dinghy – not that Kate had the least idea what that was until she saw it. He arrived to pick her up at the shop. The Ross men had always loved the sea;

it was in their blood, coded deep. Luke was the least sea-savvy of them all, but he assured Kate he could handle a sailing boat.

'My dad bought this years ago and restored it,' he said, when Kate was positioned gingerly on the wooden seat in her yellow life vest and they were gliding out into the open mouth of the firth. 'He and Nick used to come out all the time. Do you know much about sailing?'

Kate shook her head, getting used to the lurch and heave of the water beneath her. 'No, do I need to?'

'Not really, just follow my lead. It's a two-man dinghy so I will need your help.'

'What if I get seasick?'

Luke laughed. 'You won't, the firth is calm today and the forecast is OK. Stormy later, but we'll be back by then. Do you usually get seasick?'

'I don't usually go anywhere near the sea.'

For the first couple of hours Kate was concentrating so hard on learning the basics of sailing – trying not to be a hindrance – that there was little time for conversation. Eventually, she relaxed enough to enjoy herself. The sea was splendid: the rise and fall of the waves, the wind tumbling her hair, the cool green water smacking against the hull, and the sun sparking off the firth, changing its colours to teal and slate and ultramarine. The sky was blue, punctuated with soft, foamy clouds.

Luke laughed a little at her inept sailing manoeuvres; his own were fluid and practised, despite his claim not to have sailed in years. He looked perfectly at home, squinting against the sun and smiling contentedly, the forearm braced on the rudder tanned and muscled beneath the sleeve of his T-shirt. He was clean shaven today and Kate could see his dimples; he looked young and she tried to pretend they were fifteen again and just beginning.

He steered the little boat around the bay to Ardwall, the largest of the islands of Fleet, where he pulled the boat up onto the shore. Kate got out, soaking her plimsolls, and they climbed up towards the old ruined chapel, through brush and bush. She took her shoes and socks off and stretched her legs, wriggling her toes in the grass. Luke took a flask of coffee out of his backpack and held it up with a grin.

'So,' he said, gesturing at the isolated island – nothing but ruins and cormorants, rocks and sky. 'What do you think?'

'I think it's beautiful. So quiet. What's over there?' She pointed towards the nearest shore where yellow sand glimmered between the rocks and a grey stone building peeped through the trees.

'Knockbrex, I think.' His hand brushed her shoulder as he leaned across her to point. 'There's Knockbrex Castle. That's the Carrick shoreline, at low tide you can walk right across to Ardwall.'

'Have you come here before?'

Luke shook his head. 'I can't come here on my own in a two-man dinghy, and Nick and I don't often sail to romantic spots together.' Luke's eyes widened at the implication, but Kate smiled: romantic sounded fine. 'Dad brought us here once. But it made him sad. I think he used to bring my mother.'

'It's a wonder he didn't move away, when she left. If it made him so sad to remember her.'

'He was a Solway fisherman through and through. He was bred here and he wanted to die here. That was part of the problem, I s'pose. My mother wanted adventure. He taught me well . . . no son of his was ever going to get away with not knowing his way around a boat. I don't get time to sail much. Nick is the real sailor in our family.'

'He followed your father into the fishing business, was that always his intention?'

Luke leaned back on his elbows, lowering himself onto the rough, tussocky grass. 'I never had much interest in fishing but Nick always seemed to like it. It worked out fine.' If he felt any lingering resentment for his father he was careful not to show it. Kate remembered Mr Ross as a remote, frightening man, bowed down by disappointment. He spoke harshly to his boys, when he noticed them at all. She had been afraid of him on the one or two occasions their paths had crossed.

Kate drew up her knees and gazed at the Carrick shore again, strands of hair blowing across her eyes. 'But you said Nick might move to Italy to be close to your mum.'

'Yeah, he's thinking about it. The funny thing about Nick is, he always seemed so much older than me growing up, like he knew everything, and had done everything. Everyone feels like that about their older brothers, I guess. He looked out for me, you know. But he hasn't really matured any since he was eighteen. I caught up and overtook him. He's still full of hare-brained ideas and grand schemes. Dad knew that. But, ultimately, it's Dad's business – his legacy. I think that will be pretty hard for Nick to leave behind.'

Listening to him talk, Kate felt how deeply – despite their unresolved differences, or because of them? – Luke still missed his father.

'Lena is ill,' she said quietly. 'Her memory's going. It's horrible watching someone you love suffer. She won't get any better, and that's the worst thing of all, just waiting for it to get worse.'

'I'm really sorry. I always liked Lena. She didn't pull her punches, I remember. I was a wee bit scared of her as a boy.'

'We all were.' Kate exhaled softly, feeling the weight of her Lena-sadness settle in a familiar lump in her chest. 'She's still the same Lena. But she's also different, and that's hard.'

'People change.'

'Yes.' She scooped her hair back with both hands and let it fall over one shoulder. 'I . . . I didn't want anything to change here. I came back here counting on that.'

'But it did?'

'Yes. Everything looks the same, but under the surface, it's different.' She shrugged, shaking off her disappointment.

'*I'm* the same,' Luke said softly. 'And I'm right here.' His eyes met hers. He got to his feet and held out a hand to pull her up.

'C'mon.' He led her across the narrow island to a promontory overlooking the Irish Sea and they sat side by side on a rock, gazing at Ireland, hazy in the distance beyond humps of rocky islands that made up the most westerly parts of Scotland.

They came upon the moment as they had both known they would. It was natural, a smooth and seamless transition. Luke's arms around her and Luke kissing her as if he had been doing so every day of their lives. No awkwardness, no uncertainty, just hunger and comfort and reassurance.

Here I am and I am here.

Not everything had to change.

'I missed you,' Luke said quietly, when he drew back to look at her, his blue eyes deep and dark as pitch, the pupils so vast they seemed to bleed into the navy irises.

The new world – on the other side of the kiss – was unrecognisable from any they had known; there was no going back now. Kate felt the weight of the realisation.

No one else had ever looked at her with such conviction. 'I missed you too,' she replied steadily, while her heart thrummed and the blood pulsed in crazy spikes, and happy chemicals flooded her brain. 'More than I knew until I saw you again.'

Luke's voice was soft, husky. 'I thought about looking you up, but I didn't think you'd want to see me.'

A little voice at the back of Kate's head told her to tread carefully; that she didn't know where she would be come the end of summer and nor did he. He had the house to finish, she the bookshop. He had his brother, she had her life in New York.

To get embroiled with Luke again under a cloud of uncertainty might mean certain heartbreak. He had broken it once already; Kate still bore the old scars and was ready to shatter along old, weakened fault lines.

Was this just a holiday romance? A snatched opportunity to finish what they had once started? Was it worth it to have him only a few short weeks?

Then she looked into his eyes again and knew the terms mattered not at all.

Whatever the complications – even if they were living on separate continents, Kate wanted Luke Ross. She didn't trouble herself with the details, she just knew it, in every fibre; as if the knowledge of her wanting him had been there all along, woven into her soul since she was fifteen years old.

This moment right now mattered more than all the ones to come and all those behind them; it was the *only* moment she need concern herself with.

She kissed him some more, wrapped her arms around him and revelled in him, prolonging the sanctity and magic of this minute, this place, for as long as she could.

*

It was with some reluctance that Kate and Luke made their way back to the shore to retrieve the boat and sail for home. There was the sense that leaving this place was a risk; that the fragile spell that bound them on the island might not hold. But Luke had his eye on time and tide; he knew there was rain forecast for the evening and he would prefer to get safely back to dry land before the front moved in. Solway storms could be unpredictable, rising from nothing in a flash.

They sailed across the bay. Back at Isle of Whithorn they loaded the Wayfarer onto its trailer and hitched it to Luke's truck. They drove home with the windows open, humid air blowing in; the sky darkening behind them and a bank of steely cloud rolling inland from the firth. Layers and layers of cloud, unfurling. 'See, I said the weather was going to change,' Luke said.

Kate looked in her wing mirror. 'You were right,' she said. 'Well done.'

'Are you being sarcastic?' Luke grinned happily.

Kate rested her elbow on the door frame and leaned her

head out, letting the breeze tear at her ponytail and pummel her face.

Luke laughed. 'That's what Caber does when he sits in the front seat of the truck.'

'Are you suggesting I have no more sense than your dog?'

'My dog is very sensible.'

Kate was happy too: the stupid, easy banter with Luke, the sense of *rightness* about the day. She tipped her head back and smiled, let no doubts creep in to spoil her good mood.

For a while they drove in silence – good silence – but, eventually, they reached the point where a decision must be made and Luke turned to Kate and said, 'Do you want to come back to the caravan?'

'I'm hungry,' Kate said.

'We can get dinner.'

She nodded. 'Sure.'

'What do you feel like eating?' Kate didn't care and told him so. 'I probably have something at home I could throw together.'

Kate looked at him. 'Sounds good, but after the steak I have high expectations.'

By the time they reached Luke's caravan, the rain was falling full pelt, puddling unevenly in the yard and muddying the grass. Kate darted across the rain-soaked garden, half laughing and holding her jumper over her head as a shield. Luke unlocked the door, shoulders hunched and rain dripping in his eyes. A furry bundle of sheepdog hurled itself at them, one dog indistinguishable from the other. Kate crouched and attempted to stroke them, but the dogs were much too excited, their exuberant yips and barks ringing out as they shot past Kate and Luke and out into the wet yard with their tails high.

Luke shook his head and left the door ajar for them, rain thundering relentlessly on the tin roof of the caravan. He grabbed a towel from the tiny bathroom and scrubbed it across his wet hair, chucked another to Kate to ring out her ponytail. She hung her wet jumper on the back of a chair. 'Can I help make dinner?' she asked, as Luke started pulling stuff out of the refrigerator.

Luke slid a cold beer across the counter to her. 'Nope. Have a seat. Talk to me.'

Kate closed her hand around the icy bottle. 'You got an opener?'

Luke passed it to her, watched her break the cap off the bottle. 'So I couldn't help noticing, you drink now. You never used to.'

Kate took a sip, bubbles and bitterness melting on her tongue. 'Neither did you.' He nodded. 'It was a childish notion, to blame alcohol itself for my mother's problems.' The words got stuck in her throat.

'I shouldn't have asked . . .'

Kate sat on the bench seat. 'I want to tell you.' She didn't want there to be any secrets between them. 'I realised a long time ago that blaming alcohol for her problems was wrong. Alcohol became her means of coping, but there must have been something else . . . something she was deeply unhappy about. Something that made her feel she couldn't live without dulling the pain.'

'You don't know?'

She shrugged. 'Maybe one day I'll be brave enough to find out.' One day she would finally ask the questions, because one day she would be ready to hear the answers.

'For me, it was simple. Dad drank to forget my mother. There wasn't anything deeper or more complex than that.'

'My mother is complex. I still don't know what her demons were. Perhaps it was something to do with my . . . father.' The word tasted strange on her tongue – he'd never been more than a biological necessity; she didn't even have a name for him. Perhaps she'd ask that question too. Soon. 'The thing is, not drinking in case I end up like her will never show me what I am, or what I am not. I would always wonder and always worry. This way I know. I can drink a beer and it's fine. *I'm* fine.' Kate looked up. Luke was staring intently. 'Sorry,' she said, frowning. 'I didn't mean to be a buzz kill.'

'You're not. Thank you.'

'What for?'

'For opening up. There was a time I didn't think you ever would. You were so self-contained and I always wondered why you had to pretend to be someone else.'

Kate blinked. 'Did I do that? I guess I didn't know how to be myself. I'm sorry if it felt like I wasn't real, but what *we* had – the way I was with you – that was always real to me.'

'I'm sorry too,' Luke said gently, and the memory of that dreadful phone call when he had brought both their worlds crashing down around them, hovered between them. 'I should finish making dinner.'

After they had eaten, they sat side by side on the bench seat, sipping their beer and listening to music and the sound of rain. Talking about their university days and trading stories of silly things they had done.

Kate felt as if she was being led inexorably towards decisions and truths. The urge to ask him to explain was strong, but the urge to finally make love to him was stronger. 'Luke . . .' she began.

'Yeah?'

Kate felt for the bracelet that usually circled her wrist, but she had removed all traces of Ben. 'Maybe *I* changed. Perhaps I grew distant . . .'

Luke cleared his throat. This was the moment for his apology proper. He needed to apologise, to get that out of the way before things went any further.

They were adults now, with past relationships behind them; they had each tried their hands at loving other people. A wave of longing rolled over Luke and he couldn't quite force the words past his lips: who wanted to talk of old heartbreak and betrayal on a night made for new beginnings and discoveries?

Instead, he closed the gap between them and cupped Kate's face in his hands. When his lips met hers she drew him into a kiss that silenced him. She grew more certain with every second and so did her kiss. He ran a hand down her spine, feeling the ridges of bone, splayed his hands on her hips as she raised herself to straddle him, bumping her leg against the table, knocking his head on the window. Neither of them noticed these small hurts.

Kate worked her hands beneath his T-shirt and spread her fingers on the smooth, warm skin of his belly. Luke sucked in a breath and Kate grinned against his lips, swooping her thumb beneath his belt, and he grazed her lip with his teeth as he jerked at her touch. 'Kate,' he whispered, disentangling their mouths. 'Stay.'

Kate pulled back to look at him; he was gazing up at her. She remembered teenage passion, tinged with fear of the unknown, but it was different now; they were adults and they knew what they were doing.

'Or stop doing that,' Luke said, as she continued to stroke his stomach. 'One or the other.'

She nodded slowly, laughing at how nervous she still felt. For answer, she bracketed his face with her hands and kissed him again, then she reached for the hem of her top, pulling it up and over her head in a fluid, defiant gesture.

Luke laughed. 'Shit, Kate, the window!' She glanced at the un-curtained window behind his head, the lights of the interior sparkling in every raindrop and their images reflected clearly against the black, her bare skin pearly pale against the dark night. She rolled sideways, ducking out of sight, sprawling on the bench and pulling him with her, legs still tangled.

Luke reached behind him to pull down the blind. Then he shifted position and extended a hand to Kate, pulling her upwards. 'The bed is more comfortable. Not *really* comfortable, but better than this bench.'

Kate overtook him to lead him eagerly towards the fold-out bed in the back of the caravan, a dark cocoon-like space that might, in any other circumstance, have seemed claustrophobic. His sheets were creased and clean, and smelled of him.

The terms don't matter, she reminded herself. Even if this moment is all there is.

But as she lay down with Luke, she knew she was deluding herself; she was already in too deep. She was imagining their tomorrows, a whole lifetime of days stretching out ahead of them: exactly as it was supposed to be.

Chapter 20

Kate's entire body had liquefied and a sluggish, molten substance moved languidly in her veins; her muscles felt heavy, numb. She lay in Luke's embrace, his chin digging into her shoulder and his arms heavy, pinning her. She stretched one foot, trying to find a cool spot in the fever-hot sheets. She couldn't tell if Luke was asleep, or if she was. She thought they might both be drifting in and out and dreaming.

A song played in the background. There was a clean, crisp, woodsy scent to the caravan. The bed was sweat-damp and her hair glued itself to the nape of her neck. She could still feel Luke on every inch of her skin.

He breathed in her ear. She shifted, thought about getting up for a glass of water, tried to slip out of his embrace without waking him.

'Kate.' He stirred and his voice resonated through her shoulder. She liked the vibration of his voice running through her flesh. She slid out from beneath his arm.

'Go back to sleep,' she whispered. 'I'm just getting a drink.' She padded across the small space to the kitchen counter where she poured a glass of water and drank it down, then turned off the music, switched down the lights. She returned to the bed. Luke had raised himself up on one arm and was staring at her with admiration. She smiled. A sliver of moonlight lit up the grey, illuminating planes of his face and torso, bared by the sheet still twisted about his waist. His eyes were dark with sleep and longing, a slow smile curving his lips and the tiny shadow of his dimples showing at their corners: all light and shade in the gleams of moonlight slanting through the half-shut curtains.

'You're so beautiful,' Luke said wonderingly, and held out his hand to her. She went to him and slipped deliciously beneath the covers again, lay on her back with Luke over her, stroking his gentle fingertips down her cheek, her neck, the hollow of her collarbone, the curve of her breast. Kate smiled at him and reached her arms to wrap around his shoulders, pulling him down.

Luke hesitated, biting his lip.

She sensed his restraint, looked quizzically at him.

He spoke. 'Breaking up with you was the biggest mistake of my life.' His voice was soft with lament, his arms tightening around her and drawing her against him to take the sting from his words. Kate stilled, felt the contact with him all the way down her spine, his knee pressed into the back of hers and the synchronicity of their pulse beats and slow, soft breathing.

She didn't want to talk about this now, she didn't need to know. His rejection – bringing with it all the pent-up anguish of her mother's disinterest, the horrible years after, when she tried to make sense of it, when every other guy felt wrong, as Emily, steadfast and loyal, tried to put her back together.

'Luke.' She ran her fingers along his arm, closed her eyes against the remembered pain. 'You don't have to explain.'

'Yes, I do.' He tugged on her shoulder gently, pulling her round to face him. Kate rolled onto her back again, gazed up at him with a worried expression. She sighed, scooted up onto the pillow and pulled the sheet around her, feeling suddenly exposed in her nakedness.

'Luke, this is all water under the bridge. We were just kids . . .'

She didn't want to know, didn't want to peel back the edges of the wound and find it still raw beneath.

'Let me say this, please, Kate. I don't want there to be any awkwardness between us, no secrets.'

She sighed and crossed her arms.

Luke raised himself on his arm, gazing down at her. 'I need to explain,' he said. 'You must have wondered.'

'I just thought you grew tired of me,' Kate said, hiding her hurt, but not very well.

'Never. Not possible.' Luke was emphatic and she knew he meant it.

'So why then?'

'I was upset with you for going to Oxford instead of coming to see me, and I guess it felt like you were slipping away from me. Like I was losing you in increments. I suppose I was pissed off, jealous, insecure. But that was no excuse . . .'

'I don't know what you're saying.' Kate pulled away from him; why was he spoiling everything? True, she had wanted to know, but now she had a dreadful premonition that this would ruin everything.

'In the end,' Luke said, 'I just couldn't live with myself. I felt bad for doubting you. I took the coward's way out and I walked away without explaining. I knew you couldn't forgive me, you see . . .'

'What are you talking about? Forgive you for what?'

'For Emily.'

Kate was disoriented, disconnected. Was this happening? No. No, it couldn't be.

She spoke slowly, every word an effort. 'What *about* Emily?' All those months she had struggled with his decision, his refusal to speak to her, she had known there had to be something more to it, something Luke was keeping back. He couldn't just be gone from her life with no explanation.

'It was one night in Wigtown, when you were in Oxford. Emily and I . . . Oh shit, Kate, I thought you knew.'

'Tell me.' She was pressed up against the wall of the caravan now like a cornered animal, swaddled in sheets that smelled of them. She didn't want to hear it, but she had to know.

'We kissed. I thought she would have told you. I thought that you'd forgiven her. I never imagined that you didn't know.'

Kate scrambled off the bed, careless of her nakedness now in her need to get away from him. 'So, you were pissed off with me and instead of talking to me about it you kissed my best friend?'

I slept with Dan, she nearly cried. *And you drove me to it.* Her breath quickened when she thought about how she had saved herself for Luke, taken out all her anguish and frustration on one impulsive, perfect fuck.

Righteous anger thrummed through her, but beneath it the repetitive drum beat in her head: *hypocrite, hypocrite, hypocrite.* It had been so easy to fall into bed with Dan. Scorned and hurt beyond measure. Hurting Dan in return.

And Emily ... *comforting* her. Steadfast and loyal? No, a traitor, watching her tie herself in knots and never saying a word.

Kate scrambled into her clothes, her thoughts tipping into freefall now.

Emily had watched her weep over him for weeks. The sense of betrayal quickened, poisoned. '*She* should have been off limits. The very last person you ought to have gone near if you were looking for an easy shag.'

Luke had pulled on his jeans and was fighting to get his T-shirt over his head as she headed for the door. He was calling after her, trying to keep his cool. 'It was only a kiss, Kate. I was lonely and drunk and sad, and she was there. I knew as soon as I'd done it how wrong it was. I broke up with you because I was angry with myself and I thought it was all messed up. You were always flirting with Dan and I—'

Dan. Kate whirled around just as she was about to step outside into the rain. 'What do you mean?'

'I always knew you liked him—'

'I slept with him *afterwards*,' Kate said, enjoying for a split second the way his eyes blazed with jealousy. Then the awfulness of everything crashed over her like a wave. 'I slept with him after you destroyed us. I never, never would have cheated on you, Luke. But you . . . you *kissed* my best friend!'

He swallowed hard. 'Kate,' he croaked, reaching for her. 'Don't go, Kate. I guess I got it wrong. I always thought maybe there was something between you two, and Emily said . . .'

She spun in the doorway, cheeks flaming, eyes burning and brimming with tears. 'Well, I guess we both know not to trust a word *Emily* says.'

And then she was gone. The fleeting happiness they had found, sitting side by side on Ardwall looking out to sea, and in each other's arms tonight, gone for good.

*

Kate walked fast, trying to put distance between them.

Emily. The name, soft and sibilant and clinging to Luke's lips. She felt like she'd been punched. *He kissed Emily.*

Emily kissed him.

How the hell could he do that? How could she? And to keep quiet all this time. Suddenly, she wanted to go back, to know exactly what Emily had said to Luke; had she planted the seeds of his doubt; had she really set out to take Luke for herself?

No wonder Emily was so anxious about Kate's budding new romance with Luke; she was frantic in case her own secrets were exposed.

Kate reached the road and kept walking. It was still raining. Dark. Where would she go? Where was home now?

Not Bluebell Bank, with Emily, who had betrayed her; with Dan full of doubts and Lena inching inexorably away, and Fergus long since fled; with Ally living his lie and Noah fighting to find his place amongst the chaos.

That was not a Bluebell Bank she recognised. That was not home. And these were not the Cottons she had once held so dear.

Bluebell Bank was broken, the spell of her childhood shattered.

Chapter 21

Kate's anger sustained her for so long, but the rain penetrated her thin T-shirt and the combined effects of cold and shock soon made her shiver. Before long, she realised her cheeks were wet, not with rain as she had supposed, but with tears.

Of course it had all been too good to be true: Bluebell Bank, the rediscovered warmth of Emily's friendship, the rekindling of love with Luke. For a moment or two, back there in the caravan, in Luke's arms, she had imagined them to be both recreating something lost and building something new.

She hadn't even known what she was missing all those years without him; she had forgotten the intensity of their love.

Spoiled now.

Theirs was the sort of love all loves ought to be measured against, to always fall pitifully short. Now she felt its loss: a phantom, hollow ache like a missing piece of her.

The rain continued to fall, mixing with her tears and matting her hair. The night was dark and lonely. She heard the sound of tyres on the wet road behind her and quickened her pace. Of course it was Luke, pulling up behind her.

The pavement had given way to a narrow strip of verge and the trees framing the country road were dark, menacing. A pale, yellow moon shone overhead, with drifts of eerie, grey cloud floating across it. Luke leaned out of his truck window. 'Get in, Kate. At least let me give you a lift home.'

'Home? I don't have a home.' Kate knew she sounded bitter, melodramatic, but it was how she felt: abandoned, betrayed, with no one and nowhere to name her own. Just as she had started out in life – alone, with only herself to rely on – before she was spoiled and softened by the Cottons.

'You've been drinking,' she told Luke, hardening her tone and her defences. 'Go home. I'll walk. Obviously this has been a massive mistake.'

'I've only had a couple of beers,' Luke said softly. 'And it felt more like we were fixing a mistake than making one, at least to me it did.'

Kate scowled down the long road ahead of her and crossed her arms. She didn't want to let him get under her skin and his comment threatened to unravel her resolve. 'I'm going,' she said, and she wasn't entirely sure where she meant: Bluebell Bank, or New York.

'Kate—'

She stopped and rounded on him. 'Luke! Seriously, I just want to be alone. Go away. It's, like, a mile tops. I'll be fine.'

Luke struggled in indecision, unconvinced. 'No. I'm driving you back. You don't have to talk to me, but I can't just let you wander in the dark on your own in the middle of the night.' He leaned across to open the passenger door. Kate was torn – part of her wanted to revel in independence, to succumb to anger and hurt, muster a decent flounce, but also she didn't want him near her, couldn't bear his excuses.

Common sense prevailed as another bank of rainclouds rolled across the moon. The sky darkened and the rain fell more thickly and Kate surrendered, jumped into the truck without looking at him. He put the car in gear and threw her his jumper: a grey zip hoodie. Her chattering teeth gave her away. Kate put the sweater on and at once her senses were flooded by him. She closed her eyes and tried not to breathe, to think. She endured the rest of the journey to Bluebell Bank: the agony of Luke's closeness and the smell of him still on her, and the silent waves of hurt and disappointment rolling off him.

She didn't feel any better when they finally pulled up outside Bluebell Bank and she remembered Emily was within those walls.

Anger reared up, a thick and bitter taste on her tongue. Emily, who had professed to care, but had tried to take what was hers; then had stuck around to pick up the pieces when Kate's life shattered into a million fragments. Every hug, every sympathetic glance, every smile and murmur of consolation and reassurance of a brighter future just around the corner: all of it a big, fat lie, adding yet more layers of betrayal.

Luke seemed resigned to her silence. He cast her a last, regretful look as she jumped out of the truck; his eyes were glazed with remorse, all their blue fire dulled and doubtful now. 'Call me,' he said. 'Please.'

She did not reply, just tossed her ponytail and started up the drive to the sound of his truck departing. She made it to her bedroom before the tears came in a torrent once more. Thankfully everyone was in bed and Bluebell Bank lay in slumber.

Kate buried herself in freshly laundered candlewick for a storm of silent weeping. For the first time ever at Bluebell Bank she locked her doors against the Cottons.

Sleep eluded her, of course. And the rest of the long night became a grim and lonely place, a realm of dark shadows and darker thoughts: creeping and insidious and destroying everything in their wake. They swirled around her mind and sucked her under. Haunted and despairing, Kate tossed and turned, and toiled with the memories and imaginings, thoughts of Luke, Emily, Dan, her mother – all so mixed up she barely knew the truth of anything.

Those middle-of-the-night demons had a life and energy all of their own. Kate lay in her bed with an aching head and sank deeper into the pervading pall of misery until she didn't know what to do with herself and the urge to escape became a physical longing.

*

Emily felt the gnawing of some nameless anxiety as, yawning, she made tea for Lena at first light. Bracken was absent – still in the gentle care of Mike – and this little wrinkle in the fabric of the day was enough to disturb Lena's routine. She was fretful, and Emily knew there would be no stories this morning, no memory book moments.

Was her anxiety down to the absence of the dog? Her mind fast-forwarded to the time when his departure from Bluebell Bank would be permanent. She didn't want to think about Lena having to cope without Bracken. She drank her tea at the kitchen table, half her attention on her book, still vaguely unsettled. Lena was going on and on about being late for church – where she had not attended, to Emily's knowledge, in sixty years, except the occasional wedding or increasingly frequent funeral. Emily tried to tell her it was Monday, Lena's lifelong atheism having not cut it as a reasonable excuse for non-attendance.

She was casting about for a distraction from this pointless discussion, when the phone rang in the hall. At seven in the morning, this gave Emily a frisson of fear: Bracken? Or Dan calling to say it was time? Abby was two weeks from her due date, so it could be any day.

She crossed the hall and grabbed the receiver. She did not expect the dreadful, sleep-deprived sound of Luke Ross. 'Emily, I've messed up,' he said without preamble. 'I thought she already knew. I just wanted to apologise properly . . . to draw a line under the past, you know?'

'Luke,' Emily interrupted sternly, with growing dread. 'What are you talking about?'

'I'm sorry it's early. I waited as long as I could to call. I couldn't sleep. I was so worried she would do something stupid, like hop on a plane to New York and disappear again. I told her, Emily, about you and me. I thought she knew. I thought you'd told her, made her see it meant nothing—'

Emily closed her eyes and leaned against the wall. '*I* didn't tell her, Luke. How could I? She *needed* me. I couldn't have confessed to her that I was the cause of all her misery.' It felt so strange to be finally saying the words, and to Luke of all people, after so long of keeping quiet. The dread settled into solid ice in the pit of her stomach.

'You weren't the cause,' Luke said wretchedly. 'It was me. I told you, things had been weird. Kate was so preoccupied with preparing for uni, and her new friends. She didn't have time for us – you said so yourself – and then there was Dan. I was so afraid of competing with him for her affections that I gave her up, I practically pushed her into his arms.' His words came out in an uncharacteristic jumble.

The word *us* was too intimate for Emily, suggesting a collusion that hadn't existed; the kiss had been unplanned and much repented; she had tried to convince herself that made it somehow less terrible.

'Nothing actually happened between Kate and Dan,' Emily confessed, hating to admit her most egregious sin, which she had worked so hard to keep hidden. 'I only told you there was something going on to make you jealous . . . I'm so sorry, I don't know what I was thinking, Luke.'

'It did happen,' Luke said dully. 'She told me so. But only after I split up with her so that was my fault too.'

Emily was silent, thoughts churning. It didn't negate her own mistakes. But Kate had slept with Dan and kept it secret! Had she come back here and flirted and made Dan wonder even for a second? Anger reared its head; she hadn't expected that, only guilt for her own folly.

'If you had kissed anyone else but me,' she said. Or if it had just been the kiss and not what came after: all those little lies of omission. *And if not for the seed I unwittingly planted about Dan.* Or, in fact, the reality of Dan.

And if not for Kate, with her legacy of abandonment: fear of rejection at the core of her.

Emily's heart was beating fast. She was shattered and ashamed. She was also furious, with Kate *and* her brother. Something slotted into place now: a certain guardedness in Kate's eyes, the faint longing in Dan's.

Luke's words came back to her: *I was so worried she'd do something stupid, like hop on a plane to New York . . .*

'I was going to go after her,' Luke was saying, but his voice distant now, drowned by the cacophony of her frantic thoughts.

Emily closed her eyes. No, it must be her.

It hit her like a blow. New York. It was so exactly what Kate would do: put the source of her pain as far from her as possible.

'I bloody well love her,' Luke said, and that was the last Emily heard before she dropped the phone and sprinted up the stairs, panic finally breaking through the fog in her brain and reaching her muscles.

Kate would find this impossible to forgive.

As she ran, she clung to a thread of hope that she was not too late.

She should have cleared the air before now, when Kate first arrived and before she had the slightest inkling that Luke-bloody-Ross was back in town. Now Luke had decided he loved Kate again, but he would have to tell her that himself. Emily loved her too and the most pressing thing was to find her and let her know how sorry she was . . .

Emily's good intentions faded in a torment of fear that she would find Kate already gone. Had Kate ordered a taxi in the middle of the night to spirit her away from Bluebell Bank? She glanced out the window on the landing to confirm that Kate hadn't made off with Jasper.

She burst into Kate's room, devoid of its occupant as expected, only to be greeted by a sight both reassuring and terrifying: Kate's stuff was still there, packed into her suitcase, which stood expectantly by the door, her coat draped on top.

Kate was ready to run.

Chapter 22

Emily flew along the hall and into Noah's room. It was dark and Noah was sprawled inelegantly on his stomach, his face mashed into the pillow. She shook him vigorously.

He spluttered awake. 'Wha—?'

'Noah, I need you.'

Noah had barely blinked into consciousness before she was firing instructions at him for taking care of Lena and the shop. 'I need to go out.'

Noah rolled his eyes. 'Gee, thanks for the update. Couldn't you, like, leave me a note, or send me a text or something?' He slid beneath his covers again.

'I have to go find Kate.'

'Find her, is she lost?'

'I don't have time to explain. I'm going out. I'm not exactly sure where, or when I'll be back, but I need you to pay attention: you have to take care of Lena, and the wood burner is arriving at the shop today.'

Noah was looking at her sceptically, his sleep-dulled brain forming questions, but Emily was already spinning on her heel and heading for the door. 'Thanks, Noah. Oh, and you can't have Jasper, I might need him.'

She made a panicked circuit of the house, looping back and forth as she forgot things on the first lap. Clothes, a cursory wash, pulling on socks while hopping down the hall, searching for a trainer which she unearthed beneath the sofa, trying to school herself to calm so as not to alert Lena that anything was wrong.

She was out of the house in minutes. Without her stuff and with no transport there was a limit to how far Kate could have gone.

What might have seemed like overreaction to anyone else, was to Emily perfectly understandable in the context of Kate. When your childhood was solitary and dysfunctional, spent searching for scraps of love and security, any hint of emotional disturbance sparked anew that childish impulse to flee, to hide.

When things had been difficult once before, Kate had made a snap decision to flee to America; as she exited the house and began to search the grounds, Emily resolved not to let that happen again.

*

At the bottom of the garden a track meandered through the woods. At the point at which it was bisected by the stream there was a steep drop. Just past the footbridge, Lena had fashioned a rope swing over the bank to entertain her grandchildren, much to the chagrin of their mother, who fretted about the safety of the arrangement the first time she glimpsed it. Lena had assured her she would take it down and swore the children to secrecy. Over the next decade, the Cotton children continued to love this spot more than anywhere else in the grounds, even the whole of Galloway, and they continued to enjoy the rope swing without any dread calamity befalling them, save an occasional splashdown in the stream below. 'Luckily, you children bounce,' Lena had said sagely, on the occasion of a rather hard fall of Dan's, as she cleaned the grazes on his palms and shins. What story they had concocted for Melanie to explain away Dan's bruises, Kate couldn't remember.

But she *could* remember many a happy hour spent playing here well into their teens. This was where they came to light campfires and evade adult meddling.

It was here that Kate sought solace now. This was the place she had chosen to say her silent goodbyes to Bluebell Bank and the Cottons. Pausing by the old gnarly oak overhanging the stream, she knew she would be leaving, this time for good,

The swing swung still. The high bank afforded a quick, exhilarating drop, and she remembered the rope itself was tricky to master; knotted as it was into a single loop which was large enough only to accommodate one foot. Swinging off the bank was fun, but scrabbling back up was rather more difficult.

Kate had acquired the knack her first summer, encouraged by Dan's patient tuition as, time and again, he held the rope steady for her, caught her and pulled her to safety. This place was the site of Luke's first initiation into the Cotton clan on the night of her birthday bonfire – Fergus grinning and holding the rope out to Luke in challenge – and of Fergus's more inglorious moments; he was prone to showing off and landing ignominiously in the burn below.

Kate slid down the oak until her back was pressed against the trunk. She tipped her head back, staring upwards into a canopy of leaves. The memories pressed sharp here. The membrane was thin and she imagined she could hear them: Luke whooping with excitement, Emily helpless with laughter, Dan yelling as he got dunked trying to rescue clumsy Fergus; happy laughter as they lit the fire so the boys could dry themselves by the flames.

She twined her fingers in the grass woven through the roots of the big tree. She would miss this place. She found it hard to imagine a future in which she would never sit beneath this tree, never again hear the ghosts of her childhood speak to her from this spot.

Sometimes you didn't realise how precious a place was, how

every step in life was bearing you back there, until you arrived and breathed in its scent and felt its air on your skin.

But it was all ruined now. Nothing was quite as it should be.

Kate knew that Emily often returned to the favoured books of her childhood, comforted and reassured to find that the characters had not transformed between the pages in her absence; that they were as they had always been, waiting just for her: a place to drop anchor in a crazy, storm-tossed world. That was what Kate had expected from Bluebell Bank and its cast of characters: that they would have ceased to act independently once she closed the leaves of the book and trapped them within.

But they had jumped right out of the confines of the pages, living lives that confused Kate. How could they be her sanctuary, her solidity in this world, when each was struggling to find his own way?

Her throat ached but she could no longer cry. Old hurts and new churned in her mind.

The pain of Luke and Emily, of course, and a dull pang of regret for Dan. Even a brief lament for Ben. And an extra ache for her mother, who had tried for a decade to win her forgiveness but Kate had never let it be enough. She closed her eyes against the cheerful sun streaming through the leaves. Could she go back to New York, pretend none of this ever happened and pick up where she left off?

Or should she return to Edinburgh and finally make things right with Lily?

She had been irrevocably changed by this brief sojourn on the Solway. She fancied she fitted into neither world now, belonged nowhere.

She tried out the two versions of her future: eating sushi in her favourite restaurant with friends who couldn't know her the way Emily did, and whose lives would have moved on immeasurably this summer; or strolling in the Meadows with Lily, forging tentative peace.

Neither image fully fitted. Instead, she felt the sharpness of rock beneath her skin, the wind whipping her uncombed hair and Luke's laughter in her ear. His eyes, bright and warm and amused as he gazed down at her: the beach at St Ninian's Cave, when their future was so full of promise. If only she had realised how transient, how precious, those moments were.

Wallowing in her misery, she inhaled the scent of him, carried on his hoodie, which, inexplicably, she had been unable to take off. She smelled of him – she couldn't escape him at all.

Her mind flitted like a butterfly, unable to settle. Suddenly it was filled with Emily: thirteen years old and laughing with her in the dinghy, clutching the sides as it tipped alarmingly, her head thrown back, hair everywhere, eyes lit up and luminous with laughter.

Emily: the first person to show Kate her worth.

Then Emily was seventeen and her smiles were false, covering up her attempt to spirit Luke away. Anger tasted like bile. Emily had destroyed everything. Kate couldn't stay, ignore the fact that all afterwards was contaminated by that kiss. She had once lost Emily to Joe, but she had always believed that they would come back to each other. She was so ready for the email when it came. If she left now . . . but how could she not?

With malevolence at the heart of their friendship, they could not go on as if nothing had happened. Kate couldn't imagine wanting to speak to Emily ever again, but she also couldn't picture a world in which she wasn't Emily's best friend.

*

Emily found her. She was blundering through the trees, the snap and crack of twigs alerting Kate to her presence. As she stumbled into the clearing by the stream, cursing a thin branch that whipped back in her face, she glimpsed Kate wiping the last traces of tears with the cuffs of her over-large sweater.

She sagged with relief that she was not too late.

'There you are. I didn't think you could have gone far.' She went towards her, then thought better of it and stopped; she crouched some distance away on the dew-damp grass and studied Kate cautiously. 'So, Luke called.'

'Did he?' Kate's tone was flat.

'I saw your room. Suitcase packed and ready to go. Were you planning to say goodbye?'

Kate shrugged, not looking at her. 'I was planning to ask for a ride. If not you, then Dan.'

'I'm sure Dan wouldn't take much persuading to do your bidding,' Emily said caustically, then mentally kicked herself.

Kate's head snapped up. '*That's* what you have to say? A dig about my relationship with your brother?'

'I wasn't aware you *had* a relationship with my brother until Luke told me five minutes ago.' Emily knew she was saying this all wrong. Where were the heartfelt apologies and outpourings of emotion? Instead, she felt spiky, snarled up with anger of her own.

'I don't owe you an explanation. Luke maybe, but not you.' Kate drew up her legs and wrapped her arms around them, settling her chin on her knees. She turned her head away.

Emily's tone softened. 'Well, I owe *you* an explanation. And I'd really like it if you would put off running back to New York until you've heard what I've got to say.'

Kate's voice was muffled by her arms. 'Nothing you have to say could make a difference.'

'You don't know that. You came all this way . . .'

'Yeah, *stupid me*. I came all this way just to discover that you were the cause of my heartbreak. You tried to steal my boyfriend, then pretended to be just as baffled as I was when he dumped me! You patted me on the back and commiserated and you never said anything. I came all this way to find my best friend, and it turns out you were the one stabbing me in the back. Maybe you and he were seeing each other all along.'

'Don't be so dramatic! And stupid. Of course we weren't seeing each other.' A small measure of Emily's pent-up rage exploded, but she caught it in time, reined it in. Softly she said, 'OK, the bit about causing your heartbreak might be partly true. But it's not the whole story. And there are other things we have to talk about. Like Joe.'

Kate looked up, her eyes red-rimmed and determined. 'Why? Are you getting back with him? Did you find a modicum of self-respect left that he didn't completely destroy first time round? Going back to give him another shot at it?'

Emily winced. 'Just tell me you haven't booked a flight yet?'

Sigh. 'I haven't.'

'Then there's still time.'

Kate dropped her head onto her knees again. 'Time for what?'

'Time to talk. *Really* talk to each other. Come on, Kate, we'll take Jasper and go for a drive. I'll explain everything. Please, Kate, just a couple of hours out of your life, then you can do whatever you want.'

Kate shook herself, stood up and began to walk away with swift steps.

'That's right,' Emily yelled. 'Run away again, that's what you're good at.'

Kate stopped and her spine stiffened. She spun. 'Seems to me we're both pretty good at it.'

Emily gazed at her steadily. 'But we're not teenagers any more, Kate. We should have a proper discussion, like the grown-ups we are.'

Kate shook her head in despair. 'I can't, Em. I'm so angry at you right now.'

Emily took a deep breath. She was angry too; she hated to resort to emotional blackmail, but it seemed she had no choice. 'So you *are* going to run away? What about Noah, and Lena? How will I explain it to them? They need you too.'

They glared at each other. Emily's mobile rang. She swore

and rummaged in her jeans pocket to find it. She stabbed at the screen and held it to her ear. 'Yes!' she barked.

'Em, it's Dan.'

'I'm kind of busy, Dan. Can this wait?'

'Um, not really. Abby's in labour. We're just on our way to the hospital.'

'Seriously? Dan! Oh God, that's—'

'Crazy? Terrifying? Exciting? Yeah, all of the above. Listen, I have to go. I'll keep you guys posted. Are you with Noah and Kate?'

'Kate, yes. We were just . . . taking a walk. Noah's at the shop today and Lena's back home. I'll tell them what's going on. Well, except for Lena, I don't want her to get worked up before we actually know something. You want me to call Mum and Dad?'

'Not yet. No point getting them all excited either, not until there's a baby to celebrate. This could still take a while. I just wanted to share it with you. Listen, got to go, Abby is yelling at me—' He hung up.

Emily lowered the phone slowly. Kate was looking at her. 'The baby is coming,' Emily said in wonder, with a hint of triumph. 'So you can't leave.'

'The baby is coming *now*?'

'Yeah. My brother's actually having a baby! Well, in a manner of speaking.' It was strange, Emily thought. In other circumstances she would be throwing her arms around Kate. They would be jumping about like lunatics, sharing the crazy joy of it.

Kate sighed and rubbed her hands over her face. 'This doesn't change anything. I don't want to talk to you. I'm furious with you.' Her voice shook and Emily could see the pain in her eyes, feel her anger vibrating from her. If they were boys, they would have come to blows.

'I don't need you to talk,' Emily said. 'I need you to listen.' She stood up, brushed off the damp seat of her jeans. 'You can hate me all you want, but we both know you're not going to leave without a word to Lena and Noah, or without waiting for the baby to be born. So let's go.'

She began to walk away, half turning to check that Kate was following.

Kate hesitated. She felt tethered; there were too many points of attachment – Lena, Noah, Dan, Abby's baby – trapping her in this moment, forcing her to face up to the past instead of succumbing to the urge to run.

Fine, she would take a drive if that was what Emily wanted. But Emily might regret trying to make her stay; she didn't plan to hold back. And the second that baby pushed its way into the world she was gone.

Chapter 23

'So where are we going?' Kate leaned against the window looking away and feigning disinterest, but Emily could tell she was curious. They had been driving towards Newton Stewart in silence, both taking advantage of the respite to gather thoughts and garner arguments, both selfish and self-righteous in their anger. The car stewed and simmered with resentment and anticipation.

'First I'm going to fill the tank and get snacks,' Emily said briskly.

In the garage she perused a rack of CDs while she waited to pay. She experienced the usual jolt when she spotted Joe's face gazing down at her from the cover of his new album. His eyes were set deep in a melancholy, hollow-cheeked face. She touched the cover with her fingertips.

Emily knew the demons that lurked inside Joe; how he struggled to translate the feelings he captured with ease in his songs into something real. They had parted before his fame hit and the media wasn't remotely interested in her; she was his past, a nonentity, and she was happy to have it that way.

She had imagined she missed him, but she knew she only missed being loved. She did not want to be the girl wrapped around Joe when he was photographed leaving a nightclub, the paragraph tacked on to every interview; the splashy headline sensation next time he cheated with some minor celebrity or groupie who liked to kiss and tell. Emily left the CD to languish in its place – who bought CDs now anyway? – and continued to the desk to pay, feeling a sense of freedom wash over her.

Joe's hold on her was truly over.

*

Kate turned from the window to look at Emily as they headed along the coast road, picking up speed. Flashes of the Solway Firth, summer blue and sparkling with sunlight, drew her gaze. 'Aren't you going to get on with it: the *talking*?' She felt trapped now that she knew she couldn't immediately escape, but she was starting to relish the opportunity to have it out with Emily. Her mind hummed with a background track of words she had long wanted to say but never dared. One thing she was certain of, and she knew that in this her conviction would not waver: she was leaving as soon as was reasonably possible.

Any time Luke came into her mind – which was frequently – she felt the blade of betrayal pierce her heart anew and it hardened her resolve. The day unfurled before them, formless and unfilled. Kate itched for a plan, a place to be. 'We have ages,' Emily said recklessly. 'So where should we should start?'

Grudgingly, Kate said, 'The beginning, I guess. Tell me where we're going first. We can't go far; we might have to go to the hospital soon.'

'The hospital is in Dumfries,' Emily said, reaching for her sunglasses. 'We're heading in the right general direction, but babies take for ever to come. I thought we'd go for a hike.'

'A hike?'

'Yes.' Emily glanced at her then swiftly away; the vitriol in Kate's eyes hadn't faded. 'I used to moan about going on walks, but you always liked hiking in the forest park and we haven't done it since you got here, so . . .'

'Yeah, today's just the perfect time for visiting old haunts,' Kate said, slinking down in her seat and hunching her body against the window. She couldn't keep the sharp edge from her tone. Really, what was Emily thinking? That this was the moment for a gentle saunter in the hills, reliving old times and reminiscing, with Luke launched like a grenade between them? Or did she fancy that Kate would find it impossible to sever the ties that bound her here, that showing her the Solway of her youth was the perfect way to force her to reconnect to the landscape her heart still yearned for. A stroke of genius, perhaps.

'So where exactly are we hiking?'

'A hill we climbed once, just you and me.'

Kate remained in an argumentative frame of mind. 'Couldn't we just go to the beach or something?'

'We could, but is there a beach around here that *doesn't* remind you of Luke?'

Kate had to own that there was not. 'I'm wearing flip-flops,' she pointed out, waving one bare foot for emphasis.

'Do you suppose I didn't think of that? There are a couple of pairs of old hiking boots I keep in the back for when Lena and I walk the dog.' She smiled to herself; there wasn't an excuse Kate could invent that she wasn't equal to. They might never speak again afterwards, but she was quite determined they would speak today.

They settled into the drive, Kate thinking how strange it was that just a few hours ago she had been in bed with Luke, so ridiculously and perfectly happy. And now, her happiness had crumbled to dust; this wasn't how she had imagined spending the day after the night before.

Neither was hopping on a plane back to New York and, but for Abby going into labour, that's exactly what she'd be doing.

They parked the car in the shady car park at Glentrool. The

engine ticked quietly in the ensuing silence. Kate and Emily looked at each other. Then Emily opened her door and stepped out. She produced a battered pair of hiking boots which she handed to Kate along with some tatty socks. 'Put these on.'

Kate sighed and got out of the car. It was a beautiful day for hiking: warm and sunny, with a light breeze to keep it from getting too hot. She pulled on the socks and stuffed her feet into the ancient boots.

With a capable air, Emily began dividing up their supplies, handing Kate her share. 'I don't want anything,' Kate said.

Emily pressed them on her. 'Don't be silly, you can't climb a hill without taking—'

'Emily! This is ridiculous. Stop being all . . . normal, like this is just another hike. We came here for a reason and all you can do is obsess about *snacks*! If you want to talk, let's talk.'

Emily glanced around the car park; any other patrons had already headed up the hill and they were alone. 'Fine,' she snapped, locking Jasper and heading towards the trail with fast, purposeful steps.

Kate scurried after her. 'Do you mind telling me why exactly *you're* angry with *me*?' Kate felt like she was the one with the strongest claim on rage.

Emily rounded on her. 'Oh, I don't know, perhaps because you slept with my brother and didn't tell me, then came back here and messed with his head when he was all happy and settled, with a baby on the way. And because you were going to run away again, just like before. When you pissed off to America and left me.'

'OK, wait a minute. You went off with Joe and eloped before I left for America.'

'You always hated me being with Joe. You made no secret of it. I think you were jealous of how much we loved each other. You had lost Luke and . . .'

'Jealous? I think we've established where the jealousy lay. At least I didn't try to get Joe to sleep with me.'

Emily rounded on her. 'It was a kiss! And Joe wouldn't have, even if you had tried.'

There was silence as Kate processed the implication.

'Sorry,' Emily said, not sounding it at all. 'I didn't mean that.'

'You didn't mean to suggest that Luke was easy pickings?'

'Well, you were kind of distracted, neglecting him. But he loved you. It was always you. Even when . . .' Emily let the sentence drift; she hadn't meant to take attack as her best defence, but Kate had been culpable too and her injured air was infuriating.

'Luke didn't control me and I wasn't obsessed like you with Joe. Talk about an unhealthy relationship. Really, Emily, what were you thinking?' But Kate knew what Emily had been thinking: for the first time in her life with Joe she'd felt the power of her own attractiveness and it was a potent thing.

'This isn't about me and Joe,' Emily said. 'It's about Luke.'

'This I must hear. Go on then, give me your excuses. Apart from the fact you think I was neglecting him. How good of you to offer comfort.' Her sarcasm was cutting.

'I told Luke you liked Dan,' Emily confessed, braving Kate's further wrath in the interest of having it all said. 'I might have implied . . . no, I *did* imply that there was something going on.'

Kate stared at her and swallowed hard, a stillness settling between them that was worse than shouting. 'You deliberately set out to ruin my relationship with Luke.' This was more than just a kiss. This was premeditation, deliberate annihilation of her happiness.

'I . . .' Emily took a breath. 'I was horribly jealous, all right? Of you having Luke. All those summers he was there, and I liked him fine, but he took your attention away from me so at the same time I sort of hated him. And I was jealous that he loved you so much. No boy loved me, I'd barely even been kissed and you were living this epic, soaring love story. And you were popular, which I decidedly was not. You were off with someone else that holiday instead of coming to Bluebell Bank—'

'Emily,' Kate reproved sternly, still disbelieving that Em could have demolished her relationship with Luke and then kept silent all those years. All those tearful outpourings when Emily was the shoulder to cry on. 'No other friends ever really mattered to me. You were always the best. Luke didn't *replace* you. Nor did anyone else.'

The breath Emily drew was ragged, laced with pain. 'He paid me a little attention that night, and he needed me. He was lost without you and yes, it felt good that I could comfort him. I . . . I don't know why I kissed him, or let him kiss me. He was drunk—'

'Luke didn't drink back then.'

'He did that night. He was different, darker. We drowned our sorrows and talked about how much we both missed you. That's how it started, just talking and drinking, and I can't even pinpoint the moment it became something else.'

But that wasn't true; Emily well remembered the moment their kinship had transmuted into something more; flirting, kissing, then his mouth insistent on hers and Emily losing herself, losing every thread of conscience that tethered her to the self who wouldn't have dreamed of kissing Luke. She paused, put her hands on her hips and breathed hard. Her assault on the hill had left them both breathless. She faced Kate. 'That's everything,' she said. 'There isn't anything else. Now you know all the ways I betrayed you.' It was all said now, let the chips fall as they might. Emily felt something akin to relief, but she knew it would be short-lived.

It had been just a kiss. It had been astonishing, catching them both unawares, but just a kiss: a few moments of Luke's hands on her, and her senses drowning in longing. They had stopped before it became something worse, Luke ricocheting away from her as if she'd burned him, staring at her, his hand to his mouth, eyes narrowing in silent horror. Hating her for what they had done.

Emily closed her eyes and felt the imprint of his lips still, saw the look of anguish on his face. Even as she tried to absolve herself she knew that *she* had set the events in motion that night; she had made it happen but Luke had been ripe for it: teetering in his insecurity, missing Kate, doubting Kate's affections.

The kiss hadn't been the betrayal proper, *that* had come after: her silence, every comforting word and reassurance as Kate picked over the wreckage of her heartbreak.

She supported Kate through that lonely, heart-rending summer, when her quest for answers, for reasons, met with resounding silence from Luke.

It was unforgivable.

*

Kate's face was hard, her tone like steel. 'How did you know there was something between me and Dan? Nothing happened until after Luke ended things. I always had feelings for him of course, but . . .'

'I didn't really know. It was a horrible coincidence. If it helps, I don't think Luke believed me. He didn't really think you'd cheat.'

Kate shook her head. 'I didn't cheat, but it didn't take me long to run to Dan.' And, anyway, it didn't matter what she had done, only what Luke believed.

'Dan fell in love with you after that. And you left him too, you know. When you went off he was devastated.'

Kate swallowed. She dropped her head. Had Dan really been in love with her? Had she flirted and led him to believe . . .? Yes, of course; she had known it the moment she crossed the threshold of his farmhouse and set eyes on him. 'I treated Dan badly,' she admitted. 'But I don't know how you can think that I would ever want to cause him pain again. I swear to you, nothing has happened between us since I was eighteen.'

'But what's happened in his head? He's been crazy about you ever since.'

'I did *not* come here to upset things. I wouldn't do that. I told Dan as much.'

Emily narrowed her eyes. 'So you had a conversation about it? Did you give him hope?'

'No!'

Emily wouldn't let it go. 'But you and he flirted? Shared something? Even for a moment did you imagine him leaving Abby for you?'

'No! Emily, just . . . no. Once I found out he was married and that Abby was pregnant I knew that he was off limits.' But Kate felt a twang of conscience. Hadn't she revelled in her power over Dan, hadn't she, just for a second, wanted him to want her still, to flirt with her, to be conflicted because of her? Was that so different from what Emily had done with Luke? No, she would not make excuses for Emily. Or for herself.

A couple of walkers were coming down the track towards them. Kate and Emily fell silent and resumed walking, with careful, deliberate steps, smiling and murmuring a greeting as they passed. Once they had wandered out of sight, Emily put her hand on Kate's arm. Kate flinched and snatched it back, catching Emily's hurt expression as she withdrew the hand.

'I was just going to suggest we stop for a break. Over there.'

They found a place to sit on the sunny slope, gazing down over farmland towards the coast. Emily sat with her knees drawn up, taking comfort from the pose, her chin resting on the hard knobs of her kneecaps and her hair falling down around her face. When she spoke all the fight had gone from her voice. She said, 'He was kissing me and I was letting him, and then suddenly he stopped. He said your name. I . . . I wanted him to kiss me. I'm sorry, but that's just the truth. I *wanted* him to, and I tried to distract him from thinking about you. So I said you were probably with Dan anyway, and far too busy to be thinking about him. Luke was angry. His whole body went tight with fury. He got this look on his face, wild, a little crazy to be honest. Then . . . Are you sure you want to hear this?' Kate nodded grimly. 'He kissed me like he didn't even know I was there. It was weird and not at all romantic. He was angry with himself, angrier still with me. Immediately, I felt terrible. Afterwards, I thought we'd just be able to forget what had happened and put it behind us. I never expected Luke to take it so much to heart and have a complete crisis. When he broke up with you and didn't say a word about the kiss or what I had said about Dan—'

'That's Luke for you. He's like me, avoids confrontation like the plague.' Kate frowned. 'So, I guess you saw the perfect opportunity to get away with it?'

'No!' Emily was horrified. She shook her head emphatically. 'It wasn't like that. Except . . . I suppose self-preservation did kick in. I couldn't believe how close I had come to ruining everything and I didn't want to lose you. It was selfish, I'm not condoning what Luke and I did. Especially me.' Emily raised her head and squared her shoulders, tossing her mass of curls impatiently. 'I should have told you, I wanted to, but I also didn't want you to know what I had done, what I was. But, Kate, it was ten years ago and I regret it more than you can imagine. It was a terrible thing, but . . . well, I think you should forgive me. Forgive *us*.' She finished in a fierce, stubborn rush, and splayed her hands, palms up. That was all she had, Kate could do with it as she wanted.

She held her breath as she watched myriad emotions flit across Kate's face. The moment trembled with possibility, then Kate's eyes turned hard with hurt. 'You tried to take him from me. He was all I wanted and you tried to take him. I don't know if I *can* forgive either of you.'

Chapter 24

Kate lay back and tipped her head to the sky. Above her was a vastness of blue and the rounded tops of the hills stretching beyond the waving branches of the forest. Staying so intensely angry was exhausting and she found it ebbed and flowed like a tide, sometimes fading to a dull throb of hurt.

She might not be able to forgive Emily, but there were still a few things she had to know. 'About Joe . . .' she said, turning her head and glancing at Emily who had retreated behind her hair and sunglasses and was staring morosely out at the landscape as if it pleased her not at all. Kate suspected there was more to the Joe story than Emily had so far confided.

'What else can you possibly know? I already told you things weren't like I imagined. It was awful. I left. We divorced. What else is there?'

'Tell me how he made you feel, how he made you like this? I want to understand.'

That got a reaction, a swift head-turn. 'Like *what*?'

'Like half a person. Scared of the world and everything that's to come. I found you hiding out in that bookshop going nowhere, Em. You didn't even look like yourself.'

'And now . . .'

'And now, there have been glimpses of the Em I know and—' She stopped abruptly and felt the rush of tears thickening her throat. She wondered if Emily was crying behind her dark glasses. Her own anger had morphed into inescapable sadness, so acute she felt sick. The loss of Emily and Luke simultaneously was like a severed limb, something she might learn to accept, but would never fully recover from.

Emily spoke softly. 'He made me feel exactly that, like half a person. I didn't know who I was and I would have gone on tying myself in knots trying to please him. I overlooked his affairs because I always thought he would change. Or maybe I just believed it was what I deserved . . . I don't know. Bronwyn was different. She was so young. They lost me my job and my self-respect. I knew it was time to draw a line, even though it took me too long to get around to finally doing it.'

Kate frowned.

'He left me broken and I had to rebuild myself. It's been a long road back.'

'Emily, you *are* over him, aren't you?'

A quick, guilty glance. Emily removed the sunglasses and met Kate's eyes and, yes, they shimmered with tears that trembled on the edge of her lashes but did not fall. 'I'm so sick of crying over him.' She smiled and dashed at her eyes. 'I've been speaking to him, Kate. I . . . Like I said, I was relieved at first that we were over. But, after a while, I felt terrible. Some days I literally couldn't make myself get out of bed. I had moved in with Lena, but I felt so bad, Kate. And then, one day I called him and hearing his voice gave me a lift. I felt better for a while. I wanted more. Then you came and everything was different. I managed to wean myself off.' She stopped to catch her breath, turned and took hold of Kate's arm, her face fearful. 'That's why you *can't* leave again. Not over something stupid I did a decade ago. I was scared of losing you then and I still am. I don't know how to do this without you.'

'Do what?'

'The shop. Life. Everything. I was scared all the time before you came.'

Kate exhaled. 'You haven't noticed the change in you, but I have. You're a different person from the girl I found hiding in that mouldy bookshop when I arrived. You're strong, capable. You've done so much of this yourself. I was only here to guide you a bit. Now you can do it by yourself.'

'I don't want to,' Emily said emphatically. 'I thought I was so mad at you, but now all I can think is how awful it will be if you go.'

Kate pressed the heels of her hands to her eyes. 'I have to go, Emily. I can't stay now.' She was almost shouting again. 'You'll make a success of things. Now you know you don't need Joe. And you don't need me either.'

Emily thought how fragile was her recovery, how it had felt – until quite recently – as if the only thing that could ease her mind was the sound of his voice. How she had craved hearing him sing her song one more time. And now Kate would leave and Emily's guilt and doubt would fester and destroy everything.

At least you didn't have kids, Kate had said, when Emily was explaining the break-up. As if it had therefore been a clean break, a neat incision bisecting the shared parts of their lives and separating them from one another like a scalpel through flesh. Emily flinched and thought of Abby in the hospital, pushing a tiny life out of her, making a future for her and Dan that could never be dissolved.

The silence of the woods behind them became oppressive and Emily leapt to her feet. 'Let's go on.'

*

Near the summit, over an hour later, they paused for another break. Emily selected a spot where the valley uncurled, resplendent, before them and the last curve of the hill loomed at their backs. Gazing down at the bluish blur of the firth on the horizon and the stone-scattered velvet slopes, Kate smiled at Emily's choice; for surely any more cross words or hint of confrontation would seem out of place amongst the waving grass and the dense bracken, against a backdrop of so much sky: pale, pale blue and impossibly vast, with mallow-soft clouds gently scudding by.

Kate had been mulling things over the entire way up the hill. A part of her wanted to forgive Emily and ask forgiveness in return – they had both said things they did not mean. No, they had said things they meant exactly, things they ought to have aired long before. And that was good, cathartic even; but Kate just couldn't get past the image of Emily and Luke together, and the concern on Emily's face in those subsequent days as Kate begged Luke to tell her what she had done and appealed to Emily to know why she was suddenly unlovable.

She even tried making excuses for Emily – she had responded to Luke's attentions, acted on jealousy and the instincts of an overly romantic girl who had never been loved the way she craved. She hadn't wanted Luke, she had wanted what Luke represented.

'I suppose I know that you didn't set out to hurt me,' Kate said eventually. 'You acted on the spur of the moment. I can get past you kissing Luke, I think. But what happened afterwards makes our whole friendship seem like a lie.'

Emily nodded. 'I know. I was a coward. I should have just told you. You'd have hated me for a while, but you would probably have forgiven me eventually. I am sorry, Kate, for what it's worth.'

'I'm sorry too. For ignoring you and Luke and acting above myself – I know I was doing that. I wasn't sympathetic even though I could see how much you were struggling with everything back then. I neglected you and I could have been a better friend.'

Emily's face brightened, a ray of hope dawning in her eyes. 'Does this mean . . .'

Kate sighed and let several seconds tick past, the breeze catching her hair and blowing strands across her vision. 'No, Em. It doesn't mean anything. It means I still need to go home.'

Emily raised an eyebrow. She tried to push down the hurt, stifled the arguments that rose in her throat; Kate's words held a note of finality she knew she couldn't quash. She would sound pathetic if she tried. 'But where is home, exactly?'

Kate looked at her, bewilderment showing on her face. It was the first time, since those dark days of Luke, that she had seen Kate so utterly confused. Emily was used to being the weak one, the one who couldn't cope while Kate marched on capably. She considered what Kate had said, that she, Emily, had changed and could manage just fine on her own now. Yes, she decided, she probably could. But that didn't mean she wanted to.

'New York?' she suggested. 'Ben?'

'No. I don't think I should be looking backwards any more. I think I've learned that the hard way.'

God it hurt, Kate's dismissal of all this had meant. The Solway, the bookshop, Luke, Emily: all batted away with a flick of her hand and now she was ready to move on to the next thing. She pictured Kate getting on a plane and not looking back, and it pained her more than she would have thought possible.

She thought of Luke saying, *I bloody love her, Emily*, and she thought of waste and lost time. How could one misstep ruin everything?

'If not New York,' Emily said, more calmly than she felt, 'then where?'

'I didn't say not New York. I said not Ben. I was also thinking about Edinburgh, my mother.'

That wasn't so bad; Edinburgh was only a couple of hours' drive from here. But it wasn't the distance, it was what leaving symbolised. If Kate walked away she would sever all ties. Or worse, Em would be reduced to a Facebook acquaintance, allowed glimpses into her life which told her nothing at all.

'If you can't forgive me,' she tried one last tack, 'can't you try to forgive Luke? He was the one who was drunk, and . . .' She stopped short of telling Kate Luke loved her; that should come from him. If he ever got the chance now.

Kate shook her head. 'I think we just got caught up in a memory, a moment of madness based on how we *used* to feel rather than how we feel now. I'm not sure you can go back and recreate the past, not really. Maybe it should stay as it was: a memory of a magical time.'

Emily sighed and felt hope sink like a stone.

Chapter 25

They reached the summit, but neither could take pleasure in the view. Sombrely, they began their descent again.

'I think it's good you're thinking of going to see your mother,' Emily said, without a great deal of enthusiasm. Any conversation was better than none, a chance to prolong the agony of departure, and they were stuck together for now anyway; but all conversations were tarnished and dull now.

'I don't know if we'll ever have a relationship,' Kate said, knowing she sounded hard. 'I just think it's something I should do. My duty.'

Emily frowned. 'But why, if you don't think it will work? I don't understand. Maybe you should give it a proper chance. After all, it's been a long time.'

Kate fixed her eyes on the path unfolding stone by stone in front of her. It was the only way she could keep her fury from erupting. What did Emily know about it? With her perfect family who cared for her and parents who only drank the occasional glass of wine. Emily might have been on the periphery of the chaos that comprised Kate's childhood but observing wasn't the same as living it.

The truth was Kate was scared. Of loving her mother, and

of loving Luke. Paralysed by the fear of losing them all over again. The memory of past heartbreak was so acute she would do anything to avoid feeling that way again. Even give up on second chances.

Emily's words came tumbling out, as if she couldn't hold them back but was a little fearful of their impact. 'The trouble with you is that everything is black and white in your world. It's like, one tiny inkblot on a page and the entire book is ruined. You think if something isn't precisely perfect, all the time, then it's not worth anything. But people are flawed, Kate. Sometimes those flaws make us *more* able to love them. Take your mother—'

Kate's tone was chilly. 'I'd rather not.'

'Well, it's about time we did.' Emily looked braver now, and her voice was impassioned 'You know that her problems were the result of mental illness, don't you? She didn't choose to be a terrible mother.'

Kate maintained an iron grip on her emotions. 'Do you suppose I don't know that she was ill? It doesn't change anything. Not the things she did. Or the things she didn't do.'

'Of course it does. What about Lena? Would you hold her responsible for her actions if they were directly attributable to her Alzheimer's, or would you make allowances for her?'

'That's not the same thing at all.'

'Yes. It is.'

'Let it go, Emily,' Kate said warningly.

'We've never discussed it before,' Emily said with an air of having nothing to lose. 'Why not now?'

'There's a reason we haven't talked about her.'

'Yes, because you're scared.'

'I am *not* scared.' She knew that to be a lie, but she wasn't ready to admit it to Emily, who had only pretended to love her. 'It's because there's no point. You think if I forgive my mother suddenly my whole life will fall into place? It's not that simple. As it happens, I forgave her a long time ago, but . . .'

Emily nodded, getting it. 'But knowing something intellectually isn't the same as feeling it.'

Kate looked at her, surprised. 'Exactly.' She frowned and felt the confession drawn out of her. 'I look at her and I *know* that she's my mother and I admire how she's turned her life around but . . . honestly, Em, I feel nothing. Nothing. What does that say about me?'

Emily's tone softened. 'Nothing bad.'

'So why do I feel so empty?'

'Because your childhood was shit, whatever way you look at it. It shouldn't have been that way, but I think it's OK to feel . . . *whatever* you feel. Whether you choose to have a relationship with your mother is entirely a matter for you, but I think you want to. *Don't* you want to?'

There was silence, save their footsteps on the gravelly path that wove down towards the tree line. Kate whispered something, then cleared her throat and her voice grew steadier, louder. 'Yes. Yes, I think I do. Luke said he regrets not fixing things with his father before he died. Now it's too late. I guess I don't want that to happen with me and Mum.'

It was the first time Emily had ever heard Kate use that appellation. Usually she was so clinical and detached: my mother, or just Lily, when she referred directly to her at all, which was not often. Kate swiftly clammed up again and quickened her pace, stretching away from Emily a little.

Emily let her go. She had plenty to think about too and perhaps a little space was what they both needed now.

*

Emily was despondent as she walked the rest of the way alone, seeing Kate's T-shirt as occasional flashes of colour ahead. She closed her eyes and might have been ten years old, sitting with Kate that first day at the art table, paintbrushes colliding, Kate ducking her head when anyone spoke to her. She was a timid mouse of a girl, thin and pale and unobtrusive, arriving unexpectedly in the class in the middle of term when her mother fled yet another disastrous relationship and the resulting moonlit flit landed Kate in Edinburgh in a dingy tenement flat and, most fortuitously, in Emily's class.

Emily had been drawn to her even then. In that moment – with Kate apologising for clashing brushes enroute to the water pot – she had known on some deep, subconscious level she could not have explained, that Kate needed her.

And she, Emily, needed Kate right back.

When she reached Jasper, Kate was leaning against his dusty side waiting for her. She was drinking from one of the water bottles. 'What now?' Emily said.

Kate shrugged. 'I guess we go back to Bluebell Bank and wait.'

Wait for the baby to arrive. Wait for Kate's opportunity to leave.

'We have the whole day,' Emily said hastily. 'Let's spend it together. Even if it's the last one.' Kate seemed to be considering this. Emily worried it might seem a morbid concept to her. 'I'm about to become an aunt,' she pressed. 'It's a special day. A day to do something out of the ordinary. What's still on your Solway bucket list?'

Kate dug in her shorts pocket and produced a crumpled piece of paper. 'I have an actual list,' she said.

Emily rolled her eyes. 'I would expect nothing less.' She pored over the list. 'Right,' she said, eventually. 'Let's go and tick some more things off. Then we'll always remember what we were doing the day my niece or nephew was born. I just want to say, and then I'll shut up about it, I promise, that I really am sorry for how things happened. I wish everything could be different.'

'No point wishing, Em,' said Kate, ever practical. It had never seemed like such a curse before. It felt emphatic and sickening, this line she had drawn beneath Luke and Emily and her second chance at happiness. As if the line, once drawn, couldn't be erased, even if she wanted it to be.

'I would never let you down again.'

Kate's smile, as she borrowed Luke's words, was sad. 'Never is a long time.'

'I know you said you were certain you and Luke are over, but—'

Kate closed her eyes. 'Emily, please, can we not talk about him any more?'

'Sorry, but I just want to tell you – in case you really can't see it for yourself – that he's your *fucking soulmate*.'

Kate dismissed this promptly. 'Your idea of soulmates is kind of skewed so forgive me if I don't buy that. Plus, if we were soulmates it would have worked out.'

'Maybe not, maybe you weren't ready. You know, I think *I* have my eye on someone.' Perhaps, Emily thought, she could hook Kate with confidences, like they were fourteen again and whispering secrets behind the pages of *Just Seventeen*.

'You know, I really don't think this is a good idea. I should head back and check out flights.'

'No! Look, it's just a quick walk at Sandyhills, then fish and chips in Kirkcudbright.' Emily's tone went from desperate to wheedling.

Kate relented. 'Well, I guess you'd better tell me about Mike as we drive then.'

'How did you know I meant Mike?'

'You are completely unsubtle, Emily. It's written all over your face when you say his name.'

Emily tilted her chin. 'I like to think I'm an enigma. Dark and mysterious.'

Kate snorted. 'Nope. Definitely no mystery. You're an open book, Em.' The palpable untruth of her words lay bare between them, unsettling. If she was an open book, Kate thought, then she'd have known the dark truth Emily harboured. She'd have sensed her betrayal. Maybe Emily was more of an enigma than

Kate had ever realised. And maybe their friendship hadn't been built on such solid foundations after all, since they had both kept such secrets concealed: Emily and Luke; Kate and Dan. Truths rankling, slowly turning sour.

Chapter 26

The day held a melancholy note of finality, much as Emily tried to pretend it wasn't the last time they'd eat lunch together, the last walk on the beach with sand spilling through their toes and the soothing whoosh of the ocean at their backs, the last road trip arguing over music choices, Kate's feet propped on the dashboard.

She waited, lounging against a bench outside the shop while Kate went in to buy ice creams. The car park thronged around her with sun-weary people heading home after a long day at the beach. Towels and buckets and spades and other seaside debris were juggled and spilled; recalcitrant toddlers evaded grasping hands to run ahead on chubby, determined legs; a group of mooching teenage boys in baggy shorts carried a football and jostled each other, and a gaggle of girls with glossy hair and spindly legs pretended not to notice them, as they flipped their hair and laughed and passed their phones around; elderly couples sauntered along in wide-brimmed sun hats and slacks, bearing deckchairs and hampers and old-school beach paraphernalia. Emily watched this little slice of the world go by for a moment. She wished there were words to change Kate's mind. She racked her brain for them but she couldn't get past *I'm sorry* which clearly was inadequate. It came back, she thought, to Kate's inability to accept anyone or anything that was imperfect. Including herself. In this, as in so much else, Lily had a great deal to answer for.

Or maybe it was just enough that Emily had kissed her best friend's boyfriend, which everyone knew was a cardinal sin, and she deserved to be cast out of Kate's life for it.

Picking at the remnants of her nail polish, she sighed and dialled her brother's number.

Noah answered quickly. 'Hey Em. Where are you?'

'We're at Sandyhills. We had lunch in Kipford and walked round the shore to Rockcliffe, then on here. Have you heard from Dan?'

'Nope.'

'Me neither. I wish the baby would hurry up. I'm so excited to meet it.' This was only half the truth; she hoped it wouldn't come yet, because the baby's arrival meant Kate's departure. And, also, a baby would be real and an incontrovertible change in the way the bump had not; Emily was afraid of all those disquieting feelings she'd experienced around Abby and her growing pregnancy, scared of how they might come rushing to the fore and prevent her loving the child, show her most hideous face to the world. Jealousy had got her into such trouble before . . .

'So, the stove arrived at the shop fine.'

'Great, thank you, Noah. I'm sorry for dumping that on you as well. And I didn't even think about the farm.' She had been so preoccupied with making Kate linger just long enough to listen. For all the good it had done.

'It's fine, Niall from Stoneburn Farm came over to look after the place today. He and Dan had it all arranged. I'll head over and give him a hand with milking, but . . .' Emily could almost hear her brother's casual, teenagey shrug. 'It's all under control.'

'And Lena: is she OK? I thought she seemed off this morning.'

'Yeah. She's all right. I know what you mean, though. But we had lunch together and went for a walk this afternoon. It was nice. I don't usually spend time just me and her. Is Kate OK?'

Emily watched Kate negotiate the steps from the shop and gracefully dodge the folk in her way, ice creams already dripping down one hand. 'She's fine. We're on a pilgrimage of sorts. Revisiting all the old places we haven't been back to yet. It's nice.' She was aware she sounded flat and hoped Noah wasn't perspicacious enough to pick up on it. 'If you're OK holding the fort at Bluebell Bank, we might not be home until late.' She thought about telling Noah the truth, but he'd be sure to take Kate's side and he was too young to be balanced. Or maybe her sin really was that offensive and she'd just have to accept people's condemnation for it for ever more. It would become part of her and it would define her.

Emily quickly took hold of her maudlin thoughts and gave herself a mental shake.

There was a casual pride in Noah's voice at being left in charge. 'No worries,' he said. 'I might catch up with Becca later on.'

'I don't think you should leave Lena alone,' Emily objected, filled with a dull sense of foreboding she couldn't quite explain. 'Without Bracken she seems so lost.'

'I won't be gone long, Em. Don't worry. Lena will be fine for an hour.'

'OK. Maybe by the time we get home there will be baby news.'

'I guess we'll all go up to the hospital tomorrow to visit. Dan gave in and called Mum and Dad earlier and they've phoned me, like, five times this afternoon. They're practically bursting.'

'It's a big deal,' Emily said. 'First grandchild.'

'Yeah, I guess. I don't see what all the fuss is about babies.'

'Wait until you meet this one. I bet you'll be smitten immediately. I can see you as a doting uncle.'

'Hmm,' Noah said doubtfully. 'You think having a kid will mellow Dan out a bit? He and I still aren't speaking.'

'All that won't matter once the baby is born,' Emily said, playing confidence in this unborn baby's role as peacemaker, righter of all wrongs, hoping she too would set eyes on it and be smitten, cured of her covetousness. Kate reached her, brandishing two cones and licking ice cream from her thumb. 'Gotta go, Noah. See you later.'

'Yeah, later, Ems.'

'Everything all right?' Kate swirled strawberry ice cream into a point with her tongue, catching the drips.

Emily tasted hers and nodded. 'Fine. Noah's pretending to be all laid-back about everything, but I can tell he's happy being left in charge. *And* excited about the baby, though he won't admit it.'

'I'm excited about the baby too,' Kate replied. 'Though I can't quite wrap my head around the idea of Dan as a dad, can you?'

'My nutty big brother? Of course not.' Emily cast Kate an uncertain glance. 'It is weird for you? I mean, if I found out Joe was married and having a kid . . .'

'No, no. Nothing like that. Dan and I were never properly together. I mean, I'll always care about him, but . . .'

'But Abby doesn't have to be worried.'

Kate stared. 'No, Em. I told you, of course not.'

'Didn't it even cross your mind? I mean, love makes us do crazy things sometimes, doesn't it?' They began walking along the wooden decking back towards the sand. It was past five now and the beach was emptying: people heading back to holiday cottages and caravans for their tea. Emily liked the beach best in the evening. The sand was soft and cool; she kicked off her shoes and carried them in one hand, and Kate did the same, dangling her flip-flops. 'So, we'll stop at the chippie in Kirkcudbright on our way home? We'll have worked up an appetite by the time we've walked back to the car.'

'Sounds good, Em.'

Kate demolished the last of her ice cream in a bite and crunched the cone. There was a vague Luke-ache somewhere deep in her belly and now a hollow sort of feeling about Dan. 'I suppose,' she said, since Emily had been scrupulously honest with her about Luke – even the bits Kate didn't really want to hear. 'I suppose the thought crossed my mind. I mean, I always half thought of Dan as mine.'

'He was yours. He'd have done anything for you. He didn't stop pining for you until he met Abs. I didn't know that was what was wrong with him of course, but it makes sense now. I knew he had a massive crush on you when we were kids but I never realised you reciprocated. He was a mess when you left.'

'Oh don't say that.' Kate didn't like the responsibility of other people's feelings. Far better to think that she had been easily forgotten when she slipped out of the Cotton orbit for all those years.

She thought of Luke again – her mind circling back to him. She'd have to call him and tie up loose ends. That was one thing: she wouldn't flee leaving any uncertainty behind her. Regret, perhaps, but not uncertainty.

She'd tell him that it was over. Properly, definitively, for ever. She'd tell him she didn't know where she was supposed to be and there was so much unfinished business between her and Lily . . .

No, she wouldn't use her mother as an excuse; it might give him reason to hope. She'd tell him she didn't love him.

But again, no; that would be a lie and she couldn't leave on an untruth. She had feelings for him but it would never work because she couldn't get past what happened with Emily. That was the truth.

Or, her feelings were the fond, old-flame sort and their relationship was best relegated to the realm of reminiscing. Not exactly true, but plausible.

She groaned inwardly; she hadn't got a clue what she was going to tell him.

Then there were other loose ends to be tied: Dan, Lena, Noah.

Dan would be lost in new baby euphoria and would barely notice her departure, surely? She'd duck out of his life and leave him to be happy. What had happened between them – or not happened, or almost happened, she wasn't sure – was a blip, a moment. The memory of old feelings tainting the present. A fleeting what-if. She was supremely glad it hadn't amounted to more than that.

Noah she would stay in touch with, but she'd swear him to secrecy. She wanted to be there for him as he navigated the difficult choices ahead of him, and none of the Cottons really understood him.

Lena she would bid goodbye fondly, wondering if the other woman really knew who she was at all. It might be easier if she didn't. It would be the most poignant farewell of the lot because it would be the last time she would ever see Lena.

But, wait; that implied she was keeping some part of her open to the possibility of a return to the rest of the Cottons at some point in the future. She needed to shut that down immediately and accept that when she left she left for good. A fresh start, reinventing herself again. She was good at that. Was the sense of freedom she felt liberating, or just terrifying? She couldn't quite decide.

And then Lily. Maybe.

Choices. The summer was running out on her too fast. It was July and she'd expected to have another month at least; lately she'd even wondered if she'd be tempted into staying longer. Not now.

She had promised Emily she would stay for the bookshop launch but she wasn't beholden to her promises any more.

For the briefest second she allowed herself to slip into a daydream of Luke, the two of them creating something wonderful and new together, despite the odds of distance and history so stacked against them. And she and Emily working side by side in the bookshop. Then she firmly shook her head to dispel the dream.

*

It was mostly dark. The harbour gleamed blackly in the lights. The car was cosy and the atmosphere soporific; Kate was full of fish and chips and fresh air, and she felt close to falling asleep, curled up in her seat while the radio played a meandering song, loose and acoustic. Emily's eyes were open, but she was deep in thought, staring unseeingly into the distance.

At least you didn't have children together. Kate's words again.

She focused now on the dark shapes of boats bobbing in the harbour, trying to breathe, remembering the pale blue lines on the plastic strip, her heart's wild leap of joy and Joe's wide-eyed horror. A festival: long summer nights, music, dancing, cheap beer.

She turned to Kate. 'I want to tell you something.' Her voice was close to Kate's ear. She curled herself towards Kate, mirroring her.

'Mmm,' Kate murmured, drowsy.

'I want you to understand what made me run away and marry him. I know you've always wondered.'

'It confused me,' Kate admitted sleepily, her eyelids batting open with slow, heavy blinks. 'Especially only a few months after An—' She checked herself. 'After he was unfaithful.'

'It was simple. He asked me. I felt wanted, worthwhile. And . . . there was a baby. I was pregnant. I suppose I got carried away by this crazy idea of a family.'

Kate listened to the echoing depths of her silence. It throbbed like a heartbeat. Then her fingers wrapped around Emily's. She stared at Emily, curled like a comma, foetal, vulnerable, and saw, for a split second, a completely different Emily: someone's mother. 'What happened?' she whispered, in awe.

Emily's smile was fleeting. 'My dream lasted only hours. Until I told him. He wanted me to get rid of it. I refused. Days of arguments and recriminations; Joe said he just wanted to be married to me, wanted our lives to be carefree and fun. He didn't want to be encumbered. And then . . . I lost the baby anyway.'

She remembered the aftermath: feeling bloodless and boneless and so terribly tired, unable to care for anything, least of all herself. She remembered a clinging fog of nothingness, where nothing mattered and she had just enough self-preservation to cling to Joe.

'Do you see, Kate? I wasn't acting entirely without thought when I married him. I was thinking of our baby. Our future.' A baby who would be a person by now. A person who might have changed everything.

'Em,' Kate began.

'You don't have to feel sorry for me.'

'But—'

'I didn't tell you to make you feel sorry for me, or so you would stay. I told you because I don't want there to be any more secrets between us. And because I had to say the words to someone before Dan and Abby's baby comes.' She felt the surge of tears like the expectant swell of an orchestra before crescendo, felt them flow unfettered, releasing her from the terrible, long spell of silence, washing away the last vestiges of Joe and all her pent-up feelings of unworthiness. 'I've been so terribly envious,' she gasped through her sobs. 'Every time I look at Abby I feel wretched, but I don't want to feel that way. I want to love her baby. I want to be free of this.'

'Oh, Em.' Kate wrapped her arms around Emily and held her tightly. It felt like Emily's sobs were too much for her, too much for the confines of the car to contain. They shuddered together with the violence of them.

Eventually, Emily quieted. She pulled out of Kate's embrace and smiled wanly. Now the words were out she did indeed feel free. All those months of tight smiles and pretence and feeling like a horrible person for resenting Abby's every twinge and tired smile.

She turned the key in the ignition. 'We should go.'

'I'll drive,' Kate said.

'I'm fine.'

'No, you're not, but you will be. You're strong, Em. But also completely mad. I don't know how or why you kept all that to yourself. You must have felt like screaming half the time.'

'Pretty much. But I unloaded enough on you whenever you walked through the door of my bookshop. I couldn't land all that on you as well. I thought if I pretended it wasn't real, the feelings would go away.'

They switched seats without getting out of the car, crawling over and under one another, tangling limbs. 'And how did that work out for you?'

Emily grinned. 'Not so well.'

'Would you consider getting help? Counselling or something.'

Emily raised an eyebrow. 'Would you?'

Kate smirked. 'Fair point.' She reversed Jasper out of the parking space. 'Shall we go back? We can't hang around all night on the off chance of a phone call from the hospital. Likely if the baby comes during the night they won't want you to visit until the morning anyway.'

'Us,' Emily said.

'What?'

'*Us*, not me.'

Kate tried to imagine visiting the hospital, witnessing the intimacy between the three of them, thought of how close she and Dan had come to ruin . . . 'No,' she said, furrowing her brow. 'I don't think so.'

Emily was watching her closely. 'You're allowed to say it, you know.'

'Say what?'

'That you still have feelings for him. That it's hard to see him happy with Abby.'

'No,' Kate said. 'I don't think I am allowed to say that. I don't think I'm even allowed to think it.' She cast a fleeting look at Emily in the passenger seat and in that second they seemed equally broken.

Chapter 27

Exhausted by her confession, Emily snoozed in the passenger seat as Kate drove, but Kate didn't mind; she was quite happy to be alone with her thoughts for a while.

Their absence from Bluebell Bank had filled them both with a vague aura of perturbation: a shapeless anxiety as if they needed to return quickly to restore the natural order of things. She urged Jasper faster, consumed with the inexplicable need to get home, trying not to mind that Bluebell Bank couldn't be – perhaps had never truly been – her home. She felt, for all the physical distance she had put between herself and her past, like the Kate of the dirty tenement and careless mother. Which was ridiculous, as the tenement was long gone and Lily had – apparently; Kate had yet to confirm this for herself – been sober for half a decade.

Lena was alone and that was impetus enough to drive Kate's foot down on the accelerator.

No Emily, no Bracken. Having lived so many decades alone, operating to her own timetables, it must have been challenging for Lena to accept Emily's eruption into her otherwise peaceful, settled life; but since her illness, time had ceased to have meaning for Lena; without Emily to regulate the days, to root her schedule in the routines of another, where would she be? She needed Em's brisk pragmatism, the jaunty Sharpie lists and messages. Now she was as defenceless as a child.

Kate wondered if Emily felt Lena's dependence weighing on her. As they had pulled out of Kirkcudbright and headed for Wigtown, Emily had bemoaned the fact that Noah would not know Lena well enough to play the nightly game of Scrabble before bed; Kate had watched them night after night, while sketching and listening to the radio. She had been amazed at Emily's patience in the face of Lena's frustration when she took too long to come up with a word only to discover, as she began to lay out the tiles, that she didn't have the correct letters after all. Perhaps Noah wouldn't know how to make Lena's cup of tea the way she liked it, black as tar and sickly sweet.

Kate thought Emily should give Noah more credit and told her so. 'Perhaps it's time to let the others help with Lena. You can't continue to shoulder the burden alone.'

Emily had fixed her with a look as fierce and devastating as the one she had worn when confessing her lost child. 'Perhaps I can't let go,' she said softly. 'Perhaps looking after Lena is the one area of my life I have some control over, and the one thing worthwhile.'

Now Emily was sleeping and Kate was glad; Emily had needed to release so many imprisoned emotions, but the catharsis had taken its toll. For the first time Kate understood the mutual dependence that had formed between Lena and Emily, how desperately Emily craved the sanctuary of Bluebell Bank and the scraps of the lively, inexorable grandmother who had been so influential, in order to start the process of rebuilding her life.

Looking after Lena had given her purpose.

Kate thought of the history wrapped up in that house. Not just the memory book Emily was curating, with its precious stories and remnants, but the albums full of Lena's family photographs, smiling, sepia images of people long gone: parents, grandparents, her brother Austin in his military uniform. And even the rooms themselves, the furniture and long-treasured trinkets and Lena's eccentric collecting, unchanged since the first time Kate had visited as an awe-struck, nervous ten-year-old.

Lena had once woven her own life story into a book. And when it was finished she had taken it out into the yard, made a bonfire and fed the pages to the flames. Emily had been incensed by this; she could not condone the destruction of the written word for any reason, so now she was redressing the balance, with the memory book. But Kate wondered if she was more like Lena in that respect. If she had written out an account of those early years – which she wouldn't do because it wasn't her way to dwell – she would have wanted to destroy it page by page, watch flames consume the words and hoped for the hurt to perish alongside.

These last few weeks Kate had loved coming upon Lena and Emily poring over the memory book in the mornings; Emily with pen and notepad poised, scribing frantically, and Lena talking so loquaciously, waving her hands and weaving a spell with her words, losing herself in the threads of memory. Sometimes they would laugh uproariously, and sometimes they would cry together. Kate would creep away into the kitchen for her coffee and let them recover themselves before she disturbed them.

Those emergent, early morning moments were precious riches to Emily.

*

There was only the faintest strip of gold at the seam of the horizon in the side mirror when Emily scrambled out of sleep. She was exhausted from the emotions of the day, from exercise and fresh air and the effort of avoiding fatal decisions. Keeping Kate here was like preserving a wave: before you could appreciate the perfection of it, the sea was already drawing it back leaving only an imprint of its presence on the sand. She wanted Kate to be more than a memory, a fingerprint, a sense of love that touched her once and now was gone. She wanted her physical, irrefutable presence at Bluebell Bank and, most of all, she wanted her forgiveness and things back to how they used to be. No, that wasn't enough; she wanted them to be better, more even-footed, not Emily needing Kate as a crutch, not envy and trying to measure up.

The road was narrow, dark and woodsy, trees flashing past on either side; Kate was driving fast on the turns. Emily struggled into a sitting position. 'Where are we?' she asked groggily. She didn't remember falling asleep, but she now realised she had been woken by the crashing bass of music blaring from the radio. Emily couldn't wait to get back, check on Lena, take a shower and slip into bed.

'Sorry,' Kate said, with a wry grin. 'It was either this or drive us into a tree.'

Emily yawned. 'Good choice.' She fiddled with the dial and turned the music down a little. 'I'll stay awake and chat to you, keep you alert. Where are we?'

'We're only about ten minutes away.' Kate cranked her window and shuddered at the blast of cold. 'That's better. I could feel myself starting to go.'

Emily rubbed at her eyes. Part of her wanted to ask Kate to slow down, but another part was filled with an innominate dread that tugged at her. She needed to be home to see Lena; she hadn't been away from her this long since she'd come to Wigtown to care for her.

Kate had no intention or need to slow down. She loved to drive and, now she was fully alert again, took joy in careening around the corners. She was thinking about Luke and hoping her speed would banish him. She wanted to hear his voice, but she wouldn't allow herself to call, to give him hope where there was none.

This might be the last time she'd turn into Bluebell Bank's drive; tomorrow or the next day she'd be far away from here.

She tamped down the wave of sadness and pictured Luke lying in his bed in the caravan, the dogs curled up on his feet. Was he watching television, or reading a book? Did he wear glasses to read? Did he sleep in plaid pyjamas, or boxer shorts, or nothing at all? She knew so little about him.

She shuddered in the cold car and gave a jaw-cracking yawn. Bed and sleep, and tomorrow the way would be clear. Her resolve would harden once more and she wouldn't have these treacherous thoughts of what might have been; it was just tiredness making her weak.

Kate slowed around the last bend and flicked on her indicator for the Bluebell Bank driveway.

They both knew instantly that something was wrong.

The sky pulsed blue and yellow and much too bright. The night was suddenly loud, strident with sounds that didn't fit. And the smell: a smoky, charred scent that hung heavy in the air. A sense of a queasy dread consumed Kate then she looked at Emily, seeing matching horror. Neither of them said a word as Jasper bumped up the track.

Finally, Kate abandoned the car and jumped out. Emily too. They left the doors standing open and raced up the last few metres of track.

They didn't speak. There were no words; just their gasps of frantic breath as they crested the slope of the drive.

The flames were billowing like sails from an upstairs bedroom. The house blazed and burned, melting into the smoke-haze. They stalled, taking in the horror-scene: the glow of the fire emblazoned on the night sky, showers of sparks from an upstairs window, a ripple of yellow flame like ribbon and a cloud of toxic smoke, a fragment of burning curtain dancing in the draught from Lena's bedroom.

Chapter 28

There was a moment when Lena knew she ought to wake up. She struggled, trying to open her eyes.

She was drifting: in a deep, deep ocean, far beneath the surface. The water was cool and soothing on her skin and her limbs were weightless. There was no air and no need to breathe and her awareness was far away, a hazy, ephemeral thing.

There was no sound, save the ocean in her ears, a fluid, watery shushing noise like the rush of the sea in a shell, or the warm, woozy deadening when one slipped beneath the surface of a warm bath.

Lena's chest tightened, but that was stupid: she didn't need to breathe underwater. She held her breath, rode the moment until the urge went away and the world was dark and numb and safe. And pain was a far away, distant shore.

Annabelle and Austin. Faces swimming before her, alongside, drifting from the edges of her vision and slipping out of sight. The boy-man so proud in his uniform, the little girl's face full of laughter in the seconds before she began to climb the tree.

A pale, serious boy with glasses morphing into a man, and at his side a pretty, flaxen-haired woman with a capable smile. Their children: a handsome, dark-haired, stubborn boy close to her heart; and the freckled redhead only *she* could understand; the sweet child whose smile would melt hearts one day and his beautiful, strong-minded twin with her easy way with words; the girl with the bangles and a golden-haired toddler.

A man stepping out of a white haze, just the way he always used to emerge from the murk when the mist hung low over the pastures and he was making his way home to her, with his shirtsleeves rolled up and a crooked smile and a strong chin, and his arms held out and his eyes full: these were the last images to play across the screen of her mind before the smoke claimed her.

*

There were people everywhere: feet on gravel and shouting. And a great whoosh and a hiss and belch of smoke as something exploded, or gave way, the house beginning to collapse in on itself. The upstairs windows were orange-lit from within, glowing like the mouth of a pumpkin lantern with a candle flickering between its jagged black teeth.

Kate and Emily skidded to a halt in silent stupefaction, stopped in their tracks by the commotion. Emily was whey-faced and trembling, and Kate held her arm in an iron grip to keep her from tearing into the dripping, smouldering building along with the firefighters.

The scene was all chaos and confusion, and yet everyone seemed to know what they were doing. Ambulances and fire trucks and police cars, tyre tracks cutting up the grass verges, footprints, voices and the blur of radio static.

Despite Kate's hold on her, Emily took a step, as the long grass snagged her shoelaces and her plimsolls sank into the soft mud. A police officer detached himself from a small phalanx of others and walked slowly over to where they stood, already holding out his hands to urge them back from the heat and craziness.

The shock went beyond words. There were questions whirling,

the answers to which they didn't want, but for a few seconds they were mute anyway. The police officer seemed to take an age to reach them, his hands hooked into his vest, resting on his radio – an automatic gesture of readiness and authority. His face was straight, grim, and revealed nothing and everything all at once.

Suddenly, a figure came sprinting towards them from one of the waiting ambulances, hurling itself at them. They both seemed to catch Noah simultaneously so it wasn't clear who he was aiming for, or who embraced him first. 'Oh God,' he said, and kept on saying it, couldn't stop. Then, in a strangled whisper, 'Lena.'

Events didn't seem to fit into any logical sequence. There was no timeline to the next minutes and even hours. Later, Kate would look back at a jumble of glimpses that didn't quite make a full picture: serious faces, soot- and sweat-stained firefighters continuing to blast perfect, pretty arcs of water into the sodden house; a female paramedic jogging over to Noah, wrapping him in a silver blanket and trying to coax him back into the ambulance.

Noah ignored her and said, 'Luke.' Kate's heart stilled with a shuddering boom.

It was not possible – *could* not be possible – that Lena, or Luke, were ever part of that dying inferno: that sad and blackened sodden pile of stones that was once a house, whole and perfect. Kate kept looking for them, waiting for them to stumble out the front door any second, safe and alive and whole. And why would Luke be here anyway? Then she caught sight of his truck parked to the side of the drive and all the breath rushed out of her body at once.

She heard someone saying her name but she couldn't respond. Noah, in his foil coat, with soot smudges on both cheeks, caught her by the shoulders and she stared into his face. 'What?' she began. 'Why?' She touched his cheek. 'Were you in there?'

Emily's anxious face swam into focus. 'I was,' Noah said calmly. 'Me and Luke, we were both coming up the drive when . . . I called it in and he ran straight inside.'

His voice deteriorated into a sob and Emily tried to comfort him. But Kate's brain was replaying those last words over and over until they began to make some semblance of sense. 'Luke is still in there?' She broke away from them and was aware of her own movement, but not where she was going. Noah grabbed her arm.

'Wait, Kate, no! They got him out. He's in the other ambulance.' Now the police officer was talking too, gesticulating, asking them if they knew the young man they had pulled out of the wreckage.

Kate was already moving, dreamlike, towards the ambulance as a paramedic slammed the doors. The ambulance roared to life, blue lights strobing.

'No!' She knew it then, like the force of a blow, followed by a rush of certainty that spiralled through her body like adrenaline. Love. She'd felt it first at fourteen, hadn't understood its value at seventeen, had missed it all her life since and feared it when it came back to her, then let it slip through her hands again. Now it simply was.

She started to run after the ambulance, her muscles clenching into action. She managed to get a hand to the ambulance's side as it picked up speed and began the descent of the driveway. Her palm glanced off the metal, fell uselessly to her side.

And Luke was gone. Blue lights disappearing through the trees.

Kate sank to her knees in the mud. She didn't know how long she crouched there, but she felt Noah's hands beneath her arms, hauling her up. 'Kate,' he said, 'Lena!'

Kate felt two halves of her tear clean in two, her worlds divided. Luke, speeding towards the hospital in Dumfries, and the Cottons, here, needing her more than ever. She felt dizzy, compelled to jump into Jasper and tear down the drive after Luke, breaking every speed limit along the way. 'Emily,' Noah said, and it was enough to bring her back to him.

She turned towards the house – smoking now, the last embers of the fire dying slowly. She felt sickened by the sight of it, sickened further by the tableau forming on the front steps.

A trolley, accompanied by three sombre firefighters. One of the men pushing paused for a second, dragged a hand over his grey face, then looked up and caught Kate's gaze from way across the garden, and she could see in his eyes that these were the moments he hated his job, the moments he relived when sleep eluded him in the dead of night, the moments that twisted him up when he looked at the faces of his kids, his own loved ones.

Lena.

*

Emily knew it at the same instant Kate did. That bag, that flimsy piece of material zipped up around the shape of a person, contained Lena.

And Lena was dead.

'I'm sorry,' the police officer was saying, and maybe he said more, maybe he'd already asked for her name, but Emily couldn't remember. His tone carried the cadence of respectful authority: a blend of businesslike and bland sympathy. Now everything was suddenly moving in treacly time, a slow-motion film.

Some truths were too big, too horrific to be endured. Emily felt numbed. It was the only way of managing such a thing; drip-feeding the truth slowly into the brain like water, because the deluge would be too much. A person might implode under such a torrent. Shock was a blessing.

Emily felt the marshmallowy cushion of it rising around her, padding her so she could keep functioning, and nothing felt real, not the acrid smell of the fire carried on a stiff breeze, mixed with the cologne of the police officer standing next to her, or the sight of Kate coming to stand beside her with both hands pressed tightly to her mouth, not the weight of Noah sagging against her again. Little arrows of reality began to penetrate her armour as she watched the trolley's impossibly slow progress down the steps. Dead. Lena dead. Gone.

No.

Surely she'd been standing here staring at that trolley for an hour or more. Not mere seconds. How could it be moving so slowly?

Her phone began to vibrate and shudder against her leg. Dazed, she dragged it out of her pocket and saw Dan's number blinking merrily on the screen and knew at once what had happened.

The baby.

Emily let out an anguished sob and glanced from the phone in her hand to the crumbling remains of the house, to the body bag being wheeled past so excruciatingly slowly. Past, present and future were colliding in a screaming, jarring impact and nothing was ever going to be the same again.

Chapter 29

The world burst into life around Kate, too bright, too loud, too visceral; like someone ripping open the curtains on a sunny morning and rousing her unceremoniously from sleep, flooding her senses too fast. Suddenly Emily was running and there were people in the way, and Kate couldn't move to reach her because she'd shoved Noah aside and Kate caught him as he stumbled. Noah was embracing her, his whole body heaving with sobs now, his face wet against her neck and Kate could only watch, helpless, as Emily ran away from them.

Emily weaved and ducked, tried to close the distance between herself and the trolley. Heads turned to stare at her as she pushed her way through the wall of officials, and no one knew what she intended to do when she got there, least of all Emily, probably. A police officer caught her, held her gently, firmly, spoke to her softly.

Kate felt again that she was being ripped in two. Luke. Emily.

Noah stood trembling in his foil and Kate held him as the trolley carrying Lena disappeared into the waiting ambulance. No need to hurry now.

The policeman led Emily – who suddenly looked as if her legs were no longer connected to the rest of her body – back to them.

*

The police officer was called Fraser Youngs and he drove Emily, Noah and Kate to the hospital, Noah having flatly refused to wait for another ambulance. In the police car, Kate kept thinking, *Lena is dead*. And tried to force the words to have meaning in her mind.

Luke was hurt, but how badly? Fear for him tore through her like a tornado, ripping up everything in its path. She had to clench her teeth and hands to keep even a modicum of calm or she knew she'd spin into complete hysteria.

Emily took out her phone and rang Dan's number – she'd let it go to voicemail before. Her eyes met Kate's in the dark car, over Noah's head. What would she say?

Congratulations on your new baby, but Lena is dead.

She was about to bring his world crashing to a halt.

Kate pressed her nails painfully into her palms as she listened to Emily's end of the conversation; listened to her congratulate her brother and ask all the right questions, then say softly, 'Dan, something has happened.'

And the words that followed – '... a fire. Bluebell Bank ... gone. Lena ... dead' – were not the words he should be hearing tonight. It was a night for celebration, for new beginnings and looking down the road ahead to the surety of his future. Not a night for confusion and grief and horrid, catastrophic endings. Emily was crying before she finished speaking to him. 'I'm sorry,' she kept saying. 'I'm sorry I had to tell you.'

Kate leaned across a mute Noah to grab Emily's hand.

When she finished speaking to Dan, Emily cried for a while, then squared her shoulders and wiped angrily at the tears with the heels of her hands. 'I should call my parents,' she said. 'And Ally and Fergus.'

'Just wait a bit,' Kate said. 'Until we get to the hospital.'

'Abby shouldn't have had her baby tonight,' Emily said. 'It's too cruel.'

But the baby was here and healthy, and Lena was gone. It was a stark reminder that life surged on regardless. Was it cruel, Kate wondered, or something else?

You could consider it an inauspicious start for Lena's great-grandchild, or a beautiful reminder of life.

*

There was something reassuring about the noise and clatter and activity of people who had no idea that life had just screeched to a halt for the bedraggled threesome tumbling through the hospital doors and into the waiting room.

PC Youngs spoke to someone and they were led from the anonymity of the big waiting area to a more private family room: a bland, silent place where there was nothing to focus on and nothing to think about except waiting.

Emily was faced with the stark reality of Lena every few seconds, as her mind reeled away from the truth, then inevitably circled back to it again and again. She tried to think of other things: *I have a niece. I'm an aunt.* But that didn't feel real yet and, sadly, *this* – the loss – was beginning to.

PC Youngs was nearby. Sometimes Emily could see his head and shoulders as he paced up and down the corridor outside the small, square window in the door; and once she heard the blare of a radio message followed by his terse reply. At one point – she had no idea how much time had elapsed since they had arrived – he came into the room. He sat on one of the green, uncomfortable chairs with his legs wide apart, and spoke, his voice soft, cautious. 'Initial reports suggest that the fire started in the bedroom, but the place is still too dangerous for a full inspection. The fire investigation team will go in tomorrow.'

Emily put her hand to her mouth, pressing hard until her teeth dug in. Horror filled her eyes. 'Oh no,' she said. Kate put her arm around her. Noah had been whisked away to get checked out and it was just the two of them, facing the unflappable PC Youngs who had probably done this countless times: sat with broken, grieving relatives and watched their lives veering off course. He was professional, and kind, but Emily felt she hated him.

She looked up at Kate, eyes wide. 'The bedroom,' she said, and shuddered violently.

'It would have been quick,' Kate said. She looked at PC Youngs for confirmation.

He nodded, cleared his throat. 'Smoke inhalation can render someone unconscious in a matter of seconds. Of course, you'll have to wait for the post-mortem to know . . . ahem.' He coughed again. Even standing a safe distance from the burning building, his lungs were feeling the effects. Emily could feel it too, a dark, smoky taste at the back of her throat.

She stared at the officer, her eyes bright and fierce. 'I don't want them to . . . cut her up.'

'I'm sorry. In a case like this it's mandatory, I'm afraid.'

Emily's eyes closed tightly against the swell of tears.

She felt the calm, gentle presence of Kate at her side, where she had been for hours, hovering and ready for whatever Emily might need. 'Perhaps we should take a walk down to maternity and see Dan and Abby and the baby,' she said.

Emily looked wanly at her. 'I'm not sure I can pretend,' she said. 'Abby doesn't deserve to see me miserable like this.'

The door swung open. 'Abby doesn't need you to pretend,' Dan said in a hard voice. He crossed the room in three strides and swept Emily into his arms. 'Since her own family is so far away,' he continued, his voice thick with emotion, 'you guys are all she's got besides me. Abby's gutted, of course she is, but that doesn't mean she isn't delighted with our daughter. Me too. We want to show her to you. Please come.'

He held Emily at arm's length and looked down at her. His face was taut with the effort of suppressing his own feelings and staying strong: for Abby, for Emily. His eyes met Kate's and she glanced away from the rawness of him, the anger and grief and exhilaration. Emily nodded. 'I should have come up right away . . . I'm sorry. It's just . . . Oh, Dan, this is just so awful.' She buried her face in his shoulder again and he patted her back. His eyes sought Kate's over the top of Emily's head once more, and this time she allowed it.

Another ending, another final punctuation point. He had been changed immeasurably this night. Dan's expression was abashed, even ashamed. He was grief-stricken, but he was resolute. He nodded at Kate: an apology, a goodbye.

She nodded back.

*

Kate followed the police officer out of the room while Emily and Dan continued to speak in low voices, making tentative plans and beginning to talk the business of death. 'How *is* Luke Ross?' she said swiftly. 'I know I'm not family, but—'

The officer nodded solemnly at her. 'His brother should be here soon and his mother has been sent for. From Italy, I believe.'

Kate gritted her teeth. 'Please, just tell me if he's going to be OK.'

'I can't, I'm sorry. I don't know. I do know he's being treated for smoke inhalation, some burns and damage to his legs. He was hit by a falling beam. That he managed to keep going, to bring the woman out of the house is a bloody miracle. It's just a shame he was too late. Look, that's all I can tell you. When his brother gets here I'll send him to speak to you.'

Kate sighed: it was as good as she was going to get. 'Thanks.'

PC Youngs peered through the circular window into the waiting room where Emily was still in Dan's arms. 'Have you managed to get hold of her parents? We need to speak to Mrs Cotton's direct next of kin.'

'They're on their way,' Kate said. 'From Edinburgh. Thank you for all your help.'

It had been an awful phone call to Jonathon and Melanie. By

rights it should have been Dan, since he was the eldest, but Dan had been rather preoccupied having a baby. Kate knew Emily would never forget that moment of breaking the news to her father. She reflected on the phrase *breaking news* and it felt like being shattered into fragments.

The scattered Cottons were pulling back together, like magnets: moons in orbit around Lena and Bluebell Bank.

Without the gravitational force of Lena, would they pull together, or tear apart once again? Kate wasn't sure.

*

Kate stayed with Abby, while Dan and Emily went to check on Noah. Abby was sleeping and they left Kate perched awkwardly on a chair beside the bed, staring down at the pink-wrapped bundle in the cot beside her.

Emily walked along the corridor, glad of her brother at her side. They talked hesitantly about the things that needed to be done, like relieving Niall who was still managing the farm and making up the spare rooms for people coming. Their parents and Ally were already enroute; they had left it to Ally to contact Fergus.

They walked beneath the signs: *Maternity* and *Mortuary*. On the same board – opposite and apposite – where the two ends of the Cotton spectrum, old and new, would rest tonight, under the very same roof.

In the accident and emergency department, Noah was surrounded by a sea of people, but he seemed utterly alone and drowning. The depths of his grief separated him from everyone. This went beyond tragedy: too personal, too raw, too avoidable. She felt the first rising tide of guilt and had to force herself to push it away, keep it at bay. She knew Noah felt it too.

Moments and actions. Small ones and big. Turning points and decisions. And maybe you didn't ever know the magnitude until it was too late.

Like whether to grab a knife one morning before leaving for school; like running off and getting married without a thought for anyone else; like not calling your best friend all those times you wanted to; like leaving Lena alone.

And Lena, her little sister climbing that tree.

She glanced at her brother. She hoped he understood that guilt served no purpose. Death was final, and whatever congruity of events had led them to this place, to this happening, there was no way back, but no purpose in blame.

Noah was hunched on the bed behind a barricade of blankets, his face grotesque with tear tracks and soot. He couldn't look at them. 'I'm sorry,' he said, burying his face again.

'You're fine, Noah. None of this was your fault.' Emily crawled up on the bed beside him, ignoring the signs that told her not to. Dan stood by awkwardly with his hands in his pockets, while Emily shushed Noah, and stroked him and held him in her arms.

He clung to her. Finally, he raised his head and met his brother's eyes unsteadily, still the lingering guilt. 'I'm sorry for being such an idiot,' he said. 'About the farm and ... everything. I know you were just trying to help me. Congratulations, by the way.' He tried to smile and winced at the rasping pain in his chest and throat where the smoke still stung.

Dan perched on the other side of the bed and rested his hand atop Noah's. 'Thanks,' he said. 'Your niece can't wait to meet her favourite uncle, but she isn't going anywhere just now and Abs is sleeping, so you concentrate on getting better.'

'What happened, Noah? Can you tell us?' Emily asked quietly.

Noah winced. He straightened up on the bed, wriggling out of Emily's embrace. He let his hands fall loosely onto the blankets. 'I wasn't home,' he said. 'I know I said I'd only be an hour, but—'

'You were with Becca,' Emily said softly, glancing at Dan and daring him to comment. 'It's OK, I go out too, Noah. No one looks after Lena twenty-four hours a day.' Just saying her name hurt, made the tears bloom beneath her lids. If she cried again it would be a torrent, it would be unstoppable. A flood to overwhelm them all. And she needed to be strong just now, for her brothers. 'Go on,' she prompted.

'I came back from town. I was walking because you had the car, obviously. I'd kind of lost track of time.' A faint pink stained his soot-smeared cheeks. 'I don't know how late it was, but, as I was coming up the track, I could see the orange glow of the fire. I ran. Someone else was coming through the gardens and around the house. It was Luke. I don't know why he was there, but we saw each other and the fire at the same time and we both started to run towards the house. At the door, Luke grabbed me and pushed me back, told me to call the emergency services. I . . . I wanted to help him, but he had disappeared into the house and I knew we needed help quickly, so I called nine-nine-nine on my phone. It seemed to take ages to give them all the information and the woman on the phone said not to go into the house. But—'

Emily's eyes widened. 'But you did? Oh Noah!'

'I only made it as far as the hall at the bottom of the stairs. The smoke was so thick there and the fire was licking down the staircase. I could feel the heat of it on my face and it was so intense . . . I couldn't breathe. I tried covering my nose and mouth, but by then I could hear sirens and I . . .' He lowered his eyes. 'Luke managed to get Lena down the stairs, but he was hurt. I helped him drag her out, but . . .'

'You did absolutely the right thing,' Emily said, and glanced at Dan again. 'You did the best you could.'

'You did,' Dan confirmed.

'But Luke . . . and Lena . . .' Noah's eyes filled with tears. 'We couldn't save her. If I had gone straight into the house with Luke . . .'

'Then you might have been really badly hurt too,' Dan said firmly. 'And the fire brigade and ambulance might not have been in time to save Luke. Or any of you.'

'Luke made the choice to run into the house to save Lena.

And it was very brave. Both of you were very brave. We might have lost you too.' Emily pressed her hands to her mouth until the fresh wave of anguish ebbed and she stopped shaking. 'The police said the fire started in the bedroom. I . . . I don't think anyone could have saved her.' She heard her voice wobble and swallowed hard.

Strong, she reminded herself. 'Let's find a nurse and see if you're well enough to come back to the waiting room with me and Kate. None of us should be alone tonight.'

Chapter 30

'What about the house?' Emily asked PC Youngs, when they arrived back at the family room with Noah, who had been given the all-clear by the charge nurse in accident and emergency. 'Is it bad?' Kate had been shooed out of the ward where Abby and the baby were both sleeping peacefully and now accompanied them; Dan was leaving Abby to rest, enduring the agony of waiting with his siblings for the arrival of their parents who were driving through the wee hours of the morning to reach them.

Kate held her breath waiting for the answer; the Cottons could not lose Bluebell Bank *and* Lena. But PC Youngs was wary. 'I don't know, it's too early to say and I'm not a fire officer. There will be a full report in due course. They'll get the building shored up I imagine, make it safe. I think it'll be quite a job to fix up, but that's just my opinion.'

'So it's not completely gone?'

'It seemed like the east side of the building got off a bit lighter – smoke and water damage mainly. The fire didn't spread across the central corridor before they got to it. And most of the ground floor is intact. But that's just—'

'Your opinion,' Emily finished. 'Yes.' But he had given her reason to hope. If there was something of Bluebell Bank left – not just the charred bricks and burned mementoes of childhood – then there was hope for the future of the place and for them.

'Oh,' PC Youngs said. 'Before I forget, there was something...' He turned to Noah. 'When we found you and Luke outside, you had something with you. A book.' He got up. 'I'll go and get it for you. I think it's at the nurses' station for safe-keeping.'

'I forgot about that,' Noah said. 'It's the memory book, Emily. I knew how important it was to you and Lena. It was just sitting on the kitchen table. I think Lena had been reading it earlier in the evening, so I grabbed it—'

Emily turned to him with eyes huge and shining, the grey of her irises glowing violet. 'Noah, you are amazing.' She gripped him by the shoulders. She hadn't even considered the loss of the book in the greater scheme of other losses, but now, *because* of those losses, the prospect of not having that book didn't bear thinking about.

When PC Youngs came back, he had a leather-bound book under his arm and juggled four polystyrene cups of steaming coffee. Emily practically wrestled the book from him and stared at it, eyes shining with tears.

She had already cried so much, for Lena and Bluebell Bank and for them all. For the joy of a baby born at the wrong moment... and the memory of another, never born at all.

And now here was the memory book, more precious than she could ever have imagined: safe in her hands and unharmed. She turned to Kate with shining eyes. 'Look, it's not damaged at all,' she whispered.

*

Kate was glad for Emily, having the book, having Noah by her side and Dan sitting across from her – all of them lurching from one extreme of emotion to another in the blink of an eye: sorrow and joy intertwined.

But now she had been here for the Cottons, supported them to this point where they were united in their sadness and awaiting the return of those missing, she allowed her thoughts to return to Luke. It was time for her to set aside her own grief for Lena, for a moment, and to ponder that she might never get the chance to tell Luke how she felt . . .

But tell him what? How *did* she feel?

That she was still madly in love with him and always had been? That no matter what obstacles lay before them, or the stupid mistakes cluttering the past, she wanted him, and only him, for the rest of her days.

It seemed simple now. Obvious. But perhaps that was just the shock and adrenaline talking. Or the horror of what had happened had allowed her to see clearly for the first time in so long.

She had nearly lost him for good. She'd nearly set him aside for good, with no idea what for ever without Luke might feel like. She had been given a glimpse into that Luke-void as she watched the ambulance carry him away from her and she didn't like it.

She slipped out of the room, the rawness of her feelings overwhelming. In the toilet down the hall, she went to the sink, ran a basin of water and scooped it over her face, letting it drip down her neck and soak into her hair. She straightened up, blotted her face on a paper towel.

She was so tired, weariness seeping into her like deeply ingrained dirt.

Kate dropped to her knees beside the sink, pressing her knuckles into her eyes and letting the tears flow for a minute. Then she rose, splashed her face again and blew her nose, and made a cursory attempt to rearrange her hair in the mirror.

Coming out of the bathroom she very nearly collided with Fraser Youngs, in the company of a tall, scruffy man whose swarthy complexion, untidy black hair and arrangement of features bore more than a passing resemblance to Luke. 'Miss Vincent,' Fraser Youngs said. 'This is Nick Ross, he's keen to talk to you.'

Kate didn't even bother to greet Nick. 'Have you seen him? Is he OK?' she demanded.

Nick looked drained. 'I need a coffee,' he said. 'Do you want to come downstairs to the canteen and I'll fill you in on what the doctor told me?' Seeing Kate's stricken face he added, 'He's going to live.'

She could have thrown herself into this stranger's arms. She felt her knees sag and the next thing she knew PC Youngs was urging her into a plastic chair, telling her to put her head between her knees.

'I'm fine,' Kate protested weakly. 'I just need some food and to hear what Nick has to say about Luke.'

Eventually, he let her go with Nick. Kate gave PC Youngs a grateful smile as she fell into step with Luke's brother. 'So, are you like his girlfriend or something?' Nick asked, as they headed for the stairs.

Kate frowned. 'Maybe,' she said. 'Or something.' They passed beneath a clock and Kate saw it was after 4 a.m. Time was fluid and formless; it might have been any time at all.

'Doc said he's gonna be OK,' Nick said gruffly, once they were seated at Formica tables with cups of coffee that was too weak for Kate's liking – luckily she was awash with the stuff already. 'He's inhaled some smoke, all kinds of chemicals in it apparently. One of his legs is broken, and there are some burns.'

'But he's going to be fine?' That was all that mattered.

Nick nodded. 'Doctor says there might be some damage to his lungs, but they can't tell that yet.'

Kate was weak with relief. They would cross whatever bridges they must in the coming days and weeks. They would cope with his injuries, together.

She felt dizzy again, but it was just the realisation that she could see her future entwined with Luke's now. And the heady relief that Luke still had a future.

Of course, all that depended on if Luke still wanted her, and if she didn't lose her courage and run again.

'You're the chick he took sailing the other day, right?' Nick was looking at her more closely now. Kate just nodded: no point challenging him on the 'chick' part right now. 'The doctor said Luke was trying to be some kind of hero, rescuing an old woman from that fire.'

Kate nodded soberly. 'My friend's grandmother. She didn't survive.'

Nick shifted uncomfortably in his seat. 'I'm sorry. So, was he at the house to see you? Didn't he know you wouldn't be there? Was he waiting?' Nick looked perplexed as he tried to piece together Luke's movements.

What had Luke been doing in the garden of Bluebell Bank? Revisiting old haunts and hoping for an opportunity to explain himself? She shut down Nick's questions abruptly. 'We should go back up. Do you mind if I go and see Luke?'

Nick smiled; he had a nice smile, Kate thought, but not a patch on his brother's. 'I'm sure he'd rather wake up to your face at his bedside than mine. My mother is on her way,' he added. 'Guess she'd like to meet you. Luke is pretty secretive about his girlfriends usually.'

'We haven't been together long,' Kate said quickly... *and we're not really together now*. 'I need to go and check on my friend and then I'll sit with him a while if that's all right.'

For the next few hours she bounced back and forth between the ICU and the Cottons.

She liked the quiet dark of Luke's room, where she sat curled in a chair amid the reassuring beeps and pulses of the machines. The IV lines and oxygen mask didn't worry her, but were a comfort; a kind nurse with a deeply lined face had paused to reassure her and Nick that he would be off the machines soon anyway. He was doing well; when he woke he'd be off his head on morphine for the pain in his leg, but otherwise fine. Nick had lied to the nurse, said that Kate was family. Nick couldn't sit still for very long and kept disappearing off to the car park to smoke, which suited Kate fine because she preferred to be alone with Luke's sleeping form.

Jonathon and Melanie arrived a little after six. Kate went to greet them. There were tears and hugs.

'I must see my granddaughter before we go,' Melanie said, wiping her cheeks and clinging too tightly to Noah.

'Go?' Emily said wonderingly; it hadn't occurred to her they would go anywhere. They had nowhere *to* go.

'Perhaps I shouldn't—' Jonathon began, and Melanie put a hand on his shoulder.

'You can't do anything for Lena here,' she said. She walked over to her eldest son and took his face between her hands, like he was her baby still. 'Congratulations,' she said again. 'May we stay at the farm?'

'Of course,' Dan said. 'It might be a tight squeeze but we'll manage. Ally on his way?'

'Yes. He should be here tomorrow night. We can sleep anywhere, we're not fussy,' Melanie said breezily, which made them laugh because it was patently untrue. 'Let's go and see Abby and the baby, and then we'll all try to get some rest.'

'Have you chosen a name yet?' Emily said, as she followed Dan out of the room.

Dan shook his head. 'We're still working on it. Abby's pretty out of it and I'm fairly sure this is not a decision I'm trusted to make alone.'

*

Having cooed and fussed over new baby Cotton, the family were soon leaving the hospital. Kate and Emily bade goodbye at the doors to the maternity wing and Kate hurried back to Luke's side. She was there the first time he woke, high as a kite from all the medication; as he murmured her name and reached for her, she flew to his side, took his hands in hers and told him in a whisper that she was his.

She wasn't sure he'd remember the conversation later, considering his drugged state, but it felt better getting the words out. A lazy, adorable smile as Luke tried to focus on her face, his eyes dilated and fogged with sleep and morphine. 'Kate,' he slurred, grasping at her hands and tugging her closer. He closed his eyes, smiled stupidly again – beatific and addled – and said, 'Marry me.'

Luke woke up properly several hours later, still fuzzy from the long, deep chemical sleep, confused by the world he woke to: dimpled ceiling tiles and white walls and his body pinned and heavy on the bed. He glanced at the IV line running into a cannula in the back of his right hand and tried to lick his dry, cracked lips.

Nick was sitting in a plastic chair, impatient and uncomfortable, an arm flung over the back of the chair and one leg jiggling incessantly, his heavy work boot pounding the linoleum. He looked bored. His eyes fixed on Luke's and he leaned forward, suddenly animated. 'Hey,' he said, 'you're awake.'

Behind Nick's head was a window into the corridor, curtained in thin material beyond which grey shadows of figures moved: the world carrying on while Luke had slept. He turned his head. On his other side was a low padded chair with wooden arms. Kate uncurled, displacing the green hospital blanket. They had moved him out of ICU and into this ward in the night, but Kate had refused to go home.

She would leave the Cottons to adjust to their new reality and get settled into the farm.

'Luke' she said, cautious now. She got up, let the blanket puddle at her feet. Nick stood at the other side of the bed, rolling his shoulders, unsure what to do now that his brother was awake. 'How do you feel?' Kate asked, leaning over Luke.

He grunted, cleared his throat. 'Thirsty,' he croaked. 'Tired, but like I've been asleep for too long. And kind of sore.' He lifted his hand, trailing tubes, and rubbed at his chest, as if the pain was deep, in the very fabric of his lungs. 'Leg feels weird too.'

'Do you remember what happened? The fire.'

Luke nodded slowly and his voice sounded rusty when he spoke. 'Lena?' he said, hopeful.

Kate shook her head, biting down on her lip. 'No,' she said. 'No, she didn't make it.'

'I couldn't get to her,' Luke said, brow furrowing in remembered despair. 'The fire was so hot, and dark. I never thought it would be dark. Couldn't see which way to go. I was stumbling about and the smoke was obscuring everything. I went back for her, but there was a crash, that's the last I remember.'

'It's OK,' Kate said. 'You did your best. You got her out actually, but she was already . . .' A long pause. 'Noah's fine though. Take your time, you've been asleep for a while.'

'Am I . . . badly hurt?'

'You're fine,' Kate said soothingly. 'You've got some burns; I expect you'll be sore for a while. Your leg is broken, but it's in plaster and healing fine.'

Luke nodded, relaxing into his pillows as the door opened and a nurse came in.

'Hello,' she said. 'I'm Mandy. It's nice to see you awake, Mr Ross.'

Luke managed a tired smile. Mandy started pressing buttons and fiddling with the various machines around Luke, then poked and prodded at him for a few minutes which he endured in reluctant silence.

'Hmm, blood pressure is a bit up.'

'Wouldn't yours be?' Luke retorted.

'Through the roof probably. All things considered, you're not doing too badly. You must rest, though. These two have barely left your side since they brought you in.' She looked up at Kate and Nick. 'But perhaps it might be time to give him some space, now you've seen that he's all right. Mr Ross, we want to get you up and about as soon as possible, so we'll be sending in the physio later. Just now, though, I want to get the consultant to come and give you the once-over.' She looked at Nick and Kate again, expecting them to take the hint.

Nick did. 'I could use a smoke and you probably need another coffee, it's been at least three hours since the last one. You know, Luka, this chick is crazy for coffee.'

'Nicolo,' Luke said severely. 'Don't call her that. Use her name. You're nearly thirty years old for God's sake.'

'That's you told,' said Mandy with a chuckle, lifting Luke's chart and running a professional eye over it.

Nick grinned, unabashed. 'C'mon, Kate.'

She was reluctant to leave him now. 'We'll be in the canteen,' she said, trailing her fingers across his arm. 'Don't go anywhere now.' She bent to drop a kiss on his forehead before she left, glanced shyly back from the doorway and held his gaze for a moment. So many things still to say.

In the corridor she turned to look at Nick, hands on hips. 'Luka?' she questioned. 'Nicolo?'

'Italian mother,' Nick reminded her. 'It really winds him up when anyone but her calls him that. Which is why I do it, obviously.'

Kate smiled. She was starting to like Nick, though he was awkward and rarely knew the right thing to say. But he cared about Luke: that much was obvious. 'You go ahead and have a smoke,' she told him. 'I need to call Emily and check on things there. I'll meet you in the canteen, OK?'

She ducked outside to use her mobile. It was the day after a night straight out of some version of hell. Late afternoon. How long since she had slept properly? Except for a few snatched hours in the hospital chair. *Too long*. The weariness went bone deep, made her head swim.

'Kate,' Emily said, answering almost immediately.

'Hi. I just wanted to let you know Luke is awake. The doctor's with him, but he's awake and talking. He's going to be OK.'

'That's really good news. Tell him I said hello, and thank him. For what he did. For trying to save Lena.'

'I think he's having a hard time with the fact that he didn't manage to,' Kate said, leaning against the wall, her tiredness threatening to consume her, one bone at a time. 'How are you all doing?'

'OK, I s'pose. It's weird, camping out here. Abby and Dan are coming home from the hospital with the baby tonight – you could catch a lift with them actually – and Ally's arriving. I don't know where everyone is going to sleep. I think Noah and I might end up in a tent in the garden at this rate. I'm going into town a bit later to pick up Bracken. Mike's been looking after him at his house, you know. Isn't that kind? Anyway, I want Bracken with us now. He's such a part of Lena . . .' Emily's voice faded.

'Does the baby have a name yet? She's beautiful, isn't she?'

'A sweetheart,' Em agreed. 'Nope, they still haven't decided.'

'And what about Noah? He OK?'

'Hmm. I'm trying not to let him be on his own. It's going to be tough for him. For all of us, but especially for him.'

'So long as you stick together,' Kate said.

'Yeah. So are you coming back soon? You need to get some sleep, too, Kate.'

'Soon,' Kate promised. 'I'm flagging. I just want to spend some time with Luke. I still have to talk to him, tell him . . .'

'That you *like* him.' Emily was laughing now, a sing-song, teasing note to the sly question; it felt good to hear her laugh. Kate smiled and rested her aching head against the tiled wall. 'That you *love* him?' Emily pressed.

'*Bye*, Emily. See you later.'

*

It was the next day. Kate had just ordered a tuna sandwich and a Coke when Nick came into the cafeteria accompanied by a short, thin woman wearing stone-washed jeans, a black vest and a long, yellow cardigan that draped and flowed around her gracefully. She weaved between the tables, clutching her handbag in one hand, running the other through her mass of long, black hair. She had heavy features, a long face and beautiful, dark tanned skin. Her eyes were black and expressive and filled with concern.

'Kate,' Nick said. 'This is my mother, Ella.'

Ella drew Kate into a perfumed embrace, kissed her on both cheeks. 'My dear,' she said, heavily accented. 'You're the one.'

Kate wrinkled her nose. 'Which one?'

'*The* one,' Ella repeated, gesticulating. 'The one Luka has loved for ever.'

'I think you might be confusing me with someone else,' Kate said. 'Luka – Luke – and I knew each other a long time ago, but we only just met again a few weeks back.'

'No,' Ella said impatiently. 'His wallet.' She turned to her oldest son and snapped her fingers. 'You have Luka's wallet?'

'Yes, they gave me it when he was brought in.' Nick dug into his pocket and pulled out a plain, brown leather wallet. Ella snatched it from his hands and opened it, dug around amongst the credit cards and old receipts, dumping the contents on the table: driving licence, supermarket card, business cards for various stonemasons and plumbers. She found what she was looking for. 'Here,' she said, brandishing a photo triumphantly. 'If Luka doesn't love you, why has he carried this with him since he was fifteen years old?' She handed over the small, creased photo to Kate: a photo booth picture cut from a strip of four, squint edged. In the picture, Kate was sitting in Luke's lap, sticking her tongue out at the camera, eyes full of excitement. Luke was smiling enigmatically, his eyes not on the camera at all, but on Kate. She remembered posing for the pictures, diving into the booth on a whim.

She had no idea what happened to the other three, or why this one survived, why Luke had saved it when it had been his decision to end things.

She touched a fingertip to the picture, stroking the adorable, teenaged Luke. 'Yes,' she said quietly. 'I suppose you might be right.'

'Of course I am right,' Ella said. 'I am *always* right when it comes to my boys. Now take me to see my baby.'

Chapter 31

The farm was bulging at the seams, however, the close quarters were not an inconvenience but a comfort to them all. There ought to have been a veil of sadness draped over the place in the coming days, but there was not; rather, there was an overwhelming sense of rightness in them all being here together, and a choice to dwell on birth rather than death. The absence of Lena was tangible, and her favourite armchair by the kitchen fire lay empty as Bracken paced, searching for her.

Abby was ensconced in another armchair, with the baby cradled and swaddled against her, and people flocking round her, like the tides responding to the pull of the moon; the baby was the centre of everything: a pinkly wrinkled, brand-new little life, yawning and sighing and blowing spit bubbles from amongst the folds of her mint green blankets, blissfully unaware of the trauma that accompanied her advent into their lives.

Emily sat at the table with the memory book open in front of her, a teapot covered in a knitted cosy by her elbow. She was writing the last chapter, from memory of her last conversation with Lena and glancing occasionally at Abby and the baby. She had been almost afraid to look inside those folds of blankets to the child beneath when Abby and Dan first brought her home;

scared of a resurgence of those old feelings of want and loss and self-hate. But she had felt nothing of the kind looking down at her baby niece – those feelings had blown away on a Solway beach, or dissipated in the warmth and love of a dark car, floating down the river with the tide.

Noah, seated opposite, glanced up from his phone from time to time, and each time Emily felt the jolt of his guilt, stark in his eyes; of them all, Noah felt it most acutely: the sense that he ought to have been there and that he could have prevented it.

Emily caught his eye and the depths of his pain made her flinch. Becca had been here earlier and the two of them had shot off together; Noah had been smiling when he returned. Emily didn't care what tactics Becca had had to employ to cheer Noah up; if she could make her brother smile again it was all right by her.

Emily turned in her seat and looked at Dan, who was leaning over Abby to marvel again at the tiny creation lying in her lap. 'Have you guys come up with a name yet?'

Melanie turned from the sink with interest, shaking her hands free of suds. Jonathon was pacing the kitchen, the cordless phone in one hand and a bundle of papers in the other, beginning the interminable paperwork that was the accompaniment of death. Melanie touched his shoulder as she passed and they exchanged a small glance. He sighed, took off his glasses and rubbed at his eyes. Voices could be heard in the utility room and, a moment later, Ally came into the kitchen, his boyfriend Phillip behind him. That had been a turn-up yesterday: Ally arriving with Phillip in tow. Emily caught Ally's eye and smiled as he came in, bringing a flurry of dogs and the woodsy scent of outdoors. They were looking after Luke's dogs and the farm collies as well as Bracken, who had made a complete recovery.

The dogs made a quick tour of the room before settling on their respective blankets. Phillip padded into the kitchen in his socks. 'Can I make anyone a cup of tea?' he asked, reaching for the teapot again. There had been a plentiful supply of tea and food over the past twenty-four hours; it was all anyone could do to be useful and so it kept on coming.

'Thank you, Phillip, that would be lovely.' Melanie was on her best behaviour with him, playing the perfect mother-in-law. Being a grandmother suited her – Emily could see the pride radiating from her.

Kate rose from her floor cushion in front of the fire where she had been sketching ideas for a flyer for the Book Nook. 'We were just talking about baby names,' Melanie added, as Phillip and Ally began setting out another round of tea things.

There was consolation in the togetherness the ordeal had forced upon them, the suspension of normal life in some ways disquieting, and yet providing refuge in their new routines: meals and dog walks and nappy changes, phone calls and paperwork and reminiscing, and laughing when they could. Noah had thrown himself full force into the work of the farm and everyone was chipping in to help out.

Noah and Dan had had a long chat. Emily had been about to go and prise him out of the milking sheds for dinner last night, but Dan had stopped her and said it should be him. Neither of them had made it to dinner and neither divulged what passed between them, but they returned looking as if something important had been settled.

'So,' Melanie said, when she was ensconced at the head of the table. 'Let's debate names.'

'There will be no debate,' Abby said firmly, looking up in alarm. 'This is not a family decision.'

'Of course not,' Melanie soothed, stretching out her arms for the bundle. Abby relinquished her reluctantly.

'Actually, we do need your advice,' Dan said, exchanging a reassuring smile with his wife. 'We've reached a bit of an impasse.'

Jonathon collapsed into a chair, a puppet with the strings cut suddenly: it kept catching him unawares like that, the peculiar and shocking sense of loss. 'Go on,' he said, glad of the distraction.

The business of death was snarled up with so many decisions and paperwork and red tape it didn't seem like there was time simply to grieve: to miss Lena, to come to terms with the nature of her passing.

Dan sat on the arm of Abby's chair and cradled his mug carefully. 'We were thinking . . .' he began. 'And not just because of what's happened. But we want to honour Lena is some way. She gave us everything: if not for her I wouldn't have this farm and I'd never have met Abs. We've been toying with ideas, like Selena and Helena, but we can't make up our minds. Does anyone have any thoughts?'

Melanie cooed at the nameless little bundle. 'Poor little thing, she needs a name and quickly. Whatever you decide, you need to decide now.'

'I think it's a lovely idea to honour my mother,' Jonathon says, his voice a bit unsteady. 'But if you can't agree on something, please don't feel you have to stick to it. Lena wouldn't have wanted you to, if it doesn't feel right.'

Dan nodded. 'I know. It does feel right, just . . .' He shrugged and Abby covered his hand with her own, peering past him to check on the baby in Melanie's arms, feeling the magnetic pull of her child.

'Can anyone think of an alternative? I mean, did Lena have a middle name or something?'

'I have an idea,' Emily said, putting her pen down. 'What about Annabelle?'

The faces around the room wore matching expressions of mystification; even her father looked blank. Emily zeroed in on him. 'You know,' she prompted, 'Lena's little sister.'

Jonathon frowned. 'There was a brother, Austin, he was badly hurt in the war and died later from his injuries.' His eyes were weary again and he rubbed at them. Emily held his gaze.

'Yes,' she said, flipping through the pages of the memory book until she found what she was looking for. She cleared her throat, took a deep breath and read in a steady voice. The others gathered round to listen.

'*A beautiful child, with bright green eyes and golden brown hair and a voice soft and clear as a bell. She adored me and I her. How I wish she had idolised me a little less, not desired to do the things I did with such determination. I taught her to climb because she would have climbed anyway. Father understood that, though Mother did not: not at first and perhaps not at all, for the damage to her baby was a bitter blow.*

'*For so long I tormented myself with maybes and whys and wherefores, and I bargained with God to bring back the use of her legs. For once I began to listen to the sermons in church, to pray with heartfelt fervour: so that James could not understand what had happened to change me so. Everyone knew about the poor little girl who had fallen out of a tree and would never walk again, but no one knew how the darkness had permeated my soul, how the guilt chewed me up until I was but a shadow of my former self.*

'*And then she caught a fever and died. A freak thing, the doctor said, nothing to do with her accident, but I didn't believe it. After she died, I stopped eating. Stopped doing anything. No one could bring me out of it. Weeks passed. Then Mother realised she was losing another of her babies; and she was the only one with the power to bring me back. She told me it hadn't been my fault and I could see for the first time that she meant it. She saved me, with her forgiveness.*

'*I was the only one left.*

'*And I realised – not then, but later – that it is possible for something to be your fault (a technicality, as in you were there, or not there; as in there was something that you could have done, or not done, to change the outcome) and yet also not your fault; and that that is a contradiction one simply has to learn to live with.*'

Emily looked up and caught Noah's eye and she wanted to say more, but did not. All were still and silent around the table. Tears flowed in silent rhythms, as the loss of a child they hadn't even known gave them permission to cry for the woman they had.

Abby sobbed and covered her face, then reached for her own bundle, prising her from Melanie's arms with a new mother's iron will.

'Sorry,' Emily said. 'That wasn't exactly a cheerful story. I guess you might not want to name the baby after someone who died like that . . . I just thought that Annabelle was someone who mattered to Lena. But maybe you think the name is unlucky or something.'

'I never knew that,' Jonathon whispered in wonder. 'I *can't believe* I never knew that.' He fixed his eyes on Emily and his voice grew stronger. 'A name is never unlucky. A name is what you make it. How you live up to it and the way it evolves with you.'

Dan went to stand beside his father, clasping his shoulder briefly. 'Well said.' He looked at Abby. 'What do you think? Annabelle? She could be Anna or Bella when she's older.'

Abby nodded. 'I love it. It's exactly right. Thanks, Em.'

'Have you got any more stories in there I should know about?' Jonathon said, gesturing towards Emily's book.

Emily closed it, stroked the cover with reverent fingertips and smiled. 'You're welcome to read it and find out. Or, you may wait for publication and finally read an original Emily Cotton.'

*

'There's something I have to tell you,' Noah said, at dinner. 'While everyone's here.' He looked at all the faces around the table.

Melanie's head flew up, her eyes snapping fire. 'What now?' She had coped with all the revelations she could handle these past days.

'Kate and I . . .' Noah began, looking to her for support. She nodded encouragingly. 'We Skyped Fergus earlier. When everyone went out for a walk.'

'Why the big secret?' Dan said. 'I mean, I guess it would have been nice for everyone to speak to him, but—'

'It was my idea,' Kate said, no longer wary of Dan. 'I thought he should be here with you all, so I wanted to persuade him to come back for the funeral. I offered to pay for his ticket—'

Noah interrupted. 'And Fergus laughed and asked if she had any idea how much money he makes in a single season sheep shearing: *a lot*, by the way, if anyone wants to know. He said he had been thinking the exact same thing and already looked at tickets. He's flying on Sunday. I guess we can hold the funeral until he gets here?'

'Oh, my goodness!' Melanie exclaimed, covering her face with her hands, crying again, tears always so close to the surface. 'Fergus. It's been so long since we've seen him.'

'That's not all,' Noah said, as Kate jabbed him in the ribs with her elbow. 'Fergus was thinking maybe I could go back with him after the funeral. To Australia. Just for a while.'

Silence. Noah looked at his parents, his siblings, at Kate still smiling her encouragement. It had been her idea, and simultaneously Fergus's; but as soon as they'd suggested it, it had seemed so obvious to Noah. The chance to travel, to spend time with his brother. To make some money too, if Fergus could get him a job and he proved half decent at it. *Tough work*, Fergus had warned. *The toughest.*

Noah would handle it; it was time he got his head down and did something worthwhile.

'What about school?' Melanie exclaimed. 'You're too young to make a decision like this. You *need* to finish your education.' She appealed to her husband for support but he seemed mired in uncertainty. Melanie huffed an impatient breath and looked at Noah's siblings instead. 'Tell him he needs to finish school.'

Noah looked worried. Emily cast him an appraising look. 'You know,' she said, 'I think he'll get plenty of education where he's going.'

Ally agreed. 'He'll be eighteen in a few months. Maybe going halfway around the world will help him to grow up more than going back to school would.'

'Dan, surely I can rely on you to see sense?' Melanie begged, and Noah sighed, still expecting Dan's condemnation.

Dan shrugged. 'He's got a good head on his shoulders. He won't do anything stupid.' Noah stared at him, incredulous. Dan smiled. 'He'll have to really work where he's going. It'll be good for him.'

'Oh for goodness sake, am I the only one who can see things straight?' Melanie looked around the room and her eyes fell on Kate. 'I don't suppose there's any point in asking you? Or Abby. I know you'll be on Noah's side. Jonathon, I really think I should put my foot down about this.'

Jonathon, having listened to what everyone had to say, looked at Noah speculatively and saw the gleam in his eyes: the first spark he'd seen in his boy for so long. He had listened while Melanie fretted about what they would do with the boy, talking about counselling and trying to repair him; forcing him back to school against his will seemed pointless. 'You know what? I think it's a good plan.'

'The thing is,' Noah added, looking down and his plate, 'I could use the money I make for college when I get back. I was talking to Becca and she's planning to go to Dundee once she finishes school next year. She . . . she knows all about what happened at school and she understands.' His face brightened; love had given him acceptance, permission to move on. 'I thought perhaps I could take my exams and maybe go with her.' He stopped and shrugged, embarrassed. 'It was just an idea.'

Emily, who was sitting closest to him, covered Noah's hand with hers and said, 'I knew I liked Becca. Can't go wrong with a girl who likes books.' She glanced slyly at Kate, who made a face. 'Sorry.'

Kate pretended to be offended and everyone laughed.

Chapter 32

The crisp, clean scent of the new did not quite drown the papery-musk of old books. The shop was ready. Emily was ready. All those weeks of work: painting, building, renovating and rejuvenating had come to fruition. Some sort of completion; if only other things in life were so easy to measure.

Kate's favourite part had been putting the finishing touches to the decor and organising the grand party which was just about to unfold. Emily's had been sorting out the books, stacking the shelves so carefully, savouring the feel of every spine as she slid it into place and greeting every book like an old friend.

There were new books and second hand, the latter displayed in squat wicker baskets and categorised by genre to make the rummaging and rifling an attractive prospect. Emily loved the juxtaposition of old and new, the casual coexistence of the two; she loved the precise displays of brand-new books – the smell, the crispness of the pages, the gloss of the covers – but she secretly hankered for the old, the well loved, well thumbed, dog-eared and faintly damp.

The walls were covered with framed book covers. Alongside these were quotations Emily had chosen from her favourites, which Kate had copied out in her best calligraphic hand. Emily had collected inscriptions too, absorbing the stories within stories and wondering at the lives of the people who had held her books before her, enjoyed and devoured and loved them. The inscriptions were on blue index cards and pegged around the shop. There was a beautiful rocking chair in one corner, the much-admired chaise and the fat, overstuffed armchairs which had proved such a tribulation.

The shop was full of the sea: driftwood and painted pebbles and sage-green walls like the under-layers of the firth beneath a very particular sky. At a table in the backroom, children could paint their own pebble creatures – collected from St Ninian's Cave – and write stories on a postcard to accompany them. They kept the pebbles, Emily kept the stories.

In the middle of the room was the stove, and a low table with a coffee pot and selection of teas.

Kate had taken care of the branding and advertising and sent out industry invites to the opening party – much more satisfying than selling knickers, she said.

In short, everything that could have been done in preparation for the opening was done; all Emily need do was take these few moments alone to gather herself.

The family was outside in the marquee Dan had put up in the garden area, laying out the champagne and the teapots and the cupcakes, and preparing the stage for the author readings Kate had organised. Phillip and Ally had come for the weekend, but Noah and Fergus were missing: busy shearing sheep on the other side of the globe.

Lena's absence was most keenly felt, of course. Her picture was on the wall behind the counter; scowling out at the patrons because she never would smile for a photograph.

The funeral had happened a week ago, with most of Wigtown turning out for it, but more significant was the day the family scattered Lena's ashes: a beautiful afternoon of brilliant Solway sunshine. The firth was lit with silver shards and the grass shone a verdant green and the sky was huge: an impossible expanse of cloudless blue, swirling with myriad hues like paint stirred up with a palette knife.

They had scattered her from the cliff looking back on Rigg Bay, as the waves swept and pulsed against the rocks at the base of the cliff and the breath of the sea was soft and sonorous: the heartbeat of her beloved Galloway.

They had all been together: Fergus, Dan, Jonathon, Melanie, Ally, Phillip, Emily, Noah, Abby, Annabelle and Kate; their patience for one another only just beginning to fray at the edges after so long cooped up together. Luke was in hospital recuperating, beginning his long convalescence.

There had been little ceremony. They had each said a few words as they helped to scatter her to the seas below. None of them planned or scripted, just a capturing of a moment, that was all.

Emily had been grabbed by a strange sense of exhilaration and freedom and escape; and that seemed wrong, until she realised it was in fact exactly right.

Scaffolding had gone up around Bluebell Bank just the other day and the raising of the house had begun. Lena had left it to Emily, on the proviso that it not be sold but remain a refuge for Cottons. To Ally, Fergus and Noah she had left a decent sum of money; enough for Noah to put himself through college and whichever university course he decided upon – if he ever came back from his travels (Emily thought he would, the pull of Becca too strong) – and for Fergus to do whatever it was Fergus wanted: no one could predict what that might be.

Dan had the farm and Ally decided to put most of his share into a trust for Annabelle and whatever other nieces and nephews came along; it was what Lena would have done if she were able, he insisted.

Through it all – the tribulations and changes – Mike had been such a support. Emily had stopped pretending he was just the vet and begun saying his name around the others simply for the pleasure of hearing it fall from her lips. He had been steadfast at her side during the funeral and taken her out immediately after the scattering, not minding as she wove endless memories of Lena through their dinner conversation, laughing and crying by turns.

Her mobile chimed cheerfully and Emily caught it up, preparing to discuss napkins and bunting with Kate, or to reassure one of the nervous authors or – even better – to find that Mike was calling just to say hi.

The greeting died in her throat when she heard his voice. Joe.

'Hi, Em, surprise.'

'Why are you calling, Joe?' She folded her arms across her chest as if he could see her.

'It's your grand opening tonight, isn't it? I just wanted to wish you well.'

She raised a sceptical brow. 'Really?'

She could almost hear him shrug. 'Look, Em, there's no ulterior motive. I genuinely just want to wish you luck. I'm heading off on a tour of Asia tonight, so I'm going to be out the country for a while. I wanted to speak to you before I left.' He sounded more like the irrepressible college boy she had met than the turbulent, rock and roll ex-husband she remembered. 'Also, I was kind of interested in how you spent my money.'

Emily tensed. She should have known he wouldn't leave that alone, that he'd be back for another piece. That was what she got for chasing him, then denying him when he finally decided he might want her again. 'Please,' she said. 'Look, I know the way I went about it was indefensible, but this place is my dream. I love it. I'll pay you back, I'll . . .'

'Woah. Ems, it was a joke. Admittedly, not a very funny one. Look, I was curious. I mean, what woman fleeces her husband and uses the proceeds to buy a barn and turn it into a bookshop? You could have bought a fancy apartment, a car . . .'

'I didn't want those things,' Emily said quietly. 'This is all I wanted. And I am genuinely sorry, you know. I wasn't in my right mind. I should never have blackmailed you out of that money.' Joe's celebrity had been rising and Emily had been both scorned and desperate: a deadly combination. What she'd innocently termed 'the proceeds of the divorce' had in actuality been somewhat ill-gotten.

'The money's not important. You would have got the same if you'd hired a fancy lawyer, a ton more if you'd gone ahead and sold your story to some tabloid hack. Plus, I was a dick. I totally deserved it, and you deserved the money. So, if this is what you want . . . well, good luck to you. I hope it works out.'

Emily nodded. 'Thank you, Joe. I'm serious about the money, though. I really will pay you back.'

'No offence, Ems, I'm sure you'll do really well, but I doubt it's going to turn that kind of profit. Think of the money as a gift, I don't want it back.'

Emily raised her chin. 'But I need to give it. You want me to have to live with the knowledge that I blackmailed my husband for the rest of my life?' She didn't want him to have any hold over her now.

Joe smiled. 'Yeah, I do. Perhaps the guilt will remind you that you're not cut out for a life of crime. Of course, you could always go to the police and turn yourself in for extortion, but I'll deny all knowledge . . .'

'Blackmail!' Kate was marching in from the back shop where she had apparently been shamelessly eavesdropping. 'What the hell are you talking about? Who are you speaking to, Em?' Her voice rose to a comical screech: a defensive mother hen taking on the fox.

Joe laughed at the end of the phone. 'Of course, is that the redoubtable Kate Vincent I hear?'

'Look, Joe, I have to go. I've got a party to attend.'

'Yeah, well, I only wanted to wish you luck with tonight and with the shop. And to say goodbye.'

For a split second, Emily was magnetised by his voice. She let her eyes flutter closed, breathing deep.

Behind her she heard Kate make a sound that might have been a growl. 'Is that *Joe*? I'm sure Mike would have something to say about him calling you . . .'

Emily glared at her, turned her back to finish her goodbyes and hung up the phone; as usual Joe got the final word and he made it count.

'The nerve—' Kate began, bustling over to Emily like a concerned nanny. 'Are you OK? Why are you smiling and looking like that? Don't you dare look like that over Joe. What about Mike?'

'I know.' Em continued to smile dreamily at the door. 'Just give me a minute.'

'Bloody hell,' Kate blustered. 'He's a fucking boy-band cliché with his cheekbones and skinny jeans. I saw him interviewed just the other week; he needs to grow up. He treated you like crap.'

'Not a boy band,' Emily objected. 'They're "serious" musicians, remember? Also, I don't think you can use those things as an insult when they're netting him the big bucks.'

Kate looked suspicious. 'What did he say to you?'

'He whispered that I was still his muse.' His parting shot.

Kate scoffed. 'How old is he? His *muse*! Not only has he lost the right to call you that, he's also not nineteen any more. Jesus!'

'Calm down, Kate. I'm fine. I promise.' Emily turned to look at her and Kate knew, by the look in her eyes, that there would always be a tiny piece of her heart reserved for Joe, no matter his crimes.

She felt sorry for Mike; what if Joe had been Emily's one chance at happiness, and anything else would be a facsimile, a lifetime of pretending and fixed smiles?

And then Mike walked through the door, awkwardly bearing flowers – with his broad rugby-player shoulders and sensible haircut and soapy, scrubbed-up scent – and at once Kate knew differently. Because the look in Mike's eyes when he drank in

Emily – all shiny eyes and glossy curls and her curves barely contained by the gorgeous red dress they had shopped for in Glasgow – was overwhelming.

And the look in Emily's eyes was a perfect match. Not the nostalgic dreaming of long ago love, but something real and solid.

He pulled her into his arms and kissed her, told her she looked beautiful, and Emily looked deliciously happy. They broke apart reluctantly and Mike greeted Kate, a bit embarrassed by his public display of affection; he complimented her politely on her dress too and asked what he could do to help. Kate gestured to the box of wine bottles at her feet.

'You can take these out front to the marquee, please.'

Mike nodded, hefted the box and headed out the door with a backward glance, quirking a brow at Emily and making her giggle. Kate grabbed Emily's arm as she made for the door. Emily shot her a defensive glare, daring her to question. 'I can love him too,' she hissed fiercely. 'I can love him *more*.'

'I know,' Kate said. 'I can see that. But I still have some questions for you about *blackmail*?'

Emily grinned, linked her arm with Kate's and tugged her towards the marquee. 'That's a story for some other time. Right now we've got work to do; a party to host, a bookshop to run. Things to do, you and I.'

Epilogue

Kate strode into the hospital, olive-green silk swirling like a wave around her legs. The door to the ward was opened for her by a weary nurse in scrubs. 'I know visiting hours are almost up,' Kate said quickly. 'But I promised I'd stop by and see someone. I won't be long.' She had left Emily's big night for this, but she was beginning to realise the things that really mattered in life were not necessarily the big moments, the grand gestures, but the smaller ones, the seemingly inconsequential.

Like the first tentative phone call with her mum last night. Talking about nothing that mattered. The text had come as Kate was being driven back to Bluebell Bank from the hospital. It said so little. It said it all. A few insignificant, weighty little words:

It's about time I told you how sorry I am.

Lily's voice, when she answered Kate's call had been wary – afraid she might scare Kate off – but laced with barely contained excitement.

'How are you?' Kate had asked, as if she called up each week just to chat.

'I'm fine.' Soft, hesitant. 'Just in from yoga actually.'

'Yoga?'

'Mmm, I'm training to be an instructor.'

'That's . . . great. I'm . . . I'm in the country, Mum.'

'You're in Scotland?'

'Yeah, I have been for . . . a while.' She didn't want to hurt Lily with the knowledge that she'd been within reach all these weeks, and still so far away. 'I'm on the Solway, with the Cottons.'

'Of course, the Cottons.' Lily was fighting to keep her voice bland; she wasn't allowed to resent the family who had cared for Kate in all the ways that counted when she was, to all intents and purposes, absent. But Kate imagined the knowledge that such resentment was off limits didn't prevent her from feeling it.

Kate took a breath. 'Lena died.'

'Oh. I'm so sorry, I didn't know. What happened?'

'Uh, it's a long story. I was thinking perhaps I'd tell you it in person.'

Silence. 'You want to see me.'

'I do.'

The dam broke and excitement poured through. 'You can come here! Or I can come to you. Either. Whatever you like! Or we could meet in the middle somewhere—'

'Mum, stop.'

'Sorry.'

'I'll come to you. If I may.'

Lily's mask of reserve was back in place. 'Of course you may. Let's set a date. Come for lunch and stay as little or as long as you like.'

Maybe, *maybe*, Kate thought, she'd invite Lily for the book festival in September: Lily would like that. She may even spend Christmas with her. Depending how the lunch lined up for next week went.

There was a long road to recovery ahead: for Luke with his burns and broken bones; for Kate redefining her relationship with her mother, getting past Emily and Luke's betrayal and realising that what happened now and next mattered more than the mistakes of before; for Emily, ready to heal her heart and stand on her own feet.

The nurse shrugged and gestured for her to go ahead. 'Ten minutes,' he said. 'Sorry.'

'That's fine.'

Kate hurried along the corridor to Luke's private room. He was awake and watching *Grand Designs*. He looked up when she entered his room and his eyes widened. 'Hello,' she said. 'Can I drag you away from geeking out over different types of wall insulation for a few minutes?'

Luke snapped off the television. 'In that dress you have my undivided attention.' He tried to sit up straighter, but with his leg still encased in a thick white cast it was a struggle.

Kate gave a self-conscious twirl and sat in the chair beside his bed. 'The opening was tonight,' she said. 'And I missed you, so I brought you this.' She delved into her bag and produced a small package of napkin-wrapped canapés. 'I wanted to bring champagne,' she said. 'But that didn't seem so easy to smuggle past the nurses.'

Luke put the canapés aside and reached out a hand for her to come closer. She did, perching on the edge of his bed. 'Thanks for coming,' he said softly. 'I'm sorry you had to miss the party for me.'

Kate shrugged. 'I'd rather be here.' Where she had been, day after day, since the fire. 'Actually there was something I wanted to talk to you about.'

'That sounds ominous.'

Kate shook her head. 'No, it's just something . . . well, I wanted to get it out in the open because I'm not so sure you remember it. You were pretty out of it on morphine at the time.'

Luke groaned. 'Did I start singing or something? Make a complete twat of myself?'

Kate smiled, shook her head again. She tucked a strand of hair behind her ears. 'Not to my knowledge,' she said. 'But you did ask me to marry you.'

Luke coughed and his eyes widened. 'What?'

'You asked me to marry you. Right after you came round from the anaesthetic.'

He was mortified. 'I don't remember . . . I'm sorry. I—'

'Ssh.' Kate silenced him with a finger to his lips. 'I'm not telling you this to make you feel bad. I was more worried in case you *did* remember and you were still waiting for my answer.'

Luke's brow creased. 'Kate, I . . . It's not that I don't love you—'

Kate stiffened, then laughed. 'Are you trying to tell me you *do* love me, in that oh-so roundabout way? It's not exactly how I imagined your first declaration of love. Or my first proposal,' she added, almost but not quite to herself.

Luke laughed. 'I do love you,' he said, and reached out for her, caressing her cheek, sliding his fingers into her hair, pulling her face down to his. Kate brushed his lips, rested her forehead against him. 'Always have.'

Luke breathed in the scent of her hair, moved to kiss her temple, the line of her jaw, the jut of collarbone above the stiff, shivering silk of the corset. Her skin rippled at his touch. 'Perhaps,' he said, 'we *could* get married . . .'

Kate silenced him with her lips, kissing fiercely. When she released him she rounded on him in anger. 'No,' she said. 'Not like that.' She was sick of roller coasters, wanted to feel solid ground beneath her feet for a while.

She wanted mundane and ordinary. Seeing Luke's crestfallen expression, she smiled. 'I don't want to break your poor heart again without the aid of serious pain meds.'

'So . . . your answer was – *is* – no?'

'You bet. It wasn't a real proposal, and neither is this.' She sat back increasing the distance between them, saw how Luke's jaw tightened with apprehension. 'I just want to enjoy things as they are.'

'What: me flat on my back and barely able to move?'

Kate raised one eyebrow. 'Frankly, flat on your back sounds fine, but I'd prefer you able to move.' Luke smirked. 'I meant just being together. Being boyfriend and girlfriend.'

'How very adolescent.' He was laughing. He reached across the gulf of crisp, white sheets and touched her hand, tracing his fingers over her knuckles. Kate raised her eyes to his, unfurled her fingers and wound them with his.

'I love you,' she said softly. 'Let's be teenagers again, Luka.'

It was the first time he had heard the name without flinching. From Kate's lips he liked it. He tugged her down to him again, begging another kiss. She kissed him hard and when she let him come up for air, he sighed and nestled his face against her neck. 'Will you love my scars?' he said.

Kate stroked his hair. 'Every single one,' she said.

Luke nodded against her shoulder and closed his eyes. 'I promise the next time I propose to you I will be of sound mind and not high on hard drugs.'

'Sounds good to me.'

'There is one thing.' Luke pushed her gently away and looked into her eyes, all the jocularity unnerving him; he needed something more substantial from her.

Kate met his eyes. 'What?'

'Are you planning to stay a good while, Kate? Because, though I might deserve it, I couldn't take it if you left me and ran off home again.'

Kate linked her fingers more tightly with his. 'Luka,' she said. 'Don't be stupid. I *am* home.'

Acknowledgements

Getting my first novel published has been such an exciting journey. I would like to thank all the people who helped to make it happen; especially Brittany Dundas, my best friend and first reader, who encouraged me when I wavered (which was often) and helped me to finally do something with my story.

Thanks also to my agent, Jenny Brown, and my editor, Victoria Oundijian at HQ Digital, for their encouragement, insight and for often knowing what I was getting at when I didn't know it myself!

This book would never have ventured out into the light if not for The Big Pitch, at the Wigtown Book Festival. I am so grateful to the organisers of the festival – not only because it's one of my absolute favourite places to be, but also because without them I'd never have had the awesome and terrifying opportunity of pitching my novel to Jenny.

My family have been a fantastic help – Crows and Mouats alike – as I tried to write, edit and teach all at the same time, and I'm very grateful for the unending support of my husband, Chris, who always believes in me. He took me back to the Solway to propose and unwittingly rekindled my love affair with the place too.

Thanks are definitely due to Midge, because who doesn't love to be interrupted in the writing process by a gorgeous little dog pawing the laptop? I wrote this book despite her best efforts to distract me, and I'm just sorry there aren't more dogs in it – I packed in as many as seemed plausible.

Finally, I owe my love of words to Granny Hendry – my very own Lena – who taught me to play Scrabble and once wrote a book of her own, only to burn it. I only wish she could have lived to see mine in print.

Dear Reader,

We hope you enjoyed reading this book. If you did, we'd be so appreciative if you left a review. It really helps us and the author to bring more books like this to you.

Here at HQ Digital we are dedicated to publishing fiction that will keep you turning the pages into the early hours. Don't want to miss a thing? To find out more about our books, promotions, discover exclusive content and enter competitions you can keep in touch in the following ways:

JOIN OUR COMMUNITY:

Sign up to our new email newsletter:
http://smarturl.it/SignUpHQ

Read our new blog www.hqstories.co.uk

𝕏 https://twitter.com/HQStories

www.facebook.com/HQStories

BUDDING WRITER?

We're also looking for authors to join the HQ Digital family!
Find out more here:

https://www.hqstories.co.uk/want-to-write-for-us/

Thanks for reading, from the HQ Digital team